SECRET HOPES FOR THE WEST END GIRLS

ALSO BY ELAINE ROBERTS

The West End Girls Series

The West End Girls

Big Dreams for the West End Girls

Secret Hopes for the West End Girls

The Foyles Girls Series

The Foyles Bookshop Girls

The Foyles Bookshop Girls at War

Christmas at the Foyles Bookshop

SECRET HOPES FOR THE WEST END GIRLS

Elaine Roberts

An Aria Book

First published in the UK in 2022 by Head of Zeus,
part of Bloomsbury Publishing Plc.

9 7 5 3 1 2 4 6 8

A catalogue record for this book is available from the British Library.

ISBN (PB): 9781803281308
ISBN (E): 9781838933524

Typeset by Siliconchips Services Ltd UK

Printed and bound in Great Britain by
CPI Group (UK) Ltd, Croydon CR0 4YY

Head of Zeus Ltd
First Floor East
5–8 Hardwick Street
London EC1R 4RG

WWW.HEADOFZEUS.COM

To my late husband, Dave, you are loved
and missed every day.

I

August 1915

Rose Spencer stared at London's Lyceum Theatre. A man sat huddled on the steps, almost hidden by one of the pillars. He looked dishevelled and at odds with the elegance of the theatre, but she had seen him there most days. Their eyes met. Heat flooded through her. What was he doing there? Was he following her? She rushed towards the side of the building, no longer noticing the grandeur of the six magnificent pillars that appeared to hold up the giant structure at the entrance, which usually made her stop to admire the impressive cream building.

After removing her wide-brimmed hat, Rose mopped her brow with her crumpled white handkerchief before patting her blonde hair into place. She pushed open the heavy stage door and stepped inside, grateful to be in the familiar surroundings and out of the August sunshine. She smiled at the man who had made it his job to look out for her and Annie, always having a bear-like hug at the ready. 'Morning,

Bert, it's already so hot.' Frowning, she tried to gather her thoughts. 'Did you know that man's outside again?'

The stocky grey-haired doorman looked up from his newspaper and shook his head. 'Morning. Every time yer tell me I go out there and I can't see 'im, but I'll 'ave a look.'

Rose sighed, trying to ignore the bold newspaper headlines about more Zeppelin raids and food shortages.

Bert's paper rustled as he closed it and folded it in half. 'Yer early today, and on yer own.' He peered at the hat she was carrying. 'No bags of pies and rolls from yer friend Joyce today?'

Rose giggled. 'Always thinking of your stomach, Bert, but you know there's talk of food shortages right now.'

'I know – it's worrying ain't it?' Bert chuckled and rubbed his stomach. 'But I didn't get this paunch by not eating good food.'

Rose stifled a yawn. 'Annie's helping Joyce with some cooking preparation at her restaurant in Great White Lion Street. The sales on Peter's stall are keeping her quite busy at the moment.'

Bert placed his paper on the table in front of him and raised his eyebrows. 'Does that mean she'll bring some of those lovely pies wiv her?'

Rose smiled. 'I expect so.'

'That's something to keep me going this morning.'

Their laughter erupted and echoed in the hallway.

Bert raised his hand. 'Oh, I almost forgot, Miss Hetherington's looking for yer so don't let 'er rile yer up, and before yer say anything I know it's 'ard not to.'

Rose groaned. 'That's all I need first thing in the morning. It's never good news when she wants to see me.'

Bert shook his head. 'I don't know why she's so mean-spirited all the time.'

'To be honest I used to think it was because Stan gave Annie and me jobs. She doesn't see that if we hadn't sneaked into the theatre she would have been in trouble because there was no one around to do Kitty's costume repairs.' Rose laughed. 'I remember being terrified when they came into the sewing room, where we were hiding, and when Annie told them I was the best seamstress ever I just froze on the spot. Stan offered me a seamstress job and Annie was asked to be Kitty's dresser, which she didn't want because she wanted to be on the stage, but she took it and now look at us. We're all like family, and we both owe Kitty and Stan so much.'

Bert smiled. 'Yer right, we are family, and it's like I've known you and Annie all yer lives. Yer were both very brave to come to London chasing yer dreams.'

Rose smiled. 'That's kind of you, Bert, but I only really came along for the fun while supporting Annie. Anyway, I suppose I'd better go before Miss Hetherington follows the noise and I get into trouble for laughing.'

Bert nodded. 'Take care and don't let 'er put yer in a bad mood.'

Rose raised her eyebrows. 'I'll do my best, but I can't promise. She always rubs me up the wrong way.'

'Yer not alone there.'

Rose's red-painted lips tightened. 'As much as I don't want to I'd better get going.' With a wave she sped along the corridor. A sigh escaped her as she saw Miss Hetherington walking towards her. As usual, her dark hair was pulled back in a tight bun at the nape of her neck. There was no getting away from the slender, terse-looking woman.

'I'm here to see Miss Smythe.' A deep voice boomed along the corridor.

Rose turned and glanced in the direction it came from. A tall, suited man was standing near the stage door. Rose noticed the unusual pink tie he was wearing and the matching band on his trilby.

Bert opened the visitors' book he kept on the table. 'Good morning, sir. It's been a while since you were last here. No assistant with you this time?'

The man smiled as he removed his hat. 'No, she's busy back at the shop.'

Bert looked up from the page. 'Miss Smythe is expecting yer. I'll take yer to 'er dressing room, if you'd like to follow me.' He smiled. 'I remember last time you left 'ere with an armful of paperwork.'

Rose stepped aside to allow Bert and the man to walk past.

The man chuckled. Nodding his thanks to Rose, he continued his conversation. 'Miss Smythe is a good customer, who likes to keep me on my toes, but that's not necessarily a bad thing.'

Miss Hetherington smiled at the man in the suit as he walked past them.

Rose wrinkled her nose as the man's overpowering woody scent lingered in the air.

Miss Hetherington turned back to glare at Rose. 'You're late, Miss Spencer.'

Startled, Rose looked at the watch on her wrist and fought the urge to disagree with her boss. 'If that's so I'm very sorry.' She wondered what her problem was. Why was she so cold and unhelpful, and so mean to everybody? Rose turned into the sewing room and put her bag down on the side. She wanted to ask Miss Hetherington who the man was but assumed she wouldn't tell her even if she knew. After strolling over to the sink, she turned on the tap. The pipes rattled as the water struggled to come through. She let it run for a moment before filling her cup with cold water.

Miss Hetherington followed her into the room. Frowning, she watched as Rose settled herself at the table. 'Miss Spencer, there are alterations to be done today, and they need to be ready for tonight.'

'Alterations?'

'Yes, some of the men have enlisted to fight in this terrible war and the girls have left for more money at the munitions factory.' Miss Hetherington sighed. 'That means there's a lot of alterations, so the costumes will fit the new people.'

Rose frowned. 'How many are we talking about?'

Miss Hetherington's heels clipped the floor as she walked around the room, only stopping to straighten items on the table and the cotton reels in the racks. She turned to look at Rose. 'I think about six but that may not be the final figure.'

Rose shook her head. 'I'm not sure I'll be able to do that many in a day; of course it depends on what needs altering. Will you be able to help me?'

'Where is the other seamstress? What's her name?'

Rose raised her eyebrows. 'Lizzie, Lizzie Turnbull.' She picked up her cup of water. 'She's not in today.'

Miss Hetherington glared at Rose. 'And who said she could have the day off?'

Rose shrugged. 'I did. She had a family emergency and we

weren't busy so I thought it would be all right.' She looked directly at Miss Hetherington. 'And, you would have said no.'

Heavy footsteps could be heard marching along the hallway. Stan Tyler poked his head round the door of the sewing room. 'Ah, Rose, thank goodness you're in early. I wasn't expecting you in until much later, but I'm glad you're here.' Stan turned and nodded to Miss Hetherington. 'It's good to see you too, Jane. I'm assuming you've told Rose about the alterations for the costumes?'

Jane nodded and gave Stan a smile that lit up her face. 'We were just discussing it, Mr Tyler.'

Stan turned back to Rose. 'I'm so sorry to drop this on you so late. I know these things are never as easy as we think they are, but we had half a dozen actors leave last night.'

Rose frowned. 'I understand. Unfortunately I let Lizzie have the day off today, which I probably shouldn't have done without checking first but she had a family emergency.'

Stan nodded. 'Well, we have to be understanding about these things because we all have emergencies from time to time. Thankfully, we have Miss Hetherington who can help out.' He turned to Jane and smiled. 'I know it's been a while but I'm sure you'll agree we have to think of the good of the show.'

Miss Hetherington's lips tightened. 'Of course, Mr Tyler – it's times like this when we all have to pull together.'

Stan's eyes narrowed for a moment before he turned back to Rose. 'I've decided to have some of the bit-part actors double up for another role. Understandably, being actors and actresses is not the focus of many young people these days, especially when there's good money to be earned elsewhere. However, it will give the youngsters a chance to prove their salt.'

Rose nodded. 'That's a good idea. Hopefully the costume changes won't be too drastic.'

'I knew I could rely on you, Rose, and I'm very grateful that you came in early, even though you didn't know this was happening.'

'Yes, my plans have now changed but it's all about what needs to be done.'

Lizzie Turnbull rushed into the sewing room, breathless and hot. She pulled a handkerchief out of her skirt pocket and mopped her forehead, lifting her damp mousy brown hair in the process.

Rose's gaze moved from Stan and Miss Hetherington to the flustered Lizzie. 'Lizzie, what are you doing here? You're supposed to be off today.'

Fear ran across Lizzie's flushed face. 'Is it all right to come in after asking for the day off?'

Stan frowned before smiling at the young girl. He clearly didn't remember seeing her before. 'I'm sure Rose is very glad you're here after what I've just told her.' He turned towards the open door. 'I'll leave you to get on with things and I'll send the actors down to see you.' He was gone before anyone could respond.

Rose walked over to the rail of costumes. 'Of course it is, Lizzie; in fact I'm very grateful you're here. We have a lot of work to do.'

Miss Hetherington scowled as she looked between the two girls. 'Miss Turnbull, if you require a day off in future please consult with me and not Miss Spencer.' She turned on her heels to leave the room.

Lizzie sucked in her breath. 'I would have done, Miss Hetherington, but I couldn't find you, which is why I asked Rose.'

Miss Hetherington glared at the girls. 'In those circumstances you are not allowed the time off. It needs to be agreed with me. Do you understand?'

Lizzie looked down at the floor. 'Yes, miss, I'm sorry but it was an emergency.'

Miss Hetherington took the couple of steps to the doorway. 'And yet here you are. You youngsters are all the same.' She marched out of the room, her heels clicking on the floor as she went.

'Oh dear, I didn't get you into trouble did I, Rose? I didn't mean to but my mother was furious with me for asking for the day off.'

Rose shook her head. 'You should know better than to say that, Lizzie. You know what Miss Hetherington is like – even if I was in the right she'd tell me I wasn't.'

Lizzie sighed. 'I wonder what her problem is. I don't understand why she hates everyone so much.'

'Who knows. I certainly don't. I also don't understand why anybody would want to live their lives that way; from what I can make out there's more than enough misery going on in the world.'

Lizzie opened the cupboard door and took a cup from it. 'Would you like a cup of tea?'

'No thanks. I'm melting, I'm so hot.' Rose eyed Lizzie's hunched shoulders. 'Do I take it your emergency wasn't as bad as you thought?'

Lizzie stared straight ahead into the cupboard. 'Oh no, it was bad, but my mother thinks life has to go on and she's now going to need the money I earn more than ever so there'll be no taking time off for me, no matter what happens.' She paused. 'In fact I may have to leave here and see if I can get a job in the munitions factory. I don't want to but they pay so much more.'

'That would be a shame, but I understand; everyone has to do what's right for them. Annie and I would probably have to do the same if we weren't paying very low rent in Joyce's uncle's house in Seven Dials. We're fortunate that the three of us are all childhood friends. We come from the same village and when Joyce's mother died her father moved to London.' Rose paused, realising she was rambling. Her eyes narrowed as she watched Lizzie. 'I don't wish to pry, but I'm here if you want to talk. It doesn't do any good keeping everything bottled up.'

Lizzie turned around to face her new friend and boss.

Rose studied her but didn't say a word. The tears didn't look very far away.

'My ma's had a telegram.' Lizzie paused. 'My brother… he's died on the front line. Apparently he was a hero.' Pausing, she took another deep breath and blinked quickly. 'I'd rather he wasn't and had come home to us safe and sound.'

Rose stared at Lizzie's red, watery eyes. This was her worst nightmare. She dreaded getting such news from her parents. Every letter from them filled her with fear, so she had to read them at least twice. The first to scan for bad news about her brothers, and the second to actually enjoy the news her mother wrote. 'I'm so sorry, Lizzie. If there's anything I can do just say.' Rose stepped forward and put her arms around Lizzie. It wasn't long before she began to sob in her arms.

Rose patted her back gently. 'Shhhh, that's it – let it out.'

Rose and Annie strolled along Great Earl Street enjoying the early evening August weather. Car fumes hung in the air, causing Annie to wrinkle her nose. 'Sometimes I miss the fresh air and the nature smells back home.' Her fingers pushed a stray strand of brown hair away from her face and behind her ear.

'I know what you mean. I thought Peter did well when his love for you made him travel to Worcester when your mother died.' Rose turned to Annie and raised her eyebrows. 'He was clearly worried you wouldn't come back and he would lose you, and because of that I thought it wouldn't be long before you and Peter announced your engagement? I must admit I'm surprised you two aren't married by now. After all your family have met and liked him, or is Peter too busy now he's selling bread and pies for Joyce along with his vegetables?'

Annie laughed. 'He's busy, as you well know, but then so am I, so that isn't the reason we haven't done anything. There's no rush, is there?'

Rose raised her eyebrows again. 'Well what's the reason? There must be one. After all you're clearly in love with each other, so what are you waiting for?'

Annie shrugged. 'I'm not sure we're waiting for anything; hopefully we've plenty of time to worry about such things. Also, it'll need careful planning. You know... picking the right time of the year for my family to come down, or for us to go up there. I want them to be there; I can't imagine getting married without them. I would want my sister as bridesmaid along with you and Joyce.'

Rose gave a look of feigned horror. 'Well, I should hope so too.'

Annie glanced sideways at Rose. 'Why are you asking me anyway?'

Rose stared down at the pavement.

'Come on, Rose, what's with all the questions?'

It was Rose's turn to shrug. 'I don't know. I just thought you would be the first to get married but now I'm not sure it won't be Joyce and Simon.'

Annie nodded. 'Actually, it could be you and Charlie, but does it matter?'

Rose watched an old couple walking hand in hand over the road. She smiled to herself. That could be her and Charlie in years to come. 'Obviously not, but Charlie says life is short and we should live for the here and now because we don't know how long we've got.'

'I can understand that, what with bombs going off and the menfolk going off to war.' Annie followed Rose's gaze. 'I expect Joyce and Simon are waiting until Simon is really well again. I can imagine Simon will want to do it properly. They have been through so much, what with him coming back from the front so badly injured. He's a very proud man and will want to be able to walk next to her without his stick.'

Rose looked across at Annie. 'Do you think that's the reason? Do you think it matters as long as you're marrying the person you love? I mean, do you want the whole big wedding or will you just be happy that you and Peter are getting married?'

Annie frowned as she looked into the distance. 'I don't need a big wedding. I would love to have the white wedding dress but as long as my family could be with me that's all that matters.'

Rose was silent for a moment. 'I suppose that's a problem when you're living away from them. I mean where would you get married: in London or up in Worcester?'

Annie smiled. 'I suppose it depends on how much time off we can get from work. I think it will be difficult to arrange. What's this really about?'

They clung on to each other as they stepped out into the road. Car horns blared out as they ran across the Seven Dials roundabout into Great White Lion Street.

'Come on, Rose, what's going on? Are you wondering what to do about your family when you get married?'

Rose shrugged. 'No, I'm just making conversation.'

Annie glanced across at Rose, studying her features, but Rose didn't give anything away. 'Are you and Charlie setting a date?'

Rose laughed and colour rushed up her neck and into her face. 'We've talked about the future, but he hasn't asked me yet.'

Annie reached out and grabbed Rose's arm and pulled her to a standstill. 'What do you mean you've talked about it? Peter and I haven't, so if you've talked about it then why haven't you set the date? Is something wrong? You've not fallen out have you?'

Rose giggled at her friend's confusion. 'If you're asking me do we still love each other, then yes we do. He's certainly the man for me anyway, although, once we're married he might change his mind about whether I'm the woman for him.'

It was Annie's turn to giggle. 'I doubt that. You are definitely the woman for him; he can't take his eyes off you. Also, he has said some really romantic things to you even when I've been there, so he definitely loves you.' She paused. 'Were you asking about inviting my family because you've been wondering about inviting yours down for your own wedding?'

Rose jutted out her chin and pushed her shoulders back. 'Of course not. I was just curious. I can't imagine my family would come to London just because I was getting married. Let's face it, they didn't care I was coming here to live.' She moved to step forward but Annie held on to her arm and tilted her head to one side. 'What?' Rose asked.

'Rose, I want you to talk to me. I want to know what's going on inside that head of yours.'

'There's nothing to tell. I expect one day we'll get married and have children and live happily ever after, but I think you and Peter should do it first.' Rose smiled at her friend. 'Now go off and see Peter and have a good day while I go and see Charlie at his bicycle shop.'

Annie nodded. 'All right, but this conversation isn't over. I never realised you kept so much to yourself. I thought we talked about everything.'

Rose threw her arms around Annie. 'Of course we do. I'm just not that forward a person when it comes to me. I love seeing you all achieve what you need or want to do but I don't have those same feelings.'

Annie's lips tightened. 'I expect you do, Rose; you just don't know you have them.'

Rose shook her head. 'Charlie has grand ideas for me but that is a whole different conversation and we don't have time for it so just go and enjoy yourself and I'll see you back at the house later.'

Annie had a glint in her eye as she looked at her friend. 'I will, and make sure you do too, but just so you know this conversation isn't over with.'

Rose stood outside Charlie's bicycle shop in Great White Lion Street, remembering the first time she had walked there hoping to see him.

It had been a cold, wintry day. She had stood in the same spot, staring at the shop doorway. Her nerves had held her there for some time, while her confidence had gradually disappeared. After all, what could she possibly have to say to him? She had turned to walk away, disappointment swamping her.

Charlie Young's warm voice had stopped her in her tracks. 'I was hoping you were going to come in, maybe have a cup of tea with me.'

Heat had rushed into Rose's face, thawing out her cheeks. She'd taken a deep breath and turned to face him. He had stood tall in the shop doorway. There were oily streaks down his brown overall, while a rag peeked over the top of its square pocket. 'I... I was—'

'But you chickened out—'

'No, yes... yes I did.' Rose had sighed; her breath had risen in grey swirls, disappearing into the air.

Charlie had watched Rose's embarrassment. 'There's no need. I was hoping you would call in on your way to work one day.' He'd beamed as he ran his hand through his dark hair, which was longer than most men wore their hair and not greased flat. 'Come on in out of the cold. The kettle's on.'

Rose had stood there for a moment, unsure what to do.

Charlie had taken a step nearer to her and stretched his arm out in front of him. 'Come on, you've come this far.'

Rose had looked at the handsome man's outstretched hand for a second before stepping forward and lightly placing her hand in his.

Charlie had wrapped his fingers around hers and silently led her inside.

Rose remembered looking around at the many bicycles.

Charlie had followed her gaze and chuckled. 'I need a larger shop.' He'd paused and looked around. 'But then I'd probably just fill the extra space so it would look like this but bigger.'

Rose had been drawn to this man, without really understanding why. 'I don't know what I expected to see but I've never seen so many bicycles in one place.'

Charlie had raised his eyebrows. 'They're not all mine – some are here to be repaired.' He'd stepped towards the back of the shop. 'Take a seat and I'll make a cup of tea.'

Rose had watched him disappear through an open doorway.

A car coughed out its fumes, jerking Rose out of her memories of nearly a year ago. She had known on that day he was the man for her. The warmth and consideration he had shown her were things she had never experienced before. He had always acted the perfect gentleman, even though she hadn't always wanted him to.

Rose stepped forward now and pushed open the shop door. The bell rang out, competing with the clatter of spoons on crockery that reached her. 'It's only me.'

Charlie shouted out. 'It's never only you.' He poked his head round the kitchen doorway. 'I won't be a minute. I'm just making the tea.'

Rose smiled. 'There's no rush.'

Charlie appeared carrying a tray of tea things and a plate of biscuits. 'Take your jacket off otherwise, as my ma used to say, you won't get the benefit of it when you go outside.'

Rose giggled. 'My ma says exactly the same thing.'

'I expect all mothers do.' Charlie placed the tray down on the counter, on top of a pile of paperwork. He frowned as he looked from the teapot to Rose. 'I'll let you pour. Hopefully it will be strong enough for you.'

Rose nodded as she unbuttoned the blue jacket that complemented her crimson calf-length skirt.

Charlie leant forward. 'Here, let me hang it up.'

Rose passed it to him. 'I was just thinking about the first time I came here. Do you remember? I asked the most ridiculous question of someone who works in a bicycle shop. Wasn't it something like: do you like working with bicycles?' She blushed. 'It was such a silly question. Looking around at the number you have, it's obvious you do.'

Charlie chuckled. 'Yes, I remember. I said something along the lines of: I just like building and fixing things.' He waved his arms around. 'And, it happens there is a call for all of this in London.'

The teapot lid clattered against the stoneware pot as Rose lifted it. Stirring the light brown liquid vigorously, she stared down at the whirlpool she had created, as the tea grew darker. Rose replaced the lid with a thud and picked up the strainer and poured the hot dark brown tea into the cups. She looked up. 'I can't believe that was nearly a year ago.'

'It was a lucky day for me.' Charlie studied her easy, elegant movements. 'I shall always owe Joyce for introducing us.'

Rose smiled. 'You and she were friends for a long time, a bit like Annie's boyfriend, Peter.'

'Joyce walked past my shop most days, and it was always while I was putting some of my stock on the pavement. I kept saying good morning to her and tried to get her to buy a bicycle but she was having none of it.' He laughed, picking up his cup. 'She did always smile and say good morning though.'

Rose watched him fidget on his chair. 'Were you hoping a friendship might blossom?'

Charlie put down his teacup and stood up. He walked over and straightened the handlebars of a dark blue bicycle propped against another one.

'I'm sorry, I shouldn't have asked. I just thought we had known each other long enough not to have any secrets.'

Charlie took a breath. 'Not at all, you're right. The truth is I was in the beginning but, although Joyce never said as much, it was obvious it wasn't what she wanted.' He cleared his throat and turned to look at Rose. 'She always called me Mr Young, even though I told her on numerous occasions to call me Charlie. You and I had a longer conversation on the first day we met than I ever did with Joyce.'

Rose lowered her eyes. 'I'm sorry, I shouldn't have asked.'

Charlie studied Rose for a moment. 'Now you know, does it change anything?'

'No, no it doesn't.' Rose blushed. 'But I didn't mean to raise old pain.'

Charlie laughed. 'Trust me, you haven't.' He frowned as he walked back to his chair. 'Do you think you'll stay in London or will you return home to live?'

Rose smiled. 'Oh, I'll most definitely stay for as long as I can. It's so big and yet I love it. The tall buildings and statues make it very different to the village I come from and I haven't really begun to look at all the museums and galleries.'

Charlie's eyes sparkled. 'I don't think I've ever seen anyone so animated about the city before.'

Rose picked up her cup, blowing gently into it. 'Perhaps you either love it or hate it.'

Charlie followed suit. 'I don't think it's that, I think we tend to take what we have for granted.'

Rose immediately thought of her family back home. 'That's true.'

'Do you miss them?'

Rose lowered her eyes. 'Miss who?'

'Your family?'

Rose's lips tightened. 'Of course, and all my brothers, but one, signed up and are fighting somewhere. I write every day but they still don't write back; at least, I haven't received any letters so far.'

Charlie placed his hand on hers, squeezing her soft, smooth skin. 'It's not easy, but try to stay positive.' He watched her eyes well up as she struggled to keep herself strong. 'My brother also enlisted. He doesn't write much either but I try to tell myself no news is good news.'

Rose nodded. 'That's what Annie keeps saying to me. At least my parents write to give me any news they have.'

Charlie fidgeted on his stool. He ran his fingers around the inside of his shirt collar. 'I must admit not having my parents any more I do miss my brother, and I do worry about him.' He paused and took a deep breath. 'On a cheerier note, I had an old friend drop by yesterday. I haven't seen Oli for goodness knows how long but it was like old times and we had so much to catch up on. He lost his wife at around the same time my father wasn't very strong and I guess…' He shrugged. 'Anyway, it's not important right now but I think you'll like him. I said I'd give him a helping hand with some ideas he has bubbling away.'

Rose studied him. 'That's intriguing, but it sounds as though you were pleased to see him.'

Charlie chuckled. 'Yeah, we were very close growing up but sometimes things happen that hold you in a difficult place.' He picked up a biscuit. 'So, perhaps it's time we looked at some of the sights that you haven't seen yet.'

Rose blushed. 'That would be lovely. As you know I work late most evenings but Sundays would be all right.'

Charlie nodded. 'Right, well, I'll sort something out.' He paused. 'Maybe we could take in some of the museums or galleries.'

A bell chimed as the shop door opened. A young lad wearing patched trousers and a short jacket walked in clutching newspapers under his arm. 'I got yer paper for yer, Mr Young.'

Charlie stood up. 'Excellent, thank you.' He put his hand in his pocket and pulled out a handful of change. He moved it around his hand and picked out a penny. 'There yer go, and keep the change.'

The boy beamed. 'Thank you, sir.' The bell rang out again as he pulled the door open.

Charlie grinned. 'Same time tomorrow?'

The boy nodded before running out the door. The sunshine rushed in, lighting up the shop and the dust, just before the door banged shut, drowning out the peal of the bell.

Rose watched as Charlie left the paper on the counter. 'Well, you made him very happy.' She paused. 'I don't want to stop you working, as my pa used to say time's money. Oh, before I go, do you want me to pop along and pay your rent?'

'If you don't mind – it's becoming a bit of a habit.'

Rose smiled. 'I'm happy to help, and it saves you shutting the shop to go and pay it.'

'It's very good of you but you do know the landlord would come here if you didn't go to him.' Charlie laughed.

Rose shrugged. 'I don't mind doing it.'

Charlie nodded as he pushed the plate of Lincoln biscuits towards Rose. 'Help yourself.' He picked up his cup and gulped down its tepid contents.

'No, thank you. Living with Joyce means I eat far too many biscuits and cake.' Rose laughed.

Charlie pushed himself off his chair.

Rose frowned as she watched him. He looked anxious and yet she recognised the familiar longing in his eyes; was he about to take her in his arms? She held her breath as hope filled her body. She took a breath. Was he finally going to whisk her into his arms or the bedroom? Instinct told her he wasn't. Her mother would approve, saying he was a true gentleman, but she wondered how he managed to stay so controlled when she yearned to be in his arms.

Charlie walked behind the counter. 'I hope you don't mind but I've bought you a present. If you don't want it I understand. I don't want you to think I'm rushing things but…' His eyes pleaded with her. 'Please accept my present. Rightly or wrongly it was bought in good grace.'

Rose stared at him, sensing something had changed. The moment of passion had gone.

'Please…'

Rose suddenly clapped her hands together, knowing she was taking the coward's way out by not asking about it. 'I love presents. What have you bought me?'

Charlie grinned from ear to ear before looking down and opening the drawer behind the counter. 'I hope you won't be offended by it but it is given from a place of love.'

Rose frowned. 'It sounds like I should be worried.'

Charlie shook his head. 'No, although, I must admit I'm not sure if I should've bought it, even though I think it's a great idea.'

Rose stepped nearer to him. 'You're worrying me now. You don't have to give me it if you don't want to; after all presents should come with love.'

Charlie cleared his throat. 'It definitely comes with that and with good intentions.' He took a small square box from the drawer and sat it on the wooden top of the counter.

Rose glanced down at the box. It was too big for a ring. She wondered what was inside. 'Am I allowed to open it?'

Charlie picked it up. He opened it and showed Rose the delicate silver cross and chain. 'It's to remind you to take a leap of faith with your sewing. I want you to be happy and thought a cross represents a leap of faith, a belief. I was hoping that you would wear it to remind you that you are loved and that you have a talent, a creative one. I want you to think about taking that leap of faith and put it to good use.'

Rose stared down at the cross nestling inside the box. 'It's beautiful, but you shouldn't have spent your money on me.'

Charlie laughed. 'I hope one day to give you so much more, and not just money. The sign of a cross obviously represents a belief in God, but I also want this to represent the belief I have in you and that you should have in yourself.'

Rose picked up the cross, letting it nestle on her fingertips. 'It's so delicate. No one has ever given me such a present before. I don't know what to say.'

Charlie rested his hand over hers. 'You don't have to say anything.'

Rose looked up and gazed into his eyes. 'Thank you. I will be honoured to wear it and it will always remind me of you.'

Charlie lifted Rose's hand to his mouth and gently pressed his lips on it.

Rose's heart fluttered and butterflies flew around her stomach. She closed her eyes, realising she couldn't wait to give herself to this man, to lie in his arms. Maybe they didn't need to wait; after all wasn't that regarded as a little old-fashioned? She slowly opened her eyes to meet Charlie's passionate gaze. Should she suggest going upstairs?

Charlie cleared his throat, and placed her hand on the counter before slowly stepping away. 'Right, I'll go and make another cup of tea.'

A voice screamed in her head. *Do it now, speak up. Go on, what are you waiting for?* The voice was chased away by her mother's words of disapproval when someone they knew became pregnant outside of marriage.

Once again the moment had passed.

2

Mr Alexander Bowman strolled through the Dickens and Jones ladies' department, scanning the room as he went. It seemed busier than usual; he wrinkled his nose as the various perfumes assaulted him. He quickly corrected himself, hoping no one noticed. He knew the value of making his ladies feel special. He got a thrill at seeing his designs for sale but when he saw someone actually wearing them he couldn't contain himself. A smile crept across his face; those new designs had saved his job.

'Good morning, Mr Bowman.'

Alexander puffed out his chest as he turned to greet the lady. 'Oh, it's you, Mrs Todd.' He scowled at the tall, elegant brunette. 'What are you doing up here? I thought you were a customer.' He watched her fidget from one foot to the other. He had made the mistake of getting over-friendly with her once or twice, but then he'd found out she was a widow and backed away.

Eileen Todd raised her eyebrows. 'I'm sorry to disappoint you.' She lowered her eyes and adjusted the red dress that was strewn across her arm. 'I'm just taking this downstairs to get a seamstress to make some alterations.'

'That looks like one from the new collection.' Alexander pulled at the front of his chocolate-brown jacket.

Eileen forced herself to smile. 'It is, in fact, as they seem to be popular and are selling fast. I've asked Marion Simpson to help out in the sewing room. She could do with the extra money.'

Mr Bowman frowned. 'And do you have the authority to do that?'

Eileen's smiled vanished and her shoulders slumped a little.

'The answer you are looking for is no.' Mr Bowman shook his head before giving an exasperated sigh. 'Who is Marion Simpson anyway?'

Eileen tightened her lips. 'You have spoken to her before; she works a few hours each day in the ladies' department. She's a slender, dark-haired girl, quite tall and well turned out.' She paused. 'If for no other reason she would have caught your eye because she would make a good clothes horse. She's very good with a needle, and we could do with the help.'

Mr Bowman's lips tightened. 'As long as it doesn't leave us short for dealing with the customers – without them there is no business.'

Eileen pursed her lips. 'That's very true, but if we keep them waiting for their alterations then they won't be happy either. I'm afraid one doesn't work without the other.'

Mr Bowman lifted his head slightly. 'Well, I suppose it won't hurt for a while and then we'll see. However, in future you do not make any decisions without running them by me first.'

'I shall let her know.' Eileen looked down at the dress strewn across her arm. 'I don't know what inspired this new collection but it seems to have worked. I believe it's the best you've ever done; at least the customers seem to think so. Congratulations, you may have lost your way for a while but your flair for what our customers want seems to have returned.'

Mr Bowman scowled as he stepped forward. 'I did not lose my way.' He hesitated. 'Anyway, I was just on my way to see you—'

'I'm assuming not because you want any of my designs.' Eileen paused, suddenly remembering her position. 'I mean you've now found another source of inspiration.'

Alexander stopped short and stared at her. He glanced around before giving her his best smile and resting his hand on her arm. 'You will always be my inspiration, Eileen. We created some wonderful designs together but we have to keep moving forward.'

Eileen pulled opened a heavy wooden door, marked private, and walked down the stairs. 'So what did you want to see me about?'

Alexander took a deep breath and followed her. 'The next few designs I have in mind. I want to start early because, as you know, patterns will need to be made and cut, but also bringing it all together takes time.'

Eileen nodded. 'Let me pass on this dress and I'll be with you.' She strode past the many seamstresses who had their heads down concentrating at their sewing machines. There was a steady hum of the sewing needles going up and down as the ladies switched between turning the machine's wheels, and their feet working the treadles. She stopped at a young girl who was hanging a dress on a coat hanger. 'Violet, can I give you this to turn up? Unfortunately, like everything we do, it's urgent. It only needs turning up about two inches, although the young woman would have preferred about four but her mother stepped in. I've pinned it to show where it needs to be.'

Listening to Eileen, Alexander Bowman quickly opened a desk drawer. He rummaged around, lifting papers before thrusting them back inside. He forcefully banged it shut again before repeating the exercise on the next drawer down. He shook his head and drummed his fingers on the wooden table as he looked around the room. His eyes locked with Eileen's before he quickly looked away.

Violet chuckled. 'It's the fashion these days – skirt lengths are definitely getting shorter.' Reaching out, she took the dress from Eileen, and held it up to look at it. 'That shouldn't take long, Mrs Todd. Would you like me to let you know when it's done?'

Eileen nodded. 'Please, I will probably be with Mr Bowman.' She turned to walk away before glancing over her shoulder. 'Thank you.' She took a deep breath and headed to the office.

Alexander sighed as he watched Eileen march towards him. He would have to be careful. She could be his downfall. He took a breath and began shuffling several sheets of paper on his wooden table.

Eileen leant forward and studied the drawings. 'Have you lost something?'

'What?'

Eileen peered up at him. 'I thought you were looking for something.'

'Oh, er, these drawings, I couldn't remember what I'd done with them.' Alexander watched her closely, waiting for a reaction.

Eileen glanced down at the papers in front of her. 'They must have got buried because I saw these on your desk last night.' She smiled. 'I have to say, Mr Bowman, you've certainly come out of your dry spell. These are beautiful.'

The paper rustled as she lifted one for a closer look.

'Well, I don't think it was a dry spell. I just needed inspiration, and I've got that wandering around – and going to the theatre was a great inspiration.'

Mrs Todd arched her eyebrows. 'I'm very pleased for you, as I'm sure the management will be.'

'You're not feeling sorry for yourself are you, by any chance? You do know it's not my fault your designs got rejected? They just wanted something different.'

Eileen forced a smile to her lips. 'None of that matters now. I don't remember getting the credit anyway.'

Mr Bowman shook his head. 'Some of your designs are for sale in the shop, just not all of them. You have to remember we cater for a certain class of clientele here.'

Eileen frowned at him. 'You don't need to tell me about the clientele. I am very much aware of it, thank you very much. I have worked here for many years.'

Alexander bowed his head before looking earnestly at her. 'I'm very sorry we couldn't have a closer working relationship. That's my loss to grieve over, but I hope we can still be friends without any bitterness coming in to spoil it.'

Eileen looked him in the eye. 'I have learnt a valuable lesson and forgiveness is what will move me forward, and it won't hold me in a place filled with bitterness.'

Alexander fidgeted from one foot to the other. He dropped his gaze to his sketches. 'That's good, so we can move forward with these together.'

Eileen nodded. 'Of course.'

'That's excellent news.' Alexander sucked in his breath. 'It would have been a shame if we could no longer work together because then I would have to find a replacement.' He spread out the pages so he could see the last of the current designs, which he had carefully drawn from the original pad that held the sketches. He liked to reveal just a few at a time. Secrecy was paramount. Frowning, he wondered what he was going to do moving forward. 'It's time for me to start thinking about the next collection while you work on these. I have no ideas at the moment so I really need to get some sketches down, then hopefully my inspiration will follow.'

'I'm sure ideas will pop into your head; after all the last few seem to have come from nowhere.'

The sewing room door slowly creaked open. Eileen and Alexander both turned to see who was creeping in.

Eileen called out. 'Marion, is everything all right?'

Marion looked uncomfortable and she almost walked on tiptoes towards Mr Bowman. 'I'm sorry to interrupt you both, but I was asked to bring this envelope down to Mr Bowman.'

Eileen turned to Alexander. 'This is Marion Simpson.' She smiled at the young girl. 'I have arranged for you to have extra hours so you can work down here for me. If you're happy with that we'll discuss times and days later?'

Marion beamed at Mrs Todd. 'Thank you for thinking of me. I'm so very grateful.'

Alexander nodded; he reached out and snatched the envelope from her.

Marion bit her lip. Her voice was barely a whisper when she spoke. 'Also, Doctor Hardy has come to pick up a dress that was being altered for his mother, as well as one for his daughter, which he said was yellow.' Marion smiled at Mrs Todd. 'He seemed a really nice man, very polite.'

Alexander Bowman turned over the envelope, curious to see who it was from.

Mrs Todd patted Marion's hand. 'It's hanging up on the rail. The child's dress has just been pressed so that should be with it.' She frowned. 'It's a shame about his wife. I don't believe he married again – it's all quite sad.'

Alexander glanced at Eileen. He picked up his silver letter opener. Without waiting, he slipped it inside the flap of the envelope and tore it open. He pulled it apart to reveal a wedding invitation. He tugged the invite free. It was from Kitty Smythe. His lips slowly lifted at the corners as they formed a smile. He could feel a solution to his problems rolling around in his head. As it gathered momentum he realised that maybe, just maybe, everything was going to be all right after all.

Rose sat on her bed with the sun shining through the window. She glanced around her; the room was small but sufficient for her needs. She had made the deep red curtains to match the rug she had squandered some of her hard-earned cash on, but they brought colour and warmth to the drab room. Her gaze focused on the scenic painting of Westminster Bridge that was on the wall over her chest of drawers. She had been thrilled when Simon had given it to her and it struck her that Joyce's boyfriend was hiding a real talent.

The early evening was the best time for her. She opened her pad and picked up a pencil and began doodling, at first allowing ideas to form as her pencil worked its way across the page. She looked up and glanced out the window for a moment before looking back down at the paper. She once again began drawing lines to form a dress, adding structure as well as a long bow at the neck. She wrote notes next to it: what the outfit should consist of and the material that could be used. As she looked at it she realised it was similar to military uniforms, which had become the latest fashion; the long bow at the neck added a touch of femininity.

'Rose?' There was a tiny knock on the door, followed by a little voice. 'Rose?'

'Come in, Philip.'

The scratchy sound of the doorknob turning made Rose look up. 'Hello, Philip, I don't usually see you in my room. What can I do for you?'

Philip came running in and bounced on the end of her bed, causing it to creak. 'I've been sent to get you as we're going out for dinner.'

Rose smiled at Joyce's five-year-old brother. 'My goodness that time went quickly, didn't it?' She glanced at him, noticing the family likeness for the first time. She was happy Joyce had finally made her peace with her father, even if it had taken Philip to be the catalyst. Joyce's uncle Arthur had also forgiven Joyce's father for all the pain he had caused her, and allowing Ted to live with them in his house had given Joyce a chance to get to know her father again. Arthur was a different man to the one Rose and Annie first met when they came to London. He was no longer drowning his misery in alcohol while Joyce did her best to look after him; his home was now full of love again. Although, his heart still belonged to Dorothy in Worcester.

Philip nodded as he watched her pencil move across the page. 'Do you like drawing?'

Rose giggled. 'As you can see I'm not very good at it.' She turned the pages over on her pad to show Philip previous drawings. 'Look, I never draw hands or feet, or even faces. I just draw the outfits I'm trying to create.'

Philip studied the pages carefully. 'What made you decide to draw like this?'

Rose shrugged. 'I'm not sure. My older sister used to keep a diary when she was younger and pressed flowers from the fields, but that never interested me. Annie's sister learnt to play the piano, and Annie used to sing, but I was never very good at that. I suppose I was always sewing at home, darning things like socks and repairing my brothers' trousers, so one thing just led to the other.'

Philip wrinkled his nose. 'So you just started drawing?'

Rose laughed. 'My grandmother encouraged me to have a hobby. I used to make my own birthday cards because we never had the money to buy them but I soon got bored with that.'

Philip looked thoughtful. 'My grandma used to say you have to occupy your time. I didn't know what she meant.'

Rose smiled. 'She just meant find something that you enjoy doing, whether that's making something, reading a book, or in Joyce's case it was cooking and now that's what she does for a living.'

Philip nodded. He looked up at the shelves on the wall. 'You have a lot of books. Are they all ones you've drawn in?'

'Yes, some of them are not very good. I've got better with practice.' Rose paused before smiling at him. 'Shall I let you into a secret? But you mustn't tell.'

Philip's eyes widened. 'I won't tell, I promise. What is it?'

Rose peered over each of her shoulders in turn.

Philip copied her.

Rose lowered her voice to a whisper. 'Since I've come to London I have wondered whether it's actually possible to get my designs made and in the shops.'

Philip's mouth dropped open. 'So you'll be doing something you love just like my sister and Annie.'

Rose laughed. 'Maybe. It's a pipe dream at the moment but I want to try and then my grandma would really be proud.'

'What's a pipe dream?'

Rose shrugged. 'It's something that's not likely to happen.'

'I expect that's what Joyce thought.' Philip stood up and walked over to her shelf and gazed up. 'What's that on the ceiling?' He giggled. 'You haven't been drawing on it have you? I got told off once for drawing on the wall in my bedroom.'

Rose looked up and studied the brown stain. 'No, I haven't, and mind you don't trip over that bucket. I need to get Uncle Arthur to look at it because it doesn't look very good, does it?'

Philip shook his head before turning his attention back to the books. 'Why have some of them got pages hanging out of them?'

Rose laughed at all his questions. 'Sometimes I have to use scraps of paper until I get a new book. My grandmother gave me my first book to encourage me and now every Christmas she sends me a new one.'

Philip nodded. 'So why have they got numbers on them?'

Rose smiled. 'Can you count them?'

Philip looked thoughtful as he peered up.

Rose reached out and rested a hand on his. 'Go on, give it a try and I'll help you if you get stuck.'

Philip lifted his arm and pointed his finger at the books. 'One, two, three, four, five, six, and now you're on number seven.'

Rose chuckled. 'Well done. This one's number eight. Number seven seems to have gone missing, but I can see you're a clever boy.' She paused for a moment, watching him looking at her drawings. 'We should try doing something, perhaps drawing a picture of the house, or your pa or maybe the street. I know, when you go up to the village you can send us back drawings of the chickens and the trees and all the green fields; maybe you could write to us to let us know you're enjoying yourself.'

Philip's lips tightened for a moment. 'Did you like living there? I mean you came to London to live so you couldn't have liked it that much.'

Rose leant forward and wrapped her arms around his slim frame. The smell of carbolic soap clung to his skin. 'You don't need to be afraid, Philip. Us girls had a great childhood running around the farms and climbing trees.' She chuckled again. 'I was always getting into trouble, but my grandmother was my champion and would have none of it. She always stood up for me.'

Philip giggled. 'What did you do to get into trouble?'

Rose pretended to look thoughtful. 'Well, once I fell out of a tree and tore my skirt and blouse. My mother made me darn them in the hope that I'd be more careful because I had to repair the damage myself. I have to say, I don't think it made any difference.'

Philip shook his head. 'So why did you come to London then?'

'Annie was chasing her dream of being on the stage, she wanted to be a singer, so I came with her. The three of us were childhood friends, we went to school together, so it was only natural that I would come with her, and of course it was a chance to see Joyce again.'

Philip smiled. 'I still can't believe she's my sister. I'm very happy about it though.' He suddenly looked serious. 'I'm very lucky.'

Rose nodded. 'We all are, because we have each other and because we're loved.'

There was a light rap at the door. 'Rose, Philip, are you ready?'

Rose rested her finger on her lips before pushing her book under her pillow.

Philip ran to the door, glancing at Rose before pulling it open. 'Yes, Joyce, we're coming. Rose was just talking to me about drawing pictures and Annie wanting to sing, while you wanted to cook.' He grinned. 'I'm hungry.'

Joyce chuckled. 'You're always hungry.'

Philip ran past Joyce; his footsteps thudded down the stairs.

Joyce turned and followed him. She shouted, 'Go carefully. I don't want you falling.'

Rose laughed as she followed Joyce. 'He's so full of energy.'

Philip called out from the hall. 'Everyone's here so let's go. I'm starving.'

Joyce chuckled. 'Everyone's not there at all, cheeky.'

Annie smiled at Philip as she walked through from the sitting room. 'Are you being impatient?' She ruffled his hair before stepping towards the front door. The lock grated as she twisted it. The key, which hung on a long piece of frayed string, swung and thudded against the inside of the door. The hall lit up with the sunshine coming through the open door. 'Ready?'

Rose smoothed out the white cotton tablecloth, staring critically at the two interlocking B's she had embroidered on one of the corners. Leaning back against the hard wooden slats of her chair, she watched everyone tucking into their sausage and mash with great enthusiasm. The clatter of the cutlery hitting the plates told her they were making the most of their dinner in Joyce's Breaking Bread restaurant, even if the food shortages meant she had no option but to make the meals smaller. It was still a real treat to be in such plush surroundings.

Annie rested her knife and fork on the edge of her plate. 'This is lovely, Joyce. When do you think the restaurant will open for business?'

Joyce smiled. 'Thank you. The sign is going up this week – it's all very exciting. What do you think of its name?'

Murmurs travelled around the table.

Arthur looked up from cutting his sausages. 'I like the

name Breaking Bread and I think it sums up the times we're living in. It's all about coming together, sharing and caring about each other.'

Young Philip nodded. 'I fink Uncle Arthur's right, and you're always making bread.'

Everyone chuckled at the five-year-old's summing up.

Colour flooded Joyce's cheeks. 'I wouldn't have got to this amazing point without my wonderful friends and family.' She gazed over at her father. 'And yes, Pa, that does include you. I shall always be grateful to you all.'

Annie beamed. 'Have you set a date for your wedding yet?'

Joyce shook her head. 'I'm still in shock that Simon proposed.'

Annie laughed. 'Well, you must be the only one who is. You two are meant to be together, just like Charlie and Rose.' She pushed her fork down into the potato. 'When you think we only came to London just over a year ago, maybe eighteen months, and look how our lives have changed.'

Joyce ruffled her little brother's hair as he tucked ravenously into his dinner. 'Yes, it's unbelievable, isn't it? Philip is all packed up to go and stay with Pa and Uncle Arthur.' She stared down at him. 'I'm going to miss you, Philip, but I know you won't be sitting in the café all day like you used to.' She beamed. 'I still can't believe how much things have changed.' She looked over at her father. 'Are you definitely going back to the village to live, Pa?'

The wooden dining chair creaked as Ted leant back on it, letting his cutlery clatter down onto his dinner plate. 'I think so. It will be a better life for Philip – all that greenery, fields to run around in – and he can help his father on the farm collecting eggs and things like that. I realise now it was a good life but I didn't appreciate it at the time.'

Joyce tightened her lips. 'I shall miss you, and almost wish I was going back with you, but my life is here with Simon and this lovely restaurant.'

Annie smiled. 'I'm so glad you're not going, Joyce, for purely selfish reasons of course. It wouldn't be the same without you here.'

Arthur put down his fork and placed his hand over Joyce's for a moment. 'I don't have to tell you girls that you made a big difference to my life. You made me realise that I was on the road to ruin and I certainly wouldn't have got back without you.' He picked up his fork again. 'I'm looking forward to my fresh start up in Worcester with Dot. I will miss London but Dot naturally wants to stay in the village with her father, brother and the children and as we'll only be living next door she'll still be able to keep an eye on them, which is what she wants more than anything else. And with Ted and Philip living with us for a while we'll soon have that farm up and running once all the land is cleared.' He chuckled and looked over at Ted. 'So don't think you're coming up for a holiday – I'm putting you to work.'

Ted picked up his knife and fork again. 'I would never expect you to give me an easy ride. I know I've a lot of making up to do.'

Arthur chuckled. 'Well, you won't be disappointed then.' He turned to glance at Joyce. 'Anyway, I've decided not to go until after Kitty's wedding because I think it will be quite hectic for you and you'll need all the help you can get, even if it's only throwing out the rubbish.'

Ted nodded as he watched Joyce's mouth drop open to

speak. 'Don't say anything – we've had a family meeting and it's all been decided.'

Joyce shut her mouth again.

'It's certainly the least I can do.' Ted pushed some mashed potato onto his fork. 'As I said, I still have some making up to do.'

Joyce shook her head. 'No you don't, Pa, we need to just move on, and besides, everyone has already done so much for me.'

Annie frowned as she glanced over at Rose. 'Is everything all right, Rose?'

Philip glanced up from his dinner plate. 'There's a brown mark on her bedroom ceiling. I think she's been drawing on it but she said she hasn't.'

Everyone laughed.

Arthur frowned. 'Is that true?'

Rose smiled. 'What, that I've been drawing on the ceiling?'

Arthur guffawed. 'No, the mark?'

Rose nodded. 'Yes, there must be a leak somewhere.'

Arthur dabbed his mouth with a napkin. 'I'd better have a look at that then.'

Joyce glanced at Rose. 'Annie's right – you're very quiet.'

Rose forced herself to smile. 'I'm just enjoying my dinner and listening to everyone's chatter.'

Annie glanced at Rose's half-eaten meal. 'You seem troubled. Would you like to talk about it?'

Rose shook her head. 'No, I'm all right.'

Annie's eyes narrowed as she took in her friend's expression. 'It's clearly something – you're not your usual self – but I don't wish to pry.'

Rose sighed. 'Charlie...'

Annie's face lit up. 'Did he propose? No, you wouldn't look so unhappy if he had.'

Rose stared at her friend, trying to share her excitement. 'No he didn't, although for one scary moment I thought he was going to.' She sighed, wishing she hadn't said anything. 'He gave me this silver cross and chain.' She paused as her fingers touched the cross that was hanging from the fine necklace. 'He wants me to take a leap of faith, believe in myself, and my sewing. He was hoping it would remind me I have a creative talent, and should put it to good use.' Rose glanced around the table. No one was eating; they were just staring at her. 'He went on to say how he hoped to one day give me much more, and not just money.'

Annie frowned. 'That's a lovely thing to say, but do I take it, from what you said, you don't want him to give you more? I mean, I'm assuming he's talking about marriage.'

Rose cleared her throat. 'I don't know why he has to spoil things, not that he has proposed, but I thought we were happy as we are.'

Annie's eyes widened. 'But you love him, don't you?'

Rose pushed her plate aside and nodded.

Philip eyed her half-eaten dinner. 'Can I have that sausage, Rose?'

Rose smiled. 'Of course you can.'

Annie frowned.

Rose's neck was taut and her shoulders rigid.

Annie shook her head. 'I don't understand. If you love each other, why wouldn't you want to get married?'

Rose shrugged. 'I do love him but marriage is hard work. Look at our parents. They don't make time for each other because they're too busy worrying about putting food on the table for their family. Charlie is idealistic about love and marriage; he thinks life is too short to wait. What he doesn't realise is love gets lost in everyday living.'

Annie nodded. 'Our parents work hard to provide but I do know mine loved each other. They didn't show it through grand gestures – it was through a look or a touch when they thought no one was looking. They didn't always agree about things but there was respect for each other's opinion and feelings.'

Arthur coughed to clear his throat. He reached out and placed his hand on top of Rose's. 'I've made many mistakes in my life and I'm lucky to be given a second chance to put things right, where I can. One of the biggest was not looking after the love I had, taking it for granted and not talking about things. That meant there was a lot of pain and suffering with so many wasted years. I know your situation isn't the same but you need to tell Charlie how you feel, give him a chance to reassure you.'

Rose squeezed Arthur's hand. 'I know what you say is right but now isn't the time. He hasn't proposed. I need to be sure about how I feel about it. I thought I did want to but when he was talking I panicked. Anyway, who wants to get married because life is too short, or because of the war? What kind of proposal is that?'

Annie shook her head. 'Life is short. Everything can change on the toss of a coin. Look at my mother.' She took a breath. 'I expect Charlie just wants to be with you all the time, and if he's ever suffered a loss I think that's understandable because it makes you value life more – not that I know if he has or not.'

Rose looked thoughtful. 'He's lost his parents and his younger brother is away fighting.' She sighed. 'Do you think I'm being selfish?'

'No, I think you are just afraid.' Annie smiled. 'I have to say that does shock me a little because I've always thought of you as the fearless one. You've always stood up and said what you thought regardless of the trouble it got you into.'

Rose gave a small smile. 'It just goes to show saying and doing are two different things.'

Joyce nodded. 'Give yourself some time, and explain how you feel to Charlie. He loves you and as long as he knows you love him he'll wait.'

Rose bit her lip. 'That's not going to be an easy conversation. I wish I had your confidence.'

Joyce's laughter suddenly filled the room. 'Cast your mind back to me and Simon. You were very confident about us, remember?'

Rose chuckled. 'Yes, I remember.'

Charlie is a good man and you're a wonderful friend. I know you'll work it out.' Joyce looked at everyone around the table. 'Right, come on, eat your dinner before it gets cold.'

Annie frowned as she glanced over the dining table at Rose. 'Changing the subject, how's Kitty's wedding dress coming along?'

Rose sucked in her breath. 'I've had to sketch it out again from memory. I did show it to her and she still seems happy with it, but I had other ideas drawn out in that book.'

Annie pushed her knife through one of her sausages, slicing it into mouth-size pieces. 'Someone has obviously pinched it. You'd like to think if it was an accident they would have returned it, or at least popped their heads round the door of the sewing room to ask if it belonged to you.' She tightened her lips. 'You don't think it was Lizzie Turnbull do you?'

Rose frowned. 'I don't know, but I'm not sure how I'd ever find out.'

Annie shook her head. 'To think the many times I walked in on you with a pencil and a pad. I always thought you were keeping a diary.'

Rose gave a faint smile. 'It's disappointing but at the end of the day it's only a sketchbook – there's more important things to worry about. When I read in the newspaper about the Zeppelin raids in Walthamstow and Leyton Midland Road station it puts things in perspective. The homes damaged along with the lives lost or people injured, and probably while some slept in their beds. Those that did survive are probably homeless now.'

Silence reigned in the room as Rose cast her eyes over them. 'I'm sorry; I didn't mean to spoil the evening. When I think about the war, and how it's getting nearer to us, it scares me.'

Annie licked a spot of gravy from her lips. 'Maybe you're right, Arthur, life is too short with all this going on; perhaps we should be making the most of every day we have.' She stared down at her plate. 'If we're honest it scares us all. I'm a coward and I try not to think about the war. It's shameful but I've stopped buying newspapers as well.'

Joyce nodded. 'I can understand that but if we ever hope to get the vote we should be reading them, or going to watch Pathé News at the picture house; at least then we'll be more aware about what we could be voting for.'

Arthur's eyes narrowed as he peered under his lashes at Rose. 'You're stronger than you realise – we all are, but you girls definitely proved it when you decided to stay here with Joyce and I.'

Annie chuckled. 'I hate to admit it but at the time we stayed for Joyce.' The colour began to creep up her neck. 'I mean I don't think we said or did anything to get through to you; it was my brother who struck a chord with you.'

Arthur nodded. 'You're right about your brother but you all played a part in getting me back on track.'

Philip's eyes moved from side to side as each person spoke; his face was still and solemn. He tugged on his father's shirtsleeve. 'Does this mean we're not going on a train?'

Everyone round the table laughed.

Ted turned to his young son, his face full of pride. 'Yes we are but not yet. We're staying to help your sister with the wedding food.'

Philip's face lit up as he turned his attention to Joyce. 'Does that mean you'll make us some more biscuits?'

3

Rose sighed as she looked down at the crumpled French soldier's uniform on her sewing table. She hadn't been able to stop thinking about Charlie since he had given her the cross and chain. The shock of how much she had wanted to be with him, to lie in his bed, was flying around her head, day and night. She was struggling to think about anything else, and yet her reaction when she thought he was going to propose was totally unexpected; it had come from nowhere. Shaking her head, she decided she needed to stop thinking about him and how her emotions, on all sides, had caught her off guard.

Lizzie watched Rose's turmoil. 'Are you all right, Rose? You look quite tired and pale. I don't want to pry but you can trust me not to say anything if you want to talk.'

Rose forced a smile. 'Thank you, Lizzie, everything's fine. I haven't been sleeping very well. I was just wondering how these costumes get in such a state. These breeches have been ripped on the knee. Darning this in a way it can't be seen won't be easy.' Picking them up, she moved the ornamental buckle aside, and examined the frayed edges of the tear. 'I shouldn't moan; after all it's why I'm here.'

'I don't mind doing it. I'm always having to darn socks

at home so I'm quite used to it.' Lizzie picked up her needle and thread and ran her finger and thumb down to the end of the fine white cotton thread.

Rose smiled. 'No, it's all right. I don't mind doing it either; it's more about wondering how they manage it.'

Lizzie laughed. 'I expect it's because they know you're a good seamstress and everything looks new again after you've repaired any damage.'

Rose looked up at Lizzie. 'You could be right about them not worrying.' She glanced back down at the breeches, smoothing the palm of her hand over the leg before pulling the material together.

The sewing room door swung open. A heavy floral scent wafted in. It wasn't long before Miss Hetherington strode into the room, her heels tapping out her appearance. 'Good morning. There's a lot to do today so I hope you'll both be able to manage.'

Lizzie immediately lowered her head and got on with sewing the button onto the white blouse.

Rose continued to examine the breeches. 'I'm sure we'll manage; we usually do.' Sensing Miss Hetherington was still there, she looked up and her mouth dropped open. 'You're looking very nice this morning. It's unusual to see you in that style of dress.' She hesitated for a split second. 'Are you going somewhere special – maybe on a date?'

Miss Hetherington lowered her eyelashes. 'No, that time has long gone. I had my chance but it wasn't meant to be.' She snapped her eyes open, as colour filled her face. 'It's a special day for me so I treated myself to something different.'

Rose peered at Miss Hetherington. Was she reaching out to them? Remembering the numerous times Miss

Hetherington had been nasty to her, she immediately fought the urge to ask about the special occasion.

Miss Hetherington cleared her throat. 'Well, I must get on.'

Rose wondered if she'd imagined Miss Hetherington's softer tone just a few minutes earlier. She studied the tulip-shaped skirt with an overlay of contrasting colour that sat neatly on her calf. 'The shorter length suits you. Actually, it reminds me of something but I can't quite put my finger on it.'

A rare smile played on Miss Hetherington's lips, before she turned on her heels and left.

Lizzie looked up. 'Do you think she's got a man in her life?'

Rose shrugged as she stared at the doorway. 'She said not but who knows. I'm sure I've seen that dress somewhere…' The penny suddenly dropped. It was one of her designs from her missing book. Did that mean she hadn't mislaid her drawing book all those weeks ago? Had Miss Hetherington taken it? She caught Lizzie staring at her. 'Well, we'd better get on. As Miss Hetherington said we've a lot to do, although I noticed she didn't offer to help.'

Lizzie frowned. 'And that surprises you?'

Rose chuckled. 'It shouldn't do.'

The girls continued to work in silence.

Thoughts were running around Rose's head. How could she prove that Miss Hetherington had taken her book? It wasn't like she had seen her with it, and she couldn't just accuse her based on a dress. Her mind raced out of control. Perhaps she could lay a trap, but she felt sure the book was no longer in the theatre.

Annie came rushing in and immediately stopped at Rose's table. 'Have you seen old Hetherington? She's really dressed up. Do you think something's going on?'

Lizzie laughed. 'Remember to breathe, Annie.'

Annie took a gulp of air. 'Sorry, I shouldn't have rushed in like that but I couldn't believe it when she came into Kitty's dressing room. She looks more glamorous than Kitty, and I didn't think that was possible.'

Rose chuckled at her friend's flushed face. 'I wouldn't say she looks more glamorous than Kitty – that's taking it too far – but she's certainly dressed up. Apparently, it's a special day for her but I wasn't brave enough to ask why.'

Annie nodded. 'It's a lovely dress and must have cost a few bob. Perhaps she's come into money. If so maybe she'll give us all a break and leave.'

Rose was silent for a moment. 'Unless she made it.'

Annie frowned. 'I suppose that's possible but it's not a style I've seen before. Having said that I'm not an expert in these things. What do you think, Rose?'

Rose looked thoughtful. 'I would say she's probably seen a design and made it herself.'

Annie stared at her friend.

Lizzie glanced up at them. 'Do you think she's that clever? I'm sorry, that was mean of me.' The girls frowned as they glanced at her. 'The trouble is I can't imagine she could design something like that and then make a pattern to cut it out as well.'

Annie spun round to face Rose. 'Do you think she's the one—'

'She's probably a lot cleverer than we think.' Rose raised

her eyebrows at Annie. 'We need to just leave it there as we've a lot to do today.'

Annie nodded. 'I expect you're right.' She turned to walk towards the door. 'I'll speak to you later.'

'Annie, I noticed that man on the steps again this morning, so be careful when you leave tonight.' Rose looked down at the uniform on her table. 'I'm not saying he's dangerous but I noticed he's always watching when we come and go.'

Annie shuddered. 'I haven't noticed that but it does sound pretty creepy. I'll be careful, although Peter often meets me after the show.' She glanced at Lizzie. 'See you later, Lizzie.'

'Bye, Annie.' Lizzie's smile faded as she looked over at Rose. 'I'm sorry if I spoke out of turn.'

Rose picked up a reel of dark thread. 'There's no need to apologise. I'm just aware we haven't got started on these alterations yet.'

The hours passed. They gradually worked through the costumes that had been piled on the table.

Rose yawned as the day's concentration caught up with her. 'Lizzie, when you've finished what you're doing you might as well go home. It's been a tiring day.'

Lizzie nodded. 'Thank you. I must admit I'm shattered.'

There was a rap on the sewing room door and Annie immediately wandered in. 'Rose, Kitty's ready when you are.'

Rose stood up, scraping the chair legs across the tiled floor. 'That's good timing, Annie.' She stretched her back and walked around the table. 'I'll see you tomorrow, Lizzie. Take care going home.'

Lizzie smiled. 'Will do, and you.'

Annie and Rose strolled down the corridor. The only sounds were their small heels clipping the floor.

Rose yawned again. 'I could do with going home to bed.'

Annie eyed her friend. 'You do look tired.' She pushed open Kitty's dressing room door and they both walked in.

Gasping at the sight of Kitty in the white wedding dress, Rose studied it with a critical eye. She stepped back and tilted her head. 'I don't know how you manage in here, Kitty. There's not enough natural light.' Wrinkling her nose at the perfume, which had merged with the stale tobacco smoke and make-up, Rose glanced around, taking in the dingy walls with theatre posters randomly stuck on them. A rail stood in the corner with all Kitty's costumes for *The Royal Divorce* hanging on it. Playing Josephine Bonaparte gave her some luxurious frocks. The sink along with the kettle stood in the far corner with a couple of cups and a bottle of Camp Coffee. Rose looked back at Kitty's dressing table, which was strewn with make-up and creams. The only personal thing was a silver-framed photograph of Kitty as a teenager, with a beautiful smile and an expression full of promise.

Annie couldn't take her eyes off Kitty. 'It's so beautiful, Rose. You've done such a wonderful job.'

Rose didn't answer as she pulled out the soft material. 'How does it feel, Kitty? Does it fit well or do you want anything altered?'

Kitty stepped in front of the long mirror and stared at her reflection. Several layers of beautiful lace sat neatly over the fitted skirt of the white gown, giving it the look of a ball gown. The little pearl buttons holding it in place also shone on the lace flowers Rose had carefully cut out and sewn haphazardly onto the lace. The bodice fitted to perfection, and the short thin layer of lace overlay dropped over her shoulders to give the final covering for her modesty.

Panic began to rise up in Rose. 'Have I done something wrong?'

Kitty shook her head. 'Definitely not – it's beautiful. I'm sorry but I think it's worked in my favour that you lost your sketch pad. This dress is much better than the original drawing, and I loved that one. You're so clever, so talented; you're wasted here, not that I'm trying to get rid of you. Mending costumes feels such a waste of your skills.'

Rose could feel her colour rising. 'That's very kind of you, Kitty, but I've never made anything to order before. You took a real chance and I was worried I'd let you down.'

Kitty let out a girly giggle. 'That is where we differ; I never had any doubt you would deliver. This dress is absolutely beautiful, thank you. It fits perfectly. I know you're looking at it with a critical eye but you needn't worry.'

Rose frowned. 'Are you looking forward to being married?'

Kitty stayed silent for a moment.

Rose shook her head. 'Sorry, I shouldn't have asked. You obviously are otherwise you wouldn't be doing it.'

Kitty smiled. 'Don't be sorry; it's a good question.' She looked thoughtfully at her reflection in the mirror. 'People marry for lots of different reasons, some for love and some, particularly women, marry for security. To have a roof over their head and not live on the streets. I'm one of the lucky ones, and I have been for years and just didn't know it.

I'm marrying for love. I can't imagine anything better then waking up next to someone who adores you, someone who will do anything for you.'

Rose stared at Kitty. 'Would you do the same?'

Kitty beamed. 'Yes, I actually would. I've come to realise we don't always see what's right in front of us. I had to open my eyes wide to see what was there all along.'

Rose nodded. 'I suppose we get caught up in our own lives so it's easy not to notice things.' She smiled as Kitty turned to look at herself from a different angle. 'Once you're married you can wear it as a fitted dress. If you leave off the lace overlay, either one or both of them, then you'll get your money's worth out of the dress.'

Kitty stared at her reflection. 'What a wonderful idea, Rose. See, you are clever.'

Annie nodded her agreement. She leaned in for a closer look at the flowers sewn on the lace. 'Is this what Jane Hetherington caught you doing just before Kitty walked in the other week?'

Rose's lips tightened. 'Yes, she caught me cutting out flowers from a piece of lace she'd thrown away. To be honest I thought she was going to sack me.'

Kitty gasped. 'I would never allow that to happen, Rose, especially when you're working on something for me. That woman needs taking down a peg or two.'

Rose shrugged. 'Well, it didn't happen, but thank you all the same.'

Annie sighed. 'I don't know how you cope working with her. She's rude and unappreciative of all your hard work.'

'I would be lying if I said I hadn't thought about leaving, because she does get me down, but I love my job and that's what keeps me here. Charlie thinks I should become a full-time seamstress.'

Kitty swung round in her dress, her eyes drawn to the way it moved. 'I have to say, looking at this, Charlie's right – you're definitely wasted here but don't tell Stan I said that because I'll deny it.'

They all giggled at Kitty's admission.

Annie suddenly swung round to study Rose. 'You're not though, are you?' She frowned. 'After all, we're like a family here.'

Rose nodded. 'I know we are, and that's all that holds me here.'

Kitty glanced at Annie's reflection in the mirror. 'You know, Annie, as a friend you shouldn't try and hold Rose back from reaching her potential. It's hard... when you had the opportunity to stop being my dresser and live your dream of being an actress my first reaction was to kill Stan for even thinking it was a good idea, but as the stage manager cum director he was right and I was wrong. Real friends encourage each other not hold them in place.' She chuckled. 'Hark at me getting all deep and meaningful.'

Annie's tightened lips lifted at the corners. 'No, you're right, Kitty.' She turned to Rose. 'Without hesitation you came to London to support me and now I should be supporting you in what you want to do.'

Rose reached out to her friend. 'Don't worry, Annie, I'm not going anywhere. I'm not that brave.'

Annie glanced back at the wedding dress. 'Maybe you should seriously think about it though.'

There was a rap on the dressing room door. They all jerked round and stared at it, as the turning handle creaked round.

Annie was the first to kick into action; she ran over and stood in front of it. 'Who is it?' The door pushed against Annie's body; her feet didn't move.

'What's going on? It's Stan. I want to come in.'

Annie glanced over at Kitty, who was frantically shaking her head. 'I'm sorry, Stan, can you come back in about half an hour?'

There was no answer.

Annie frowned. 'Stan, are you there?'

'Yes, yes I'm here.' Stan's voice was barely a whisper. 'Is everything all right? Is Kitty all right?'

Annie fought the urge to pull the door open. 'Everything is more than all right, Stan.' She smiled. 'Your fiancée is trying on her wedding dress and it's bad luck for you to see it before the day.'

'Do you like it, Kitty?' Stan's happiness shone through his words.

Kitty laughed. 'Oh my darling, I more than like it; I love it. It's beautiful as you will see on our wedding day. Rose has done a wonderful job.'

Stan chuckled. 'I can't wait, but I'll come back in half an hour. I don't want to spoil your moment with the girls.' He pulled the door shut and his heavy footsteps faded away.

Alexander Bowman stared out of the window in the Dickens and Jones boardroom. The September sunshine was fighting to get through the afternoon cloud. He fleetingly wondered if it was going to rain. He gazed down at the hustle and bustle of Regent Street; for the first time he noticed women queuing at the butcher's. How was a man meant to live without a good meal? He sighed as his gaze wandered; he never tired of looking out at the busy London Street. He loved living in the city, the aromas of the food mingling with the scent coming from the flowers that were for sale up and down the street. He watched the sellers at their barrows trying to attract customers to buy their wares. There was always so much going on, unlike the sleepy village he came from. He smiled as he remembered standing open-mouthed the first time he saw a street performer.

He turned and looked around the large room that was dominated by a long table. Alexander wrinkled his nose at the smell of beeswax hanging in the air, wishing he could open a window to get the true smell of the city. After a moment he smiled. He'd done well. He didn't suffer any pangs of guilt that he hadn't acknowledged the help he had received along the way; after all no one made it on their own. It was sad that his marriage was soon to be over but she had served a purpose. Her money had enabled him to buy the best suits, to dine in the finest restaurants, and to mix with the right people. The door handle creaked as it turned. Mr Bowman pulled himself upright and painted on his best smile as the door opened.

'I'm sorry to have kept you waiting, Mr Bowman, but I have been speaking with the owners.'

Alexander's heart was pounding in his chest. Was he about to get the sack? He hadn't expected to see Mr Woodford. He was as high as it got in Dickens and Jones. The rotund, grey-haired man marched quickly towards the table, belying his advanced years.

Mr Woodford dropped a stack of papers onto the highly polished table and pulled out an ornate wooden chair at the head of it. 'Come, take a seat. We have things to talk about and I don't have much time.'

Alexander looked around at the dozen or more chairs and wondered which one he should sit on.

Mr Woodford glanced at him and sighed. 'Just pick one and sit down.'

Alexander quickly stepped forward and pulled out a chair nearest to him, but a couple down from Mr Woodford. The soft leather cushioned seat and back wrapped around him.

Mr Woodford spread out a couple of the sheets of paper he had brought in with him. 'Well, Mr Bowman, what can I say? Six months ago I was thinking I'd have to ask you to leave us but you seem to have turned things around.' He pushed the papers towards Mr Bowman. 'These are the latest sales figures on your clothing line. I don't know what's happened but it seems nothing short of a miracle to me. I'm curious, have you had some help with these latest designs?'

'No, sir.'

Mr Woodford patted his suit jacket and sighed. 'For heaven's sake, now I've left my pen behind.'

Mr Bowman pulled out a silver fountain pen and placed it in front of Mr Woodford. 'You're welcome to use mine.'

Mr Woodford picked it up and appeared to weigh it in his hand. 'This is a very nice pen. It must have set you back a bit.' He took the top off and scribbled on the paper in front of him. 'It writes nice too.' He chuckled as he handed it back. 'We must be paying you too much.'

Mr Bowman took the pen and tucked it away inside his jacket pocket, thankful his wife's solicitors hadn't noticed the pen was missing from their office. 'It's important to make the right impression, sir.'

'That it is, that it is.' Mr Woodford studied Mr Bowman for a moment. 'I've heard a rumour that the seamstress manageress…' He glanced down at a piece of paper. '… Mrs Todd, was helping you, so I wondered if she had any part in these latest creations.'

Alexander nodded. 'Mrs Todd is a valuable asset, and while she did help with the previous designs I can assure you she had no hand in this latest line.'

Holding one of the pages at arm's length, Mr Woodford studied it for a moment. 'I know nothing about women's fashion so I can't really comment on any of it, but I'm told by my wife and daughters that the range is quite magnificent.'

Alexander puffed out his chest. 'Thank you, sir.'

Mr Woodford nodded. 'Well I'm glad to hear it, as it's probably saved your job, especially as your soon-to-be ex-wife is like family. Had you failed I would have been under a lot of pressure to let you go. However, business is business and if the sales of your new range continue you could find yourself with a bonus cheque at the end of the season.' He placed the paper down on the table and peered over his glasses at Alexander. 'It's important we keep ahead of our competitors, so are you now working on the next collection?'

Alexander fidgeted in his chair. 'Yes, I'm already giving it quite a lot of thought.'

Mr Woodford's lips flattened slightly. 'You need more than thought, Mr Bowman. This is quite a cutthroat business and we need our customers to keep returning to us.'

'Yes, sir, I always make sure that our customers get a very personalised service.' Alexander weaved his damp fingers together and rested them on the table, taking a breath, knowing he had to sound confident if he was to be successful. 'While I have you here, I wonder if I may be so bold to ask if we could discuss taking on another seamstress.'

Mr Woodford pushed his glasses further up the bridge of his nose as he peered down at the designs and the sales figures that were in front of him. 'Is it really necessary?'

'I believe so. With the success of the collection has come the need for more alterations as well as putting together the new collection.' Alexander fought the urge to rub the trickle of sweat that was running down the back of his neck. 'I want to put forward the best I can but I also need good staff to do that and a talented seamstress wouldn't cost very much against the return we would get.'

Mr Woodford nodded. 'If you feel you can deliver a similar collection with such great results then I think you can pretty much have what you want, within reason.' His eyes narrowed as he studied Mr Bowman. 'I must admit to being more than a little intrigued as to how you managed to turn it around. One minute we were having discussions about sacking you and the next we're praising the sales of your clothing range. It's certainly quite bewildering.'

Alexander lifted his head slightly and pulled back his shoulders. 'All designers have times where they feel they can't create. Thankfully my creativity seems to have returned.'

Mr Woodford gathered the paperwork together. It rustled as he bounced and shuffled the ends of it on the table until they were neatly stacked. 'Well, I can't pretend to understand it all but I'm very pleased and, more importantly, so are the board. As long as you keep delivering, your future is safe with Dickens and Jones, and from what I hear you need this job so make sure you look after it.'

Alexander scowled, biting down on his tongue until the iron taste of blood filled his mouth.

Mr Woodford stood up. 'Now I must get on.' He hesitated for a moment. 'Perhaps we can have a drink at the club later, but I have no desire to get caught up in the tribulations of your marriage.'

Standing up, Alexander followed his lead. 'Yes, that would be lovely. They seem to have messed up my membership but I'm in the process of sorting that out.'

Mr Woodford frowned. 'That's unlike them; they are normally on the ball. Would you like me to have a word?

Mr Bowman vigorously shook his head. 'Oh no, I wouldn't want you to be bothered with such a trivial thing. It's all in hand but thank you for offering.'

'Very well. Let me know when it's sorted and we'll have a chat and a drink.' Mr Woodford headed towards the door. 'Keep up the good work and I'm sure we'll speak again soon.'

Mr Bowman breathed a sigh of relief as he headed towards the door. Now he definitely had to make his plan work.

Annie smoothed down the skirt of her long mauve bridesmaid dress before peering into the small church, and watched Stan looking around at its stained-glass windows. The sanctuary had seating for around two hundred people. The altar was small and the aisle narrow, but that gave it an intimate feel.

There was no best man. When Annie had asked Stan about it he had confided he didn't need, or want, the fuss let alone someone telling him to look after Kitty; he had been doing that ever since he'd met her. Annie had been surprised how much they had wanted it to be very personal and not have throngs of people in attendance.

'It's warm out there.' Rose patted her forehead with a lace handkerchief as she walked through the church doorway into the cool vestibule, clutching the couple of stems of orange blossom tied together with white ribbon across her Bible with one hand and patting the back of her hair with the other. Her blonde unruly locks had been rolled into a chignon and flower decorations had been pushed into it. The dark oak church door had been pushed back against the grey stone wall.

Rose stepped forward, and followed Annie's gaze. As she glanced around, thoughts of what her own wedding might be like popped into her head. Was this where she would marry someday, or would she go back home to the village? Her stomach churned as excitement took over. She took a couple of deep breaths to silence her thoughts. 'It's good to be in the shade at last. I did worry that the weather might change especially as it's been a warm September so far, but I'm so pleased the sun stayed out for them today.'

Annie nodded as she turned round and nudged Rose, who swung round and saw Kitty enter the church vestibule. Rose drew in a sharp intake of breath. The luxurious wedding dress was a perfect fit.

Kitty's eyes became watery. 'Do you think Stan will love it?'

Annie stood stunned for a moment; she couldn't believe what Kitty was saying. 'You look so beautiful, what is there not to love?' Annie shook her head. 'You do know you could turn up in a potato sack and Stan would love it. He's waited a long time for you to realise the love of your life has always been right under your nose.'

Kitty turned to Rose. 'I owe you and Annie so much; you've both changed my life and become my family. I don't want to ruin my make-up by crying but I can't thank you both enough.'

Rose sniffed, trying to hold back her tears as she stepped forward to fiddle with Kitty's long veil, straightening it at the back.

Annie smiled. 'You don't have to thank us. Just be happy – that's what we all want for family and friends.' The sound of the organ playing Mendelssohn's 'Wedding March' inside jolted them all into action. 'Be happy.'

Kitty leant in and wrapped her arms around each girl in turn. She finally stepped back and giggled. 'I can't believe I'm actually getting married.' She took a breath.

Rose peered round the doorway and caught Stan looking anxiously in her direction. 'Well, we'd better not keep Stan waiting any longer.'

Kitty nodded.

The girls moved into a single line and started walking slowly in front of Kitty, in time to the music.

Stan's face lit up as he saw his bride walking towards him.

Neither seemed to notice the gasps from the congregation as they caught sight of the bride; they only had eyes for each other.

Kitty, flushed with happiness, finally stood next to the man who was on the brink of being her husband. Her gaze was full of love as she looked into his eyes. There was no doubt she would love this man forever.

Stan smiled. 'You're beautiful.' He blinked quickly and cleared his throat as he took her hand. 'I love you.'

Kitty looked at him through blurred eyes. 'I love you too and always will.' She turned and handed Annie her Bible and posy of orange blossom. The sweet, simple floral scent filled the air around them.

Joyce stood by the kitchen door of her Breaking Bread restaurant and cast her eye over the tables that were set for the guests who were about to arrive.

'It looks grand, Joyce. Today is going to be a glorious success.'

Joyce frowned at her father. 'Thank you, although I wish I had your confidence, Pa, but the place does look good.'

Rose strolled over towards them, stopping to straighten a crisp white tablecloth and napkins on one of the tables. 'I think you've done Kitty proud. She'll be over the moon when she arrives in a moment for her wedding breakfast. Won't she, Annie?'

Annie beamed. 'Most definitely.'

Joyce looked at her friends. 'You should've stayed in the church for longer and enjoyed watching Kitty and Stan get married. I'm sure we would have managed.'

Annie smiled. 'I'm sure you could've done but we wanted

to help. Anyway, we did see them get married, and had photographs taken with them; we just didn't stay around after that. Kitty and Stan will understand as they say the show must go on and today they are both the stars.'

Arthur walked through the open kitchen doorway. 'I'm assuming they'll be here any time now. Shall I pour the champagne Stan gave us for the toast into the glasses?'

Joyce shook her head. 'I don't think it'll be needed until after the meal. We could put jugs of water down on the table.' She scanned the room once again. 'I feel quite nervous. I hope I don't let them down.'

'You won't.'

Annie beamed at Rose. 'You know Kitty looked fantastic today. That dress was so beautiful – you've clearly kept your talent hidden from your friends.'

Rose's face immediately turned scarlet. 'I don't think I have, at least not intentionally. I didn't know I could do it until Kitty asked me to. I was so nervous about getting it wrong.'

Annie looked around at her friends. 'I don't think any of you have got anything to worry about. I'm very lucky to have such talented friends.'

The restaurant door flew open and Stan carried Kitty inside. There was a lot of laughter as they almost fell through the doorway.

'Stan, put me down.'

A man followed them in. 'Yes, put her down, Stan. You don't want to ruin that beautiful creation she's wearing.' He chuckled. 'I may never forgive her for not buying her dress from me, and to think I thought we were friends.'

Kitty laughed. 'Stop it, Alexander, you know we are. Jealousy is an ugly thing, as well you know.'

Stan lowered Kitty to the ground. He leant in and gave her a kiss. 'Hello, Mrs Tyler.'

Kitty giggled. 'Hello, Mr Tyler.'

Mrs Todd beamed at the happy couple before turning to Mr Bowman. 'Thank you so much for inviting me to come with you. It's been such a wonderful wedding and the dress is beautiful.'

Mr Bowman stared at Mrs Todd. 'You are lucky; unfortunately my wife was unavailable to come with me.' He sighed. 'And at least you get to see why Kitty didn't come to us for her wedding dress, and that's a great loss to Dickens and Jones.' He glanced over at Kitty and smiled. 'You truly look like a princess, my lovely.'

Kitty tilted her head. 'Why thank you, kind sir.'

Rose stepped forward to tidy the veil.

'Don't worry, Rose, I'm going to take it off – well if you don't mind helping me that is.' Kitty reached up to the silver tiara she was wearing.

Alexander eyed the young girl fussing around Kitty. 'Wait, are you the Rose who designed and made Kitty's dress?'

Rose could feel the heat rise up in her face. 'Yes.'

Annie stepped forward. 'Why don't you sit down and it will make it easier to remove the veil for you.'

Rose smiled at Annie. 'I'll let you do it because you are better at hair than me.'

Alexander's eyes sparkled as he stared at Rose. 'You have a wonderful talent and I can help you to take it further.' Alexander thrust his hand inside his jacket pocket and pulled out a small white card. 'Take this. You are wasted at the theatre; I want you with me at Dickens and Jones and I'll not take no for an answer.'

Rose's heart was racing. 'Thank you, sir, but I couldn't possibly leave the theatre.'

Alexander thrust the card at her again. 'You, my dear, can achieve so much more.'

Charlie coughed gently into his hand. 'Why not take it in case you change your mind?'

Alexander raised his eyebrows as he turned to look at Charlie. 'That is an excellent idea; at least you'll know where to find me when you realise I'm offering you a dream job.'

Kitty gave him a mischievous look. 'You'll have to make it a good offer, Alexander. Rose is going to be famous.'

Rose's colour deepened. 'I don't think that's true.'

'Oh, trust me, it is.' Kitty beamed at Rose. 'A journalist was outside the church. He wanted a photograph, so I told him he could only have one if he mentioned the dress designer.' She giggled. 'I told him all about you.'

Alexander shook his head. 'We can talk about what you want to get out of it when you come to see me.'

Charlie took Rose's hand in his. 'She's very talented and should have her own collection.'

Alexander frowned. 'You are quite right. Miss Spencer is very talented and I'm just the person to hone her creativity and teach her how things work in a prestigious shop.'

Charlie nodded and glanced at Rose. 'It sounds like a great opportunity for you.'

Kitty smiled at Alexander. 'Where's your wife? I hope you realised the invitation was for two?'

Alexander grinned. 'Of course. She sends her apologies, but she had a prior engagement.'

Simon picked up a knife and tapped one of the glass flutes a couple of times. 'Welcome to Breaking Bread. If you would all like to take your seats we will start to serve the food and drink. Thank you.'

4

'Morning, Bert,' Annie and Rose chorused as they walked through the open stage door of the Lyceum Theatre.

'It's still quite warm out there for September,' Annie quipped as she pulled at the bottom of her soft cream blouse. 'Do you want the door left open?'

Bert put down his newspaper. 'Yes please. It gets stuffy in here. I think it's the make-up and the smell of the paint that gets splattered around every day, as well as all the hot air.'

Rose smiled. 'You don't seem very happy this morning. Is everything all right?'

'Yeh, it's just 'er innit. I don't know what you two 'ave been up to but Miss 'etherington is looking extraordinary these days and I don't know what's worse – the 'appy or snappy one. I tell ya what: I don't trust 'er not as far as I can throw 'er. Somink is going on. Do you fink she's got a boyfriend?'

Annie shrugged. 'How would we know? We'd be the last people she'd tell.'

The clatter of heels further along the corridor caught their attention.

'Do you think that's her?' Rose looked at Annie. 'If it is

I might go home again. I just can't face her every day. She gets me down too, Bert.'

Bert followed her gaze down the corridor. 'It sounds like 'er. Yer sit 'ere for long enough yer get to recognise the footsteps.' He looked back at Annie and Rose. 'Don't yer go letting 'er get you down. She ain't worth it. Although I'm curious about why she's suddenly dressing up for work.'

Rose shrugged. 'Last time she told me it was because it was a special day but who knows, maybe she's meeting someone or going to a restaurant.'

Bert raised his eyebrows. 'I don't know but it's the talk of the theatre. Mind now yer mention the special day fing – someone said she dresses up about the same time every year, only for a few days like, and then she goes back to 'er usual self. Not that I'd noticed that.'

'That sounds intriguing. I wonder what it is.' Annie glanced from Bert to Rose. 'Do you think she has stolen your book? Do you think that's why she's suddenly wearing all these fancy clothes?'

Rose tightened her lips. 'I have no proof. I only know the outfit she had on the other day looked very much like something I had drawn.'

The three of them stood and waited with bated breath for the figure to show themselves along the corridor. It wasn't long before they saw Miss Hetherington heading their way.

Rose gasped as she saw the outfit she was wearing.

Annie and Bert both swerved round to look at her.

Annie shook her head and frowned. 'It's one of yours, isn't it?'

Rose shrugged. 'I drew something similar, but that doesn't

mean it was mine; maybe my imagination is very similar to other people's.'

Bert tutted. 'They may well be but they're certainly not like anything Miss 'etherington's ever worn to work before.' He glared at her as she came towards them. 'Trust me, I see 'er every day and suddenly she's coming into work looking quite glamorous. I tell yer something ain't right.'

Rose was tight-lipped for a moment. 'Maybe she has a man in her life lifting her spirits.'

Bert threw back his head and guffawed with laughter. 'I can't imagine that man exists.'

Annie straightened her shoulders and thrust out her chin. 'I think we should confront her once and for all.'

Rose frowned as she looked at her friend. 'And how are we going to do that without getting the sack?'

Annie shrugged. 'There must be a way. I should talk to Kitty or Stan; maybe they could—'

'No, I don't want everybody involved; you know what this place is like for gossip. No, this is my problem and I have to find a way of dealing with it, even if that means walking away.'

Bert frowned. 'What does that mean "walking away"?'

Rose shrugged, rubbing her damp palms down the sides of her black calf-length skirt. 'Charlie thinks I should be moving on. He thinks I have a real skill and it's wasted here.'

Annie gasped. 'You're not going to leave though, are you? I mean I know Miss Hetherington gets you down but…'

Rose lowered her eyes. 'I don't know what I'm going to do but London's a large city paved with opportunities so why shouldn't I spread my wings a little further?'

Annie stood silent for a moment. 'I don't know what to say, except I don't want you to leave, and she shouldn't have the power to drive you out.' She paused. 'I know I should be encouraging you, like Kitty said, but I can't imagine not working with you every day.'

Rose tilted her head. 'I like working here but I must admit avoiding the daily arguments is getting harder.' She paused before whispering, 'And maybe it's time I tried for my own dream of making clothes that I love.'

Miss Hetherington approached them carrying a bundle of papers, juggling them in her arms as she tried to look at her wristwatch. 'Ah, Miss Spencer, I'm so glad you could make it in today.'

Rose sighed. The hair on the back of her neck stood on end. 'I make it in every day, and I'm always early. I would appreciate you not making those sorts of comments because I'm getting pretty fed up with it.'

Miss Hetherington's eyes held a steel-like quality, while a small smile played on the corners of her mouth. She moved her papers from one arm to the other. The bundle started to slip and slide from her grasp and landed on the floor.

Annie rushed forward to pick them up for her, quickly followed by Rose.

'Thank you, Miss Cradwell, at least someone here has some manners.'

Rose picked up the pages one by one and came across a wallet lying open underneath them. A photo of a young man was staring back at her. It was cracked down the side, she guessed from where it had been pushed in and out of the wallet so many times.

Miss Hetherington snatched it from Rose's hand and snapped it shut. 'I believe that belongs to me.'

Annie gave her a steely glare. 'Miss Hetherington, have you seen Rose's sketch pad?'

'Seen it? I didn't even know Miss Spencer had one.'

Rose pulled back her shoulders and jutted out her chin. 'It's usually in the sewing room but it's gone missing.'

Miss Hetherington glared at Rose. 'What makes you think I would know, or care, about where it is?'

Annie glanced from her friend to Miss Hetherington. 'It contains some drawings that Rose has done.'

'Drawings?' Miss Hetherington arched her eyebrows. 'I'm not interested in your drawings. Whatever next?'

Rose stood her ground. 'I've looked everywhere for it.'

Miss Hetherington frowned. 'You clearly haven't done a very good job looking for it if you still haven't found it.'

Rose shook her head. 'The dress you're wearing today matches one of the sketches, and it's not the first one you've worn either.'

Miss Hetherington's face reddened. 'I do not have to explain myself to you but just so you know I bought this, so you're clearly not as clever as you think.'

The pulse in Rose's temple throbbed and the invisible band tightened around her forehead. 'I'm sorry, but the dresses are identical.'

Miss Hetherington's eyes widened. 'You need to be very careful, especially as it sounds to me like you're calling me a liar.'

Rose turned away from them and stormed outside. She threw herself down on one of the cold steps outside the theatre and snapped her eyes shut. No tears, she told herself, no tears. They pricked at her eyelids but she squeezed them tighter.

'Are you all right?'

Rose didn't move. Her throat tightened as she fought against crying.

'I know I'm not so well turned out as you but you don't have to ignore me.'

Rose opened her tired eyes and looked in the direction the voice was coming from. Stiffening, she clenched her hands, instantly recognising the man who sat every day behind one of the theatre's pillars. 'I wasn't ignoring you.' She hadn't thought about the dishevelled man on the steps when she sat down. 'I'm sorry, but it's already been the sort of day you shouldn't get out of bed for.' She folded her arms in front of her. Her fingers gripped the softness of her blouse.

The middle-aged man nodded. 'No need to be sorry, I'm used to being invisible to people.' He smiled, which was only just visible through his out-of-control beard. 'I just wanted to make sure you were all right.'

Rose inhaled deeply, taking in his pungent breath. 'That's very kind of you.' She watched the people walking by. 'I'm just tired of not knowing what to do with myself and putting up with things I shouldn't have to.' For the first time she turned to look at the man properly. His coat was torn and he had a grubby blanket across his legs. His bushy beard had grey strands threading through the brown hair. She frowned; maybe he wasn't the threat she thought he was. 'Do you live on the street?'

The man studied her for a moment before nodding. 'You

need money to live in a nice home and I've struggled to get a job.' He ran his fingers through his tangled hair.

For the first time Rose noticed half of his little finger was missing. 'What's your name?'

Silence reigned between them for a moment.

The voices of stallholders shouting to sell their wares rung out, mingling with the spluttering of the car engines on The Strand. People chattering and laughing as they walked past the theatre filled the space between them.

He frowned as he glanced at her. 'It's Michael.'

Rose smiled. 'Hello, Michael, it's lovely to meet you. I'm Rose.'

'I know. I see you and your friend Annie arrive here every day, along with some of the others.'

A clock chimed in the distance.

'It's time…' Michael glanced over Rose's shoulder. 'It's time I left.'

Rose followed his gaze and watched Miss Hetherington step out through the open stage door.

'Don't let her rudeness make you move on.'

Rose turned to look back at Michael but he was gone. Sighing, she stood up and made her way back to the stage door and the work that was waiting for her.

Rose's heart was pounding as she marched along Great White Lion Street. Beads of perspiration were forming on her forehead. Her mind had gone round and round in circles all day. She had convinced herself that Miss Hetherington had stolen her book with all her ideas for clothes sketched inside it, along with details of material to use. She shook her head, but there was no evidence to confront her with – only the dress she wore today. It had to be thought through; after all she could be given the sack and then what would she do?

Charlie's bicycle shop soon came into view; she would discuss it with him. Rose knew Annie wouldn't be happy because they'd always discussed everything, but she wouldn't want her to leave the theatre so would advise her not to rock the boat, or she'd want Kitty to deal with it.

Rose watched Charlie as he stepped out of the shop and started chatting to a young boy. Charlie held the handlebars of a blue bicycle while the lad climbed up and sat on the saddle, reminding her of Philip's first time on one. Rose waited and watched as Charlie adjusted the seat before ruffling the boy's hair. The lad gazed up at him open-mouthed before a smile spread across his face. The boy was beaming as he cycled away and Charlie began walking the rest of the bicycles inside the shop. A smile played on her lips.

Charlie suddenly stopped and looked up. He grinned as he watched her walking towards him. 'Oh my goodness, what a sight for sore eyes, and to what do I owe this pleasure?'

Rose, flushed with colour, grinned. 'I just thought I'd come to see you; maybe we could have a cuppa together, if you're not too busy.'

Charlie took Rose's hand in his. 'I'll never be too busy to see you. Come in and take a seat while I wheel these last few inside. It's good timing because I'm just closing up.'

Rose smiled. 'I can help.' She took the handlebars of a small blue bicycle that was standing behind him against the wall. 'This is about my limit though.' She laughed.

Charlie grinned at her. 'It all helps.' He followed her inside with his bicycle while closing the door with his foot as he walked in. He turned to lock the door and changed the sign to closed.

Rose frowned as she stepped over a black stain on the floor, wrinkling her nose at the potent smell of oil. 'Charlie, I don't want you closing early because I paid you a visit.'

Charlie glanced over his shoulder and gave her a winning smile. 'Oh, I won't miss out on any business. I don't know how many you think I sell in a week but you could probably at least halve it to what it actually is.' He paused. 'I'll make us that cuppa. I might even have some cake.'

Rose shook her head. 'No cake for me, thank you.' She smiled. 'I don't think Joyce has heard about food shortages, when it comes to cake and biscuits. I'll have to let my skirts out if I don't stop eating them.'

Charlie leant back and eyed her from top to toe. 'You're beautiful, inside and out, so don't change a thing.'

Rose could feel the colour rising in her face.

Charlie smiled. 'Anyway, to what do I owe the pleasure of this visit? Not that you need a reason of course; I'm always happy to see you.'

Rose frowned. 'I'll tell you when we're settled.' She smiled. 'I only came because you make a lovely cup of tea.'

Charlie shook his head. 'I don't care about the reason as long as it gets you here.' He pulled out a chair for Rose.

'You know, Charlie, no one has ever spoken to me the way you do. I don't always know how to respond, but I love your kindness.'

Charlie frowned. 'I hope you see it as more than kindness, otherwise I'm in big trouble.'

Rose nodded. 'If that's true then we're both in trouble.'

She stepped over a chain on the floor.

Charlie bent down and picked it up. 'Sorry, I was fixing a bicycle that someone had brought in.' It clattered as he dropped it on the counter. 'I need to sort some of this out. The trouble is when I think I don't need something it turns out I do.'

Rose laughed. 'It's always the same. I used to keep material offcuts but I never used them.' She picked up a strange-looking tool, turning it over in her hand before placing it back on the counter. 'I don't mind helping you to have a sort-out, although I've no idea what some of this stuff is.'

Charlie chuckled. 'I might hold you to that.'

Rose glanced at Charlie. 'That young lad looked happy as he pedalled away. It's good that you've sold one; it's one less to bring inside.'

'It wasn't exactly a sale, but wasn't it great to see him so happy?'

Shaking her head, Rose smiled. 'You'll never get rich if you keep giving them away.'

Charlie adjusted the pedals of the bicycle nearest him. There was a clang of metal as it fell against another one. 'I know but who said I wanted to be rich?'

Rose laughed. 'You're terrible.'

'Anyway, it's good to be able to give something back to the community. I wish I could do more, but you never know, maybe one day this shop might become the centre for this community. I'd love that.' Charlie paused. 'Anyway, what do you want to talk to me about?'

Rose's lips tightened as her fingers traced the grain of the wooden counter. 'I can't remember if I told you before but I have several books that I use to sketch out ideas for women's clothes. No one has ever looked in them, well, except Kitty and Annie of course.' She looked up and caught him staring at her.

Charlie smiled. 'Go on.'

Rose tightened her lips. 'This all sounds silly now I'm saying it out loud.'

Charlie shook his head. 'Don't worry about that. If it concerns you then it concerns me so spit it out.'

Rose stared at the counter and took a deep breath. 'Well, there's no easy way to say this, even though I feel awful for thinking it, never mind saying it out loud to someone I care about.'

Charlie frowned. 'Stop worrying and just say it.'

Rose took another breath. 'I had a sketchbook that I kept at work. I'd do rough drawings in it when ideas came to me, and, well the thing is—'

'Yes…'

'Well, the thing is it went missing some time ago…'

Charlie studied Rose. 'From the tone of your voice I'm assuming something has happened today, but it wasn't you finding it.'

Rose shook her head. 'No, it wasn't. Miss Hetherington came into the sewing room wearing a dress that I'm convinced is from my missing book but I can't prove it, and it's not the only time it's happened.'

Charlie pulled back his shoulders. 'What are you going to do?'

Rose shrugged. 'That's just it, what can I do? I've no proof, especially as I don't have the book.'

Charlie paced up and down in the tiny gap between the bicycles and the counter. 'There must be something we can do. She can't be allowed to get away with it.'

Rose lifted the corner of her mouth. 'Well, I've thought of nothing else all day and I've come up with nothing. I obviously can't just accuse her or I'll end up getting the sack.' She sighed. 'Luckily there weren't that many drawings in it but it's not the point.'

Charlie stopped pacing. 'Have you started another book?'

Rose frowned. 'Of course, whenever I have a moment I'm doodling.' She opened her bag and pulled out her book and passed it to Charlie.

'I feel honoured you're letting me take a look.' Charlie stared at the front cover for a moment. 'Number eight?'

Rose blushed as she peered at the large black number. 'I know it's silly but I number them, only for myself. It's interesting to look back at my old ones.'

Charlie opened the book and flicked through the pages.'

Rose fidgeted as the silence dragged on. 'As you can see I'm not very good at drawing.' She gave a nervous laugh. 'But then you should see some of my earlier stuff.'

Charlie looked up. 'I'm no fashion expert.' He chuckled, stretching out his arms, while glancing down at his plain white shirt and black trousers, before studying the pages again. 'But these drawings look impressive to me.'

Rose shrugged. 'I don't know about that, but if someone was interested in my books they only had to say.'

Standing upright, Rose walked further along behind the counter. Glancing down at the open newspaper, she gasped at the pictures of bomb damage around Deptford, Greenwich, Charlton and Woolwich. She scanned the article, and it told her forty bombs had been dropped in and around South East London, killing eighteen people. Shaking her head, she slammed her hand down on the counter. 'I'm so selfish. It says here eighteen people have died and forty bombs were dropped and I'm worrying about a stupid drawing book.'

Charlie took the couple of steps that separated him from Rose. 'Don't say that – there's always bad things going on but it doesn't mean what you're feeling is less important.'

Rose stared up at him, her eyes flashing with a steel-like quality. 'But no one is going to die because a drawing book has been mislaid, or someone has stolen an idea. Let her have it – I don't care. None of it is important – they're just clothes.'

Charlie shrugged. 'I can't deny everything you've said is true but it's still stealing and why should she get away with it?'

Rose sighed. 'I don't have the answers. All I know is it's not that important. Anyway, Miss Hetherington was in a good mood, better than I've ever seen her before, so maybe it's worth paying the price to stop her picking on me and everyone else.'

Charlie shook his head. 'I need to think about it. Keep this book safe. I hope the other six are.'

'They're in my bedroom. The book I'm using is always close by, even if it's only in a drawer at work.'

Charlie handed the book back to her. 'If you ask me, the sooner you spread your wings and find yourself the better.' He paused for a second. 'You're always quick to help others. I mean Joyce and Annie wouldn't be where they are without your encouragement.' He smiled. 'You must realise you could do anything you want.' He pointed at the book.

'You could have your own collection, and end up working in high fashion.'

Rose shrugged as she walked back to the chair he had pulled out for her. 'Maybe, we may never know.' She slumped down. 'What I do know is I like the people I work with and not many can say that. We're like a family.'

'Family and friends are important...' Charlie bit his lip. 'Look, there's something I want to talk to you about.' His gaze stayed fixed on the counter. 'I've been wanting to talk about it for some time. I've thought long and hard about how and where, and if I'm honest it was never going to be here. It feels like life is too short to wait. Let's face it, we could all get blown up tomorrow. We have to grab happiness and make the most of every day.'

Colour flooded Rose's cheeks as she whispered, 'What?'

Charlie took her soft hand in his and got down on one knee.

Rose gasped. Her hand flew to the silver cross and chain around her neck.

'Rose, I love you with all my heart and I believe you love me too, at least I hope you do – otherwise this is going to be very embarrassing.'

'I do.'

Charlie's face immediately relaxed and lit up with a smile. 'Rose Spencer, I promise to love and protect you for as long as I live. It will be a great honour if you agree to become my wife.'

Rose stared at him opened-mouthed. Her head jerked up as a car backfired, the explosive sound stealing the silence and the moment.

There was a thud on the shop door.

Startled, Charlie peered over his shoulder at the boy outside.

Thrusting herself up off her chair, Rose rushed over to her jacket and put it across her shoulders. 'I'll get the door.'

Joyce glanced around the dining table. How things had changed. 'I love Sundays and us all having breakfast together. No one has to rush off to work or anywhere else.' She picked up her knife and, holding the egg in the eggcup, she gently tapped the edge of the blade against the side of it until it cracked and she was able to slice the top off. She watched her father do the same for her brother, Philip. She couldn't help smiling at them both; he was a different child to when he first arrived on her doorstep. All that seemed such a long time ago now and yet it wasn't.

Rose's concentration wavered as she thought about Charlie's unexpected marriage proposal. For about the tenth time she wondered why she had run out of the shop like the devil himself was after her. She had given up trying to understand it. She loved him with all her heart and it was about time Charlie knew that. Rose watched everybody tucking into their breakfast and fought the urge to share the news with her friends. First, Charlie had to be told her answer was yes; that is, if he still wanted to marry her.

Ted looked up at Joyce. 'I've been thinking now might be a good time for Arthur and I to take Philip back to the village.'

All eyes were on Joyce, waiting for her to react, but she said nothing.

Ted cleared his throat. 'I mean, while spending the night

in the basement with you all is lovely, the Germans have dropped too many bombs over the last few nights. I don't want to frighten anybody but according to the newspaper another forty-one bombs were dropped the other night, killing twenty-two people. Thankfully it wasn't more. I understand one of them only just missed Great Ormond Street Hospital. Although it shattered the windows it could have been so much worse. To be honest I would like us all to get out of London because the Germans are clearly trying to take out the seat of power.'

Arthur's gaze travelled between Joyce and her father. 'I know you have the restaurant now, but you could always come with us even if it's just for a holiday.' He paused and glanced over at Rose and Annie. 'Of course Dorothy would be glad to see all of you, so you could all come up for a break.'

Annie gave a faint smile. 'It would be lovely to see Auntie Dorothy and my father but I just don't think I can get away right now.'

Rose frowned. 'To be honest I try not to think about the war, but the policemen shouting and ringing his bicycle bell to raise the alarm and us scurrying into the basement at night does seem to be becoming a bit of a habit.'

Ted watched his daughter, as she silently listened to the chatter around the table. 'I would love for you to come with us but I do accept your future is with Simon, and I know you're going to be very happy with him. Although, I hope when you decide on the wedding date you will let me walk you down the aisle like the proud father I am.'

'Of course.' Joyce's smile was chased away by the sadness that suddenly flitted across her face. 'I don't think it would be a good time for me to leave London. As you say I have the restaurant to think about and I do all the baking for Peter's barrow. The sales in the market are wonderful and it's helping to keep the restaurant going until things pick up there.' She paused, looking down at the scraping of butter on her bread. She looked up again and glanced at her brother Philip.

Philip was all smiles as he looked adoringly at his father. 'Does that mean I get to feed the chickens, and collect their eggs?' He was thoughtful for a moment before glancing over at Joyce. 'Of course, I have to be very careful with the eggs otherwise they'll break.' He looked down at his egg on his plate. 'They're not so easy to break once they've been boiled though.'

Everyone beamed at the five-year-old they had all come to love.

Annie put her spoon down on her plate. 'The chickens are lovely, Philip. I used to talk to them and was always sure they were listening to me.'

Philip frowned. 'Why? They can't answer you.'

Annie chuckled. 'No, they can't but it used to help me to talk to them, and I think that's mainly *because* they couldn't answer me.'

Arthur looked at Joyce; her eyes seemed full of sadness. 'You know you and the girls can come and stay any time. I regard you all as family and I want you to remember that.'

Joyce reached out and put a hand over Arthur's, and gently squeezed it. 'I know, Arthur. It doesn't matter that you're not blood family; you'll always be my Uncle Arthur. I promise to come up and visit.' She glanced over at Ted. He looked sad, as though he knew what was coming. 'As much as this hurts me to say, I think we do need to think about Philip and his safety, first and foremost. When you think just over a year ago none of us knew what a Zeppelin was, and now they seem to be dropping more bombs in London than ever.' She hesitated for a second. 'I think it's right that you go up to Worcester and stay safe.'

Ted's lips tightened as Joyce spoke. 'I was hoping you might come with us even if it's only for a short time, but I do understand about the restaurant, your cooking and of course then there's Simon. I know your life is here but it doesn't mean I'm happy to leave you behind. I've finally got my family back together and I don't want to lose you again.' He bit down on his lip. 'I do hope you'll still come up to see us.'

Joyce could feel the tears pricking at the backs of her eyes. 'You try and stop me. I thought I had no one so I'm not going to let my family just disappear.'

The room was silent for a moment; there was not even the clattering of cutlery to break it.

Joyce took a deep breath. 'When do you want us to move out so you can sell the house?'

Arthur shook his head. 'I haven't told you yet but I've made a will and everything I own is being left to you. If I've learnt nothing else in my life I know that possessions don't and can't replace the people you love. I sold a couple of properties before the war started, and thankfully I didn't manage to drink all the money away, so there will be enough left for Dot and I to live on, especially as I've bought the property next door to Annie's family. Dot loves being back home so she'll be close enough to look after her father and brother, and we'll be able to live off the land.'

Joyce's mouth dropped open. 'I don't know what to say. Does Dot know? I mean please don't feel you have to do that – you've already kept a roof over my head when you didn't need to.'

Arthur shook his head again. 'I've discussed it with Dot, and she agrees with me. You looked after me, even when I was awful to you, and I hope Ted doesn't mind sharing you and Philip with me.'

'I would never mind. You've been good to my family when I wasn't.'

Arthur gave a wry smile as he glanced over at Annie. 'I might even get your father to come in with me and sell any excess food straight from the farm.'

Rose's eyes widened. 'If you could persuade my family to do that as well I'd be very happy.' She laughed. 'That would wipe the smile from Mr Butter-wouldn't-melt-in-your-mouth. He takes advantage of the farmers because he knows they need to sell their vegetables in his shop.'

Ted laughed. 'Maybe we could open a farm shop; you know, sell the items everyone grows as well as eggs.'

5

Rose and Charlie looked over the Westminster Bridge railings at the boats chugging along the River Thames. Young lads waved at them as the boats got nearer the bridge. Beaming, Rose waved back. She stared down at the river, which had glistened in the summer when the sun had beaten down, causing little sparks of light to reflect off of it. Now it was autumn the water was dark and far from inviting. She glanced at the man who had become the love of her life, wondering if he was going to mention his proposal and her hasty exit, or whether she should be the one to do it.

'You know, Charlie, this was one of the first places Peter and Joyce brought Annie and I.' She turned to glance over at Westminster Palace. Big Ben started chiming. As the bongs rang out across London she counted how many times the bell rang. 'Eleven o'clock.' She studied the skyline in front of her. 'I love this area of London. It's so full of history, not that I know much about it but the buildings alone are probably full of it. You know, when Annie and I first arrived from our village it felt so big. Everything seemed to tower over us. Everywhere was so busy and full of life, but one of the first things that hit me about this city, particularly when we started walking around it, was the amount of green space. The parks are wonderful and so unexpected.'

Charlie smiled at the wonderment on her face. 'You're right of course. I suppose living here all my life I just take it for granted and don't give it any thought.'

Rose turned back to watch the boats. 'It's so relaxing.' She sighed. 'I've had quite a busy week and Miss Hetherington has been driving me mad. She just doesn't stop going on.'

Charlie lifted his hand and rubbed her back gently. 'I don't know why you're still there. She's clearly got a problem with you, and from what you tell me, has done since the day you started.'

Rose frowned but didn't take her eyes off the water. 'I'm still there because I love my job, and she's the only thorn in my side.'

Charlie bit down on his lip. 'Have you tried talking to her?'

Rose gave a humourless laugh. 'Yes, but she doesn't listen and has told me outright that she's not happy that I got my job by sneaking into the theatre, even though at the time we were trying to get Annie a singing job.' She giggled. 'We just happened to be hiding in the sewing room when the star and the stage manager came in with an urgent repair.' She paused. 'Of course we didn't know who they were at the time but Annie told them I could do it. I was terrified but thankfully it all went well.'

'So Kitty and Stan obviously saw something in both of you, otherwise they wouldn't have given you the jobs. You're a good friend and always willing to help others, but you should have more faith in yourself. Did you ever have a dream like Annie and Joyce?'

Rose lowered her eyes and shook her head. 'The Spencers don't have dreams; we just get on with the life we've been given and make it work.'

Charlie shook his head. 'If you don't mind me saying so that sounds like something a father would say.'

Rose looked up. 'It's the family mantra. My three brothers and sister were brought up on it, just as I was.'

Charlie stared at Rose. 'And there's nothing wrong with that unless you want something different, and you shouldn't feel guilty for that.'

Rose chuckled. 'Except I've never thought about what I want because there was never an option to do something different other than to work on a farm, and be a farmer's wife.'

Charlie squeezed her hand. 'And there's nothing wrong with that, except one day I'm hoping you'll agree to be Mrs Charlie Young.'

Rose stared into the dark rippling water of the River Thames; she shook her head as she wondered what answers she was hoping to find.

Charlie immediately put his arm around her. 'I should have been more romantic when I proposed; even leaning over the railings of Westminster Bridge would have been better than the shop.'

Rose couldn't look at him. 'Stop worrying about it.'

Charlie put his finger under Rose's chin and lifted her face to look at him. 'I can't help but worry that you still haven't said yes, but you haven't said no either.'

Rose gazed into his eyes; they were full of love for her. She immediately felt anger surge through her. 'I don't know what's the matter with me.' She snapped her head to one side. 'I love you to bits and yet getting married scares me.'

Charlie shook his head. 'Are you angry with me?'

Rose's eyes widened. 'No, I'm angry with myself, mainly because I don't understand why I feel this way.'

Charlie frowned. 'You do know I would never do anything to hurt you?'

Rose nodded. 'I love you and my job. I worry once we start our lives together all that will be lost.'

Charlie pulled her into his arms. 'Not if we don't allow it. I don't think you understand what you mean to me. I would give my life for you.'

Tears threatened to spill over as Rose peered up at the man who had stolen her heart. 'I love what we have and I'm so frightened of losing it. I've never felt so loved and I worry, once you live with me, your feelings will change.' She closed her eyes as Kitty's words screamed in her head.

Charlie's arms tightened around her. 'You need to know you bring out the best in me and we will be good together. You just have to give us a chance.'

Rose pulled back. 'I expect you think I'm foolish.'

'No, I don't. It's a big step but I only want to make you happy.' He paused and grinned at her. 'I want to make that my life's work.'

Rose smiled at him. 'I've never met anyone who talks like you. My family are practical and just get on with things. No one really talks about anything important, at least not in my hearing.'

Charlie frowned. 'It doesn't mean they don't. They might be trying to protect you or, in their eyes, prepare you for life's knocks.'

Rose shook her head. 'I don't think so. They don't seem to worry about anything. They weren't worried about me coming to London whereas Annie had an argument with her father.'

Charlie stared at Rose. 'And, I expect, Annie would have preferred her family to be more like yours and you wish yours were more like hers. We all wish for what we haven't got but it doesn't mean your parents got it wrong; everyone's just trying to do the best they can.' He squeezed Rose close before taking a breath and quickly continuing. 'You've made a break from the farm so now's the time to think about what you want to do. I know you enjoy your job, and from what I've seen you're very good at it, but I also know from your books and Kitty's dress you could do so much more. You're almost wasted at the theatre; you have a real talent.'

Rose could feel the heat rising up her neck. 'Thank you, but I would miss everybody if I left.' She turned away and leant against the black iron railings of the bridge, and watched the tranquil scene of the boats rippling through the water.

Charlie stayed silent for a minute as he watched one of the larger boats approach the bridge. 'Just because you leave doesn't mean you can't keep in contact with people. It doesn't mean you can't ever go back for a visit.'

Rose lifted her gaze to his. 'I know, it's just a bit scary because the theatre has been a safe haven since we've arrived. Everyone has been so kind to us. I almost feel like I owe them and shouldn't turn my back when they need me the most.'

Charlie shook his head. 'I understand that, I really do,

but Miss Hetherington is making your life a misery, and is that what you go to work for?'

Rose chuckled. 'Of course not.' She reached up and rested her hand over his. 'But it's like a family and with the war going on and people leaving to join up or to get better pay in the factories, especially the munitions factory, I'd feel like I was deserting them.'

Charlie nodded. 'I just want you to be happy and to achieve the best you can. I don't think you understand what a skill you actually have. The fact that the star of the show wanted you to make her wedding dress must make you see you have a talent. You actually designed it specifically for Kitty Smythe, and if it weren't for the war that would be headline news in the newspapers.'

Rose giggled. 'You're so sweet but I have to say I don't think it would ever be headline news or even make the paper's back page.'

Charlie tightened his grip on her hand. 'I was trying to make a point. Kitty is a big star. Why do you think that bloke from Dickens and Jones wants you? I understand it's not the big news it would have been before this war began, but it's still news.'

Rose's mouth dropped open. 'Oh my goodness, I didn't look to see if my name was in the newspapers, did you?'

Charlie laughed. 'Yes, and I kept a copy of it to show our children.'

Rose blushed. 'Why haven't you shown it to me?'

'I suppose I assumed you'd seen it and just weren't saying anything.' Charlie shrugged. He opened his mouth to speak but closed it again.

'I can't believe it.' Rose shook her head. 'I don't buy

newspapers. They tend to be full of war news and that just worries me.'

'Well, I've got several copies.' Charlie smiled. 'You're famous now, and don't forget your parents might have seen it too, and if they haven't we'll send them one.'

Rose stared straight ahead. 'I don't think they would think anything of it. I don't think it would impress them at all; that's even if they read about it.'

Charlie studied her for a moment. 'I am sure they would be very proud; after all why wouldn't they be? Anyway, papers or not, you need to ask yourself what you want to be doing this time next year. We could always make room in my shop for you to have your own business. What do you think?'

Rose tightened her lips. 'Charlie, I wish I had your confidence but I don't think any of us can plan that far ahead. The war feels like it's getting closer to us every day.'

Charlie wrapped his arm around her slender waist. 'I know, but don't you realise that's why we have to live for the here and now? That's why I asked you to marry me: I want us to make the most of every day we have because none of us are promised tomorrow.'

Rose peered across at the man she loved so deeply. 'If the question is still open then my answer's yes.'

Charlie's face lit up. His eyes sparkled with love. 'You've just made me the happiest man in the world but please only marry me because it's what you want.'

Rose beamed at him. 'It is. My love for you was never in doubt. I was just frightened of spoiling what we have.'

'That will never happen.' Charlie picked Rose up and swung her around.

People stopped and stared, some grinning from ear to ear.

Charlie put her down. Looking around he shouted, 'You are looking at the happiest man in the world. We're going to be married, and have lots of children.'

Everyone around them started clapping and cheering.

'Congratulations, well done,' voices shouted from the crowd that had gathered.

Rose's face was suddenly crimson as she smiled at everyone. 'Thank you.'

Charlie waved. 'Thank you.' He shouted as he stood tall and proud. 'Come on, let's get out of here. We can maybe sit under a tree in Hyde Park.' He grinned and waved as everyone started to move on.

Rose took a deep breath. 'That sounds like a good idea.' She stepped away from the railings and slipped her hand under Charlie's arm, squeezing the sleeve of the soft wool of his coat beneath her fingers.

Without a word he grinned down at her and rested his hand over hers.

Rose smiled. He was right: they were meant to be together. The love they had was real.

Charlie caught her smiling. 'No regrets?'

Rose beamed. 'No, definitely not, and I'm sorry I kept you waiting.'

Charlie laughed. 'I won't say I wasn't worried because I was, but I do think life will always be interesting with you by my side.' He squeezed her hand. 'We could give the theatre a miss tonight and have a cosy night in together. What do you think?'

Rose's smile wavered. 'I… I can't put into words how tempting that is, but—'

'Ahh, the but…'

Rose's brows pulled together. 'The thing is Annie got us the tickets, and I said we would meet her outside by the stalls in the interval.' She paused. 'It just wouldn't feel right not to go, sorry.'

Charlie rested his hand on his chest. 'No, you're right and it should be me saying I'm sorry. I shouldn't be so impatient to have you all to myself, especially when we have a lifetime ahead of us.'

Rose stood on tiptoes and kissed Charlie's cheek. His bristles pricked at her lips. 'Thank you.' She paused. 'I still haven't heard from my brothers but I shall write and tell them I'm getting married. That should get a response.'

Charlie chuckled. 'Let's hope they like me.'

Rose laughed. 'Of course they will. You know Simon has come back and doesn't talk about what it's like on the front line.'

'I know, but have you thought he might not be talking about it to stop you and Annie from worrying about things? If you think about it logically, he's trying to protect his girlfriend as well as both of you.'

Rose and Charlie walked slowly as they approached the Lyceum Theatre. A cold wind blew down Wellington Street, pushing paper and rubbish along with it. Rose pulled at the collar of her coat. She glanced around but couldn't see Michael sitting on the steps. There was no sign of him. Was he there but hiding? She hoped he was warm inside somewhere. People were chattering with excitement as they queued to get inside the theatre. Their laughter carried through the air, while food smells from the stalls wafted up the street, tickling her taste buds. Rose reached out and pulled on the sleeve of Charlie's coat as they walked towards the stage door of the Lyceum Theatre.

Charlie frowned as he was brought to a standstill. 'What's the matter?'

Rose smiled as she tilted her head slightly. 'Nothing, I just wanted you to know I've had a wonderful day. Walking with you around Hyde Park and seeing the beautiful autumn colours – the golds and deep reds – was beautiful.'

Charlie smiled. 'That's because you are looking at it all with a designer's eye.'

Rose squeezed his arm. 'I don't know about that but I've missed the autumn colours since I've been in London. The seasons here tend to be shown by how bright the day is or whether there is snow on the ground or not.'

Charlie placed his hand over hers. 'I'm pleased you've had an enjoyable day because so have I. You've made me so very happy. Tomorrow we shall buy a ring so the whole world knows we are in love.'

Rose giggled. 'You are funny. Come on, let's find Annie and tell her our news.'

Charlie opened the stage door so Rose could step inside.

'Hello, Bert.' Rose beamed.

Bert looked up and grinned. 'Hello, this is a lovely surprise. Can't yer stay away from us?'

Rose smiled. 'Apparently not.' She stepped aside. 'Annie gave us two tickets for tonight's show so we thought we would pop in to say hello and wish everyone good luck before we take our seats.'

Bert laughed. 'Yer must know it word for word.' He

reached out his hand to shake Charlie's. 'Hello, it's nice to meet yer.'

Charlie nodded. 'And you.'

Rose smiled. 'I probably do, Bert, but I don't often see the actors in the costumes I seem to be continually repairing.' Rose clasped her hand in Charlie's. 'Anyway, it will be good for Charlie to see it.'

Bert nodded. 'I better let yer go then, otherwise we'll still be 'ere nattering when the show's finished.'

'We have some news we want to share with you and the others.' Rose blushed.

Bert grinned at the pair of them. 'Oh yeah, what's that then?'

'We're getting married.' Rose jumped up and down, clapping her hands together.

Bert stepped forward with his arms outstretched. 'This is wonderful news. Congratulations.' He wrapped his arms around Rose and squeezed her tight. 'I'm so 'appy for yer both.' He stepped back and reached out for Charlie. 'Well done – yer got a good un 'ere so make sure yer look after 'er.'

Charlie grinned. 'Oh don't worry, I will.'

'Hello, what's going on here then? I thought I heard you squealing.'

Everyone looked round to see Annie in her French costume ready to go on the stage.

Rose grinned as she took the couple of steps towards her friend. 'I said yes. Charlie and I are getting married.'

Annie beamed as she rushed to hug Rose. 'That's wonderful. I'm so happy for you both.' She peered over

Rose's shoulder at Charlie. 'Congratulations, Charlie. I hope you'll both be very happy.'

Rose stepped back and looked over at Charlie. 'We've got to set the date, but we're not going to wait long.'

Bert gave Rose a sideways glance. 'Err, yer not in—'

'No I'm not in the family way, thank you very much.' Rose tried to look indignant but just grinned. 'We just want to be together and there's no point in waiting.'

Annie glanced over at Charlie, who was grinning from ear to ear. 'You're quiet. You're smiling but is everything all right?'

Charlie gave a little laugh. 'Most definitely. I'm the happiest man in the world and enjoying seeing my bride-to-be so happy and excited.'

Annie's name was called from behind the stage.

'I'm so sorry, I've got to go, but we'll most definitely celebrate after the show, and you two have got to take your seats or you'll miss the beginning.' Annie clapped her hands together. 'I'm so happy for you both. I think it's the first time ever that I haven't wanted to be on the stage.'

Rose laughed. 'Go on or you'll end up in trouble, and don't forget we'll see you in the interval. We'll be outside by the refreshment stalls. We'll get you a drink.'

Annie's named was called again.

'I've got to go but I'll meet you outside.' Annie wrapped her arms around her friend again. 'We have so much to talk about, like your wedding dress and flowers.'

Rose giggled. 'Go on, off with you.'

'If I must.' Annie gave Rose another squeeze before turning and running down the corridor towards the stage.

Rose laughed as she turned to Charlie. 'You wait until Joyce knows. They are going to be impossible to live with until everything is organised.'

Charlie chuckled. 'You love it really. Come on, we had better get to our seats.'

Bert laughed. 'Charlie, just leave it to the women. They'll be in their element. Enjoy the show.'

Rose gazed at Charlie as he opened the heavy wooden door for her to leave the Lyceum Theatre. 'What did you think of the show, Charlie? Annie's very good isn't she – especially as she has several parts now there's a shortage of actors. *The Royal Divorce* is a good play.'

Charlie looked down at her and smiled as he held on to the door handle. 'It's very good, but I think the best thing is the costumes.'

Rose giggled. 'You're terrible.'

'What? I just think you did a good job and someone should be praising you for it.' Charlie stepped through the open doorway and followed Rose out into the street. 'We don't have long before the second part begins so shall we get a drink and maybe something to eat from one of the stalls?'

Rose nodded as they walked down the road to The Strand. She pulled at the collar of her coat as the cold night air cut through her. 'Thank you for a wonderful day, Charlie. I've loved every minute of it.'

'Me too, especially being on Westminster Bridge with you. It will always hold a special place in my heart.'

Rose felt the shiver run down her spine. 'It will for me too.' She gazed up at him.

Charlie nodded. 'I want you to know that I love being with you and before much longer we will be wed; that is, if you still want me. I've always wanted a family with lots of wonderful children running around, a home full of laughter.'

Rose could feel the heat rising up her cold face. 'You had better get selling some of those bicycles then, Charlie.'

Charlie's breath came out in grey swirls as he cleared his throat. 'We'll manage; after all we've got our love to keep us going.'

Rose giggled. 'You're such a romantic.'

Charlie's love for her was written all over his face as he peered at her through his long dark lashes. 'I've never been called that before, and I can tell you I've been called many things in my time.'

They both laughed as they walked onto The Strand and headed for a stall to get a drink.

Charlie thrust his hand into his trouser pocket and pulled out a key. 'I have a gift for you. This isn't something I've ever done before but I want you to know how serious I am.' He held out his hand; the key was lying in his palm.

Rose gasped. 'What is it for?'

The corners of Charlie's lips lifted. 'I'm not sure it's romantic but it's the key to my shop, which means it's the key to my heart as well. If we're to be married it's going to be yours as well as mine.'

Rose's finger and thumb wrapped around the cold metal. 'I don't know what to say, except I've been blessed since the day we met. Thank you for everything.' She threw her arms around him and held him tight. 'I love you.'

Charlie pulled back, his eyes full of passion as he peered

down at her. 'We had better get our refreshments before I change my mind and take you somewhere more private.'

Rose stared at him. 'My mother would kill me but at this precise moment I don't care.' She reached up to run her hands through his hair just as a man knocked into Charlie's back.

'Sorry, I wasn't looking where I was going.'

Charlie nodded at him as he walked past before looking back down at Rose. 'I think your mother will be pleased that your virtue has just been saved.' He shook his head and pulled away. 'Come on, let's get a drink.'

They stood in line waiting for their turn to be served, listening to the chatter and laughter around them.

Charlie peered up into the clear night sky. A large grey cigar-shaped object was gliding majestically through the darkness. He yelled as loud as he could while pushing Rose to move away. 'Take cover, everyone, there's a Zeppelin above us.'

Rose lost her balance but Charlie's voice echoed in her head and she kept running. The ground under her feet shook; grey billowing smoke followed her along the road, closely followed by glass shattering. Bricks and wood rained down and flames were licking at her heels. The stench of burning was all around her. Loud hacking coughs could be heard as smoke and dust filled her lungs until she couldn't breathe.

Rose stopped, bending over and fighting for the oxygen she needed. She pulled her handkerchief from her pocket and put it over her mouth. Standing upright, Rose expected to see Charlie next to her but he was nowhere to be seen. Straining to see through the thick dusty fog that was now surrounding her, her eyes darted one way then another.

'Charlie?' She stepped forward, pulling up sharp in front of the rubble that blocked the road. Smoke and flames skewed her vision, but she could see bodies lying motionless. She sucked in her breath and screamed at the top of her voice. 'Charlie?'

She ran back to where the stall had once stood. Her voice trembled as she yelled out again. 'Charlie? Please be all right, please.' Smoke caught in the back of her throat. She couldn't stop coughing. Rose lifted her handkerchief to cover her nose in a bid to block the smoke and the stench of charred bodies. She took a step forward, her ears ringing as the rubble and glass crunched underfoot. 'Charlie?'

The screams of the survivors mixed with names being called out.

People were shouting instructions. Rose kept going, lifting debris from bodies. She was relieved the police and ambulances had arrived. 'Charlie, where are you?' She sobbed. She sucked in her breath, straining to hear his voice.

'Rose, is that you?'

Rose hurried towards the small, weak voice. 'Charlie, I'm here.' She bent down and removed the bricks and wood that covered his body. Looking up towards where she had seen an ambulance pull up, she saw a man pick up and cosset a little girl in his arms. He ran towards a car, as her arm flopped down. Her bright yellow skirt shone in the darkness. 'Help, can I get some help here?' She gently took Charlie's hand in hers; his eyes closed. 'I love you, Charlie, just you stay strong. We have a wedding to plan.'

'I'm sorry.' Charlie's eyes fluttered open a little. 'Promise me… you'll help yourself… to achieve the best you can… be happy.' His eyes slowly closed.

Rose could feel his life ebbing away as she gazed down at him through blurred, watery eyes. 'Charlie, talk to me, please don't leave me. I need you.'

'I... love... you.'

Rose sobbed as his hand went limp in hers; the tears were rivers on her dusty face. 'Charlie, please don't go. I love you. Please stay. Think of all the wonderful children we're going to have.'

Hands were suddenly on her shoulders, hugging her tight.

'No, I can't leave him while he's unconscious. He's going to be all right; I know he is. He just needs to see a doctor.' Rose gripped Charlie's limp hand tight as she sobbed. 'He has to be. We're going to get married and have lots of children.'

'Come on, you've got to let them look at him and take him to hospital.'

Rose glanced up to see Annie crying as she looked down at her. Another time Rose would have laughed at seeing her friend in full French costume in the middle of The Strand but she hardly noticed.

A lady came over to them. Her face looked grey as she took in the scene in front of her. 'My name's Alice.' She bent down and reached for Charlie's wrist, holding it between her fingers and thumb for a couple of minutes before shaking her head. 'I'm so sorry. I'm too late. He's with God now.' She looked shaken, as she stood upright. 'Let me take a look at you.'

Rose shook her head, not letting go of Charlie's hand. 'I'm fine. He saved my life.'

Annie sniffed as the tears rolled down her cheeks. 'I'll look after her.'

Alice nodded. 'Make sure she has some hot sweet tea. She's had a terrible shock.' She turned to walk away. 'If you change your mind, come and find me.'

Annie kept her arms around her friend. 'Don't worry, I'll keep an eye on her. Hopefully there's still people you can save.'

Conflict ran across Alice's face. 'I'm so sorry.' She patted Rose's arm and stepped away.

Rose turned and looked at the devastation for the first time. There was a large crater outside The One Bell public house, and flames were coming from it, illuminating the street. Glass and rubble crunched under foot as the police, doctors and nurses rushed around trying to help everyone. People stood around, some watching in stunned silence, some sobbing.

Rose spoke in low tones as she looked around her. 'We were laughing and enjoying ourselves and this happens. He wanted me to be his wife and he was telling me he wanted a big family – that's what we were laughing about.' She stared down at Charlie's dust-covered face. 'How can this have happened?' She leant forward and sobbed over the man who had loved her.

Annie looked around her, not knowing how to help her friend.

A policewoman was talking to Alice as they crunched past on the debris. 'I've heard they've hit quite a few places in London, but Woolwich has suffered the most. I expect they were after the munitions factory there, but they weren't successful; although, apparently, the army barracks took five hits.'

Annie bent down and stroked Rose's back. 'Come on,

Rose; let me get you out of here. Charlie saved you, he loved you, but as we know, whether we like it or not, we will soon be in the way.'

Rose was silent for a moment. She looked up at Annie; her tear-stained face was red and blotchy. 'I can't just leave him here, not like this.'

'Charlie wouldn't want you to stay here. You need time but please let me help you.'

6

Rose lay still on her bed. Was it really two months ago the Zeppelin had dropped its bombs in The Strand? Her eyes screwed tight, trying to hold in the tears that were seeping through her lashes. She clutched her damp pillow tight to her body. 'Oh, Charlie, how could you leave me?' Anger flooded through her. 'Why, oh why did this have to happen?' She sobbed into the empty room, screaming at the top of her voice. 'This isn't fair. Why did you have to be a hero?' She wept into her pillow. How was she going to continue without him? If only they had stayed at home like Charlie wanted. They shouldn't have waited for the right moment to get married, or to lie next to each other.

The pictures of that evening reeled through her mind over and over again, like a Pathé News report at the picture house. Anger had surged through her when she first got home after the explosion. She should have been stronger and stayed with Charlie until they had taken him out of the rubble; instead she had cried over him before kissing him goodbye.

Annie and Joyce had taken over arranging Charlie's funeral for the week after the bombing, while Rose had buried herself away in her room. She still couldn't stop thinking about Charlie's coffin being lowered into the ground. Annie and Joyce had stood either side of her, holding her up as the heavens had opened and rain had fallen to mingle with her tears.

Rose had waited all night for exhaustion to take over as she listened to the rain beating its own rhythm against the window, but it hadn't. The constant drip splashing into the bucket went unnoticed. She had curled herself into a tight ball, worrying about Charlie on the ground and the rain lashing down on him. He had saved her life at the expense of his own. The love they had was gone, ripped away from her before it had firmly taken root. How she wished she had died with him. Her heart felt like it was being ripped out of her chest all over again.

There had been no time to introduce him to her family. They would never know what a kind and loving person he was, and she would never know what their children might have been like. She rolled onto her back. Her body ached with grief.

Rose opened her eyes and stared into the room's semi-darkness. A chink of the grey morning was breaking through where the curtains didn't quite meet. The shadowy shapes of the furniture looked threatening. The curtains suddenly fluttered and the windows rattled as the wind outside collided with them. Voices carried up from the street, children shouting, playing war games and laughing.

Rose had got up and dressed in the dark, unable to bring herself to open the curtains and start the day. Instead, she had lain back down in her clothes. It was a nightmare that she couldn't wake up from. Did it really happen? Was Charlie really gone? Tears rolled down, pooling in her ears, as she lay so still staring up at the ceiling. Her face was sore and her eyes ached from all the tears that had left their salty taste on her lips night after night.

A door banged shut, but Rose couldn't tell where it came from. Her mind drifted back to the plans they had talked about. Had they tried too hard not to rush things? None of it mattered now; he was no longer here and had taken all their plans with him.

There was a light rap on her bedroom door.

Rose froze, holding her breath; she had no desire to see anyone.

Annie's voice whispered through the closed door. 'Rose.'

The handle turned slowly, creaking loudly in the silence. Rose stared at the door before quickly closing her eyes. Could she get away with pretending to be asleep? Rose peered out from underneath her lashes, but said nothing.

The quieter Annie tried to be the noisier she became. She gently pushed the door open but the hinges screamed out in the silence. Annie stopped dead, peering into the darkness. She wrinkled her nose at the mustiness that hung in the air, reminding her of the first day they had moved in. Annie walked on tiptoe towards the bed, the floorboards creaking under foot. She let out a sigh of frustration as she moved further into the room. Annie dropped down into the nearby wooden chair and sat there staring at her friend. 'I know you're awake, Rose. I also know you don't want to talk to me or anybody else, but you shouldn't be on your own any longer. It's not what Charlie would have wanted for you.'

Rose held her breath; her eyes stung with unshed tears wanting to escape again. She squeezed her eyelids shut but it didn't stop them. They trickled out from the corners. 'Just go, Annie; you have the show to do. You can't let Stan and Kitty down.'

Annie shook her head. 'Don't worry about the show. I won't let anyone down, especially you. I want to take away your pain. We're friends, and friends are always there for each other, as you have been for me. It's now my turn to be here for you. I know there's nothing I can do to change anything. I can only give you a hug and let you cry as much as you want, but I'm not going to leave you on your own in this room any longer.'

Rose groaned as she ran her fingers over her face again. 'He saved my life, Annie; I don't understand why he saved me because I don't want to be here without him. If only we had stayed together we would've died together. At least we would've been in each other's arms; instead I'm here and he isn't. Our lives have been ripped apart by something that has no bearing on us. I didn't ask for this war, neither did Charlie and yet we've been caught up in it. At least Simon came back to Joyce. It's just not fair. He didn't even want to go to the theatre!'

Annie lifted herself out of the chair, noticing the untouched cup of tea on her bedside table from the previous evening. She knelt on the floorboards next to the bed and clasped Rose's hand in hers. 'There's nothing fair about any of this. Don't try and make sense of it. Charlie saved you because he loved you. It wasn't your time to leave us, and that's all you need to know.'

Rose began to sob again; her whole body shook on the wooden bed. 'Annie, I loved him too, but how am I meant to get through all this? I made us go. We could have been at home together, and then he'd still be here, but oh no, I felt we should go.'

Annie swallowed hard and blinked quickly. 'You can't keep blaming yourself. None of us knew the Germans were going to drop bombs that night.'

'It hurts so much.' Rose shuddered. 'One minute we were talking about the play, getting married and having a family. Our future was full of love and happiness; we were listening to the laughter and the chatter around us. He told everyone to run, and I thought he was behind me, but when I turned round he wasn't. I don't understand. One minute we were together and suddenly there was no we.'

Annie stroked her friend's arm. 'I don't have the answers for you, Rose. I wish I did. I heard a policeman say bombs had been dropped all over London. And I know you're going to miss Charlie, but know he died a hero. He saved a lot of lives by shouting out before the bombs hit the ground.'

Rose's lips tightened. 'I understand that, but to be honest with you it doesn't mean anything because he's no longer here.'

Annie nodded. 'I know, I know. Close your eyes and try and get some sleep.'

Rose peered up at her friend. 'Every time I close my eyes I see Charlie lying in the rubble. I see that little girl limp in a man's arms, her bright yellow dress smeared with blood. I'm not sure I'll ever sleep again.'

'Maybe it's time you left the house.' Annie stood up. 'One, or both of us, will go with you.' She took the couple of steps towards the window and dragged the curtains open, allowing the greyness of the day to flood into the room, revealing the layer of dust that had settled on every surface. 'We need to get you out of here. We've allowed you to be on your own for too long.'

Rose shook her head. 'I can't, I can't.'

Annie's lips pressed together. 'Yes you can, and to be honest I won't take no for an answer. I'm doing this as your friend, and for Charlie. He encouraged and loved you, and I know none of us would want someone we love to be locked away like this. It's time you honoured Charlie by at least getting up and out of this house. Work will be a good distraction for you; it stops us from thinking about all the hard stuff. I'll go and make you a cup of tea.' Annie walked over to the door and looked back. 'After that you are definitely going outside, even if it's only so I can clean this room.'

Rose caught a glimpse of the cross and chain Charlie had given her. The chain was stretched out on her bedside table. The sketch pad, which was next to the chain, was covered with a layer of dust. Shaking her head, she reached over and picked up the delicate piece of jewellery and stared down at it resting in the palm of her hand. *Be brave; take the leap of faith*. Rose could hear his words being repeated in her mind. She shook her head, knowing he would be upset that she had turned her back on everything. 'Take a leap of faith,' she repeated to herself. 'I don't know if I can do that, Charlie. You're expecting too much of me.' She sniffed. 'But I'll try, for you. Annie's right: it's what you would have wanted. But I truly wish you hadn't saved my life and I'd died in your arms.'

'But it wasn't your time, Rose. You still have a lot to give.' Joyce stood in the open doorway holding a cup of tea, her eyes red with unshed tears.

'So did Charlie.' Rose began to sob again.

'Maybe, but look what he'd already given you in the short time you knew him.' Joyce stepped further into the room and sat on the edge of the bed after placing the cup and saucer down on the bedside table. 'He'd shown you true love, and you felt that. There's no better gift than that.'

Rose nodded as her tears silently rolled down her cheeks. 'I know.' She sniffed. 'But we had plans.'

Joyce leant in and put her arm around Rose, pulling her close.

After a moment, Rose lifted her head and gazed at Joyce before looking down at the silver cross resting in her hand. 'He gave me this, and told me to take a leap of faith, to do more with my sewing and achieve the best that I can.'

Joyce nodded. 'And you will, in time.'

Rose stared down at the precious gift Charlie had given her. 'I don't want to let him down but…'

Joyce squeezed her friend's shoulders. 'I know, but please remember you're not on your own.' She pulled back after a few minutes. 'Look, why don't I bring you some hot water so you can have a wash, then we'll go out for a walk. The fresh air will do you good. What do you think?'

'I don't know if I feel able to go out just yet.' Rose gripped the cross in her hand and bit down on her lip. 'I can hear the voices outside; everyone's laughing and talking. Their lives have just gone on and yet mine feels like it's over.'

Joyce stared at Rose's clenched hand. 'If the roles were reversed what would you want Charlie to do?'

Rose took a deep breath and sat up straight. The pain was tangible. Once again she opened her fingers to look down at the cross and chain in the palm of her hand. Red welts were visible and stung where it had been gripped. She bit down on her lip until the pain and the iron taste of her blood told her to stop. 'I would want him to carry on living and be happy.'

Joyce passed her a handkerchief. 'Your lip's bleeding.'

Rose ran her tongue over the blood before reaching for the handkerchief and dabbing her mouth with it.

Joyce studied her friend. 'Are you going to take the leap of faith then?'

Rose stared down at the cross and chain but didn't say a word.

Shivering, Rose pulled up the collar of her winter coat as the wind cut through her like a hot knife through butter. She walked briskly with Joyce by her side. Great Earl Street was as busy as ever, cars chugging by, while a horn sounded in the distance. Horses and carts rattled along, while the wind carried the stench of the manure that sat in piles in the road. Sellers stood behind their barrows, shouting out to get the attention of the people passing by. Rose looked around her. Nothing had changed, and yet her world had stopped turning. She had wanted it to end with Charlie's but everybody else's had continued as normal.

She glanced at Joyce. Was the wind blowing the cobwebs away? Did she actually feel better for being outside? She shook her head. 'It's hard, Joyce. I feel like my life has fallen apart and yet everybody's out here as though nothing has happened.'

Joyce nodded, thrusting her arm through Rose's before glancing around the street. 'I know that's how it looks but

I expect some of these people have already lost husbands, brothers, fathers, uncles and sons in this rotten war, but they still have to continue whether they like it or not. After all, what's the alternative?'

Rose peered around at everybody going about their business. A man's belly laugh sounded close by. She turned quickly and looked at the grey-haired man. After a moment the man he was talking to turned and walked away. As the grey-haired man walked towards her she noticed his pallor was ashen and his stoop was lower than before. His laughter hadn't reached his sad eyes. There was no life in this man, no twinkle in his eyes, and she began to understand that it was all a front. People didn't want you to be miserable. They were worrying about trying to earn a crust so they could feed their children, and themselves, with the food shortages getting worse every day.

Everyone cared but they didn't need or want to have to worry about their friends as well. They were trying to survive and not think about how their lives had been turned upside down. She knew then what she had to do.

They reached the Seven Dials roundabout. Joyce pulled her close. 'Let's walk down Queens Street for a change. I can't remember the last time I walked down there.'

Rose glanced at Joyce, as she whispered, 'You don't have to avoid Great White Lion Street you know. I'll have to walk down it at some point.'

'But not today you don't.' Joyce squeezed her arm and gently pulled her along. 'It's going to be all right, Rose. Annie and I are here for you.' The grey swirls of her breath disappeared into the cold air.

Rose sighed. 'I know, but you can only do so much and

the rest is up to me. I need to go back to the theatre and face it all.' Even as she spoke she could feel the tears were waiting to flow again.

'You don't have to go today. Of course you don't have to go at all. You could take up that man's offer of a job in Dickens and Jones.'

Rose shook her head. 'You sound like Charlie now. I just don't think I could do it.'

Joyce stepped back to let someone pass on the pavement. 'I know, but maybe you should take that leap of faith Charlie wanted – you know, a fresh start. Of course you'll probably feel better amongst people you know.' She tugged at the scarf around her neck. 'What you have to remember, Rose, is that sometimes people see something in us that we don't see in ourselves. Look at me – I thought I was stuck serving breakfasts all day, and now I'm cooking in my own restaurant. You have to realise that only happened because you all encouraged me, and made me see I wasn't on my own. You just don't know what you can do until you have to.'

Rose walked on in silence. Without looking, she stepped out into the road and a car horn beeped loudly several times.

Joyce tugged her back.

'Sorry, Joyce, I wasn't concentrating.'

'You could've been run over.'

Rose didn't speak, but immediately wondered if that would have been such a bad thing.

Joyce looked at Rose's pale features. The cold air had failed to bring a rosy glow to her face. 'Perhaps we shouldn't have come out. I thought it might do you some good.'

Rose forced a smile. 'Don't worry, Joyce, the walk has

done me good.' She paused and took a deep breath. 'If we walk down Kings Street we can head for Covent Garden and The Strand...'

'What? You want to go to the theatre now?' Joyce scowled, not hiding her dismay. 'When I said let's go for a walk, I didn't mean for you to go back there.'

Rose nodded. 'I know it doesn't make sense to you but I just can't believe he's gone.'

Joyce looked at her friend and was lost for words. 'All right, we'll go there now, but the minute it gets too much we're leaving.'

Rose frowned. 'Take it from me, don't wait too long to marry Simon and live your life to the full because you don't know how long you've got. None of us do.' She rubbed her hand across her face. 'I feel like my heart has been ripped out and stamped on.'

Joyce peered over at Rose's pale features. 'I know. There are no words to make it better but know Charlie saved your life for a reason. He loved you and wanted you to achieve so much. He believed in you so don't let him have died for nothing.'

Rose shook her head. 'That's just it, I'm not sure I can achieve what he wanted. I'm not as brave as you and Annie.'

'Maybe you will or maybe you won't, but one thing is for sure: in time you will take the first step because Charlie wanted you to and you love him so you won't want to let him down.'

They walked on in silence for a moment.

Joyce rubbed her hand gently down Rose's arm. 'It's hard. I was devastated when my mother passed away, and there's never a day when I don't wish she was still here with me.' She watched Rose for moment. 'The best way you can honour Charlie is to continue to live your life and fulfil the dreams you talked about. I know some of it won't be possible but he loved you to bits and you should follow through with the plans you both talked about regarding your own life. Does that make sense?'

Rose nodded. 'I don't know if I'm strong enough to do that.'

Joyce smiled. 'None of us know how strong we are until we have to deal with certain situations and then you'd be surprised where the strength comes from.'

Rose glanced over at Joyce. 'So much wisdom shows you have already lived a life that has challenged you.' She paused. 'He really believed in me, more than anyone else I have ever known.'

'Then you mustn't let him down.'

Rose sniffed. 'I'll try not to. To be honest it's going to be difficult to go back to the theatre. It will always be the place where I lost the man I loved.'

Joyce nodded. 'You have friends there who will support you, unless of course you decide to go to Dickens and Jones instead.'

Rose shook her head vigorously. 'Oh no, I'm definitely not brave enough for that, no matter what Charlie wanted.'

Paper swirled around Rose and Joyce's feet as the cold wind blew down Wellington Street. The imposing building of the Lyceum Theatre stood tall ahead of them on the right. A couple of people were milling around on the steps leading up to the large entrance doors. As they strolled down the hill a man stood up and walked towards them. He was dishevelled, needing a shave and a haircut. His clothes were grubby and his trousers were torn. His scrawny frame looked as though he hadn't eaten for weeks.

Joyce delved into her handbag and grabbed her purse. 'Don't worry, Rose, I'll deal with this.'

Rose frowned as she glanced at Joyce. 'What?'

The man's voice carried urgency. 'I was hoping to see you. I've hardly moved from this spot for weeks.'

Rose stared at him, taking few minutes to register who he was.

Joyce shook her head. 'I'm sorry, but my friend—'

'You don't remember me, do you?'

Rose nodded. 'Yes I do, it's Michael. We chatted on the steps a few months ago.'

Joyce tightened her hold on Rose's arm and eyed the man suspiciously. 'Rose, we should get home; after all it's freezing out here.'

Rose kept her eyes fixed on the man in front of her. 'You must be frozen. Don't you have anything warmer to wear, or a thicker coat?'

Michael took his left arm out of his coat pocket; the sleeve was long as the coat was too big for him. 'I'll be all right – you get used to it.'

Rose shook her head. 'Tomorrow I'll bring you a blanket or find you a coat from somewhere.'

'Thank you, but there's no need.' Michael hobbled uncomfortably from one leg to the other, trying to hide his pain. 'I was worried you got caught up in that blast, especially when your friend still came to work and you didn't. I nearly went in and asked but I couldn't bring myself to.'

Rose stared down the street. 'I was here when the bomb went off.'

'Well thank goodness you're all right; there was a huge hole in the road. Thankfully it doesn't look like the Lyceum was damaged. Of course I'm only going by the outside, it could be a right old mess inside.'

Rose turned to Michael, unsure what to say, but then her words tumbled over each other. 'We were in The Strand, so were lots of people. It was the interval...'

Michael shook his head. 'You must have been terrified.'

Rose shrugged. 'It all happened so quickly, there was no time to feel frightened.' She paused, trying to swallow past the lump in her throat. 'Charlie saved my life, and others. He pushed me away.'

'Thank goodness, maybe one day I can meet your hero.'

Tears pricked at Rose's eyes, just waiting for the signal, but she blinked quickly and took a couple of deep breaths. 'He didn't make it.'

Anger flitted across Michael's face. 'I was hoping I'd left all that behind but it seems not.'

Bert's booming voice came from behind Rose, jerking her into moving. 'Rose, are yer all right? Is this man bothering yer?' He bounded down the steps.

Rose looked up as he rushed towards her. 'No, Bert, don't worry, it's Michael. I'm sorry I don't know your full name, but he sits here most days.'

Bert drew level and threw his arms around her, giving her his trademark bear hug. The signal was given and Rose sobbed into his chest. 'It's all right, let it all out.'

Rose's body shook as he comforted her.

Bert eyed Michael.

Michael met Bert's suspicious gaze. 'It's Michael Dean.'

Bert nodded. 'Yer must be blooming freezing. There's nothing of yer.'

Rose stepped back and ran her gloved hands across her face. 'I said I'd bring him a thicker coat or something to wrap around him tomorrow.'

Bert looked at the young girl he'd come to love like his own daughter before glancing over at the man. 'You can 'ave my coat.'

Michael shook his head. 'No, sir, thank you, but I couldn't possibly take it.'

Bert chuckled. 'Trust me when I say I've enough fat on me to keep me warm for several winters, and given the size of yer you'll be able to wrap it round yer several times. Wait 'ere.' Bert squeezed Rose before turning to go back inside the theatre.

'Thank you, sir.' Michael turned to gaze at Rose. 'I have no words but if there's anything I can do?'

Rose pulled a handkerchief from her pocket and blew her nose. 'Thank you but there isn't. I shouldn't have come today.' She sniffed.

Michael nodded. 'They've repaired the road so there's nothing to see.'

Joyce studied Michael and watched the pain flitting across his face. 'Would you rather sit down?'

Michael's lips tightened slightly. 'No, thank you.'

Bert trundled back down the steps. 'Here yer go, this'll keep yer warm, well warmer than what yer wearing at the minute.' He handed the coat over to Michael, who slung it over his arm. 'Are yer not going to put it on?'

Michael gave a half-smile. 'I will later. If I put it on too soon I won't get the benefit of it later when the temperature drops again.'

Rose wanted to laugh and cry all at the same time as Michael's words had matched Charlie's when she first entered the bicycle shop.

Bert nodded at Michael before turning to Rose. 'Good job I went back inside cos I forgot that posh old fella came looking for yer – 'e left a card.' His hand stretched out, holding a business card. 'He's been 'ere a few times to see Miss Smythe.'

'I don't know anyone who's posh.' Rose frowned. Taking it from him, she read the name emblazoned on the card. 'Alexander Bowman. He's the man from Dickens and Jones who loved Kitty's wedding dress.'

Bert raised his eyebrows. 'He was adamant I shouldn't forget to give it to yer – 'e even told Miss 'etherington that 'e would be stealing yer because yer were wasted in the theatre, and I can tell yer 'er face was a picture.'

Rose couldn't resist smiling. 'Well, he's got a cheek.'

Joyce took the card from Rose. 'Has he? Charlie wanted you to take a leap of faith and maybe it's time you did.'

Michael peered at them. 'It sounds like Charlie wanted you to reach for the sky. You've already discovered how quickly things can change, when you least expect it, so grab life while you can. You've nothing to lose by trying.'

Bert nodded. 'He's right, but I'd miss yer. Are yer coming in?' He stretched out his arm towards the theatre.

Rose shook her head. 'Not today, Bert.'

Joyce peered furtively at her wristwatch. 'Can you let Kitty know Annie won't be in until later? She has things to do.'

Bert nodded, wrapping his arms around Rose again. 'Yer take care now.'

Rose stepped back and gave a watery smile. 'I will, thank you. Hopefully I'll see you all soon. Bye, Michael.'

Joyce linked her arm through Rose's and they stepped forward together. They retraced their steps back to Great White Lion Street. 'I need to pop in to the restaurant for a couple of hours. Will you come with me?'

'Don't worry, Joyce, I'll be all right.' Rose looked along the street. 'You're a good friend and coming out has helped to clear my head.'

Joyce hesitated, watching Rose closely.

'Go on, I promise everything will be all right.'

Joyce nodded and squeezed Rose's arm. 'I'll be as quick as I can.'

'Stop worrying – now go.' Rose watched her friend march up the road, waving when she turned round to check on her. She walked a few yards towards home before coming to a standstill. She stared at the shop. The paper rolling along the pavement and the clatter of wheels and hooves on the road went unnoticed. The cold wind was getting stronger, howling between the buildings and rattling windows. It almost knocked her off her feet but still she didn't move to enter into Charlie's world.

She took a breath before looking down at the blue woollen gloves she was wearing. Reluctantly, she pulled one off and thrust her hand inside her handbag. Rooting around inside, her fingers wrapped around the cold metal of the shop key. The steel sent a chill through her fingers as she clutched it. Pulling it out, she stared at it before looking up at the bicycle shop. The door was locked, and inside was hidden by the dark curtains, which Charlie had pulled together so the Germans couldn't see any light that might be on. The sign on the door said closed.

She had to go in. There were things to do, practical things like going through his paperwork. Memories of Charlie standing in the doorway smiling at her, holding out his hand for her to take it and be brave enough to walk inside flooded her mind. Her vision became blurry. She dropped the key into her coat pocket. It was too hard. Rose wondered how many times the landlord had knocked for his rent. It was time to pay it out of her savings, at least until she knew what was happening with the shop.

'Hello, Rose, silly question but are you all right?'

Rose jumped at the voice behind her; taking a deep breath she turned on her heels to face Peter's piercing blue eyes staring at her. 'I don't know, Peter.'

Peter ran his hand over his mousy blonde hair before stepping forward and wrapping his arms around her.

Rose breathed in the cold air and earthy smell that clung to his soft black corduroy coat.

Peter gently squeezed her tight. 'Everything will be all right, eventually.'

Sniffing, Rose stepped back and looked up at him. 'Will it, Peter? It's all so hard – even getting out of bed feels beyond me. When will it start to get better?'

Peter shook his head. 'I don't have any answers. Charlie's gone, and that's as bad as it gets, but you have good friends who love and worry about you so let them help. I know Charlie was only in your life for a short time but try to remember the good things he gave you, the love, the laughs and his endless devotion. He wanted what was best for you, and nothing less. Try and keep that legacy going.'

Taking her handkerchief out of her coat pocket, Rose nodded. 'I know you're right; it's just so difficult. When I first wake up my memory seems to take a few minutes to catch up. I forget he's no longer here but then it jumps back into the forefront of my mind and it's like I've only just lost him all over again.' She looked over at the shop. 'Then there's this. I need to contact his brother. It's already been too long but I can't bring myself to step inside and go through his things.'

Peter frowned. 'Would you like me to do it? I don't mind. It's been shut a long time so I expect there's a lot of post on the floor.'

Rose shook her head. 'It's something I should do. I've just got to be braver than I am.'

'Shall we go in together – I mean now while we're here?'

Rose forced a smile. 'Thank you, but you have a stall full of food to sell and I've already held you up. Actually, what are you doing here?'

Peter gave her a sheepish look. 'I saw you walking in this direction and wanted to make sure you were all right. Annie's worried sick about you.'

Rose took a deep breath. 'I'm sorry, I don't mean to worry everyone.'

'It's only because they love you.' Peter pulled her into his arms again and gave her a quick squeeze before stepping back. 'Try to occupy your time as much as you can and don't be on your own for too long. If you don't know what to do, follow Charlie's lead, because he only ever wanted the best for you; but make sure it's right for you too.'

7

Annie pulled the edges of her cardigan together before glancing at Rose as they sat in front of the unlit fire in the sitting room. She stood up and walked over to the window and stared out, but there was nothing to see. Car horns sounded and people could be heard shouting but the thick grey fog hid most of it from view. 'The only good thing about December is Christmas, and that's not going to be the same this year.' She sighed. 'It's freezing in here; maybe we should go out for a brisk walk. We could go to Hyde Park. It's cold, but we can wrap up warm and it might brighten up later if this fog lifts. It might do us good, and warm us up.' She marched into the hall, her slippers not making a sound.

Rose stared straight ahead.

Annie frowned as she strolled back into the room carrying their coats. 'Is there something else you would like to do today?' She dropped the coats onto the sofa.

Rose sighed. 'Peter's told you, hasn't he?'

Annie sat down. Lacing her fingers together, she rested her hands on her lap. 'I'm not entirely sure what you're referring to, but if you're talking about seeing you outside Charlie's shop then yes he did. We're all worried about you.

We could help with the shop; you've just got to tell us what you want us to do.'

Rose sighed as she glanced across at Annie. 'The shop isn't mine to do anything with. I should be paying the rent until I can find Charlie's brother, but I don't know where to start.'

They sat in silence for a few minutes.

Rose stroked the cold silver cross and chain that hung around her neck. 'I thought if I didn't read about the war I could pretend it wasn't happening; after all it's mainly happening in other countries.'

Annie nodded, lowering her eyes as she spoke. 'I know, I think the same. It's the only way to not worry about our brothers.' She looked at Rose. 'You do know you're not on your own? Joyce and I are here for you, as indeed are Peter and Simon.'

Rose sighed and pushed herself up out of her chair. 'I'm going to go and have a lie-down.'

Annie jumped up. 'No, I'm sorry. We've only just got you out of that room. You did well when you went out with Joyce and today it's my turn. You may not want to go back to the theatre to work, and to a point I do understand, but you are not going to shut yourself away anymore. It's not doing you any good.'

Tears pricked at Rose's eyes.

Annie stretched out her hand, but just held back from trying to comfort her friend. 'I don't mean to be tough on you, Rose, but you're only hurting yourself and the people who care about you.' She paused. 'I have thought about writing to your mother because you aren't listening to us.'

Rose slumped back down on the chair she had just vacated.

Annie tightened her lips. 'I'm not trying to be mean but Charlie wouldn't want you to hide away, and you know that.'

Rose peered up at her friend. 'Yes, well, he isn't here, is he? It's hard, Annie. I feel like I'm dragging myself around. I'm exhausted with the effort it takes just to get out of bed.'

Annie's face relaxed as she knelt at Rose's feet. 'Look, you know I love you like a sister, and there's nothing I wouldn't do for you. I can't begin to understand what you're feeling. I struggled when I lost my mother but I had my father to worry about and that's what got me through it. I know you don't have that but I'd rather see you go back to your family than see you slowly dying in front of me. Trust me when I say the last thing I want is for you to go back home but I don't want to lose you either.'

Rose sat very still, staring down at her feet.

Annie lowered her voice to a whisper. 'Would you rather go home to your family where you can be looked after properly?' She looked down to see Rose wringing her hands together.

Rose stared at them, all movement suddenly stopped. 'No, I don't. It would feel like Charlie never existed.' The whites of her knuckles poked through her pale skin as she gripped her hands tight. 'I know lots of women have lost someone because of this rotten war; it's just so unfair.'

Annie nodded. 'It is, Rose, but there's nothing we can do about it. When my ma passed I used to continually ask myself what she would want me to do; maybe you should be asking yourself what Charlie would do or what he would say to you.'

Rose blinked quickly. 'I know what he'd say.' She peered

at her friend. 'He'd be saying come on, life's too short to be miserable. Get on and chase your dream.'

Annie nodded. 'I think that's true.' She paused before taking a deep breath. 'The hard part is always picking yourself up and trying to start again. I know what I'm about to say sounds awful but it comes from a place of love.' She hesitated, before continuing. 'To sit in your room for weeks on end avoiding everyone is easy but it's not who you are. I can't stand by and watch it; it's too painful.'

Rose squeezed her eyes shut.

'You're an unbelievably brave person, and always have been. You were the driving force that got me to London and got Joyce to admit her love for Simon, and to believe she could become a proper cook.' Annie clasped Rose's hands in hers. 'I know your heart has been broken and your life seems to have no meaning anymore, but it does to the people who love you. If you can't fight back for yourself then please do it for Joyce, your family, and me. Charlie would be the first to say you still have so much love to give and he wouldn't want you to be strangled by his passing. He would want you to start smiling again, start living and achieve the best you can. You are a strong person so please don't lose yourself.' Annie took a breath. 'I'm sorry, I've gone on but you'll never know how worried I am about you.'

Rose took a breath. She opened her eyes but didn't look up. 'No, it should be me saying I'm sorry. Every day feels such a struggle.'

Annie wrapped her arms around her friend. 'I know it is. I can see that. I don't mean to sound cold, I just want you back.' Pulling away, she stood up and forced a smile to her lips. 'It doesn't look like we'll be needing this then?' Annie reached out and grabbed Rose's coat. She slung it across her arm as something fell out of one of its pockets. She bent down and picked up the card. 'Alexander Bowman.'

Rose shook her head. 'Bert gave me the card when I was outside the theatre with Joyce.'

Annie nodded. 'I heard he had been in to see Kitty, and I think he popped in to see Miss Hetherington as well.' She shook her head. 'He's persistent, I'll give him that.' She studied the card. 'I'll put it back.' She fumbled with the coat before pushing the card back inside the pocket. 'What do you think you'll do?'

Rose frowned. 'About what?'

Annie flopped down on the sofa. 'Well, will you come back to the theatre? They miss you. Or will you go and work for Mr Bowman?'

Rose sighed. 'I have no idea what I'm going to do.' She paused. 'If I'm honest I can't face dealing with Miss Hetherington's mean spirit every day.'

Annie nodded. 'Well, I suppose now is a good time for a fresh start, and your friends will always be there for you. Although I shall miss you, as will everyone at the theatre.' She sighed. 'Charlie lit the fire of possibility so you should at least stoke it and give it a try.'

Rose frowned. 'You know Charlie thought I could achieve anything I wanted. He's the first person, apart from my grandma, to believe in me.' Her cheeks became flushed with colour. 'You know, when I think back to all the times Mr Butterworth thought he could say what he wanted to us...' She shook her head. 'He was just a bully, and my grandmother was the only person I knew to have the spirit to stand up to him. He never liked it and used the fact our parents, and other farmers around the village, needed him to sell their produce in his shop to get away with it.'

Annie's lips curled. 'I was always getting into trouble for upsetting him. He always seemed to make it to the farm before we got home.'

'Tell me about it.' Rose glanced at Annie. 'I can't go back to the theatre and Miss Hetherington. It's like working for a Butterworth.'

Annie took a breath. 'Then you should give Mr Bowman a try. He seems lovely and pretty desperate for you to work at Dickens and Jones.' She stood up again. 'If you don't want to go out we could do some baking. That would shock Joyce.'

A faint smile played on Rose's face. 'She would probably faint if we did that but it would be a good way of saying thank you to her for being there for us.'

Annie smiled. 'Let's do it then. I'll hang up our coats.'

Rose gripped the cold metal key in her coat pocket. The freezing wind cut through her. The pavement still glistened with the previous night's frost. There was no escaping it: it was time to steel herself to go inside the shop. She pulled the key from her pocket and stared down at it. A lump formed in her throat. This wasn't how it was meant to be; they should have been together, laughing.

'Is Charlie all right? The shop's closed and I 'aven't seen him for ages.'

Rose jerked at the young voice behind her. Pushing the key back into her pocket, she turned round.

'He never missed buying a paper from me. I'd come to the shop and he'd always give me a penny, even though he only 'ad to give me 'apenny.'

Rose stooped, not noticing the hem of her coat was on the pavement. 'Charlie won't be coming back.' She took a breath, trying to control the wobble in her voice. 'The bomb that exploded in The Strand… He saved a lot of lives but it cost him his life.' She blinked quickly and whispered, 'He saved my life.'

The boy stared at her, but said nothing.

Rose watched her words hit home. He suddenly looked tearful. 'Would you come inside with me?'

The boy shook his head. 'I can't.' He lifted his arm. 'I've all these papers to sell.'

Rose raised her eyebrows. 'I understand. It's just that I'm a little scared to go in by myself.' She stood upright and looked back at the shop.

The boy tugged at her coat. 'I'll come in wiv yer, but I can't stop. Charlie would want me to 'elp 'is girlfriend.'

Rose blushed as she looked at him. 'Thank you.'

The boy stared wide-eyed. 'Charlie was always kind to everyone.' He scuffed his shoes on the pavement, lifting the silver, glistening frost into a small heap. 'What will 'appen to 'is stuff?'

Rose shrugged. 'I don't know.'

The boy stepped forward. 'Come on then, open up. It ain't gonna get any easier the longer yer stand 'ere. Yer just gonna freeze to death.'

A tear dropped onto Rose's cheek. 'You're right about that.' She brushed her gloved hand across her cheek and pulled the key from her pocket. Stepping forward, she put it in the lock. It grated as she turned it. When it came to its resting place she pulled it out and twisted the handle. The hinges creaked as she pushed open the door.

'Go on, miss, yer can do it.'

Rose frowned at the young lad, suddenly wondering what his name was. She turned to peer into the semi-darkness. Taking a deep breath, she stepped inside, and over the many letters scattered on the doormat. It looked just the same; nothing had changed but then what was she expecting?

'Are yer all right, miss?'

Rose walked towards the counter and leant against it. The air was stale and a thick layer of grey dust covered the surfaces. Cobwebs hung from the corners. She furtively scanned the room for spiders.

'Miss, can I get yer somefink?'

Rose turned to face the young boy and shook her head. 'Thank you for coming in with me.' She walked to the window and pulled back the black curtains. The greyness of the day immediately threw its light across the shop. 'Perhaps I can buy a newspaper from you today?' Rose dropped her cloth handbag on the counter. The disturbed dust particles immediately swirled into the air. She waved her hand in front of her face before opening her bag.

'Yer don't 'ave to.'

Rose forced a smile as she pulled out her coin purse. 'No, I want to.' She opened it. Her slender fingers caused the coins to chink together before she pulled out a silver sixpence and held it out for the boy to take.

'They're only an 'apenny.' The lad folded a newspaper in half and passed it to her. 'I don't 'ave any change yet.'

Rose shook her head. 'I don't want change or the paper. I don't want to read about this never-ending war.'

'But you've paid for it.'

Rose waved the sixpence at him. 'Sell the paper to someone else. Look on it as a thank you for your kindness.'

He reached out and took the sixpence. 'Thank you – yer kind just like Charlie.' He stared down at the coin for a moment before looking around. 'It's like he's still 'ere.'

Rose followed the boy's gaze. 'I know.' Her chest tightened. Had he really gone? Had he really left her? Was she going to wake up from this nightmare?

'Will yer be all right if I go?'

Rose forced a smile. 'Thank you for coming in with me; you were very brave.'

The boy nodded and turned towards the door. 'Charlie is with the big boss in the sky now and he'll look after yer, just like he's looking after me, as me ma says yer just gotta have faith.'

Rose watched him go as Charlie's voice rang out: *Let me take your coat or you won't get the benefit of it when you go outside*. She spun round expecting to see him smiling at her, but he wasn't. Only his tools and bicycles filled the space, dulled by the several layers of dust. With trembling fingers, she pulled off her other blue woollen glove and fumbled with her coat buttons. She strolled round to the other side of the counter. Rose flopped down on the chair.

It dawned on her it was nothing without him. What was she going to do with all these bicycles? It was overwhelming. She fought the urge to run away. With a heavy heart, she glanced down at the counter, and that's when she saw it. A telegram, which was lying on top of papers scattered across the wooden surface. It had been scrunched together. She picked it up, smoothed it out, and scanned it before gasping.

CORPORAL HENRY YOUNG HAS BEEN KILLED IN ACTION. HE DIED A HERO FIGHTING FOR HIS COUNTRY.

Stunned, she read it again. Charlie hadn't mentioned it. Was that because of her own brothers? Rose dropped the paper onto the counter.

A clock chimed in the distance. The cold air rushed in, chasing out the stagnant smell before catching the door and banging it shut.

'Come on, you can do this, and there's the rent still to pay.' Rose slipped off her coat and rested it on the chair. She moved the crumpled telegram to one side, not allowing herself to read it again. She scanned the papers, which were mainly orders and invoices. Unaware of the time, she patiently sorted through the paperwork.

Rose jerked as the shop door swung open and the bell rang out and chimed again as it shut.

'I've come to see Charlie. Is he around?' The young man frowned. 'I've been here a number of times in the last few weeks but each time the shop was closed, which is quite unlike Charlie, especially as we had an arrangement to meet up.'

Rose's gaze darted around the shop as panic gripped her. 'No, I'm sorry, the shop is closed.'

He nodded. 'I'm Charlie's friend, Oliver, or Oli as he liked to call me. We were at school together. I came on the off chance but I can come back tomorrow.'

Rose sighed. 'I'm sorry, I haven't explained myself

properly.' She hesitated before looking up, his image blurring as she tried to focus. 'I'm sorry, Charlie has passed away. He… he…'

Silence stood between them for a moment.

'I'm sorry, I didn't know.' Oliver shook his head. 'I can't believe it.' He frowned. 'I've been away… and we've only recently caught up with each other.' His eyes glistened. 'Are you Rose, Rose Spencer?'

Rose nodded as she peered up at his ashen face. 'Charlie was so happy you had popped in to see him.' She took a breath. 'I'm sorry you weren't told but I'm afraid it hit me hard and my friends organised the funeral.'

Oliver stepped forward, fighting the urge give her comfort. 'No, you weren't to know. Charlie is… was a lovely man. If there's anything I can do please say.'

Rose sucked in her breath. 'Thank you, but there's nothing anyone can do.'

Sadness trampled across Oliver's face. 'I don't want to cause you upset but can I ask what happened to Charlie?'

'It was the bomb in The Strand. He shouted out but…'

Oliver gasped. 'I was… I mean, I'm so sorry.'

Rose nodded. Her heart was pounding. 'We had plans…' Her voice dropped to a whisper. 'But it was clearly not meant to be.'

Oliver shook his head. 'Life can be so cruel at times.'

Rose's gaze drifted to the telegram.

Oliver's eyes followed hers. 'Our fathers were friends so we were always together until… Anyway, none of that matters now. Look, I can't change what's happened but I can help on a practical level.' He paused before taking a deep breath and forcing a smile. 'Charlie told me he'd proposed to you but thought he'd scared you off. Apparently you ran out the shop as though the devil was after you.'

Rose blushed.

Oliver rested his hand on hers. 'He was frightened he'd ruined everything.' He shook his head. 'He was clearly in love with you. He told me what with Henry dying and all the bombs going off he didn't want to wait.'

Rose closed her eyes as she remembered the day Charlie proposed to her. 'I was frightened of getting married. I didn't want his love for me to change. I thought it might once he got to know me better.'

Oliver squeezed Rose's hand. 'He was a lovely, kind and humble man who loved you dearly.'

Rose looked up at his soft grey eyes. 'He was, and I did say yes, but he was taken not long after that. So he was right: life is short and you never know when someone is going to be ripped away from you.' Tears rolled down her cheeks.

Oliver walked around the counter and wrapped his arms around her as she sobbed into his soft woollen coat. 'You gave him the best gift of all; you gave him your love as well as your trust that everything would be all right. What more could anyone want?' He rubbed his hand up and down her back. Stepping back, he reached inside his trouser pocket and pulled out a white handkerchief. He shook it out and passed it to her. 'I'll go and get you a cup of tea from the restaurant over the road. I'll ask if they can make you a sandwich as well, then I'll be back to see what I can do to help.'

The bell chimed as Oliver opened the door and it shut again after him.

Sniffing and reminding herself this was not the time for tears, Rose frowned at a drawing scrawled on a scrap of paper. A few minutes later she jumped as the doorbell chimed again.

'I've got you a tea and an egg sandwich. I hope that's all right?' Oliver frowned as he studied her pale features. 'Sit down and eat. I don't want you fainting.' He placed the two cups on the counter and pulled a wrapped sandwich out of his pocket. 'Sorry if it's a bit squashed.'

'That was quick.' Rose smiled. 'Only if you'll share it with me.'

Oliver chuckled. 'That wasn't the idea.'

Rose eyed the two cups. 'Well, you have a drink and you can't expect me to eat on my own. Charlie would never have agreed to that.'

Oliver raised his eyebrows. 'You're not pulling at my heartstrings, are you?'

Rose blushed. 'No, maybe I just don't want to be here on my own. Memories are rushing at me. I need a distraction. That's if you have the time?'

Oliver nodded. 'I know Charlie would want me to look after you. That's probably what brought me here.'

'Thank you.'

'I was just thinking about some of the mischief we used to get up to at school.' Oliver gave her a wistful look. 'We never went straight home like we were meant to. I suspect our mothers used to despair we would ever amount to much.'

Rose smiled. 'And yet here you are, looking every inch a doctor or a solicitor.'

'That's scary.' Oliver chuckled. 'My father used to say, "If you spare the rod spoil the child," so that tended to focus my mind, especially the older I got.' He paused as he looked around him. 'Charlie used to help his father in this very shop so when his father died it was natural for him to take it over.' He sighed as he walked around, stopping at a photo of Charlie and his father outside the shop surrounded by bicycles. 'He was a great friend.'

Rose forced herself to smile in a bid to stop her lips from trembling. 'He had a kind heart.'

Oliver laughed. 'Indeed he did. I suspect he gave more of these bicycles away then he ever sold.'

Rose giggled. 'Yes, I caught him doing exactly that. I told him he'd never get rich.'

Oliver glanced across at her. 'I can tell you his answer would have been something like, "Who said I wanted to be rich?"'

Rose nodded. 'That's almost word perfect.' She glanced back at Charlie's drawing. 'He was obviously making plans to make room for me in this shop.'

Oliver strolled back to the counter and studied the drawing. 'He talked about you and your sewing. He was so proud, and I think he told anyone who would listen.'

Rose gazed out of the window; the day was getting duller as the grey clouds got darker. 'None of it matters now he's gone.'

Oliver stared at the pain etched on her face, but said nothing.

Rose suddenly turned to face him. 'I don't know what to do with all this stuff.' She waved her arms around. 'I don't even know where to start.'

Oliver took a step nearer to her. 'Why don't you leave

it with me to sort out? Charlie was my closest friend and I promise not to make any big decisions without talking to you first.'

Rose nodded. 'Thank you.' She sighed, feeling like a weight had been lifted from her shoulders. 'Do you know whether he has any family? I only knew about his brother.'

Oliver stared down at the tiled floor. 'His mother died when he was quite young; I believe it was pneumonia. His father lost interest in life after that, which is why Charlie came to work here so he could keep an eye on him.'

Rose could feel a lump forming in her throat. 'That's so sad.'

'Yes, grief can do terrible things to you. It's hard when you lose someone you love.' Oliver picked up his cup and sipped his tea, grimacing at the lukewarm liquid. 'Right, drink your tea and eat your sandwich. I'll look out the back, otherwise we'll never get started, never mind finished.'

Rose's heart was pounding as she stood in Regent Street, opposite Dickens and Jones Department Store, staring up at the large four-storey building. Its balconies and pillars gave it a regal look, along with the pots of flowers either side of an ornate clock. On the top floor a sculpture of a lion stood on its hind legs holding a flagpole within its paws.

Rose glanced at the white calling card she was holding: Mr Alexander Bowman of Dickens and Jones. Did she have the courage to go inside this magnificent-looking shop? She shook her head. What had happened to all the bravery she felt? After all she was only going to have a look. Going into Charlie's shop yesterday had been the hardest thing she would have to do.

Charlie's voice shouted above all the turmoil inside her head: *Spread your wings, find yourself, and move on. You've got more to give.*

Rose sighed before dashing across the road, narrowly avoiding the cars, coughing as car fumes filled her lungs. 'Am I doing the right thing, Charlie?' Her head throbbed from thinking about the leap of faith Charlie had talked about.

Rose stopped and gasped at the shop window. The lengths of material, lace and ribbon enthralled her. She clutched the cross and chain she was wearing before walking away as people streamed out onto the street. Rose wrinkled her nose as various perfumes wafted into the air.

'You made it then? I wasn't sure you'd come.'

She turned and saw Michael sitting by one of the windows. 'I wasn't sure myself. I didn't expect to see you here.'

Michael studied her. 'It's good to have a change of scenery.' He pulled his blanket and Bert's oversized coat around him. 'Most days I walk to Selfridges.'

Rose tilted her head. 'I suppose I can see why, their customers are better off than most.'

Michael frowned. 'That's not why I go. Have you been there?'

'No, although I've heard it's a wonderful shop.'

Michael's eyes narrowed. 'It's more than that – they have a war window.'

Rose looked stunned, imagining military uniforms and bombs on display. 'A war window?'

Michael shook his head. 'They put war news up. Crowds gather there every day to read it.'

Rose blushed. 'Sorry, I should have realized.' She peered up at the shop. 'Shall we get out of the cold, maybe get a coffee and some food in Dickens and Jones?'

Michael chuckled. 'I love your innocence, Rose, but they probably won't let me in.'

Rose sighed. 'You're probably right, but we can find somewhere else.'

Michael frowned. 'You don't have to worry about me, Rose. I get by.'

Rose shook her head. 'Oh, so you can worry about me but I can't worry about you?'

'It's different; the first time we spoke you were upset and I wanted to make sure you were all right, but now you've also experienced a terrible loss and I know what that feels like.' Standing up, Michael brushed the dust from his worn clothes and wrapped Bert's coat around him like a blanket.

Sadness gripped Rose; she wondered what had happened for Michael to be living on the street and how he'd lost half of his finger. 'Come on, I don't know about you but I'm freezing. Let's at least get a hot drink.'

Michael laughed. 'Freezing? It's the beginning of December. You wait until winter really sets in.'

Rose pulled at his arm. 'Come on, I saw a café up the road. We'll get some breakfast.'

Michael bristled. 'I don't need your charity.'

Anger surged through Rose; heat filled her cheeks. 'What makes you think I'm offering? I was being friendly, as I assumed you were by looking out for me, but I was clearly mistaken.' Muttering, she strode away. Suddenly, her arm was gripped and she staggered to a halt.

Michael stared at her, immediately letting go of her arm. 'I'm sorry.'

A car door swung open and a man jumped out, almost colliding with Rose. 'Oh, I'm sorry, are you all right?'

Rose paled as she met Mr Alexander Bowman's gaze. 'Yes, thank you.' She moved to sidestep around him.

'Wait, it's Rose, isn't it?'

Rose's colour deepened.

Mr Bowman's eyes lit up and a grin spread across his face. His hand rested under her elbow as he turned her towards the shop. 'I trust you were coming to see me.'

Rose glanced over her shoulder at Michael, who nodded. 'Well, I—'

'Excellent, you're holding my card.' Mr Bowman grinned.

Rose raised her eyebrows. 'I'm sorry, Michael.'

Mr Bowman led her into the shop. He unbuttoned his black coat and loosened his pink scarf from around his neck. He removed his hat with the matching pink band just above the brim. 'You won't regret it, and who knows where it might lead.'

Rose gasped at the lines of shining glass cabinets. Ladies in black skirts and white blouses stood pristine behind counters. Handbags stood on shelves and silk scarves were draped across them. Regal pillars stood tall around the shop. Rose's eyes widened at the swirling staircase. Everything seemed bigger and brighter than any shop she had been in before.

'Welcome to Dickens and Jones, Miss Spencer.'

Rose stared at the sparkling jewellery on display. The

air held captive an array of perfumes that were sprayed to entice the ladies. The fragrances hit the back of her throat; she coughed to clear the overpowering taste. 'Mr Bowman, I haven't come here to start work—'

'But everyone wants to work here. It's an honour to even be considered.' Mr Bowman studied her. 'Look around. Why wouldn't you want to? We're owned by Harrods, and that's an exceptional shop.' He paused. 'I'll take you to meet Mrs Todd; she manages our seamstresses.' He eyed Rose. 'Mrs Todd and I have seen Miss Smythe at the theatre a couple of times. I rather assumed when she married her dress would be one of ours, but I was clearly wrong.' Mr Bowman took Rose's hand, placed it under his arm and stepped forward. 'Our customers always come first, and we want them to have a wonderful shopping experience.'

Something stirred inside Rose. 'I would like to see the haberdashery. The window display looked quite magnificent.'

'Of course.' In a matter of minutes they were standing in front of many rolls of material.

Mr Bowman glanced around. 'Please excuse me for a moment.'

Rose kept her gaze fixed on the display. 'Of course.' She reached out and stroked the different materials, feeling the textures and softness.

A young woman stepped forward. 'Can I help you?'

Rose beamed at the woman, dressed in the uniform of long black skirt and white-buttoned blouse. 'This is wonderful. How do you get any work done?'

The assistant smiled. 'It is hard, especially when you enjoy sewing as much as me. Would you like to look at something in particular?'

Rose gazed at the shelves. 'Oh no, thank you, I'm happy to just browse.'

The woman nodded. 'I'm Miss Simpson, should you change your mind.'

Rose watched her walk away and smile at a customer. It wasn't long before Mr Bowman strolled into view wearing a very wide smile.

He rested his hand under Rose's elbow. 'So when are you going to bring your skills to Dickens and Jones?'

Rose immediately thought about Charlie. Was this the leap of faith he wanted? 'That depends; I'm looking to have my own collection. I have many books filled with designs that are ready to go.'

Mr Bowman beamed. 'You're making the right decision. Bring them in so I can assess them. Now, let me show you where all the creative work happens. There's a lot to learn.' He walked purposefully towards a door marked private, which he held open for her. They descended the well-lit stairs. Mr Bowman turned the handle; the springs echoed against the whitewashed brick walls. 'Welcome, Miss Spencer, to your place of work. Mrs Todd oversees everything down here, although I pop in from time to time.'

A hanging rail ran the length of the room, holding many garments on coat hangers. A shelf was above it with clothing neatly folded on it; each had paper pinned to it. Lines of mannequins were waiting to be dressed. The rows of treadle sewing machines sat like soldiers. It was a large room, especially when compared to the theatre's sewing room; maybe Charlie had been right.

'Mrs Todd, may I formally introduce Miss Spencer, who will be starting work here in the next day or two?'

Mrs Todd peered over her glasses. 'Well, it's lovely to meet you. I must say Miss Smythe's wedding dress was absolutely beautiful.'

Rose blushed, immediately recognising her. 'Thank you, that's kind of you. I'm sorry we weren't introduced at the wedding and hope you won't be disappointed with me.'

'Time will tell.' Mrs Todd raised her eyebrows. 'We never employ anyone without seeing their sewing first hand, we have a reputation to uphold.'

'Of course.'

Mr Bowman scowled. 'That won't be necessary, we've both seen her work.'

Frowning, Rose didn't know what to say. 'I don't wish to be treated differently. I'll happily sew something for you but I'm not here for my sewing skills, I'm here to design women's clothing for Dickens and Jones.'

Mr Bowman took a deep breath. 'Happy or not it won't be necessary; I want you to start immediately.'

Rose watched the seamstresses working in silence; was that Mr Bowman's doing, or was Mrs Todd another Miss Hetherington?

Mrs Todd cleared her throat, jolting Rose back to their conversation. 'Why are you leaving the theatre?'

Mr Bowman glared. 'Don't bombard her with questions, she's leaving because it's a great opportunity and her creativity can shine here.'

Rose's gaze darted between them.

Mrs Todd stayed silent for a second. 'I assume you can use a sewing machine?'

'Of course, and sew neatly with a needle and thread.' Rose glanced around the room.

'Follow me.' Mrs Todd led Rose to a sewing machine, with a table close by. 'This will be the machine you'll use most of the time. I'm afraid I can't spend as much time with you as I would like today, but you can familiarise yourself with everything we do here.' Mrs Todd followed Rose's gaze. 'We do many alterations, which I'm sure you can help with. For our wealthier customers we send our best seamstresses to their home. We don't expect them to come here for fittings.'

Rose's eyes widened. 'Well, that won't be me because I don't know my way around London.' She paused. 'Would I be able to use a sewing machine in my own time?'

Mrs Todd raised her eyebrows. 'You're a little forward for my liking. Don't you have one at home?'

'Sorry.' Rose blushed. 'In answer to your question, no I don't.'

Mrs Todd eyed Rose. 'We'll have to see how things go.'

8

Joyce, Annie and Rose huddled together on the doorstep waving off Arthur, Ted and Philip in the taxi as it drove away. The wind that blew across them was damp and cold.

'I was hoping the day would get warmer, or at least brighter.' Annie looked up at the thick cloud that looked full of rain and showed no sign of letting any sunshine through. 'I hate these dark grey days.'

Joyce stared along the road, rubbing her eyes with her fingertips. 'It's going to be strange not having them all here. I know it's been a struggle at times but I've got used to them being around, and I had hoped they would stay for Christmas.'

'I know.' Annie put her arm around Joyce's shoulders. 'There would never have been a good time for them to leave, but at least you've had a chance to get close to your brother and enjoy having your father back in your life. You now have a family that you didn't know you had so make sure you stay in touch with them, and Arthur.'

Rose nodded. 'Annie's right – Arthur clearly sees you as family even though you're not blood.' She stopped waving as the taxi disappeared from view. 'It's right that Philip moves up to Worcester. Hopefully they'll be safer in the village than here in London.' She looked thoughtful. 'Actually, if we'd had any sense we would've gone with them.'

Joyce and Annie both stared at Rose.

Joyce shook her head. 'I couldn't leave Simon. It took a long time for us to finally admit our feelings to each other, let alone talk about getting married, so I couldn't just walk away from him no matter what happened here in London.'

Rose turned away to walk back indoors. 'No, I couldn't have walked away from Charlie either. He had my heart; however, I do worry about my family. It doesn't help that those blooming brothers of mine never seem to put pen to paper no matter how many times I write to them.'

Annie was the last one to step over the threshold; she closed the door behind her. 'The main thing is that you know they're as safe as they can be, and before you say anything, I know you're hearing it from your parents but at least they're passing any news on to you. I expect your brothers don't want to worry you, just like my brother, David, doesn't want to worry me. I suppose it's more important that my father knows he's safe. I know he's receiving the parcels of chocolate and socks, because my father writes and tells me. I've even posted books to him, although I don't know if he gets a chance to read anything. My father tells me he looks forward to receiving the parcels and they all share out any chocolate or food they get.'

'My family say the same thing to me. It's just frustrating that I don't hear from them myself.'

Joyce took a deep breath. 'Well, perhaps it's time we all had a cup of tea. My mother used to say that would make everything better, and even though I've never been convinced that's the case we have nothing to lose by trying.'

Annie and Rose silently followed Joyce into the kitchen.

Annie opened a cupboard to take out the crockery that was needed, using her elbow to shut it again with a thud. The cups and saucers clattered together when she placed them on the scrubbed wooden table.

A drawer grated on its runner when Rose opened it to get the teaspoons.

Joyce turned on the tap and the cold water gushed out; she filled the kettle up before she put it on the range.

Rose played with the cross and chain that was hanging from her neck.

Annie bit her lip as she surreptitiously watched Rose. 'Do you want to talk about it?'

Rose jerked at the sound of Annie's voice.

Joyce looked round from the sink. 'What's happened? Is everything all right?'

Rose forced a smile. 'Of course.'

Annie shrugged. She wanted to ask if Rose was thinking about Charlie but was frightened to. 'You can share your thoughts; after all we're on our own. Have you been thinking about your sketch pad?'

Rose let go of the cross before pulling out one of the wooden chairs and flopping down on it. 'I can't believe that woman won't admit she stole my book. It's a terrible thing not to trust people you work with.'

Joyce shook her head. 'If you reported the theft she would probably get the sack.'

Rose studied the grain of the wooden table for a moment. 'I couldn't do that. Not admitting what she's done is wrong, but I couldn't get her the sack. Everyone has to eat.'

Annie rested her hand over Rose's. 'If it isn't that

troubling you then what is it? And don't say nothing because something clearly is.'

Rose peered up at her friend. 'As you know Charlie gave me this cross and chain.' Her hand immediately moved to her neck and caressed the silver metal.

Joyce watched Rose's troubled face. 'It's beautiful, but why is that causing you so much worry?'

Rose forced a weak smile. 'It isn't. As you say it's beautiful, but he said I should take a leap of faith and leave the theatre world because I'm capable of much more.'

The girls were silent.

Rose took a deep breath. 'I went to Dickens and Jones yesterday. Mr Bowman offered me a job.'

Joyce raised her eyebrows. 'Mr Bowman?'

Rose gave a half-smile. 'He was the one who came to Kitty's wedding and admired her dress. It was that day he left me his card and told me there would be a job for me if I wanted it. Anyway, I went along yesterday, just to have a look. I wasn't expecting to talk to anyone about work but he got out of his car and recognised me.'

Annie's eyes widened. 'What happened?'

Rose shrugged. 'I can tell you my heart was pounding. I thought I was going to keel over.' She laughed. 'He took me inside the shop. It's wonderful. Everything looks, feels and smells so rich but Charlie's words keep coming back to me and I wasn't sure at first but I accepted the position.'

Joyce frowned. 'So what are you worrying about?'

Rose gazed at her friends. 'That's just it – I don't know. The one thing I do know is I can't put up with Miss Hetherington anymore.'

Annie stood up and leant against the kitchen side. 'If I'm

honest I don't want you to leave the theatre. I love knowing you are just down the corridor but I also know that's very selfish of me. If we can chase our dreams why shouldn't you?'

Rose made a funny sound in her throat. 'I wish Charlie was here to talk to. I don't want to let him down. Why did he have to be a hero?'

Joyce stroked Rose's back. 'The question is would Charlie have forgiven himself if he'd just run away without alerting everyone?' She shook her head. 'I don't think he would have done. That would have eaten away at him and over time the man you loved so much could have disappeared.'

Rose nodded. 'I know you're right. I just miss him so much.' She closed her eyes and tried to shut out the clatter of pans and crockery. The aroma of the food cooking in the range made her feel nauseous.

Annie placed the white china teapot in the centre of the table and surrounded it with cups and saucers.

Joyce turned and peered at Rose. 'Right, dinner won't be long. Thankfully all the preparation was done earlier.' She pulled out a chair and sat down while Annie poured the tea into the cups. Joyce glanced at the empty chairs. 'It's not the same without Arthur, my father, and Philip. I'm already missing them and mealtimes won't be the same anymore.'

Annie nodded. 'I know what you mean but I expect Philip will have a wonderful time in all those fields and climbing trees.' She smiled. 'Let alone talking to the chickens.'

'You're right, of course, but it doesn't stop you missing people.' Joyce's face was suddenly ashen. 'Sorry, Rose, that was thoughtless of me.'

Rose forced a smile. 'It's all right – stop worrying.'

Joyce drained her cup of tea, standing up; she placed the cup back on its saucer. 'Right, let me check the dinner.'

Annie followed her lead and stood up. 'I'll get the dinner things out of the cupboard.'

Joyce nodded.

Rose stared at her cold cup of tea.

The thud of cupboard doors was quickly followed by the clatter of crockery and cutlery and the table was laid.

'Right, Annie, sit down.' Joyce placed a bowl of cabbage and carrots in the centre of the table. 'I'm sorry it's meat and potato pie again, and more potato than meat I'm afraid.' She sighed. 'It isn't much but it's getting harder to get fresh food these days. Peter has been very good but I can't push my luck because it's not fair on everybody else.'

Annie smiled. 'I don't suppose Arthur and Ted will notice it on the farm. That's the joy of growing your own – we never went short of vegetables.'

Joyce laughed. 'It's a shame we can't get them to post some to us.'

Annie glanced over at Rose. 'Are you still thinking about Dickens and Jones?'

Rose shrugged.

'It'll do you good to get back to work.' Annie frowned. 'Do they know at the theatre that you're leaving?'

Rose lowered her eyes. 'No.' She paused. 'Mr Bowman is paying me a lot more and there are more opportunities for me to make clothes for customers.'

Joyce smiled as she reached over and took Rose's hand in hers. 'That's excellent news. It means you're following Charlie's advice. You're taking that leap of faith.'

Rose gave a small smile.

Annie stared at her friend's pale face. The dark rings under her eyes told her she still wasn't sleeping properly. 'It could be a good thing, something new for you to concentrate on.' She spooned some cabbage onto her plate. 'So when are you going to tell them at the theatre? To be honest I don't think anyone will be that surprised. I get the impression they've been expecting it since you made Kitty's wedding dress.'

Rose looked sheepishly at Annie. 'Can I take the coward's way out and ask you to tell them?'

Annie picked up her knife and fork. 'Of course. I don't mind telling them but don't you want to see them before you leave? After all they've been very good to us both.'

Rose stared at the bowl of vegetables. 'I know, but I can't face it – at least not yet.'

Joyce nodded. 'I'm sure they'll understand. You'll be able to sort it out won't you, Annie?'

'I shall do my best.'

The tension in Rose's face ebbed away. 'Thank you. Make sure they understand that I don't mean to let them down and if anything is urgent I'll sew for them at home.'

Annie smiled. 'Don't worry. I can't imagine it will be a problem and if they get that busy old Hetherington is going to have to pick up a needle and thread.' She loaded her fork with pie. 'I take it you liked what you saw at Dickens and Jones. I would have come with you if you'd said you were going.'

Rose forced a smile. 'I didn't know. I just went out for a walk and next thing I knew I was in Regent Street outside the shop.' Her eyes lit up. 'You should see the material they sell. There was reams of it, and I've never seen anything like it.'

Joyce chuckled. 'Your eyes have lit up. They're sparkling like stars in the sky, so it seems Charlie was right to push you to move on.'

Rose shook her head. 'Well if I'm honest I'm not sure it's the right thing to do but I'm doing what Charlie wanted and that's enough for now.'

The girls fell silent.

Joyce was the first to recover. She started spooning vegetables onto Rose's plate. 'Come on, eat up. If you're starting a new job then you've got to keep your strength up.'

Annie gripped the handle of her umbrella with both hands as the freezing wind changed direction. The icy rain sprayed onto her face. 'We picked a good day to go Christmas shopping.'

People held their umbrellas tight as they tried to avoid the spikes hitting others as everyone rushed along the pavement. Men, with their coat collars pulled up and hats pulled down to cover their faces, charged along with their heads down. Coal men were drenched as they slung heavy bags of coal on their backs, the usual black dust dampened down by the weather. Cars drove through pools of water, spraying it up onto people's feet as they raced along.

Water sprayed up Joyce's legs, soaking the hem of her coat. She frowned as she shook it, while holding on to Rose's arm. 'I know this weather is awful but we're running out of time. Hopefully the rain will ease soon.'

Rose frowned. 'Michael will be soaked through if he hasn't found shelter somewhere.'

Joyce gave Rose a sideways glance. 'I'm sure he must have.'

Annie stepped behind Rose to let someone pass. 'Maybe we haven't seen him because he's found somewhere to live.'

Rose shook her head. 'Possibly, but it's unlikely. He's probably moved on somewhere else, but I hope he's all right.' The continual thud of the rain on her umbrella seemed to have lessened to become more musical. Was it her imagination or was the rain easing?

Joyce frowned. 'It's a shame because he appeared to be quite a caring man when we saw him. I wonder what his story is? You know, why he's in that situation. You'd think someone would be missing him.'

Rose looked pensive as they strolled along Oxford Street, weaving in and out between the stalls and other shoppers. Not noticing the usual tantalizing smells coming from the barrows. 'I wonder if there's a way we could find out.'

Annie peered at Rose. 'You mean apart from talking to him.'

Rose smiled. 'I know that's the obvious way but I don't think he'd tell us.'

Joyce glanced in a haberdasher's window. 'We need to gain his trust so we can help him, and I can tell you something else we need to do—'

'What?' Annie frowned.

Joyce laughed. 'Get out of this awful weather. Let's get this shopping done so we can go home and get dry.'

Annie glanced at Joyce. 'As always straight to the point.'

Joyce pulled Rose near to the shop window. 'Where do you want to start? Do you know what you want to get?'

Rose shook her head. 'If I'm honest, I haven't given it much thought.'

Joyce glanced across at her friends. 'I might send Dot some material and threads.'

Rose beamed. 'That's a good idea; maybe we could pool our money and send it from all of us.'

Annie nodded. 'I like that idea. We could have a look in John Lewis. I believe they have quite a selection.'

Rose nudged Annie. 'That was me who told you that.'

'Ahh, I knew someone had.'

Joyce giggled. 'Come on then, let's at least get that one done. Then we need to think about the men…' She immediately fell silent.

Rose rested her hand on Joyce's arm. 'Stop worrying, Joyce. Christmas is coming whether I like it or not, and I don't want to spoil it for everyone else.'

Joyce tightened her lips. 'I know that but it doesn't mean we have to add salt to the wound. I'm sorry.'

Rose shook her head. 'Don't be. Now let's get on with this shopping. It's a shame the rain has kept the carol singers away, especially as it's easing now. I could do with listening and maybe joining in on a few.'

Annie glanced across at them. 'Maybe we could sing some when we get home.'

Joyce stuck out her hand. 'It seems to have stopped raining, or at least it's only spitting lightly.' She closed her umbrella and gave Annie a mischievous look. 'You've a great singing voice so you could start now and I'm sure everyone would join in.'

Annie placed her hand on her chest. 'It's one thing to do it on stage but I couldn't just start singing now.'

The girls laughed at Annie's horrified expression.

Rose chuckled. 'What do you mean? You've done it before.'

Joyce turned to a woman standing near a vegetable stall. 'Would you like to hear my friend sing some carols?'

The woman gave a toothy grin. 'Now, that would brighten things up.'

Joyce turned to Annie. 'There you go, pick one and we'll join in.'

The woman looked up from bagging some potatoes. 'Go on, lady, you'll make our day.'

Annie blushed and looked at her friends. 'You will sing with me, won't you?'

The girls glanced at each other before chorusing, 'Of course we will.'

Rose stepped aside. 'What are you going to sing?'

Annie frowned. 'You mean what are *we* going to sing?'

Rose raised her eyebrows. 'Yes, of course that's what I meant.'

Annie gave her friends a suspicious look.

Rose sighed. 'Well?'

Annie glanced down at the puddles of water at her feet. 'How about "O Come All Ye Faithful"?'

Rose could feel her throat tightening. 'That's one of my favourites.'

Annie reached out and gave her friend a hug. 'I know it is.' She stepped away; pulling back her shoulders she took a deep breath.

O come, all ye faithful,

Annie's first line was barely a whisper but the lady on the stall suddenly burst into song, waving at everyone to join in.

Joyce nudged Rose and they burst into song as well.

Joyful and triumphant,
O come ye, O come ye to Bethlehem.
Come and behold Him,
Born the King of Angels...

People stopped and sang along before carrying on with their business. When the carol was finished someone started singing 'Away in a Manger' and the whole street was singing along. The girls carried on singing as they began walking along the road, hearing the joy in everyone's voices.

Joyce watched Rose through her eyelashes. For the first time in ages she noticed a sparkle about her. She turned to Annie. 'Look what you've done. Everyone is smiling and a lot of people have joined in with the singing.'

Annie blushed. 'You did it – it was your idea – but I have to admit everyone seems to be happier. I don't know why that surprises me because I love to sing; it lifts my spirits.'

Joyce nodded. 'I think we all did it together. The war has dragged people down and everyone needs something to lift them, and singing is free.' She noticed the John Lewis shop further along the road. 'Come on, let's get these presents bought so we can wrap them and get them ready to post.'

Annie pushed open the door to John Lewis and immediately smiled. 'Look at all this, Rose; this must be like heaven for you.' She glanced over her shoulder. 'I think picking the material for Dot isn't going to be as easy as we think. There's an awful lot to choose from.'

Rose laughed. 'Never mind Dot, I might buy myself some.'

They all stepped forward and spread out in front of the many shelves holding the rolls of material.

Joyce shook her head before looking over at her friends. 'Are we going to send lace and ribbon as well?'

Rose beamed. 'I think we should send her as much as we can afford, and we mustn't forget a couple reels of thread as well.' Smiling, she moved along the shelf gazing at the rolls of material, occasionally reaching up and touching one.

'How many yards of material do I need to buy to get a dress made?' A well-spoken customer spoke to the assistant next to her. Her coiffured hair was neatly hidden under a narrow-brimmed hat.

The shop assistant gave her an anxious look. 'Erm, it depends on the width of the material and the style of the gown.'

The customer shook her head. 'It's no good. I need to find someone to organise it. You have some lovely material here; perhaps if I leave you my card you could find someone for me.' She opened her small handbag and pulled out a calling card. 'Here's my details but, please, I want the person to be checked out. I need to trust whoever comes into my home.'

The assistant looked down at the card. 'Of course, Miss Allen. I can ask around for you. I'm sure we can find you a good seamstress.'

Rose walked over to Miss Allen and touched the fabric she had been studying. Rose pulled the roll out and placed it on the table nearby. She expertly unrolled it a couple of times. She let it run over her fingers before turning to Miss Allen. 'Look how this flows over my hand, it's beautiful. It would make a lovely gown.'

Miss Allen smiled at Rose. 'You sound like you know what you're talking about.'

Rose nodded. 'I like to sew. It's very relaxing and rewarding.'

Annie glanced over her shoulder at the two women. 'I don't wish to be rude but if you're looking for a seamstress they don't come any better than my friend. She made Kitty Smythe's wedding dress.'

Rose blushed.

Miss Allen turned to face Annie. 'That's wonderful and exactly what I'm looking for. My usual seamstress… is no longer available. Consequently, I have to find another one, someone who is reliable and excellent with a needle.' She paused, glancing at the three girls who were staring at her. 'Is it possible to meet your friend?'

Annie frowned before whispering, 'Of course, she's here and you've already been talking to her.' She thrust out her arm to indicate Rose.

Mr Bowman tried to pull his coat collar closer to his neck. Groaning, he pulled his flat cap down over his eyes and peered over his shoulder before lowering his head, shocked at how busy Great Earl Street market was with the wintry evenings drawing in. He didn't expect to see anyone he knew but he still stepped behind the garments and the accessories on the stall.

'Come on now, I can't go home till all this bread has

gone,' a man's voice yelled out over people's chatter as they walked past.

'Never mind his bread, what about my flowers? Come on, treat yerself, yer wife, yer mother, or even yer mistress. I don't care; I'll sell 'em to anybody.'

Laughter filled the air around Mr Bowman.

There were pockets of men huddled together, deep in whispered conversation. The shop awnings that were normally down protecting the windows from the heat of the sun were folded back for the winter. Mr Bowman watched people weave in and out between tables and barrows that were scattered all over the pavement. The four-storey buildings lorded over the people below. Some had signs emblazoned on the brickwork, advertising their business as far as the eye could see. Everyone appeared to be wearing many layers against the cold wind as they worked their barrow. Mr Bowman took out his handkerchief and blew his nose, catching a whiff of the floral smells mixed in with the hot food and fresh fish.

A child's scream made him jump. He jerked round and stared in the direction it came from but he couldn't see anything untoward. He shook his head; he couldn't afford to get involved even if he did.

A scrap of a boy yelled out. 'Get yer newspapers 'ere.' He picked up a folded one and held it outstretched. 'Come on, folks, give me an 'apenny and I'll give you a newspaper. Come on, I ain't got many left. It'll give yer somefink to read when the peeler comes around later ringing his bell telling yer to get in yer basement cos the Germans are coming again.'

Mr Bowman glanced at the boy; his scuffed shoes had seen better days and his trousers were too short.

Mr Bowman sighed and turned to the owner of the stall he was standing next to. 'I need to go.' He frowned. 'I need the money you owe me.'

'Yeah, yeah, just give me a minute; me customers come first.'

Mr Bowman pushed through the clothing hanging from the rails to glance down at the table. He eyed a brooch and earrings before picking up a necklace. 'This looks like it's good quality.'

The man turned to him and smiled. 'Yeah, I only have good quality 'ere yer know. It's not the real thing but only someone who knows their stuff would know that, especially from a distance.' He turned to take some coins from a lady. 'Yer ain't got sixpunce 'ave yer, love? Only it'll save me change.'

The customer opened her coin purse and searched for the small silver coin with her gloved fingers. 'Yeah, I 'ave.' She picked it up and passed it over to him.

The man smiled as he took it. 'Thanks. That's lovely.' He counted out a couple of larger coins into her hand.

The woman picked up the folded dress and put it in her shopping bag before nodding at Mr Bowman. 'Some of this jewellery looks genuine. Yer could treat yerself, or someone else.' She turned round and walked into the crowds that were still hovering, clearly hoping to get a bargain from the fresh food stalls.

The man smiled at Mr Bowman. 'She's bought a few items from me. Sometimes I throw in a brooch or somefink to keep 'er sweet.' He picked up the pearl necklace. 'This is a good 'un. Yer can 'ave it if yer want.' He pulled out his wallet. 'Right, I'll give yer a couple of quid, which is more than I can afford.'

Mr Bowman scowled at him. 'You owe me a lot more than that.'

The stallholder frowned. 'Yer need to understand it's not moving as quickly as it did before this damn war started.' He scowled. 'If it's not enough yer can always take 'em back.'

Mr Bowman's lips tightened. 'You know I can't do that.'

'Then yer just got to accept what I say then, ain't yer.'

Mr Bowman snatched the two-pound notes from him. 'Well, you need to understand the power doesn't all sit with you because I'll find another outlet for my goods.'

Annie eyed the man wearing the flat cap haggling with the stallholder as she came level with him. She couldn't see his face properly but he looked vaguely familiar. She turned to Rose and Joyce. 'Still we've had a good day shopping, and I think I've got everything I needed to get.'

Rose nodded. 'I must admit I'm quite tired but I think Dot will love the material and threads we've bought her.'

Annie glanced over at the stall again but she couldn't see the man wearing the flat cap. 'She will, although living on the farm she would probably have preferred something more practical.'

Joyce shook her head. 'I expect that's true but who wants a practical present?' She chuckled. 'That just sounds plain boring to me.'

The stallholder gave the girls his best smile. 'Come on, ladies; get your bargain prices here. I've got good-quality clothes for a fraction of the price you'd pay in the shops.'

Mr Bowman eyed the girls from behind the dresses hanging up; he immediately turned his back on them before stepping away from the stall.

Annie smiled. 'Sorry, we've spent all our money already.'

Rose turned to look at the dresses hanging up. She stepped nearer the stall and peered up at a long silver dress. The sequins shimmered as the dress moved in the breeze. 'This is beautiful.' She turned to Annie. 'It looks familiar.'

Annie and Joyce walked towards the stall.

Annie gasped. 'Are you saying—'

'I don't know, and it can't be. I mean how could it end up on a market stall?' Rose ran her hand under the material and gazed at the silver sequins. 'This would have taken hours to sew. It's beautiful.'

The stallholder beamed. 'It's yours for a snip. Wouldn't you like a beautiful gown like this for Christmas?'

Rose smiled. 'I'd love it but as my friend has already said we've spent all our money on presents.'

Joyce looked up. 'You have some lovely jewellery. I'm assuming the gemstones aren't real.'

The stallholder guffawed. 'At them prices, darling, definitely not.'

The girls looked at the array of brooches, necklaces and bracelets.

Rose picked up a brooch. 'You wouldn't know to look at them.' She studied the dark blue stone surround by tiny pieces of clear glass. 'I think I'll get this for my grandma. She'll love it.'

'All right, lovely, are you sure I can't interest you in the dress? A beautiful girl like you would certainly turn heads in it.'

Rose blushed. 'As beautiful as it is, I'm afraid it's a no. I'll just take the brooch, thank you.'

9

Annie stood in The Strand. Once again memories of that terrible evening rushed into her head. The bomb had dropped, changing people's lives forever. She stared straight ahead as she remembered all the destruction it had caused. The missing windows were now repaired and the hole in the ground had been filled, but the devastation was still in people's hearts.

Voices carried on the wind as paper boys shouted out the news headlines. Men in suits rushed along the road. A couple of policewomen could be seen ambling together, smiling and stopping to chat to the ladies and children. The cold wind rattled around them. Large puddles and water running along the side of the road were evidence the rain hadn't stopped all night.

Peter rested his arm around Annie's waist and closed his eyes for a moment. 'I'll never forget that night and the fear that I might 'ave lost yer.'

Annie didn't move. The chaos, the screams and the groans of injured people would always stay with her. 'That awful night has carried on for some.' She had sat all night with Rose, and when sleep had eventually come Annie had listened to her crying. Annie had dozed intermittently on the wooden chair; she remembered her body aching from sitting in one position all night.

Peter turned to look at Annie. 'And 'ow's Rose?'

Annie tightened her lips for a moment. 'How do you think she is?' She took a deep breath. 'I'm sorry. She's devastated. They had plans, you know, marriage and children. It's not been good.'

'Yer not on yer own.'

'I just feel so helpless.' Annie shook her head; the war had definitely arrived on their doorstep. There was no more pretending it wasn't happening. Her brother immediately sprung to mind, along with Rose's brothers. No doubt they were experiencing much worse. No wonder Simon didn't want to talk about it. 'She's making slow progress. At least she's leaving the house now.'

Peter nodded. 'That's good.'

Annie groaned. 'I don't know what to do to help, and if I'm honest I haven't done since it happened. I don't want to let her down.' She sighed. Her voice was little more than a whisper when she spoke. 'I've got to go. I have to tell Miss Hetherington that Rose won't be back. I should have told them already, but I had hoped she would change her mind.'

Peter took Annie's hand in his. 'Doesn't it make yer think about 'ow fragile our lives are?'

Annie gazed up at Peter. 'I've always thought my life was in front of me, but then so did Charlie and Rose. We've been shown how it can all be ripped away in an instant, and we shouldn't take it for granted.'

Peter pulled her in close. He wrapped his arms around her and kissed the top of her head. 'Yer know this isn't 'ow I wanted to propose to yer but I want us to start our life togevver. I don't wanna wait, I want us to get married as soon as possible. What's 'appened to Rose could easily 'appen to any one of us. Yer know I love yer, and there's nothing I wouldn't do for yer, but please say you'll marry me.'

Annie pulled back, her eyes watery with unshed tears. 'I love you too, Peter, and I hope you know that I want to spend the rest of my life with you but now isn't the right time.'

Peter's head dropped as he stepped away.

Annie grabbed his arm and stopped him from walking off. 'Peter, I can't go back and tell Rose we're getting married. That would be like adding salt to the wound. I just can't do it, no matter how much I want to. Please try and understand. I need to look after Rose. We've been friends since we were small and she has always been there for me and now it's my turn.'

Peter frowned. 'I know, I was being selfish. It scares me that we may never 'ave the life we want together because of this damn war.'

Annie lifted his hand to her lips and left a light kiss on it. 'I know. It frightens me too, and we're not the only ones in this situation, but it doesn't mean we shouldn't do the right thing by the people we love.'

Peter took her in his arms again. 'I know yer right, but please don't forget I love yer.'

Annie held him tight. The roughness of his coat scratched at her cheek. 'I could never forget because I love you just as much, if not more.' She gave him a squeeze before pulling her head back to look at him. 'I really do have to go but I need to know we're all right.'

Peter smiled. 'We're more than all right. Come on, I'll walk yer up to the Lyceum and then I'd better get back to 'arry and me stall.'

Annie and Peter walked hand in hand up Wellington Street to the Lyceum Theatre. Peter pulled open the heavy stage door. He leant towards Annie and kissed her cheek. 'Hopefully, I'll see yer later.'

Annie nodded before walking into the theatre. The door clicked shut behind her.

Bert glanced up. His newspaper rustled as he closed and folded it. 'Hello, Annie, 'ow's Rose? I 'aven't stopped thinking about 'er. I've 'ardly slept a wink since I saw 'er outside.'

Annie removed her gloves and rammed them into her coat pockets. Swallowing hard, she tried to dislodge the lump that was forming in her throat. She took a deep breath. 'She's slowly facing things but she'll not be coming back to work here.'

Bert shook his head. 'I only met her fella the night they came in to see the show. They seemed so 'appy together.' He fidgeted, his chair creaking under his ample weight. 'It's so sad. Rose is a good girl and deserves all the 'appiness in the world.' He stared down at the ground. 'I can't believe it.'

Annie stepped forward and rested her hand on his arm. 'I know. We all feel the same, but all we can do is be there for her. At the moment she's feeling compelled to follow Charlie's advice.'

Bert nodded. 'I shall miss her. Rose is quite a character, but right now she has to do what's right for her.'

'That's just it. I'm not convinced she thinks it is the best thing for her but she has to try.' She lowered her eyelashes. 'I shall miss knowing she's only down the hall.'

Bert stood up and dropped his newspaper onto the seat of his chair. 'We'll all miss Rose, and I don't suppose for all of her behaviour old 'etherington will be very 'appy about it.'

Annie sighed. 'No, and I hold her responsible, but it could be the right decision for Rose. We just have to wait and see.'

Bert nodded. 'It's so 'ard for her, 'aving their futures together taken away like that...' He lowered his head. 'My guess is the change in job is the distraction she needs, and no one will be surprised. Rose has a real talent that was wasted 'ere – that much was obvious even to me when I saw Kitty's wedding dress.'

Annie's chest tightened. 'I'm not sure she's ever going to get over losing Charlie. I had no idea how much she loved him or how far their plans had progressed. This war has a lot to answer for.'

'That's true, so very true,' Bert agreed.

'Well, I better go and pass on the news to Stan and Kitty. I might let them tell Miss Hetherington.' Annie shrugged and let her hand rest on Bert's arm for a moment.

The sound of heels clattering along the corridor made Annie step back.

'Tell me what?'

Annie sucked in her breath as she stared at the cold, formidable woman who stood in front of her.

'Tell me what?' Miss Hetherington's face didn't flinch under their scrutiny. 'Miss Cradwell, is Miss Spencer with you today?' Miss Hetherington's shrill voice echoed off the walls. 'I know it's a difficult time but she's not the only one to have lost someone dear to them.' Miss Hetherington stared at Annie. 'She needs to get back to work instead of feeling sorry for herself. You youngsters seem to make everything a drama instead of just getting on with things. Life is hard and there's nothing you can do about it.'

Annie's anger raged through her veins. She clenched her hands by her sides until her fingernails dug into her palms. 'I think you'll find that Rose has never made a drama out of anything, and the only time off she's had was when my mother died. I know you didn't approve of her coming to look after me, but that's because you're a cold fish who knows nothing about friendship. I will not have you talk about my friend like that. It's because of you she's leaving. You're an unfeeling person, and you need to look at yourself before you continue to spread your wickedness.'

Miss Hetherington glared at Annie. 'I don't know who you think you're talking to but you'll not get away with it. You might have the ear of the important people round here but you've overstepped the mark this time.'

Annie took another step forward. 'I'm sorry to be rude. It's not how I was raised, but some people don't listen unless you are, and unfortunately you are one of those people. You're just a bully who has got away with it for far too long.'

Miss Hetherington's lips tightened for a moment. 'She'll be back. After all she needs to work – it's not as though they were married.'

Annie pulled back her shoulders and lifted her chin, fighting the urge to shout at her. 'I don't expect you to understand how Rose feels but she has lost the love of her life; in fact she hasn't just lost him, he was ripped away from her. She's heartbroken but, as I said, I don't expect you to understand.'

Miss Hetherington lifted her head as the brutal words were hurled her way. 'Miss Cradwell, you need to be very careful. You're judging people on things you know nothing about and never will.' She turned on her heels and paced back along the corridor.

Bert frowned. 'I think you 'it a nerve there.'

Annie shook her head. 'I don't care. She's heartless and has made Rose's life a misery for far too long. I'm sure she would have thought about coming back if it wasn't for her.' She sighed. 'I had better go and tell Kitty and Stan.' Annie felt she was carrying a heavy burden, one she didn't know how to deal with. She ducked into a bathroom to compose herself for a few moments before emerging. The theatre had an eerie feel about it this morning. The only sounds were her heels clipping the tiles as she walked along the corridor to Kitty's dressing room.

Kitty poked her head round her open dressing room door. 'Ah, there you are, Annie. I was just coming to look for you.'

Annie raised her eyebrows; her voice was flat when she finally spoke. 'Is something wrong?'

Kitty studied her for a moment. 'No, I'd just heard you were in the building.' She hesitated. 'If you don't mind me saying you don't look too good. I'm not sure you should be here after the news I've just heard about Rose.' She stepped back into her dressing room so Annie could follow her.

Annie shook her head. 'If you heard, that must mean Miss Hetherington has already been to talk to you and Stan. Now there's someone I could act totally out of character for.'

Kitty laughed. 'Couldn't we all, my dear.' She sat down on the chaise longue and lit a cigarette.

Annie watched the grey smoke spiral up to the yellow-tinged ceiling. She took a breath, coughing as smoke filled her lungs. 'I take it she told you Rose isn't coming back?'

Kitty poked out her tongue so her fingers could pick a speck of tobacco off it. 'I can't say I'm surprised; losing Charlie will always be connected with being here. Also, Mr Bowman has made no secret he wanted her to work at Dickens and Jones. He recognises talent when he sees it.'

Annie flopped down onto the dressing table chair. She removed her coat. 'I know. Your wedding dress was beautiful, but I can't help thinking now isn't the time for making big decisions. I worry she might regret it.'

Kitty patted Annie's hand. 'You worry too much. Rose can come back anytime. She may have left us but we haven't left her. She has to do what's right for her to get through this awful time.'

Annie nodded. 'I just don't know what to do.'

'Just be there, listen and watch to make sure she's eating and looking after herself. That's probably what she did for you when your mother died.' Kitty drew on her cigarette. 'You have to let her grieve and how long that takes is different for everyone.' She paused. 'She's probably doing the right thing. The distraction of a new job will keep her mind off things.'

The invisible band around Rose's chest tightened as blood raced through her veins. She took a couple of deep breaths, the visible grey swirls quickly disappearing into the overcast day. Rose pushed open the heavy door, which was the staff entrance to Dickens and Jones. The door creaked. A slender brunette turned to face her.

Miss Simpson smiled. 'Ahh, so you decided to come and work here then.'

Rose blinked quickly and forced a smile. 'Yes, Mr Bowman can be very persuasive.' She paused. 'It's Miss Simpson, isn't it? We haven't been introduced properly. I'm Rose Spencer.'

Miss Simpson smiled. 'Don't look so worried – you'll be all right. And please call me Marion. You'll find management call everybody Miss this or Mrs that and they'll expect you to do the same, but if they aren't around I wouldn't worry about it.'

Rose nodded. 'Thank you. I'd better get used to it. I'm just used to being called Rose, so don't be surprised if I don't answer straight away.'

Marion chuckled. 'Come on, I'll show you where we hang our coats. I hope you like working here. It was quite a big thing when Kitty Smythe didn't buy her wedding dress from us, so everyone is intrigued to meet you, and of course it means you have quite a reputation to live up to.'

Pressure immediately wrapped itself around Rose. Perhaps this wasn't a good idea. She gave a nervous laugh before raising her eyebrows. 'Don't believe everything you hear.'

Marion smiled. 'No, it's all good, honestly.'

Rose shook her head. 'Thank you, but I'd rather everyone made their own minds up about me.'

Marion nodded. 'Do you know where you're going?'

Rose shrugged. 'To be honest I'm not sure.'

'I'll take you down to the sewing room first. I'm sure Mrs Todd will look after you.' Marion raised her eyebrows. 'I haven't seen Mr Bowman yet so it should be quite a gentle start for you.'

Rose followed Marion down the steps to the sewing room.

Marion pushed open the door and immediately smiled as Mrs Todd looked up. 'I saw Miss Spencer arrive so I thought I'd bring her straight down to you before the day becomes too busy.'

Rose could feel everyone's eyes on her but tried to focus on Mrs Todd. She almost stood to attention, while her fingers gripped the softness of her woollen coat. There was no whirring of the sewing machines or quiet chatter. She took a deep breath, trying to hold down the sickness in the pit of her stomach.

Mrs Todd stood up and strode towards them.

Rose studied the pristinely turned-out woman. Her hair was rolled into a neat bun at the nape of her neck, while her hemlines were still at her ankles, bucking the new fashion of having them end at the calf.

'Thank you, Miss Simpson.' Mrs Todd guided Rose to step forward before turning to clap her hands at the seamstresses. 'Can I have your attention please?'

All the seamstresses shifted their gaze from Rose to Mrs Todd. Some of the young ones murmured to each other.

Mrs Todd stepped nearer to Rose. 'I would like to introduce you all to our newest recruit to the sewing room, our new seamstress, Miss Spencer. As you all know every day is a busy day so I'm sure you'll all make her feel welcome and introduce yourselves during the course of the day.'

Rose breathed in the floral scent Mrs Todd was wearing. She forced a nervous smile to her lips as she stared wide-eyed at them all. She wanted to correct Mrs Todd; after all hadn't she taken the brave step to be employed as a designer and not a seamstress? But she decided it wasn't the time.

'Welcome.' They all spoke as one.

Rose nodded. 'Thank you.'

The silence was slowly swept away as the women whispered to each other.

Mrs Todd clapped her hands again. 'There's time for chatter later.'

The seamstresses turned to face their sewing machines and their feet began pushing the treadle boards back and forth. It wasn't long before the whirring noise filled the room and all conversation between them was drowned out.

Mrs Todd nodded as she looked on them all with satisfaction. 'We have a good team here so I hope you'll fit in with them. It's very busy; we do many alterations, some big, some small. We also make Mr Bowman's clothing range from scratch. It's a lot of work but definitely worth it.' She smiled. 'I've been lucky to put forward some designs and, once Mr Bowman has tweaked them, they have been good enough to be included in his collection.'

Rose beamed. 'That's wonderful, you must have felt so proud.' She glanced around her, noting again the mannequins, the hanging rails and the shelves. For the first time Rose noticed a large bin with different colours of material hanging over the sides.

Mrs Todd tilted her head slightly. 'Unfortunately since then I've struggled... to... er... find the time to carry on with that side of things.' She took a breath. 'Still, it doesn't matter because Mr Bowman has enough creative talent for all of us. Anyway, we like to try and clear each day's work on the same day. It isn't always possible but in those cases what isn't completed takes priority the next morning.'

Rose nodded, glancing at the near-empty hanging rail before looking back at Mrs Todd. 'What would you like me to do first? Only I think Mr Bowman—'

'Mr Bowman isn't here at the moment so you can start by taking something off the rail and doing the alterations required.' Mrs Todd pursed her lips. 'If you don't understand what is required then please come and talk to me.'

Rose held in the sigh that was threatening to escape.

Mrs Todd continued, 'There will also be items on the shelf above to keep an eye on.'

'Ah, Miss Spencer, it's good to see you this morning. I had hoped you might have started work here before today, but never mind you are here now.' Mr Bowman's voice boomed out from the open door. He strode towards them both. 'I trust Mrs Todd is looking after you.'

Rose nodded. 'Yes, Mr Bowman, Mrs Todd has been explaining about the alterations.'

Mr Bowman beamed. 'That's good. Mrs Todd is an excellent seamstress and we'd struggle if she wasn't here.'

Rose glanced at them both. 'She was telling me she's tried her hand at designing clothes as well.'

Mr Bowman's lips tightened. 'Yes, well, the first lot needed changing quite a bit before we could make them for our customers, but then it has to be said she did improve rather substantially.' He turned and smiled at Rose. 'Under my guidance, you'll also be visiting some of our more influential customers in their homes to sketch out their requirements.'

Rose swallowed hard. 'I don't know London very well.'

Mr Bowman patted Rose's arm. 'You are not to worry about such things. I will be with you at all times.'

Rose nodded.

'Mrs Todd, I'll look after Miss Spencer so you can get on with your work. We have things to discuss.' Mr Bowman smiled at Rose. He placed his hand on her elbow and guided her to his office. 'Do you have any of your designs with you? It would be lovely to cast an eye over them to see where you are in your ability to produce more than one wedding dress.'

Rose shook her head. 'I don't but I am always coming up with ideas. I do have several books full of them, some good and some not so good.'

Mr Bowman looked down at the papers scattered over his desk. 'Perhaps you can bring them in and I'll give you my professional opinion; remember, I'm here to guide you and offer any help I can.'

'Of course. I'm lucky to have this opportunity.' Rose hesitated. 'I noticed the large bin in the sewing room. It looks like it contains all colours of material. What is that for?'

Mr Bowman smiled. 'It's for the offcuts of material we don't need anymore, mainly because they are either too small or they are at the end of a roll so the colours may not exactly match with a new roll.'

Rose nodded. 'I know it's cheeky to ask but are we allowed to take those or do we have to buy them?'

Mr Bowman studied her for a moment. 'As my pa used

to say, "If you don't ask you don't get." I consider them to be available to the staff at no cost; after all, they will only get thrown away so someone might as well make use of them.'

Rose stood outside the bicycle shop, the cold wind taking her breath away. She knew in her heart this would be the last time she came here.

'Wanna newspaper, miss?'

Rose jerked round and saw the young lad who had come into the shop with her that very first time after Charlie died. He looked frozen. She wondered why he wasn't wearing a winter coat. Peering at his scuffed-out shoes, she noticed they were full of holes. 'I haven't seen you for a while. Are you selling many newspapers?'

The young lad smiled at her. 'Depends on the weather. I don't sell many when it's raining, but I ain't doing too bad, thanks.'

Rose smiled. 'Would you like to come in out of the cold for a moment? Maybe I could fix you a hot drink.'

The young lad shook his head. 'No thanks, miss, I'll miss me early morning rush if I don't get me skates on.' He eyed her for a moment. 'Unless of course you need me to come in Charlie's shop with you again?'

Rose tilted her head and smiled at the boy. 'You were very kind to me that day. I couldn't have gone in there without you.' She opened her purse and moved her fingers around inside, causing coins to chink against each other. Her fingers searched out and tightened around two small silver coins. 'Here, I don't want a paper but take these sixpences. It's not much but I know you probably miss Charlie buying a newspaper from you every day.'

The lad nodded. 'He was a good customer.' He reached out and took the silver coins. 'Thank you, miss, it's very kind of you.' He thrust the coins into his trouser pocket. 'I must get on but if you ever need any help with anything I'm always in this area.'

Rose smiled. 'Why thank you. You've been very kind to me too.'

The boy turned away before glancing over his shoulder and waving at her.

Rose waved back before turning to face the door of the shop. She pulled the key out of her bag and inserted it into the lock. Taking a deep breath, she turned the key. The mechanism grated as it turned. 'Come on now, you can do this. It's probably the last time.' She pushed the door wide open and stepped inside. She wrinkled her nose at the musty smell that greeted her. She looked around and noticed a lot of the bikes had gone. Oliver had obviously been busy. She left the door open and walked out the back of the shop to open the back door; the cold air whooshed in, causing her to shiver. 'Come on, today is about being practical.'

Looking around the kitchen she found a box and started filling it with cups and other crockery. She realised Charlie hadn't had much, but he had still been happy with the little he had.

'Hello? Hello, Rose, are you in here?'

Rose rushed back into the shop, stopping short of the counter. 'Oliver, what are you doing here?'

Oliver frowned. 'I was walking past and saw the door was open, but now I'm here I might as well be a helping hand if you need me.' He looked around. 'There's not many bikes left. I found another bike shop that was willing to take most of them and I think he might take these as well as some of the spare parts. I will not lie – I did give some of the older ones away to some local children.'

Rose smiled. 'Knowing Charlie, he would have given them all away so there's no harm done.'

Oliver nodded, as he gave a little chuckle. 'That's so true. That's why he didn't have very much, but he was a happy man and true to himself. When I take these last bits to the owner of the other shop I will have some money to give you for everything.'

Rose shook her head. 'The money doesn't belong to me. Having said that I don't know who it belongs to.'

Oliver gave a faint smile. 'On the contrary it definitely belongs to you because you've been paying the rent on the shop since Charlie's been gone.'

'That was my choice; I could have sorted everything out much quicker but I just couldn't face it. Clearing the shop has gone much better than I expected and that's thanks to you and your kindness. It's hard to believe it's only been about three weeks since we first met.'

Oliver took a breath. 'It's a shame it was in such difficult circumstances but I'm glad I've been able to help.' He paused. 'Charlie would have wanted that.'

Tears pricked like spears at Rose's eyes as she stepped behind the counter and pulled out a wad of paperwork that needed to be gone through. She swallowed hard. 'I think I'll take these home and go through them at my leisure; maybe it's best you hold on to the money for now in case there are any bills that might need paying.'

Oliver nodded. 'I don't mind holding on to it for now, but you must let me know if you need it. I can tell you I won't be happy if I find out you've been paying the bills out of your own money, because it isn't necessary.'

Rose looked down at the paperwork before glancing back at Oliver. 'If we don't need the money then maybe it should go towards something good, like helping the wounded soldiers who come back from the war. I think Charlie would have liked that, or something to do with children.'

'I agree. I'll look into it and see where we can send it.' Oliver reached up for the photograph of Charlie outside the bicycle shop. 'Are you keeping this photograph?'

Rose stared at him for a moment. 'I would like to, unless you want it. You knew him a lot longer than me.'

Oliver shook his head. 'I would have taken it if you didn't want it, but maybe we might come across some other photograph I could have.'

Rose nodded. 'I don't intend to come back to the shop after today. Charlie wouldn't want me to hang on to it and be miserable.'

'I think you're right. He definitely wouldn't want you to be miserable but his drawings would suggest he wanted you to work for yourself inside this shop with him.'

Rose stepped out from behind the counter; she paced to the back of the shop. 'That's just it – with him, and he's not here. I think to work in the shop would hold me in a place that would continually remind me of what is lost. Also, I couldn't afford the rent on the shop, long term.'

Oliver nodded. 'I do understand. When you're done I can take the keys back to the landlord. Of course you'll have to give me his address.' He stepped nearer to her. 'I want you to know if you need anything or you just need a shoulder to cry on I will always be here for you.'

Rose flushed with colour and stepped back. 'Thank you, it means a lot.'

Oliver brought his hands together, his fingers interweaving as they pressed their edges against his lips. 'If you don't mind me being presumptuous, Rose, I have a proposition for you.'

Rose gasped. 'Sorry, I…'

Oliver fidgeted from one foot to the other as he realised what he had said. 'No, it's me who should be sorry for giving the wrong impression. I just wanted to ask you how you would feel about altering some clothing?'

Rose blushed. 'My apologies. I should have known better. Whose clothing are we talking about? And how much is there?'

Oliver studied her for a moment. 'Some of the soldiers I work with at the hospital have lost limbs and their clothing can be an accident waiting to happen. Also, some have lost so much weight that their clothing is too big. I would like to try to raise money or gather clothing for these men to have before they leave the hospital. Most of them will never go back to fight so I would like them to leave with the best possible chance of recovery and for getting work.'

Rose immediately thought of her brothers. Her eyes widened as she realised it had never occurred to her that they would come back broken and unable to survive on their own. She could feel the tears pricking at the backs of her eyes. She blinked quickly in a bid to stop them from falling. 'If there's anything I can do then I'm more than happy to do it. They are lucky to have you in their corner.'

Oliver shrugged. 'They have all lain their lives on the line for us so it's the least I can do; however, I would appreciate your help.'

Rose nodded. 'Of course, it's about time I got involved. It never occurred to me that I could help in such a way. Do you want me to come to the hospital to pick up their clothes? Do I need to talk to the men to see what needs altering or will you be able to write that down for me?'

Oliver raised his eyebrows. 'If I'm honest I haven't thought about the practicalities of it but we could try with me dropping the clothing off to you and see how that goes.'

'That sounds fine, but I will need details; for example, how much needs to come off the sleeve or a trouser leg, how many inches need taking in. In some instances it might be easier for me to come to the hospital.'

Oliver nodded. 'I can see that, but maybe we'll start off small and see how we get on.' He paused. 'Maybe you could come with me to the shelter I help out at? It's for injured men.'

Rose frowned as she wondered what she would see inside. 'I didn't know such places existed.'

'There's no need to worry. They are good men, but thanks to the war they do have problems.' Oliver paused. 'You would be quite safe and I can assure you I will stay with you until you feel comfortable with them.'

Rose shrugged. 'I'm sure it will be all right. It's just the unknown.'

Oliver nodded. 'Of course.'

Rose took a breath. 'Well, I'll gladly help but right now I need to get cleaning; otherwise I'll have to come back another day. So please forgive me. I don't wish to be rude but I need to get on.'

Oliver smiled and unbuttoned his jacket. 'Right, what is it you want me to do?' He removed his arms from his jacket and hung it on the back of the door before facing her again. 'I don't know if I'm gonna be more of a hindrance than a help, but I want to do something.'

Rose giggled. She reached out for the long-handled broom that was propped against the wall, and passed it to him. 'I'm not going to say no to any sort of help, so sweeping the floor it is.'

Oliver took the wooden broom handle and chuckled. 'My mother will never believe this when I tell her.'

10

Rose took a deep breath, the cold December air filling her lungs causing her to cough as she pushed open the staff door to Dickens and Jones.

'Ahh, thank goodness you've arrived.' Mr Bowman's voice carried along the corridor.

Marion and Rose turned to see him racing towards them.

'Miss Simpson, can you let Mrs Todd know that I'm taking Miss Spencer with me to see Mrs Hardy?'

Marion frowned. 'Yes, sir.'

Rose stared at Mr Bowman. 'But, sir, I don't have any sewing things on me.'

Mr Bowman shook his head. 'You won't need them. She wants you to design something special for her.' He lifted his hand, which was clutching a tape measure. He turned to Marion. 'Why are you still here?'

'Sorry, sir.' Marion stepped quickly along the corridor, her heels clattering on the red and black tiles.

'I trust you have your sketch pad with you?'

Rose nodded. 'I do.'

'Excellent. Come, Miss Spencer, we must get a taxi to Bury Street. We can't keep Mrs Hardy waiting.'

Mr Bowman marched on ahead. When she caught up

with him he was holding open the car door for her. Rose climbed in. 'Thank you.'

Mr Bowman's officious voice rang out. 'Bury Street please.' He climbed into the taxi and slammed the door shut behind him.

Rose gazed out of the window as the car chugged along Oxford Street. She was mesmerised by the comings and goings of the crowds that were already forming. It wasn't long before the road became New Oxford Street and they turned off into Hart Street and were taking the first left into Bury Street. Rose's insides were somersaulting.

'Right, Miss Spencer, let me do the talking. Only speak when a question is directed at you, and keep your answers short but polite.' He leant forward to speak to the driver. 'Just here will do, thank you.' The taxi came to a standstill. Mr Bowman thrust some coins at the driver and opened the door before stepping out. He narrowly missed a lad on a bicycle, who dropped the envelope he was holding.

Rose followed Mr Bowman. Stooping down, she picked up the letter. Turning it over, she saw it was a telegram. Pictures suddenly flooded her mind. Was it the same lad who knocked on the shop door when she ran away from Charlie's marriage proposal? Nausea washed over her. Did Charlie hear about his brother on that same day?

Mr Bowman sighed. 'Come, Miss Spencer, we don't have all day.' He looked up at the black ornate railings framing the front of the six-storey red-brick house. The many large sash windows had decorative scrollwork above them. The black front door stood tall and imposing.

Rose handed the telegram to the boy, who nodded his thanks before cycling off. She watched him go, taking a deep breath to stop the nausea rising in her throat. 'Does Mrs Hardy always have home visits?'

Mr Bowman raised his eyebrows. 'All our customers get home visits when they want something made for them. That's one of the reasons they keep coming back to us.'

Rose frowned as she looked up at the flamboyant man standing next to her. 'I know I'm here now but who usually does these visits?'

Mr Bowman glared at her. 'You ask too many questions. Mrs Hardy wanted you, and what Mrs Hardy wants Mrs Hardy gets.' He fiddled at the pink woollen scarf tucked inside the neckline of his coat. 'Right, let's get in out of this cold weather.' He stepped towards the front door before looking round at Rose. 'Stand up straight and shoulders back – you look like you're carrying the weight of the world on them.' He lifted the shiny doorknocker, before letting it drop with a thud. 'You need to learn how you present yourself is everything.'

Rose kept her eyes fixed on her black serviceable shoes. Maybe she should buy some new ones and make herself some new clothes, especially if visiting posh houses was to be part of her job. The rattling of a curtain being pulled back from the other side of the door made her take a breath.

The lock clicked and the door swung open. 'Ahh, Mr Bowman, good morning. Mrs Hardy is waiting for you in the sitting room.'

Rose looked up at the grey-haired lady dressed all in black as she stepped aside.

Mr Bowman gave a slight nod. 'Thank you, Mrs Franklin.'

Rose followed Mr Bowman inside. 'Good morning.' She stood aside in the large hallway so the front door could be closed. The smell of beeswax hung in the air, drowning out the scent of the lavender standing between two church candles on a console table.

'Let me take your coats and I'll get some tea for you both.'

Mr Bowman began to unbutton his coat.

Rose's eyes widened. 'Thank you, but I'd rather keep mine on.'

Mrs Franklin reached out and took Mr Bowman's, carefully placing it over her arm.

Mr Bowman scowled. 'Come, Miss Spencer, take it off. We can't keep Mrs Hardy waiting. I'm sure Mrs Franklin has more important things to do than to stand here waiting for you.'

For a moment Rose wasn't sure how to react but sensing Mr Bowman glaring at her, she slowly unbuttoned and removed her coat and handed it to Mrs Franklin. 'Thank you.'

Taking it, Mrs Franklin opened a large oak cupboard door and hung them on the hooks inside it. She turned and smiled at them. 'Follow me, I'll take you to Mrs Hardy.'

A girl came running into the hall, her brown curls bobbing up and down on her shoulders.

'Catherine, you are meant to be resting. If you're not careful you'll end up in trouble.'

Catherine lowered her eyes. 'Sorry Mrs Franklin, I just get bored.'

'Have you finished reading the book your grandma gave you?' Mrs Franklin shook her head before smiling at the young girl. 'You can bake some biscuits with me later.'

Catherine beamed.

Mrs Franklin indicated they should follow her into an elegant front room and take a seat.

Rose perched herself on the edge of the armchair. Looking up at the glass chandelier, she wondered whether it was gas or electricity. Heavy, sumptuous curtains hung at the windows, stopping the wind finding its way in. A fire crackled in the grate. The Victorian tiled fireplace was a mass of colour. The blues and yellows of the tiles matched the flames as they snaked up the chimney. Every so often the fire would spit out an ember onto the hearth. Above the fire grate was a marble mantelpiece that had candles and silver-framed photos sitting on it. Rose wanted to have a closer look but she knew that wouldn't be the right thing to do. A large portrait of an older man stood above the fire.

'Good morning, Mr Bowman, Miss Spencer.'

The demure voice startled Rose. 'Good morning, Mrs Hardy.'

Mr Bowman stood up. 'It's lovely to see you again Mrs Hardy, looking as beautiful as ever.' He paused and turned to look at Rose still seated on the armchair. He waved his hand at her. 'As you can see I have brought Miss Spencer to meet you and discuss your requirements.'

Rose jumped up. Unsure what to do, she gave a little curtsey.

Mrs Hardy smiled at Rose. 'Please sit down, child. You don't need to stand on ceremony in my home.'

Rose glanced nervously at Mr Bowman, who nodded at her. She sat back down, wondering if she would get used to all this. She thought about her family and how poorly they lived. Would they believe how careful she was being before she spoke? Was she betraying them and the freedom she had grown up with? It was that same freedom that had made her think they didn't care about what she did. After all, hadn't she always said and did what she thought was right regardless of who was involved? They had been happy for her to come to London to support Annie's bid to be a singer, whereas Annie had argued with her father who had wanted her to stay in the village and be a farmer's wife.

Mr Bowman's gaze moved between the two women. 'Miss Spencer has brought her pad with her and will show you some ideas and sketch out anything you might suggest.'

Rose quickly undid the clasp of her bag and pulled out her pad. She flicked it open and began turning the pages over, unaware that Mr Bowman was peering over her shoulder.

Mr Bowman smiled. 'You have some lovely ideas in there. I think you will go far under my guidance.'

Rose gave a tentative smile. 'Thank you, sir.' She fought the urge to snap the book shut, knowing she had to learn to trust the people she worked with and stop thinking about her lost designs.

Mrs Hardy beamed at Rose. 'I'm so pleased. It's an exciting time for you.' She glanced at Mr Bowman. 'Why don't you leave Miss Spencer here? I'm sure a man of your stature has more important things to do than to sit and listen to us talking dresses.' She gave a melodic laugh. 'I will make sure Miss Spencer gets back to you in one piece.'

Mr Bowman almost preened himself. 'That's very kind of you to say so, Mrs Hardy, but I really couldn't make such an imposition.'

'It's not an imposition, Mr Bowman. I know you are key to Dickens and Jones's popularity and I would hate for my favourite shop to fall apart while you're away.'

Mr Bowman smiled. 'Well, when you put it like that, I suppose I should get back.' He turned to Rose. 'I trust you will remember our earlier conversation, and I'll see you back at the shop.'

Rose nodded, realising Mr Bowman had stood taller with the flattering words. She could learn a lot from Mrs Hardy.

Mrs Hardy walked towards the sitting room door. 'I won't be a moment, Miss Spencer.'

As they walked out of the room Rose let out a big sigh. She leant back in the armchair, which seemed to wrap itself around her. A rattle of crockery caught her attention and she sat bolt upright.

Mrs Franklin came into the room carrying the tray of tea things.

Once again Rose didn't know if she should say something. Mr Bowman's words were shouting in her head.

Catherine ran into the room and flopped down onto the sofa.

Mrs Franklin frowned at the young girl. 'Catherine, if your grandma saw you sit down like that you would get into trouble. Remember you're a young lady and should sit down accordingly.'

Catherine looked heavenward. 'I'm not a young lady; I'm seven so that makes me a child. Anyway, Grandma isn't here so she didn't see me, unless you're going to tell on me?'

Mrs Franklin shook her head but struggled to hide the smile that was tugging at the edges of her lips. 'No, I'm not going to tell on you, but remember you're meant to be resting.' She turned to Rose and gave a wry smile.

Mrs Hardy strolled into the front room; there was a click

as the door closed behind her. 'Catherine, I believe you're meant to be resting and reading the book I set you.'

Catherine's nose wrinkled. 'I will, Grandma, I promise. Will Miss Spencer be able to make me a dress too?'

Mrs Hardy shook her head. 'I don't know what I'm going to do with you, and your father doesn't help.'

Catherine looked wide-eyed at her grandmother. 'Pleeeasee.'

Mrs Hardy shook her head. 'I expect a treat is in order as you've been through a lot in the last few months. Maybe we could replace the dress that got ruined, especially as it was your favourite.'

Catherine sat upright and clapped her hands before jumping up. Wincing, she threw her arms around her grandmother. 'Thank you.'

Rose smiled at the child's excitement.

Mrs Hardy's lips thinned for a moment. 'Catherine, I know you are excited but you're not meant to be throwing yourself around.'

Rose's smile was quickly chased away as she wondered what was wrong with the little girl. Despite her good spirits she was obviously in pain.

Joyce gazed into the dancing flames of the fire. The once black coal was ashen and crackled as it shifted position in the grate. She sighed, knowing she should prod it with the poker. The marble hearth had a scattering of small pieces of ash that the fire had spat out. 'I love being in this sitting room.' She looked around her. 'Being surrounded by Arthur and Dot's things makes them still feel close.'

Rose glanced over at her. 'I know what you mean. I missed Dot when she left the theatre.' She smiled. 'It's strange I never realised she was Annie's aunt. She was great company when we sat sewing for hours on end.' Rose paused, staring into the distance. 'When I think back it was obvious. I remember her asking about the village and our parents, and yet I didn't make the connection. I just thought she was making conversation with me. But then neither did Annie. She certainly didn't recognise Dot, but it had been years since she ran away from home and, to my knowledge, no one knew she was in London.'

Joyce peered at Rose. 'I wonder what she would make of you working at Dickens and Jones.'

Rose shook her head. 'Who knows, but I'm trying to concentrate on getting my designs out there.' Hearing footsteps and rattling crockery, she jumped to her feet as Annie pushed open the sitting room door. 'Ah, well done, Annie, I'm gasping for a cuppa. Be careful you don't trip over those boxes of Christmas decorations.'

'Here it is. There's biscuits as well; I think we deserve a treat.' Annie placed the tray down on a small table and began handing out the cups.

Rose took hers and nodded her thanks before sitting back down again. She sipped the steaming tea. 'That's a good cuppa, thank you, Annie. It feels like it's been ages since I just sat without sewing or knitting.'

Annie picked up her knitting and sat down with her tea. 'You certainly seem to get a lot of alterations to do.'

'Yes, Oliver dropped off several bags from the hospital.' Rose paused. 'It hits home how many lives are never going to be the same ever again; in fact he's asked me to visit a refuge with him on Sunday.' She took a deep breath. 'I also still have paperwork to go through from Charlie's shop as well. I've brought it home but haven't got round to looking at it yet. Oliver managed to sell the bicycles and all the spare parts Charlie had collected. A couple of the older bikes he gave to some local children. I was thinking of donating the money but I haven't decided where yet.'

Annie gave Joyce a sideways look. 'Wait a minute. Oliver?'

Rose could feel the colour and the heat creeping up her neck. 'Don't get overexcited. He's Charlie's friend. He's helped me sort out the bike shop and now he's delivering clothing for alterations, so I'm seeing a lot of him at the moment.'

Joyce smiled. 'So, he's turning out to be rather a good friend.'

Rose lowered her eyelashes. 'Apparently, Charlie told him all about me and how he had proposed.' She stared into her half-drunk cup of tea before looking up and watching Annie's fingers deftly move the knitting needles in and out of the woollen stitches. 'Have you and Peter decided to set a date yet for your wedding, or at least to get engaged?'

'No.' Annie stopped knitting but didn't look up. 'We've talked about it and Peter wants to get married sooner rather than later. He's anxious about conscription.' She sighed. 'The trouble is there's too much going on, and anyway I'm not sure if I can get my family down here, or if we could get to Worcester.'

Rose frowned. 'You two have been in love almost since the day you met and I know in an ideal world you'd want your father to walk you down the aisle – that's what all girls want. However, you need to think about how you'd feel if Peter suddenly had to go to war.' She sighed. 'I'm sure your family could get here tomorrow if they had to and there's less to do on the farm now it's winter. They could ask my parents to pop over and feed the chickens. I'm sure they won't mind.' She glanced over at Joyce. 'And what about you and Simon?'

Joyce looked across at Annie, who shook her head. 'We haven't decided yet.'

Rose let out a big sigh. 'Haven't you two learnt anything? You don't know how long you've got with this rotten war. If you love them then get on with it. You could even have a joint wedding, because my guess is it will be pretty much the same people going to both. If you're waiting because of what happened to Charlie then that's not what I want.' She paused. 'If you don't wish to get married then that's a different thing altogether.'

Annie put down her knitting and stared at her friend. 'Rose, you must understand we care about you and we're trying to do the right thing.'

Rose's gaze switched between her two friends. 'I'm sorry, and I appreciate that, but putting off your wedding because of me isn't right. I don't want either of you to live with regrets. There have been times when I truly wished Charlie and I hadn't waited. I will never wake up in his arms. I wish I hadn't been a prude, or had my mother's voice in my head, because then I might have known.'

Joyce gasped. 'Did he want you to then?'

Rose shook her head. 'No, at least he never suggested it, but I often thought about it.' Her throat tightened. 'But it is now something I will never know. Trust me when I say if you love your man then don't wait, particularly not to save my feelings.'

Annie and Joyce looked at each other, but remained silent.

'Have I shocked you?' Rose chuckled as she looked at them both. 'Does that mean I can't be a bridesmaid?'

Annie giggled. 'Rose, you've never stopped shocking me, even when you were younger backchatting the shopkeepers, but we're still friends. You're your own person. It's one of the many reasons why I love you so much; you help me to be brave and try things. I've told you before if it hadn't been for your encouragement I probably would never have made it to London, and then I wouldn't have met Peter.'

Joyce tilted her head as she listened to Annie. 'You've always been a good friend, Rose, even when you wanted to help things along and said things that I would have preferred to be kept between us.'

Rose giggled. 'Yes, but if I hadn't said them you wouldn't be with Simon now and he would never have known about your dream to be a cook.'

Joyce shook her head and gave a small chuckle. 'Yes, you're good at pushing your friends to achieve, just not at pushing yourself.'

Rose smiled. 'I like to help, so just set your wedding dates so I can buy a new dress. I'm happy to make your dresses for you but, equally, I won't be offended if you'd rather I didn't.'

'Thank you. We'll see.' Annie picked up her knitting needles again.

Rose sipped her tea. 'Annie, have you seen Michael outside the Lyceum recently?'

Annie shook her head. 'No, but it's been so cold I haven't actually hung about. Have you not seen him around then?'

Rose frowned. 'No, I do worry but I don't know where to start looking. I just hope he's in the warm.' She looked pensive as her finger tapped her lips. 'I might ask Oliver to look out for him.'

The girls nodded.

Annie turned to Joyce. 'How's the restaurant going? Is it keeping you busy?'

'It's steady; it wasn't really the right time to open a restaurant but it'll be all right. Baking for Peter's stall brings in a bit of money, and it's definitely easier to cook at the restaurant than at home.'

Annie took a sip of her hot tea. 'What about you, Rose? How's it going at Dickens and Jones?'

Rose shrugged. 'To be honest, I'm not sure. I'm almost certain my sketch pad has ended up in the hands of Mr Bowman. It seems odd that all the designs I think are mine seem to have come from Dickens and Jones, even the one Miss Hetherington was wearing. Mr Bowman's their designer so what other conclusions are there? I just can't figure out how he got hold of them. It's frustrating because I just keep going round in circles. His assistant, Mrs Todd, has got something going on but I don't know what that is either.'

Joyce smiled. 'Your life is always full of mystery.'

Rose chuckled. 'I don't think it is. I'm just nosy and pick up on things.' She glanced at her friends. 'I haven't been there very long so it's hard to make a judgment yet.' Rose fidgeted in her chair.

Annie's eyes narrowed. 'You must have some idea.'

Rose sighed. 'I know Charlie would talk about giving it a chance.' She paused. 'Mr Bowman took me to Bury Street to meet Mrs Hardy, who wants me to design and make dresses for her and her granddaughter.'

Annie watched the sadness flit across her friend's face. 'Well, it's a step forward to realising your dream of making the clothes you want.'

Rose nodded. 'Mr Bowman made it clear I wasn't to speak unless I was spoken to. I suppose he's trying to teach me how to deal with the customers, which is something I've never had to do before.' She gave a lopsided grin. 'But I'm certainly being kept busy.'

Annie nodded. 'Was Mrs Hardy difficult to deal with then?'

Rose gave a faint smile. 'No, actually she was very nice, as indeed was her granddaughter who was clearly in pain at times.'

'What's wrong with her?' Annie picked up a biscuit and bit into it, flicking the crumbs on to her saucer.

Tears immediately sprung into Rose's eyes. 'I don't know and didn't like to ask.'

Annie nodded. 'I know you're thinking about Charlie right now but please focus on what you had with him and not what you're missing. He wouldn't want you to be miserable, he'd want you to fulfil your dreams.'

Rose peered towards the window. 'I know. I'm keeping myself busy.' She looked back and forced a smile.

'Charlie would be so proud of you.'

Rose sucked in her breath. 'Anyway, how's everything and everyone at the theatre?'

Annie smiled. 'They're missing you, even Miss Hetherington, although she'd never say so.'

Rose gave a wry smile. 'Yeah, I'm sure she is!'

Annie giggled. 'No, I think she really is. She's having to spend more time in the sewing room and poor Lizzie is going through it.'

Rose shook her head. 'Maybe I shouldn't have left Lizzie on her own with her.'

Annie looked at her friend. 'It's up to the old bat to learn; after all, she's not a very nice person. She needs to recognise that, and be kinder to people. I also think she was shocked when you didn't come back.'

Joyce's glance moved between her two friends. 'Maybe there's a reason she's like that. You don't know what people are going through.'

Rose looked pensive for a moment. 'You're right, Joyce. We should be kinder, but if I'm honest it's hard when someone is constantly finding fault and being horrible to you.'

Annie nodded. 'She made Lizzie cry, and now she has to face her every day. At least before she had Rose to protect her.'

Rose shook her head. 'Don't. I feel bad now; perhaps I shouldn't have left.'

'Lizzie has to learn just like the rest of us.' Joyce paused. 'There will always be someone who misuses their power. All you can hope is they learn to be kinder. I wonder what happened to Miss Hetherington to make her so angry with everyone.'

Annie sighed. 'Heaven knows but I can honestly say she's mean to everyone.'

Rose chuckled and put her cup down on the small side table. 'That's the only saving grace: you know it's not personal, but it's tiring to work with her day in and day out.' She stood up and ran her hands down her skirt before peering up at the tall Christmas tree standing in front of the window. 'We need to decorate this tree otherwise we'll be the only house with no decorations up. I found everything we needed in the basement and brought it up. I enjoyed doing it last year.'

Joyce smiled. 'Arthur's moved on quite a lot since then, I'm so proud of him.' She opened a box and picked up a glass bauble. 'Come on, let's get decorating the tree and maybe we can sing some carols as well.'

Rose stood outside a four-storey building. Rivers of water ran down the edge of the road and large puddles were forming as the rain speared into the ground and anything that got in its way. Holding her umbrella tight, she battled against the wind and the rain pummelling it.

Oliver pulled up his coat collar in a bid to stop the cold drips running down the back of his neck. The paint on the large sash windows was peeling away. The black wooden front door was ajar onto the pavement and revealed black and white tiled flooring, which was splattered with water. As Oliver approached the front door of the shelter for homeless soldiers, he turned and glanced at Rose. 'Ready?'

Rose looked solemn as she nodded before shaking and closing her umbrella.

'I'll stay close by until you at least feel comfortable with everyone.' Oliver studied Rose. 'I'm wondering how you'll feel after seeing these men. Some are quite severely injured, whether that's physically or the nightmares they suffer day and night, but all of them have nowhere to go.'

Rose took a deep breath. 'I'm sure I'll be fine; it's not me we should be concentrating on. Shall we get out of this awful weather?' A car sped past splashing dirty puddles up on the pavement.

Just as Oliver was about to push on the front door it swung open.

A grey-haired lady was sprawled at the bottom of the stairs. A thin man, who'd had his head shaved, was bent over her.

'Oh, thank goodness you're here, Oliver. Ruby's had a fall.' The heavy man, who had his arm in a sling, stepped aside allowing Oliver and Rose to move into the narrow hallway. He then turned to look at the man bent over Ruby. 'Jack, help is here.'

A dark-haired man rushed forward, pushing Jack out of the way and blocking Oliver from getting nearer to the stairs. 'We don't need help so you can just get out.'

Oliver rushed forward, pausing only to glance over his shoulder at the heavy man. 'Do you know what happened, George?'

The dark-haired man had a face like thunder. 'I said get out.' He stood in Oliver's way.

Oliver's eyes were like steel. His voice was menacing. 'Brian, Ruby needs help so I suggest you get out of my way.'

The heavy man – George – stepped nearer to Oliver, leaving Rose safely at the front door. 'Brian, get out of the way and let the doc look after Ruby.' George shook his head as Brian glared at him. 'Bloody fool, you'll end up on the streets if you ain't careful – we all will.' He took a step nearer to Brian and Oliver. 'None of us were here, but I assume she fell down the stairs. She was out cold when we got to her.'

Jack frowned as he stepped back. 'She's going to be all right, ain't she?' He gripped his stomach as he watched Oliver step around Brian and drop to his knees.

Brian stepped nearer to Ruby. 'We can look after her. We don't need any outsiders coming in here.'

Jack grabbed the man's arm. 'Brian, it's Oliver. You remember, he's a doctor and can help Ruby, just like he helps all of us.'

Brian scowled as he watched Oliver before looking up and glaring at Rose. 'What about her?'

Jack followed Brian's gaze. 'I'm sure she's all right. She's come with the doctor.'

Rose stood rooted to the spot but her gaze darted around. Her hands felt clammy as the hairs on the back of her neck stood to attention. She wrinkled her nose as she breathed in the overpowering smell of disinfectant, which collided with the beeswax scent. She watched Oliver take control. His eyebrows furrowing together gave the only signal he was concerned.

Oliver studied Ruby for a moment before gently brushing her grey curls off her forehead. 'It's all right, Ruby. Lie very still while I examine you.'

Ruby groaned. 'Thank goodness you're here. You need to keep an eye on Brian.'

Oliver dropped his voice to a whisper. 'Try not to move, and stop worrying about him – you're my concern right now. I'll do my best not to hurt you but I must make sure nothing is broken.' He ran his hands expertly down her arms and legs, gently squeezing the skin under her cardigan and long skirt. 'Are you in pain anywhere?'

Ruby bit her lip. 'I ache all over, but it's probably just bruising.'

Oliver didn't look up; his eyes were fixed on Ruby as he continued to examine her. 'I think everything is all right. I expect it's more the shock of falling and bruising.'

Ruby grimaced as she shifted her leg position. 'I would have just got up.'

'I think it was wise to be checked over first, especially as you were unconscious when I arrived. You can't be too careful.' Oliver smiled. 'I think we'll get you up but you need to take it easy for a few days.' He looked over at Rose. 'Can you help me lift Ruby up?'

George stepped forward. 'I can do that.' He looked at Rose. 'I don't mean to be rude but there don't look like there's much of yer and I don't want you hurting yourself.'

Rose opened her mouth to speak.

'Always a gentleman, George.'

'Thank you, George, but I am stronger than I look.' Rose gazed down at the old lady on the floor.

Jack shook his head. 'It's better that I do it. At least I have two working arms.' He stepped forward again. 'What do you want me to do?'

Oliver looked up at the young man whose face looked ravaged with pain. 'If you're sure, Jack, we need to be careful but if we can put our arms under hers we can gently lift her into a chair.'

'I'll get a chair.' George rushed down the hall and disappeared through a doorway.

'Is there anything I can do? Can I fetch something? Would you like a cup of tea?'

Oliver glanced in Rose's direction. 'We'll get Ruby up and then I'm sure she would love a cuppa. See if there's any sugar to make it sweeter for shock.'

Ruby screwed up her face. 'Aww no sugar – don't you go worrying about that. I could never drink a cuppa with sugar in it.'

Jack grinned at her. 'Now I know you're okay.'

George marched along the hall with a wooden Carver dining chair. Rose wanted to help him but she guessed from his previous comment he was a proud man and wouldn't thank her for offering.

Breathless, George placed the chair near Ruby. 'There you go.'

Oliver looked up at Jack. 'Ready?'

Jack stooped down. 'When you are.'

Oliver nodded. 'On the count of three.'

They both hooked their arms under Ruby's.

Oliver nodded. 'One, two, three.'

Ruby groaned as they lifted her. George quickly stepped forward to place the chair under her. Jack and Oliver slowly lowered Ruby onto it.

Oliver frowned as he studied Ruby's screwed-up face. 'I don't need to ask how you are feeling now; your face says it all.'

Ruby took a deep breath. 'I'll be fine. It's going to take more than a fall to keep me down.'

Jack frowned. 'Sit there for a minute, and catch your breath. If you feel up to it we can move you to the sofa shortly.'

Rose gave a brief smile. 'If someone can tell me where the kitchen is I'll make a cup of tea for you all.'

Oliver smiled. 'Sorry, Ruby, I haven't introduced you to Rose.' He glanced at Rose. 'Rose, this is Ruby Blake, the magnificent lady who owns and runs this wonderful house. Ruby, this is Rose Spencer who has been busy sewing for us and for the men who are still in hospital.'

Ruby nodded. 'You are doing a wonderful job, and I can tell you the men here will always be grateful to you. People would be amazed what a difference having their clothes altered to fit makes to them, and actually to all of us.'

'Thank you, Mrs Blake.' Rose nodded.

'Please, call me Ruby.'

Rose smiled. 'I wish I'd realised I could help before; unfortunately it hadn't occurred to me, but I'm glad Oliver asked me to do it.'

A loud bang came from outside. Rose turned round to shut the front door, assuming it was a car backfiring. When she returned her attention back to Ruby, Jack was slumped next to the stairs shaking uncontrollably.

Oliver was knelt down next to him. 'It's all right, Jack, you're at home and safe now. It was a car backfiring. Take some deep breaths. I will stay with you until you feel better.'

Ruby's lips tightened as she peered over her shoulder. 'Jack, it's Ruby. Talk to me, lad.'

George watched Rose's colour drain from her face. 'He suffers with shell shock, poor bloke. The slightest thing sets him off. That's the war for yer. I'd rather lose a limb than have that.'

Ruby shuffled on her chair. 'Jack, I'm probably going to

need your help getting into the sitting room. Can you help me?'

Rose's heart pounded in her chest and her head was throbbing.

'Ruby's trying to distract him, and that sometimes works.' George shook his head. 'Don't worry, he'll be all right. Why don't we go and make that cuppa for everyone?'

Rose nodded.

11

Joyce's head jerked up as the closed restaurant door rattled hard against the frame and lock. The wind didn't give up as it battled to get inside. The rain lashed against the window as the daylight faded. She glanced across the round table at her friends. 'The weather sounds horrendous out there. It's a good job we don't have far to go home, otherwise we might have been sleeping here tonight.'

Annie nodded. 'I'm already fed up with these grey days. Roll on the spring.'

Rose fiddled with the edge of the crisp white tablecloth, slowly rolling it up before letting it go again. 'I met the most incredible woman today.'

Joyce held the teaspoon as she swirled the hot dark brown liquid around in the teapot. The chink of it occasionally hitting the china broke the silence. She stopped stirring and looked up. 'You've caught my interest – tell us more.'

Annie's eyes widened. 'Yes, who is it?'

Rose smiled. 'She runs a shelter for injured soldiers. Isn't that wonderful? Oliver took me there. I must admit to feeling a little bit anxious but the men I met were so caring and they clearly love the owner – Ruby.'

Annie raised her eyebrows. 'I didn't know they existed. I assumed it was a women's refuge you was going to.'

Rose watched Joyce pour tea into her cup. 'You know it's heart-rending to see the physical injuries some of them have sustained, never mind the things they've seen and heard that they can't get out of their heads.'

Joyce stared at Annie. 'Simon doesn't talk about the war. He never mentions his time in France.' She paused. 'I've tried to get him to talk about it, mainly because I thought it might do him good but I think he's trying to lock it all away in the depths of his mind.'

Annie frowned. 'It scares me to think that's how Peter could end up.' Her eyes became watery. 'Let's face it, when he gets called up he won't come back the same man, if he comes back at all.'

Rose reached out and took Annie's hand in hers. 'We have to pray he comes home safely like we do for our brothers. Broken bones heal but the mind takes time.'

Annie looked tearful as she nodded.

Rose squeezed Annie's hand before moving hers away. 'Anyway, I didn't tell you about Ruby to bring you all down.' She forced a smile. 'Apparently when her husband died she was left a small fortune so she originally bought the house to help the homeless – you know, provide them with food and a bed, but with the war going on she has taken in injured soldiers who struggle to find work. Oliver's a doctor so he goes in at least once a week to make sure they are all well – at least as well as they can be – and he doesn't charge them.'

Joyce tilted her head. 'I was just going to say how can

they afford to pay a doctor. It's admirable he gives his time for free.'

Rose nodded. 'He's very caring. Anyway, what I wanted to ask you is whether you would consider doing something to help them.'

Annie's lips tightened for a moment. 'I'm more than happy to help but I'm not sure what I can do.'

Rose chuckled. 'Oh, I'm coming to that.'

The girls laughed.

'Of course you are.' Joyce picked up her cup and sipped her hot strong tea.

Rose grinned before raising her eyebrows. 'I don't know what you mean.'

Annie shook her head. 'Come on, spit it out. You've obviously got it all worked out.'

Rose beamed at her friends. 'I haven't, not really.' She paused as the seriousness of the situation took hold. 'The thing is, Ruby's had a fall and needs to rest but that means there's no one to cook for these men.'

The girls frowned.

Rose held up her hand. 'Now, I'm not suggesting we go there and cook meals because everyone still has to go to work, but I wondered, Joyce, if there's anything that you could come up with where the men could just stick something on or in the range?'

Joyce smiled. 'Of course. The biggest problem will be getting hold of the food.'

Rose nodded. 'I suspect there will be some at the house. I'll check.' She paused. 'I don't think there's any money to pay you but—'

'I don't need paying.' Joyce looked indignant.

Rose smiled. 'I was hoping you would say that. Unfortunately cooking isn't something I'm very good at. I've been lucky enough to never have needed to do it so I've never tried, and it doesn't feel right to use them to try out my cooking skills.'

Joyce reached out and clasped Rose's hand in hers. 'I'm more than happy to help. Just tell me what you need me to do, how many people I need to cook for and where I need to take the food. If it's possible I would prefer to cook at the house.'

Rose smiled. 'I knew you would want to help; you're such a good person. If you saw the injuries these men carry it would make you weep. I've been told they don't like to talk about their experiences, but you can see the pain etched on their faces, and the dark rings under their eyes tell you they have nightmares.' She shook her head. 'You know some of them drop to the floor when they hear a car backfire because they think it's bombs or gunfire. It's so sad, and it makes me feel I should be doing more, although I have no idea what.'

Annie nodded. 'You do so much already, I'm not sure you could fit in doing any more.'

Rose's lips flattened. 'We can all do more. I've been guilty of trying to ignore the war instead of doing my bit.'

Annie frowned. 'That's not just you, Rose. We're all guilty of that because we don't like to think of our loved ones suffering. In fact it's an unbearable thought. I know my brother is away fighting but I can't bear the thought of him being shot at, or injured, and seeing things that no one should see in their lives.'

Joyce squeezed Rose's hand. 'Annie's right. It's too painful to think of people we love suffering no matter where they are or what they're doing.'

Annie took a breath. 'Anyway, I'm not much good at cooking but I could go in and do a bit of cleaning for her.'

Rose grinned. 'I knew you would both rise to the challenge.' She looked thoughtful as she tapped her finger against her lips. 'Do you think it would be a stretch too far to teach the men to do things for themselves? You know, cook and clean? I know it's seen as women's work but at least they would be able to look after themselves if they had to.'

Joyce smiled. 'Good luck with that idea and while I don't hold out much hope for its success I do think it's worth trying. After all, Arthur managed to make a pot of tea and wash up before he left us.'

Annie chuckled. 'And clear tables in the café.'

Joyce nodded. 'Yes, I do him a disservice because he came on a long way from the drunk he was. Bless him.'

The girls sat in silence, each lost in their own thoughts.

Rose picked up her cup and wrapped her fingers around it. 'Arthur is a good man; he just lost his way for a while.'

Joyce nodded. 'Right, so where do we start with helping Ruby? I mean will she want our help?'

Rose frowned. 'I think so but I'll talk to her and find out. In the meantime we might need to think about how we can help with Christmas dinner.'

'The men might need a crash course on what to put in the oven and when.' Joyce chuckled.

Annie sniffed the air. 'Is that bread I can smell?'

Joyce smiled. 'Yes, Annie, I was up early this morning. Peter sells so much of it on his stall; I'm lucky he's helping me because the restaurant is quite slow. I suppose I shouldn't expect anything else with a war going on.'

Rose nodded. 'Hopefully things will pick up once it's over, and everyone will have a lot to celebrate.' She paused, taking a deep breath. 'I noticed on my way here that Charlie's shop was still boarded up. It breaks my heart to see it like that, although I don't know what would be worse: seeing it like that or someone else occupying it.'

Joyce reached out and squeezed Rose's hand. 'Sorry, I must go and check the bread. I can't afford for it to be overcooked.'

'No, I'm sorry. I didn't mean to get all maudlin. It doesn't change anything.' Rose stood up. 'Let's sort out this bread and get home. I'll get up early tomorrow and try and see Ruby to put forward our offers of help.'

Rose sighed as she strolled into the women's department in Dickens and Jones. It had been a long day. She had lost track of how many gowns she had altered for the last-minute Christmas shoppers.

Marion Simpson walked over to her. 'It's unusual to see you up here without an armful of clothes.'

Rose smiled. 'I'm just stretching my legs. I've hardly moved all day.'

Marion nodded. 'It's been really busy up here, so I know that means you've all been snowed under in the sewing room.'

'Yes, and it seems everybody wants everything yesterday.' Rose strolled towards the rail of women's dresses. She stopped and stared at a mannequin wearing a silver evening dress, the many sequins sparkling in the light. 'I didn't notice this dress yesterday.'

Standing behind Rose, Marion sighed wistfully. 'It's beautiful isn't it? Mr Bowman is such a clever man. I don't know how he does it.'

Rose glanced over her shoulder at Marion. 'Does he design all the dresses we sell?'

Marion shook her head. 'No, but he has collections that sell very well.'

Rose frowned, remembering the one and only time she had seen this dress before, but how did the same dress end up on a market stall? 'This is stunning. Is it possible I could see some more of his gowns?'

'Of course. Are you thinking of treating yourself?'

Rose turned round, catching a whiff of orange blossom perfume. 'I don't know about that. I expect they cost way above what I can afford.'

Marion nodded. 'They are expensive for the likes of you and me but our customers love his designs and they sell very quickly. Come on, I'll show you some of them. I've heard a whisper he's now working on some new designs but it's all very hush-hush. Only Mrs Todd is allowed to know about them at the moment but it's already creating quite a stir.'

A silver-haired lady came over to admire the gown on the mannequin. 'Isn't it beautiful – do you have many left?'

Marion smiled. 'Yes, ma'am, I'm sure we have your size.' She walked over to the rail. Glancing at the dresses, she expected to see the silver one standing out against the more traditional colours.

'Is everything all right, Miss Simpson?'

Marion froze. 'Yes, Mr Bowman.' She turned to face

him. 'A customer was admiring the silver dress on the mannequin.' Marion frowned. 'The lady has asked to see one in her size but we don't seem to have any available, which surprises me because I thought we had a few left.'

Mr Bowman studied the two girls before turning to smile at the customer. 'It is a beautiful dress but unfortunately we seem to only have the one on the mannequin, which I can let you have at a reduced price. Alternatively, Miss Simpson will be able to show you other stunning gowns from my collection.' He turned to Miss Simpson. 'Make sure you assist this young lady to find something to complement her beauty.'

The customer blushed as she rested her hand on her chest. 'Thank you, sir. I'd heard you're quite a gentleman.'

Rose raised her eyebrows as she watched Mr Bowman at work.

Mr Bowman gave a small bow. 'My ladies are very important to me. My gowns are here to enhance a woman's beauty.' He turned to Miss Simpson. 'Please show this wonderful lady some of our magnificent dresses.' Glancing back at the customer, he said, 'Please excuse me.'

The customer beamed and followed Miss Simpson's lead.

Mr Bowman turned to Rose, before speaking in a low voice. 'Miss Spencer, why are you up here? I'm sure you must have work to do.' He cleared his throat. 'How have you been getting on with Mrs Hardy? I trust you are giving her your undivided attention. She's a valued client.'

Rose stared at Mr Bowman. His red silk scarf hung loosely either side of his black suit jacket, making his matching red tie stand out against his pale pink shirt. 'Mrs Hardy is going to pick out a couple of gowns she loves so that gives me a starting point to know what style of clothing she likes.'

Mr Bowman tutted. 'That's very commendable, but we don't want to give her the same as what she already has. We want to dazzle her with something totally new.'

'Yes, sir, I shall do my best.' Rose glanced over at the silver dress again.

'I hope so.' Mr Bowman followed her gaze. 'I've gone to a lot of trouble to get you here so don't let me down.'

'No, sir, I'll do my best to keep Mrs Hardy happy.' Rose bit her bottom lip and clenched her hands together in front of her. 'I understand you're working on a new collection. If I may be so impertinent, sir, it would interest me to see how a designer works. I have only ever followed my imagination and never done it professionally before.'

Mr Bowman eyed her. 'I'm sure but I prefer to work alone. You will just have to let your imagination run wild and then rein it in where necessary.'

Rose glanced back at Mr Bowman. 'The trouble is nearly everything I design appears to have already been made.'

Mr Bowman's eyes narrowed. 'That, Miss Spencer, is where your talent should be coming in, so might I suggest you concentrate on the job in hand rather than wandering around the shop?' He stepped nearer to Rose and lowered his voice. 'Don't forget to leave me your pad so I can check your designs. The sooner you do that the sooner we can get them out as part of a collection. After all, it's why you are employed here and I would hate to have to let you go because you aren't producing the goods.'

Rose's heart was pounding in her chest. His musky scent engulfed her and nausea started to rise from her stomach.

'Ah, Mr Bowman, just the man I want to see.'

Mr Bowman pasted on his best smile and turned around. 'How lovely to see you, Mrs Hamilton, and what can I do for you today?'

Rose decided to take advantage of the situation and raced to the door that led to the stairs down to the sewing room.

Mrs Hamilton's face lit up. 'My daughter has given me a delightful grandson; he's almost three months old now. I know she's worrying about her husband who's away fighting so I want to buy her a gift to try and cheer her up.'

Mr Bowman nodded. He held up his hand and beckoned for a nearby assistant to come over. 'Do not worry, Mrs Hamilton, you have come to the right place. You will be in safe hands, with one of our best assistants.'

Rose stopped and listened to Mr Bowman and wondered how he could sound so threatening and then switch to adoring in a matter of minutes.

'Mr Bowman.'

Rose watched a suited man marching towards them before glancing at Mr Bowman, who pushed back his shoulders and straightened his tie.

'Mr Woodford, this is an honour. It's not very often we see you on the shop floor.'

'No, but I wanted to catch you before we closed for Christmas.'

Mr Bowman nodded, keeping his smile fixed on his face. 'Of course. What can I do for you?'

Mr Woodford frowned as he pushed his glasses further up his nose. 'Since our meeting in the boardroom a few months ago I've noticed some discrepancies, which I can't make head nor tail of.' He glanced over his shoulder. 'This isn't the place to be talking about it but when the shop reopens I want a full stocktake done. We seem to be having a lot of rolls of material coming in and yet… I'm not sure what it is, but something isn't right.'

Mr Bowman's gaze didn't waver. 'I'm sure whatever the problem is, I will be able to explain it.'

'Let's hope so.' Mr Woodford raised his eyebrows. 'I hear that you've taken on the young girl who designed Kitty Smythe's wedding dress?'

Rose turned away.

Mr Bowman's voice followed her. 'Yes, that was the seamstress I talked to you about.'

Mr Woodford chuckled. 'Well, if she's as good as everyone says she is she won't be a seamstress for long. You better watch yourself as you'll have competition for your job.'

Rose listened open-mouthed before running down the steps.

Mrs Todd looked up from the material she was holding. 'Rose.' She beckoned her over. 'I was just thinking, as it's Christmas Eve, why don't you take yourself off home? I've told the rest of the girls to go. We'll be shutting in about ten minutes and if there's anything last minute to do I'm sure I'll cope.'

Rose frowned. 'That's very kind of you but are you sure? I really don't mind staying and Mr Bowman is upstairs.'

'I'm very sure. You've all worked so hard leading up to Christmas, and it's the least I can do.' Mrs Todd smiled. 'Don't look so worried.'

Rose nodded. 'Well, I could go home and work on something for Mrs Hardy. I'm thankful she didn't want the dresses for Christmas.' She turned and grabbed her coat.

'I'll try and avoid Mr Bowman. I don't want to get you into trouble.'

Mrs Todd chuckled. 'Don't you go worrying about him.'

Rose frowned. 'Before I go can I just ask a quick question?'

'Of course.'

'Is any of Mr Bowman's collection available anywhere else?' Rose slipped her arms into her coat and began fastening the buttons.

Mrs Todd laughed. 'Definitely not. Dickens and Jones owns everything. Why?'

Rose concentrated on pushing her hands into her woollen gloves. 'I just wondered.'

Mrs Todd nodded. 'Now, go off and have the best Christmas you can under the circumstances.'

'I will, and I hope you do too.' As she turned to walk away she glanced back at Mrs Todd. 'I don't wish to pry but if you're on your own tomorrow I'm sure you'd be more than welcome to spend the day with me and my friends.'

Mrs Todd studied Rose for a moment. 'That's very kind of you but I'm spending the day with my two daughters and my grandchildren. Thank you for asking though – it's very kind of you to invite someone you barely know.'

Rose nodded. 'I don't know about that, but it's a hard time of year to be on your own.'

Mrs Todd frowned. 'My husband died several years ago and my sons-in-law enlisted so it's a worrying time for my daughters.'

'It is. My brothers are away fighting as well.' Rose took a breath. 'Still, I'm glad you're with your family and I'm sorry about your husband.'

Mrs Todd gave a faint smile. 'Thank you. Now get off and have a good Christmas.'

Rose nodded. 'Thank you, and you too.' She waved as she left the sewing room. She ran up the stairs before pushing open the staff entrance to step out on to Regent Street. The cold air took her breath away. She wrapped her woollen scarf around her neck. As she stepped out amongst the shoppers she stopped to admire the Christmas window. A decorated tree stood in pride of place. The baubles shone in the light. The wrapped gifts were haphazardly placed underneath it.

'It looks good. Does it make you miss your family?'

Rose glanced over her shoulder and saw Michael standing there. He looked grey and cold. 'Michael, I have been wondering what had happened to you. I haven't seen you around for a while.'

Michael grimaced. 'It's been cold and wet so I've been hiding in the underground stations, although I keep getting moved on. Apparently it's not good for travellers to see people like me.'

Rose shook her head. 'Come home and spend Christmas with me and the girls. Joyce will enjoy having someone to fuss over and it'll stop them watching me all the time.'

'Don't you think you should ask them first?'

Rose shrugged. 'Maybe, but if I leave you here I'll probably be roaming the streets all night looking for you. They won't mind.' She wrinkled her nose. 'Although you'll have to have a bath first.'

Michael chuckled. 'In this weather it's hard to say no to an offer like that.'

Rose smiled. 'Let's get going then. It's blooming freezing out here.'

Rose sat by the unlit fire in the dining room staring at the Christmas tree, mesmerized by the candlelight reflecting and dancing on the glass baubles that hung on its branches. She had been sat there since the early hours wondering whether she should have gone home to her family for Christmas. She could have done all the things she had moaned about as she grew up, like attending the carol service, helping her mother with all the cooking and sewing, and delivering food to the older people in the village. Rose sighed. She hadn't appreciated the good she was doing then, but then there was Michael. She had never met anyone like him before. How did he end up living on the streets of London? He seemed to have a gentle, caring soul.

The stairs creaked; Rose glanced towards the door, waiting to hear the footsteps. The door swung open.

'Morning, Rose, happy Christmas. I didn't expect to see you up so early this morning. Simon was a great help getting the food to the refuge.' Joyce stood in the doorway and glanced around at the lit candles, which had nearly burnt away, before stepping further into the room. 'The men and Ruby seemed pleased with our efforts.'

'Happy Christmas, Joyce. That's good. I should imagine Simon was pleased to be part of it as well.' Rose bit down on her lip. 'I'll make some tea for us while we wait for Annie and Michael.' She fidgeted in her seat. 'I expect you were shocked to see Michael sitting next to the fire when you came home last night, although you hid it well,' Rose blurted out. 'I know I should have discussed it with you first but it was so cold I just couldn't leave him out there. I just couldn't.'

Joyce smiled. 'Stop worrying, Rose. You look tired. Have you been up most of the night worrying?'

Rose stared at her friend. 'Partly. I stayed up to wrap my presents but I've also been wondering why Michael is living on the streets and where his family is, and why he isn't living in a shelter like Ruby's. I've also been thinking about my own family.'

Joyce perched on the edge of an armchair. 'It's understandable – I mean wondering about Michael – but what was it about your own family that kept you awake?'

Rose shrugged. 'I don't know. I don't think I ever appreciated my family enough. When I spoke to Charlie about them he said people can only do their best.'

Joyce smiled. 'Charlie was probably wiser than his years; I suspect he had a tough life. I never thought I'd say this but I think my father was trying to protect me, although I struggled to understand that at first.'

Rose chuckled. 'It makes you wonder what sort of parents we would be – not that I'm likely to find that out now.'

Joyce raised her eyebrows. 'Don't say that. None of us know what's ahead of us, which is just as well. We can all weather any storm if we help each other, and more importantly, Charlie wouldn't want you to feel alone.'

Rose bit back her tears. 'I know.' She jumped up out of the chair. 'Come on, it's Christmas Day. Let's get some happiness going.' She peered at the tree. 'Look at all those presents waiting to be opened.'

Joyce laughed, before stopping abruptly. 'Oh my goodness, we haven't got anything for Michael.'

'Happy Christmas, and you've given me the best present I could wish for: a warm welcome and a comfy bed to sleep on. What more could a man ask for?'

Joyce spun round. 'I'm sorry, I didn't realise you were there. Happy Christmas to you too.'

Rose grinned. 'Morning, Michael, happy Christmas. I take it you slept well?'

Michael chuckled. 'The best. I'd forgotten what it was like to be relaxed and warm.' He gazed at Joyce. 'Thank you for taking me into your home. I know I was forced upon you but I do appreciate you not throwing me out last night.'

Joyce raised her eyebrows. 'It's not a problem, Michael. Rose wouldn't have brought anyone home if she didn't feel safe.'

Michael nodded. 'You can trust me; I have never stolen anything in my life. However, it might be a little forward of me but I wondered if I could take advantage and have another bath? The worst thing about not having a home is water isn't always freely available and, despite my dishevelled appearance, I do like to keep up with the news and be clean.'

Joyce gave a small smile. 'Of course you can. I'll boil some water on the stove for you. My uncle Arthur didn't take all his clothes with him so I'll have a look to see what's in his room. I suspect most of it will be too big but it might do while I wash the clothes you're wearing.'

Rose beamed. 'When they're washed I'll repair them for you.' Charlie's words jumped into her mind. Her parents had done the best they could and she had been brought up to care about others.

'Right, I'll go and put some water on to boil and then I'll go and rifle through my uncle's clothes.' Joyce looked thoughtful. 'Sit down, otherwise you'll make the place look untidy.'

Michael chuckled as Joyce headed towards the kitchen. 'You have some lovely friends.'

Rose nodded. 'I'm very lucky, but you must have had family and friends. What happened for you to end up on the street?'

Michael's eyes widened.

Rose blushed. 'I'm sorry, I shouldn't have asked. Sometimes I speak without thinking about how it affects others.'

The floorboards on the stairs creaked as someone ran down them. 'Morning, happy Christmas.' Annie beamed as she ran in. 'I love Christmas.'

'Happy Christmas.' Rose and Michael smiled as they spoke in unison.

Annie looked around the semi-darkness of the room. 'Shall I open the curtains, or are they shut for a reason?'

Rose laughed. 'No, I just haven't opened them yet.'

Annie strolled over to the window and pulled the heavy green curtains back. She sighed. 'Another grey day. I'll go and make the tea then maybe we can have breakfast. Maybe we could sing some carols or something after that.'

Rose shook her head as Annie rushed out of the room. 'She's like a small child this time of year. Being on the stage is the right place for her.'

Michael stared at Rose. 'It's good to have fun people around you. It helps to lift you when you're down.'

Rose studied Michael for a moment. 'You sound as though you've experienced a good family life and that just makes me more curious about why you are living on the street.' She watched his conflict trample across his face. 'Sorry, it's nothing to do with me.'

Michael frowned. 'No, it isn't, but there's nothing to tell.' He stared at his feet; his shoes were worn with holes that let in water. He looked up and glanced around the room, taking in the expensive ornaments, the plush curtains with matching cushion covers sprawled over the sofa and chairs. 'I wouldn't expect you to understand.'

Rose watched him closely; she knew what he was thinking. 'Don't judge us by what you see here. Things aren't always what they seem.'

'I'm sorry. I know that better than anybody.' Michael sighed. 'People walk past me every day; I'm invisible to them. They think I'm dirty so they might catch something if they get close to me.'

Rose nodded. 'And yet you spoke to me.'

Michael shrugged. 'You were distressed at the time, and I was just checking you were all right. I must admit I did get angry when you ignored me.'

Rose smiled. 'I didn't ignore you, I didn't hear you and that's totally different. I was too caught up with my own feelings about Miss Hetherington.'

Michael pulled himself upright. 'You have a lovely home.'

Rose thought she saw a glint in his eyes. 'Actually, it's Joyce's uncle Arthur's. Annie and I are lucky to have rooms here.' She closed her eyes and took a breath. 'Has Miss Hetherington ever tried to shoo you away from the Lyceum?'

Michael laughed. 'No, but then I try to stay out of everyone's way. Don't tell anyone but Bert sometimes lets me in to have a wash. He's a good man.'

Rose chuckled. 'He is, he has always been lovely towards me and Annie, trying to protect us like a father would.'

Michael nodded. 'I can believe that – he's got a good heart.'

'As indeed do you, Michael.' Rose paused. 'Do you have any family in London?'

'No, my father got sick when I was a child and they couldn't afford a doctor so he died. My mother and I ended up in a workhouse for a while but I think she constantly worried we would be separated. She hated it there so we left, like thieves in the night.'

Rose shook her head. 'That's so sad.'

Michael puffed out his chest. 'I don't need your sympathy. It's just the way life was and it could have been worse.'

Rose stared at the proud man standing in front of her. 'Is your mother still—'

'No, she passed years ago, working herself into the ground taking in washing, sewing and cleaning other people's houses. There was nothing of her when she died.'

Rose could feel the tears pricking at her eyes. 'I'm sorry. It's so sad.'

Michael shrugged. 'Yeah, well there's lots of sad stories out there so don't get caught up in mine.'

Joyce poked her head round the door. 'The bath is ready when you are. Take your time; there's no rush. The tin bath isn't huge so I hope you don't struggle to get in it. I've also left a razor in case you wanted to have a shave, but please don't feel you have to.' She disappeared again.

'Forgive me, I don't wish to be rude but I would love to get in the bath while the water is hot.'

Rose nodded. 'Of course.' She watched Michael disappear and couldn't help feeling there was more to his story than he was saying.

12

Rose glanced at Joyce. 'Do you think Michael's all right upstairs? He seems to be having a long bath.'

Joyce laughed. 'He's probably enjoying a long soak. Wouldn't you in his position?'

'I suppose so.'

Annie frowned as her hands ran down her plush red Christmas skirt. 'Rose, you're not happy unless you're worrying. I'm not sure when you turned into this worrier I see before me.' She shook her head. 'You were always so spontaneous it used to frighten me.'

Joyce gazed between her two friends. 'That was exactly what brought you to London, so don't totally lose it.' Sadness flicked across Joyce's face. 'I hope my father and Arthur are giving Philip a good Christmas. I do miss them, which sounds a little bit strange when you think they haven't been in my life for that long.'

Annie reached out and stroked Joyce's arm. 'It's understandable but I'm sure they'll be having a good day. They're probably spending it with my family. I can't imagine Auntie Dot would leave my father to his own devices on Christmas Day, or actually any other day.' She smiled.

Rose nodded. 'Annie's right. Come on, it's Christmas

and we're all missing someone but we have to make the best we can of it, so let's have some smiles, and what makes us smile? Singing.'

The sitting room door squeaked as it was pushed open.

The three girls turned to look in that direction.

Michael frowned as he peered around the door. 'I thought I heard voices. I don't want to interrupt, but is it all right if I come in?'

Rose's eyes narrowed as she studied the man in front of her. 'Of course. Come in, you don't have to ask. Take a seat. I have to say you look completely different without your beard; in fact you remind me of someone but I can't quite place who.'

Michael sat down on the nearest chair. 'I just have one of those faces. I nearly didn't shave it off because it does keep my face warm in this weather.' He stared up at the tree; a smile crept across his face. 'I haven't seen a tree like that outside a shop window for years.'

'It does look beautiful.' Joyce smiled as she caught the smell of carbolic soap. 'Did you enjoy your bath?'

Michael grinned. 'I most certainly did, thank you.' He peered down at the baggy black trousers and white shirt he was wearing. 'Your uncle's clothes aren't too bad a fit. The trousers are big but the braces are keeping them up. I appreciate and give thanks for everyone's kindness.'

Rose nodded. 'It's entirely our pleasure.'

Joyce clapped her hands together. 'We might sing some carols later so I hope you have a good singing voice?'

'I haven't sung anything for some time.' Michael fidgeted in his chair.

Rose chuckled. 'Don't look so worried; Annie's the only

one here who can really sing. Joyce and I just enjoy it. I've found it lifts my spirits.'

Annie stared at the colourful wrapped presents under the tree. 'Can we open a present before dinner? I know we usually wait but it will be exciting to open one now.' She bit her bottom lip for a second. 'That's if you don't mind, Michael?'

Michael chuckled. 'Mind? Why should I mind? I'm having the best Christmas I've had in years.'

Joyce giggled as she watched Annie's face light up. 'Go on then, take your pick.'

Annie jumped up and ran over to the tree and pulled out a crumpled package tied together with red ribbon. Her face was full of excitement as she squeezed the parcel. 'This is mine. It's very soft whatever it is. Shall I open it?'

Rose smiled. 'I think it's clear you want to so as it's from me the answer is yes.'

They all laughed and watched as Annie gently pulled the ribbon to spring the package free. She ran the ribbon between her fingers. 'I shall keep this – it's a beautiful colour.' She dropped it on the floor next to her. There was a rustle as the brown paper was pushed open.

Everyone was silent as they waited to see what was in there.

Annie squealed with delight. 'Oh my goodness, Rose, you shouldn't have done. It's beautiful.'

Joyce grinned. 'What is it?'

Annie giggled. 'Sorry.' She lifted the pale blue blouse away from the paper. 'It's beautiful, and those buttons have a real shimmer to them.'

Rose smiled. 'I don't know if you remember but they are

the buttons you picked out of the tin that time you came into the sewing room.'

Annie nodded. 'I do. How very sneaky of you. I love it. Thank you.'

Michael's gaze wandered between the girls. 'Did you make that, Rose?'

Rose looked over at him. 'Yes, thankfully I made it before Charlie died. I would have struggled to think about making it in time for Christmas afterwards; in fact any sort of celebrations and presents would have been out of the question.' She took a breath. 'Annie came into the theatre's sewing room as I was looking for a matching set of buttons and she pulled them out. I then made the blouse to fit the buttons she liked.'

Michael raised his eyebrows. 'Well, from what you say about Charlie, and from what I can see, he was right – you do have a real talent.'

Annie pulled a rectangular package from under the tree. 'Rose, I think you should open this one. I expect you know what it is but it will represent a new year for you.'

Rose gave a faint smile as she took it from Annie.

Michael frowned. 'It sounds intriguing.'

Rose turned the parcel over in her hands. 'My grandmother gives me a special present every Christmas.' She glanced at Michael. 'It hasn't changed just because I'm in London.' Rose ripped the brown paper to reveal her new sketch pad.

Annie beamed. 'New designs here we come.'

Everyone laughed as Rose hugged the book to her for a moment before opening the cover. 'Bless her, she's written in this one.'

'Lovely.' Joyce smiled. 'Do you want to share it?'

Rose blinked rapidly. 'To my very special granddaughter, may you achieve all that you want, but more importantly, be happy.'

Annie nodded. 'That's lovely.'

'She's a lovely lady.' Rose stared down at the words before closing the book.

Joyce glanced at Michael. 'I know we don't have a physical present to give you but I would like to give you a meal for two in my restaurant.'

Michael opened his mouth to speak but Joyce held her hand up.

'There's no time limit on the meal so if you find yourself a lady friend you can bring her along, and she doesn't need to know it's on the house.'

Michael stared down at the deep pile carpet. 'I don't know what to say except it isn't necessary for you to feel you have to give me a present. What you're doing now means more than you can ever know.'

Joyce smiled. 'And that's very kind of you to say so, but I can tell you I will come looking for you if you don't take up my present. If you don't have a lady friend then you can have the meals on two separate occasions.'

Michael looked up. 'Thank you, that's very kind.'

Rose felt a glow of pride wash over her. 'That is such a good idea. I can do something like that too.' She tapped her finger against her lips. 'I know, I'm going to be doing some alterations for Dr Hardy's wounded soldiers in the hospital so I'm sure I can either make you something or alter some clothing to fit you. I might be able to pick up some remnants of material from work.'

'I could arrange for you to see a show in the theatre,'

Annie burst out. 'Oh this is fun, although it's a shame you don't get to unwrap the presents today.'

Joyce giggled. 'Or, Annie, if Michael has a meal with a lady friend you could come to the restaurant and sing at their table.'

Laughter filled the room.

Michael gazed around at them all. 'You are all wonderful people but I think you're getting carried away. Honestly, believe me when I say none of it is necessary.'

Rose smiled. 'It's not so much fun when it's necessary. It feels good to give rather than take, whatever it is.'

Annie nodded. 'That's true.'

Rose lowered her head to peer under the Christmas tree. 'It's your turn, Joyce – pick something to open.'

Annie craned her head to see the presents. 'Make sure it's one tied with dark green ribbon.'

Joyce frowned. 'I should be getting on with dinner.' She suddenly grinned. 'But who can resist opening a present?' After taking the couple of steps nearer to the tree she stooped down and picked up a few of the presents and put them back down again. 'Mine must be hidden.'

Annie giggled.

Joyce picked up a rectangular package that had her name on it. 'I wonder what this is?' She gently shook it.

Annie clapped her hands. 'Come on, open it.'

Everyone laughed at her excitement.

Rose shook her head while smiling broadly. 'You're terrible. It's from you so it's not like you don't know what it is.'

Annie giggled as she glanced at Rose. 'I know, but Joyce doesn't.' She turned to Joyce. 'I really hope you like it.'

Joyce nodded. 'I'm sure I will.' She pulled at the end of the dark green ribbon and watched the bow disappear. After pulling the ribbon apart, she slid her hand under the folds of brown paper and revealed the box inside. 'Oh my goodness, Lily of the Valley perfume. I love it, thank you.' Joyce gazed at the green and white flowers before opening the box and smelling the scent. 'It smells lovely and fresh. Thank you so much, Annie, I love it.'

'What a lovely gift,' Rose said.

Smiling, Joyce stood up took a step towards the doorway. 'I'm very lucky, thank you, but I think I'd better check on dinner. It smells like it's nearly ready. I just hope the vegetables haven't overcooked while I've been in here instead of being the cook.' She left the room and headed for the kitchen.

Annie got up off her knees and stared down at her present. 'Thank you for my beautiful blouse, Rose.' She held it up in front of her. 'The material is so soft.'

Rose frowned. 'I hope it fits, but the good thing is I can alter it if there's a problem.'

'It looks fine.' Annie moved towards Rose and wrapped her arms around her. 'Thank you again.'

Rose smiled as Annie's floral scent washed over her.

Annie pulled away. 'I suppose we should go and see if Joyce needs some help.'

Rose nodded. 'That's a good idea; after all she has done all of it so far.' She stood up. 'Come on, Michael, in case you hadn't noticed, there's no standing on ceremony in this house.'

Half an hour later all the best dishes had been carried to the dining room, where the table had been laid with the best crockery and cutlery.

Michael sat down at the dining table. His eyes gradually widened as he glanced around the table at the array of china dishes filled with vegetables. He peered round at the girls. 'This all looks wonderful, and smells delicious. I'm so lucky, thank you for letting me stay.'

Annie blinked quickly as she watched his wonderment of what stood before him. 'We're all blessed. Joyce is a wonderful cook so tuck in before it gets cold.'

Joyce blushed as she picked up the carving knife and fork. 'We're fortunate to have a friend who has a stall so we don't go short of potatoes and other vegetables. Meat, on the other hand, is harder to get hold of. This isn't a very big chicken but hopefully there will be enough to go round.' She began carving the chicken and placing slices onto the china plates.

'I can't believe how lucky I am.' Michael stared wide-eyed at everything. 'This is a banquet compared to what I'm used to. I shall do the washing up afterwards.'

Joyce laughed. 'That's always welcome. I love cooking but I hate all the washing up that goes with it.'

Rose gasped. 'That's it, Michael.' She grinned. 'Maybe you could do a couple of hours for Joyce every day – that's if she can afford to employ someone. Or, we could ask around if anyone has any jobs for someone to wash up or anything else for that matter. At least it would be a start for you.'

Joyce beamed. 'Why didn't I think of that? It's a brilliant idea. I can only offer you about two hours a day at the moment and a meal as well.' She turned to Michael. 'What do you think?'

Michael shook his head. 'It's a wonderful offer but you

are already doing so much for me. I don't want you to feel obliged to give me work as well.'

Joyce gave a small laugh. 'Don't worry about that because I can't afford to pay you much but it would be a great help to me.'

Michael chuckled. 'Then I would love to take you up on your offer.'

Rose clapped her hands. 'Today is truly a good day.' She glanced down as she put some carrots onto the decorated china plate. 'I don't think we've used this service since last Christmas.'

Joyce frowned. 'That's because I'm frightened of breaking it. Don't forget it belongs to Dot and Arthur.'

Walking down the stone steps to the sewing room, Rose took a deep breath. Her palms were damp as she flexed her fingers. Beads of perspiration were forming on her forehead. 'Stop worrying,' she mumbled. 'It's going to be all right.' Rose pushed open the sewing room door before stepping inside.

'Ahh, good morning, Miss Spencer.' Mrs Todd stepped towards Rose.

'Good morning, I'm sorry I'm late. I took a wrong turn and wasn't sure where I was.' Rose unbuttoned her coat. 'It's freezing outside.'

Mrs Todd glanced up at the large clock on the wall. 'You're not late, but Mr Bowman is a stickler for timekeeping.'

Rose nodded. 'Of course.'

Mrs Todd smiled. 'Did you have a good Christmas?'

'Yes, thank you.' Rose hung her coat on a hook. 'It wasn't

the same as being home with my family but we made the best of it. How about you?'

Mrs Todd beamed. 'I always enjoy being with my family so we made the best of it, despite the food shortages.'

Rose chuckled. 'My friend Annie gets very excited at Christmas so she kept our spirits up.'

Mrs Todd laughed. 'We all need someone like that.' She pursed her lips. 'I hate to talk about work but Mr Bowman is working on his new collection and I'll be assisting him. I need to work out the pattern pieces to be cut.'

Rose smiled. 'I'm happy to help if I can. I'll even stay late.'

Mrs Todd arched her eyebrows. 'Thank you. It's good to have someone who knows the process and has done it from scratch.'

Rose shrugged. 'I just sketched out Kitty's dress and then put it all together. I still have a lot to learn.'

Mrs Todd smiled. 'And we both know it's not that simple. How are you getting on with Mrs Hardy?'

Rose tightened her lips. 'I've tacked together a dress for her granddaughter but didn't ask enough questions about her own style of clothing. Although, she did say she'd select a couple of her frocks to show me. Do you think it would it be all right to go back there after work to find out what she likes?'

Mrs Todd tapped her finger against her painted red lips. 'Usually it's by appointment only; after all they could have guests.' She looked thoughtful. 'Maybe knock on the door. If it's not convenient make an appointment for another time.'

Rose smiled. 'That's a good idea. I've got the dress with me so I'll go after I've finished here.'

Mrs Todd glanced around her. 'I'd just pop along now before the madness starts. If Mr Bowman asks I'll say you had to go back this morning with the granddaughter's dress.'

Rose nodded. 'Thank you.' She turned on her heels, grabbing her coat and bag before running out of the sewing room.

'Rose, is everything all right?'

Rose spun round and saw Marion Simpson striding towards her.

'You look like you're in a hurry.'

Heat began to fill Rose's cheeks. 'I'm just running an errand before I start work, so if anyone asks you haven't seen me. Mrs Todd knows I'm off out.'

Marion arched her eyebrows. 'You're not a spy for the Germans, are you?'

Rose chuckled. 'Of course not, although would anyone admit it if they were?'

Marion laughed. 'No, I don't suppose they would. You'd better get going before Mr Bowman comes in.'

Rose nodded. 'I'll see you when I get back.' She turned and made her way to the exit. Pushing open the heavy door, she shivered as the cold air swept inside.

It wasn't long before Rose was in Bury Street. She bit down on her bottom lip. Maybe this wasn't a good idea. Would Mr Bowman be mad at her for coming back unannounced? The front door suddenly flew open. Rose stepped back. Had she knocked on the door? Was she so preoccupied that she didn't remember doing it?

'Good morning, Miss Spencer. Is Mrs Hardy expecting you today?'

'Erm, no, Mrs Franklin.' Rose hesitated. 'I don't wish to

intrude but there were a couple of things I forgot to ask. I'm afraid I'm new at all this.' She blushed. 'Anyway, I wondered if Mrs Hardy was free to see me, or maybe I could make an appointment for another time. I've also brought the dress I've made for Catherine for sizing.'

'Of course. Come in out of the cold, and I'll check.' Mrs Franklin stepped aside. 'You have an unusual accent. If you don't mind me asking, where's home?'

'It's a small village in Worcester.'

Mrs Franklin smiled. 'From a village to a city – that's quite a change for you.'

Rose nodded. 'I love London though, not that I don't love the village, but there's so much to see here.'

'I should think it's very different. I've heard it said that in villages everybody knows everyone's business.' Mrs Franklin smiled. 'I expect that can go either way, depending on how you feel about it.'

Rose tilted her head. 'Yes, as a child it's like the whole village are your parents so you can't get away with anything.'

Mrs Franklin laughed, her eyes lighting up as the throaty sound filled the hallway. 'Maybe the Hardys should move to a village.'

'Mrs Franklin, what are you laughing at?'

'Nothing.' Mrs Franklin smiled. 'Miss Spencer's here to see your grandma.'

Catherine looked up at Rose. 'Can I call you by your first name? It's much friendlier.'

'Catherine, it's bad manners to ask. You should wait to be invited.'

Rose smiled at the little girl who seemed to be older than

her years would suggest. 'Of course you can. It's Rose, Rose Spencer.'

Catherine giggled. 'It's very nice to meet you Rose, Rose Spencer. And are you married?'

Mrs Franklin snapped, 'Catherine, you don't want your father to find out you've been rude do you? You've been brought up to have better manners than that.'

'What? I only wondered.' Catherine's bottom lip quivered.

Rose stepped forward and peered at Mrs Franklin. 'It's all right. I don't mind, honestly.' She forced a smile and tried to hide the sadness that swept over her. 'No, I'm not married.'

'Neither's my pa. He was but my ma died just after I was born.'

Rose's mouth dropped open a little.

Catherine kept her eyes fixed on Rose. 'My gran is always trying to find him a wife but he's not interested. He should get married again; after all one day I'll have a husband and then he might have to live on his own, especially if he doesn't like him, unless Mrs Franklin will look after him.'

Mrs Franklin gathered herself together. 'Catherine, enough. I don't know where you get all this nonsense from but Miss Spencer doesn't need to hear your father's life story.'

Catherine peered up at her. 'I heard Gran talking to her friends; she thinks I'm not listening but I usually hear most of what they're saying. She said she wouldn't always be around. What does that mean?'

Mrs Franklin shook her head. 'We'll talk about this later. It's no surprise you're always getting into trouble.' She turned to Rose. 'Is there anything in particular you wanted to ask Mrs Hardy?'

Rose gripped her bag in front of her. 'I wondered if she

had selected the dresses she particularly liked. It's helpful to know if there's a style she's drawn to.'

Mrs Franklin smiled. 'Catherine, let your grandmother know Miss Spencer is here and what she's asked for.'

Catherine turned and ran up the stairs, her footsteps cushioned by the dark green carpet.

'I'm sorry about Catherine.'

Rose smiled. 'There's no need to apologise. She's young and has picked up everyone's concerns.'

Mrs Franklin nodded. 'Please come through and sit by the fire.' She led the way into the sitting room. 'Let me take your coat. I'll hang it up while you warm yourself.'

Rose's eyes were drawn to the fire. The flames danced and the coal crackled in the grate, while the grey smoke spiralled up the chimney. 'It's lovely and warm in here.' She unbuttoned her coat and slipped it off, relieved the feeling of intimidation from her previous visit was missing.

Mrs Franklin took it from Rose as Catherine ran into the room. 'Grandma won't be long. She said she'd bring a couple of things down with her.'

'Excellent.' Mrs Franklin left the room to hang up Rose's coat.

Catherine perched on the edge of an armchair. 'Do you like sewing?'

Rose smiled as she sat down. 'I love it.'

'I think I'd get bored with it.' Catherine pulled her legs up under her.

Rose laughed. 'I thought the same when I was younger, but now I love creating something from a length of material. It's wonderful to look at when it's finished.' She paused. 'Do you sew?'

Catherine shook her head. 'Neither does Grandma; at least not like you do.'

Rose nodded. 'I started off darning socks and repairing ripped trousers for my family. Would you like to learn?'

Catherine shrugged. 'Grandma doesn't have time to teach me things like that. She says, unless things change for women I shall need to marry well so I don't have to do it.'

Rose stayed silent, not sure what to say.

Catherine eyed Rose, and gave a mischievous smile. 'Would you teach me?'

Mrs Franklin stepped into the room carrying a tray of tea things. 'Teach you what?'

Catherine's eyes lit up. 'I was asking Rose if she would teach me to sew; after all if I don't become prime minister then I might have to darn socks and repair ripped trousers for my family.'

Rose choked back the giggle that was about to erupt from her.

'Hmm, I'm sure Miss Spencer has enough to do.'

'Who has enough to do?' Mrs Hardy glided into the room with several items of clothing draped over her arm.

Catherine glanced up at her grandmother. 'I've asked Rose to teach me to sew but Mrs Franklin thinks she has enough to do.'

'I expect that's true.' Mrs Hardy glanced across at Rose. 'Good morning, Miss Spencer. Are you too busy to teach Catherine?'

Rose wondered how she'd ended up in this situation. 'Good morning, Mrs Hardy, that would depend on how often I'd be required. I mean I work full-time at Dickens and Jones.'

Mrs Hardy nodded. 'Of course. I'll give it some thought. Well, here are two of my favourite dresses.' She placed the dresses on the armchair, and held each one up in turn.

Rose gasped, immediately recognising them. 'They're beautiful. May I ask where you bought them?'

'Dickens and Jones, of course, and not that long ago. Thankfully Mr Bowman is coming up with some beautiful clothing again. I was seriously thinking about shopping elsewhere.'

Rose's eyes widened and she was at a loss for words. Fumbling, she opened her bag. 'Er... I've put together a dress for Catherine.' She glanced at Catherine. 'I hope it's the bright yellow you wanted.' Rose grabbed the bag and pulled it out. 'If you could try it on for size, that would be helpful.'

Mrs Hardy frowned. 'Of course. Catherine, be careful when you slip out of your dress.'

Catherine beamed. 'It's exactly what I wanted. It's the same colour as the one that got ruined.' She stepped out of her pale blue dress, leaving it crumpled on the floor.

Rose drew in a sharp intake of breath at the horrendous sight of the red welts and scarring on Catherine's body. She lowered her eyes and kept herself focused on the dress as she held it open for Catherine to step into. Worrying about catching the injuries, Rose gently pulled it up onto her shoulders.

'Stand still, Catherine,' Mrs Hardy admonished as pins were added to alter the fit. 'It will look lovely. Thank you, Miss Spencer.'

'Hello, what's going on here then?'

Rose froze as she recognised Oliver's voice coming from the doorway.

'Pa, this is my new dress. Rose is making it for me.' Catherine twirled in front of him.

Oliver frowned at his daughter. 'Rose? Shouldn't it be Miss Spencer?'

Rose kept her gaze on Catherine while forcing herself to smile. 'I don't mind, honestly.' She stood up, her head immediately filled with the sight of Catherine's scars. She wondered why he had never mentioned Catherine and what had happened to her. Did he have something to hide? She opened her mouth to speak but closed it again, unsure what to say.

Oliver fixed his gaze on Rose as he stepped nearer. His eyes shone and his voice was low when he spoke. 'Rose, it's an unexpected pleasure to see you in my home.'

Rose's smile wavered as she glanced up at him. Was he enjoying her discomfort? She shook her head as she suddenly felt angry with herself, but she didn't understand why. 'Hello, Oliver... Mr Hardy... I didn't realise...' She turned to Mrs Hardy. 'Thank you for showing me your dresses. I need to get back to work so, Catherine, if you can carefully step out of the dress.'

Mrs Hardy frowned as she looked at her son and back at Rose. 'I didn't realise you two knew each other, but that aside, you haven't drunk your tea yet.'

'No, I'm sorry, but I really must get back to Dickens and Jones.' Rose rammed the dress into her bag.

Rose squeezed the rag she was holding; she had taken her time to dust all the figurines in the sitting room cabinet, determined to distract herself and not dwell on Catherine's scars. It had taken longer than usual because she had made up stories to amuse herself and then rearranged them. It was a good job the girls weren't in, otherwise they would think she had real problems. She laughed, and ambled into the hall before opening the front door. Rose shivered as she shook the cloud of dust from the rag outside, while trying to make sure the wind didn't blow it her way. As she stepped inside again, the wind caught the front door, banging it shut.

Rose found it strange being in the house without Joyce or Annie; she flopped onto the armchair by the fire and stared at the dancing flames licking the grey coals in the iron grate. She didn't notice the smoky smell or the ash spitting out onto the hearth. Mesmerised, she got lost in her own thoughts. The front door slammed shut. Rose jerked round to stare at the sitting room doorway.

'Hello, Rose.' Joyce came rushing in, rubbing her hands together. 'It's freezing outside. Have you been in long?'

Rose glanced up at the clock on the mantelpiece. 'I'm not sure what time I got home but I did take the liberty of lighting the fire. I hope you don't mind.'

Joyce chuckled. 'Mind? I'm very thankful.'

'How's Simon?'

Joyce beamed. 'He's improving all the time. In fact... no, sorry, it doesn't matter.'

Rose frowned. 'What? Tell me. I didn't think we had any secrets.'

Joyce stared down at her feet. 'Things have changed, thanks to this war.'

Rose shook her head. 'Don't give me that, Joyce. You were full of happiness and now you clearly think you shouldn't be. Whether we like it or not life goes on, so if you have some good news I would like to hear it.'

Joyce nodded. 'I don't want to upset you, that's all.'

Rose shrugged. 'I have to learn to live with my loss but that doesn't mean everyone has to carry it. Now give me your news.' She watched the conflict cross Joyce's face. 'Have you set a date for your wedding?'

'Simon wants to, but I'm not sure it isn't too soon.'

Rose stared into the flames as the bright colours danced in and out of the coal. She sighed. 'Joyce, it's not too soon. Don't put your life on hold. That's the one thing Charlie didn't want to do, so set your date and enjoy planning it. Enjoy becoming Mr and Mrs Hitchin. You've waited long enough.'

Joyce's smile chased the problem away. 'Are you sure?'

Rose jumped up and hugged her friend. 'Of course I'm sure. I hope Annie isn't delaying marrying Peter for fear of upsetting me. I hate the idea that everyone is walking on eggshells around me.'

Joyce hugged Rose tightly. 'We all care and feel so helpless, and there's nothing we can do to make it right for you.'

Rose nodded. 'No, there isn't but that's all the more reason to move your lives forward. I have no doubt that's what Charlie would have wanted. Don't attach guilt to your happiness.' Rose stepped back. 'So what sort of wedding dress do you want me to make for you?'

'No, I couldn't ask you to do that. I'll just wear something I already have. Anyway we haven't set the date yet.'

Rose shook her head. 'Let me make you something. It doesn't have to be a dress like Kitty's; it can be anything you like, but it will be my gift to you.'

Joyce nodded, saying nothing. Her bottom lip trembled and her eyes filled up with tears as she sat down.

Rose patted her friend's hand. 'Don't get soppy on me now.' She returned to the armchair she was sitting on before Joyce came home.

A draft blew into the sitting room and the flames of the fire danced in it. The front door slammed shut. 'It's only me,' Annie's voice rang out. 'It's absolutely freezing out there.'

Joyce turned in her chair to face the open doorway, and yelled out, 'We're in the sitting room.'

Annie rubbed her hands together as she strolled in. 'Ah lovely, a fire.' She walked over and stood in front of it for a few seconds. 'That's lovely and warm. I can't believe how the temperature has dropped.'

Rose frowned as her thoughts immediately jumped to Michael. She wondered where he was, and hoped he had found shelter somewhere. 'I don't know how anyone copes outside in this weather.'

Annie looked across at Rose. 'I looked out for Michael today but he wasn't outside the Lyceum. I did ask Bert if he'd seen him but he hadn't, at least not for a week, maybe longer.'

Rose tightened her lips. 'I do hope he's all right.'

'He comes to the restaurant and washes up.'

'That's a relief.' Rose sighed. 'At least we know he's safe.'

Joyce nodded. 'I haven't seen that brother and sister walking around the market for ages either. I know the boy was determined to look after his little sister, and they were scared of being split up if someone took them in, though I can't help but worry about them. When I first saw them begging they were soaked through and looked so scrawny.'

She shook her head. 'I can't help feeling giving them food and money wasn't enough. I should have insisted they come and live here.'

'Joyce, that must have been about a year ago, and if I remember rightly they did tell you they would run away if you'd tried to force them to live with someone.' Rose paused. 'It's hard because you want to help, but I for one don't know what to do for the best.'

Annie glanced at Rose. 'Is everything all right?'

Rose forced herself to smile. 'Of course, Joyce and Simon are thinking about dates for their wedding, so we were just discussing her wedding dress.'

Annie jumped up and down and clapped her hands together. 'That's wonderful news. I'm so happy for you.' She rushed over and wrapped her arms around Joyce; she squeezed her tight before pulling away. 'It's so exciting. Have you decided when?'

Joyce laughed. 'No, not yet.'

'What sort of dress will you have?' Annie looked thoughtful as she peered under her eyelashes at Rose. 'Will you make it for Joyce?'

'I've already offered, but Joyce said she didn't want a traditional dress.'

Annie's eyes widened as she stared back at Joyce. 'Why not?'

Joyce laughed at Annie's look of astonishment. 'It just feels like a waste of money.'

Rose watched Annie's confusion. 'I've offered to make it as my gift to her so it wouldn't cost her anything.'

Joyce closed her eyes for a moment. 'Rose, I don't want to put you through all that. You've already been through so much.' She sniffed and dabbed her eyes with her handkerchief.

Annie reached out and squeezed Joyce's arm. 'How's work going, Rose?'

Rose glanced at Annie before sighing. 'I was at the Hardys' again today. I wanted to ask about the styles she liked, and to do a fitting for her granddaughter's dress.' She paused and closed her eyes.

Annie's eyes narrowed as she stared at Rose. 'Has something happened?'

Rose's lips tightened and she opened her eyes to glance over at her friends. 'While I was at the Hardys' home, the little girl, Catherine, had to get undressed to try on the frock I'm making.' She paused and took a couple of deep breaths.

Joyce's eyes widened. 'What?'

Rose shook her head. 'Her back was covered in red welts and scarring. There was so much of it. I was quite shocked.'

Annie opened her mouth to speak but said nothing.

'Do you think someone in the family is doing it? Maybe her father or even the grandmother?' Joyce hesitated. 'It wouldn't be the first time something like that had happened in a family home.'

Rose shrugged. 'I don't know but that's another thing: it turns out Oliver is her father.'

'Oh my goodness.' Joyce's eyes darted left and right.

Annie held up her hand. 'That doesn't necessarily mean anything. I'm not saying Oliver did it but look at Matthew Harris.'

Joyce frowned. 'Matthew Harris?'

Annie sighed. 'The pianist at the theatre.'

Rose nodded. 'How can we forget him?'

'It was the name that didn't ring any bells.' Joyce raised her eyebrows. 'But I'll never forget what he did.'

Annie shook her head. 'When I think about it I had a narrow escape, but the point is I thought he was a kind man, wanting to help me with singing lessons, and look how he turned out. I could have died when he locked me in that cupboard.'

Rose gripped her hands in her lap.

Joyce leant forward and plumped the cushion behind her. 'Why don't you just ask him about them?'

Rose shook her head. 'I don't know him well enough to do that, and would he admit it if he was doing it?'

Annie nodded. 'That's true. He's very unlikely to come out and say, "I beat my daughter to within an inch of her life."'

Joyce waved her hand in the air and raised her voice. 'But you can't do nothing if she is being beaten. She's a child for goodness' sake.'

Rose sighed. 'No, you're right. I just can't believe he would do something like that and she's such a confident, happy child.' She paused. 'No, she must have got them some other way; maybe she was involved in an accident or something.'

They all sat in silence for a few minutes.

Rose's mind raced around trying to match the actions to the kind man she had come to know. 'Anyway, it turns out Doctor Hardy went to school with Charlie and his brother. Their families were friends.'

'When did you find that out?'

Rose watched Annie trying to work things out.

'I mean, you haven't known him long.'

'No, it was a bit of a shock when he first arrived at the shop. Apparently, he had been trying to see Charlie for weeks and didn't know he'd died. He thought the shop was shut for money reasons.'

Annie shook her head. 'That must have been awful for him.'

Rose nodded. 'He stayed with me all day and helped go through things. He talked about Charlie's family and his childhood, which was nice. Sorry, I should have told you but to be honest I didn't expect to see him again after that day. Although, he did come back and helped me clear the shop. He even took the keys back to the landlord for me.'

Annie gave a faint smile. 'It sounds like you've made a new friend. He was clearly a good friend to Charlie.'

Rose's lips tightened. 'And like all good friends he wishes he had seen more of him, but as always life gets in the way.'

Annie frowned. 'I know that feeling with my mother. It's heartbreaking to live with that regret.'

Rose stepped forward and hugged her friend. 'It's no good punishing yourself. We all think we've got all the time in the world, but as we know, it's not for us to know how long we have. We just have to make the most of the time we do have, and that's always difficult to juggle.'

Annie stepped away. 'Yes, and you need to remember your own words and that Charlie would want you to be happy, although I accept it's early days, but I don't want you to forget you deserve to be happy too.'

'I know.' Rose took a deep breath. 'I'm sorry, I should have told you at the time about Doctor Hardy, and I don't know why I didn't.' She swallowed hard as she remembered that difficult day. 'Except, at the time it was hard talking about Charlie without wanting to cry.'

Annie reached out and squeezed Rose's arm.

Joyce shook her head. 'I can't believe it's the doctor then, because you said he was such a kind man, and surely Charlie wouldn't have been friends with someone who was violent. He was such a gentle soul.'

Rose frowned. 'None of it makes sense but I will try to find a way to ask about them, so let's just move on and talk about something else. Let's talk about Joyce's wedding.'

Joyce grinned. 'No, Simon and I need to discuss things first so just hold on to your excitement for now.'

Annie smiled and nodded at Joyce. 'It will be good to have something to look forward to.'

Rose's eyes widened. 'You could always start arranging your own wedding. There's no reason why you and Peter couldn't tie the knot now.'

Annie's colour deepened. 'I think it's time we had a cuppa, don't you?'

Rose laughed at her friend's embarrassment. 'You can't avoid the subject forever.'

13

It had been a slow start to January for the seamstresses in Dickens and Jones. Some were only just returning after having time off for Christmas, all voicing how they were glad to see the back of 1915. There was a lot of chatter about how Christmas hadn't been the same without their menfolk, and thanks to the food shortages some hadn't managed to have the traditional Christmas dinner. Gradually the work had started to come downstairs and the hum of the sewing machines had taken over.

Rose's eyes narrowed as she stared down at the many pieces of material she had pinned and tacked together. She glanced at the pattern pieces and tilted her head.

'How are you getting on?'

Rose jumped.

'I'm sorry, I didn't mean to startle you.'

Rose peered over a shoulder and gave Mrs Todd a weary smile. 'I was in a world of my own.' She sighed and looked back at the dress before turning round to face Mrs Todd. 'I think there's a problem with this design. It feels like it doesn't fit together properly.'

Mrs Todd stepped forward and looked at the dress that

was laid out on the table. 'It might be all right when it's finally sewn together.'

Rose nodded. 'I did think it might come together at the end, but I've got this niggling doubt.'

Mrs Todd picked up the drawing that Mr Bowman had done. 'I'm not sure.' She deftly moved the material around the table, smoothing it out with her hands. 'You could be right; maybe it needs a bow or something.'

Rose picked up a pencil; turning the paper over she started to draw the dress out again with an extra couple of side panels and a large bow draping down the back of it. The dress immediately became recognisable to her. 'Do you mean something like this?'

Mrs Todd nodded. 'Yes, I think that's improved it. You've certainly got an eye for it.' She paused, eyeing the sketch.

Rose smiled. 'We make a good team.' She moved the paper to one side. 'I'm glad that's sorted out because I've got so much to do. Mrs Hardy is keeping me busy on her own. Thankfully I've done most of the work on her dresses at home.'

'Mr Bowman is putting too much on you. I'll have a word with him. You can't do everything.'

'Don't worry; it'll all get done. Mrs Hardy is very understanding.'

Mrs Todd frowned. 'I'm not convinced Mr Bowman will be if he finds out Mrs Hardy is being kept waiting.'

Rose raised her eyebrows. 'She's not. Mrs Hardy's had the original two dresses and loved them but she keeps adding to her order.' Her eyes narrowed. 'I haven't had a chance to tell Mr Bowman yet. You're not going to tell him are you?'

Mrs Todd shook her head. 'No, but he has to understand

you can't do everything.' She looked thoughtful. 'I'll ask Marion, er Miss Simpson, to sew Mrs Hardy's dresses. If you design them, make sure the pattern is correct, and ensure they're finished to a high standard; that should ease the pressure.' Mrs Todd paused. 'Mr Bowman doesn't need to know anything about it.'

Rose nodded. 'Thank you, I'd appreciate the help.'

Mrs Todd glanced towards the office and saw Mr Bowman holding up a string of pearls, which seemed to have his undivided attention as he rolled his fingers along them.

Rose followed Mrs Todd's gaze, and watched Mr Bowman peering at the necklace. He stared at Rose before quickly lowering his hand.

'What are you two gossiping about?' Mr Bowman's voice boomed across the sewing room as he marched towards them. 'There's no time for that. Get on with what you're paid to do.'

Mrs Todd scurried back to her table without a backwards glance.

Mr Bowman's gaze followed her. 'Useless woman, I don't know why I keep her on.' He turned to Rose. 'Haven't you finished this yet? You were working on this when I left a couple of hours ago.' He shook his head. 'It must be finished and dressed on a mannequin, with accessories, today. Mr Woodford will be down later to look at the collection so far.' He delved into his jacket pocket and pulled out the pearl necklace Rose had seen him with earlier. 'Be careful with this and guard it with your life. I've borrowed it from the jewellery department, and it's expensive. Mr Woodford will sack us both if it goes missing.' He placed the pearls against the black dress. 'They'll look excellent, almost regal, with that gown, which will help sales.'

Rose nodded.

Mr Bowman turned to walk away.

'I have a problem.' Rose paused as Mr Bowman turned back and gave her a steely stare. She pulled back her shoulders and lifted her chin. 'I came to a standstill because I felt something was missing from this gown.'

Mr Bowman stared at Rose. 'Are you questioning my designs?'

'No, sir, I wouldn't dream of it. I just thought—'

'You're not paid to think; you're paid to sew.' Mr Bowman's face reddened. 'I don't know how many times I have to say it but these gowns have to be finished today.'

Rose picked up the piece of paper and thrust it in front of him. 'Do you want a large soft bow added to the back, and the extra panels sewn in the sides? I believe they finish it off.'

Mr Bowman snatched the paper; he was silent for a moment. 'They were always in my design. Is this how you made a name for yourself? Taking credit where none is due?'

Rose flushed as anger flowed through her veins. 'No, sir, and it wasn't part of the original drawing you gave me, as you'll see when you turn the paper over.'

Mr Bowman threw the paper down on the table. 'I don't know what's going on here. If Mrs Todd is sabotaging my designs she will be out the door, as indeed will you.' He turned to march away.

'Is that a yes then, sir?' Rose peered down at her drawing.

Mr Bowman scowled as he glanced over his shoulder. 'Yes, now get the dress finished.'

Rose shook her head but said nothing. She picked up the soft, silky material and began machining it together.

A few hours later she was pulling the long black flowing gown over the mannequin.

The sewing room was empty, and the seamstresses had long gone home, when Mr Bowman came marching towards her. 'Have you got the necklace with you?'

Rose nodded. 'It's in my pocket. They are beautiful. My mother always said pearls were for tears and never wanted any for that reason, not that she could ever afford them.'

Mr Bowman's mouth tightened as he checked his wristwatch. 'Mr Woodford will be down shortly so hurry up and put the necklace on the mannequin.'

Rose pulled the necklace out of her skirt pocket. Her fingers fumbled with the tiny catch until she managed to undo the clasp and open it up. She gasped in horror.

They both stood there open-mouthed. The pearls pinged and rolled around the floor, filling the silence.

Mr Bowman yelled. 'What the hell have you done?'

Rose's fingers gripped the broken necklace.

Mr Bowman's mouth dropped open as he fought for breath. His hand came up and rested on his chest. 'I can't breathe.' He bent over. 'What have you done? Mr Woodford will sack us when he sees the pearls.'

Rose clenched her jaw. 'I don't know what happened… I swear I only undid the catch,' she mumbled.

Mr Bowman swung into action. 'We need to pick them up. I'll put them in the drawer until I can decide what to do.' He stooped down and started picking up the loose pearls. 'Come on, help, before we both get the sack.'

Rose felt the pulse throbbing in her temple. 'What will happen?'

Mr Bowman scowled at Rose. 'Sshh, let me think.' He stopped picking up the small pearls and stared ahead. 'You'll just have to offer to pay for them.'

Rose rubbed the back of her neck. 'I don't have that sort of money.'

Mr Bowman shook his head. 'Well, if you want to keep your job I'll have to trust you, I suppose.'

Rose mumbled, 'What do you mean trust me?'

Mr Bowman gazed down at the pearls in his hand. 'I'll pay for them but you'll need to give the money back every week out of your wages.'

The clatter of cutlery hitting the plates filled the kitchen as the three girls tucked into their dinner.

Annie smiled. 'It's funny how the three of us have got used to eating in here instead of the dining room. Although I still like to eat in there, it is easier to sit at the kitchen table.'

Rose laughed. 'It's not surprising really – it's a magnificent room with Arthur and Dot's fine ornaments and cabinets.' She looked around her. 'I think Michael thought we were rich when he saw it all.'

Annie nodded. 'We are lucky that Arthur is happy for us to continue living here.'

Joyce laid her knife and fork on the edge of her plate. 'I forgot to say I had a letter from Uncle Arthur. It doesn't matter how hard I try I seem to struggle to just call him Arthur.' Chuckling, she picked up her fork again. 'They all seem to be settling down into their farm life very well. Apparently, Philip loves it. I think it's safe to say they won't be coming back in a hurry.'

Annie smiled. 'I bet he doesn't know himself with all that space to run around in after being in London. I don't think we realised how lucky we were growing up.'

Rose used her knife to slice into the pastry of the meat and potato pie. 'Do any of us? We all think there's something better out there and our parents know nothing. It must be part of growing up to think like that.' She pressed her fork into a small amount of the pie. 'It's good Philip has the chance to see another side of life, just as it was for us. It helps to decide where and how to live.'

'I do miss them though.' Joyce poured some more gravy onto her plate. 'Maybe one day soon we can go and visit them. That would be good, wouldn't it?'

Rose giggled. 'You could both get married while you're there. At least it would make it easier for both your families.'

Annie shook her head as she laughed. 'I'll say one thing for you, Rose, you don't give up.'

Rose looked across the dinner table to her friend. 'Anyone would think you didn't want to get married, and if that's true you should just be honest about it.'

Annie smiled. 'Actually, we're going to set the date soon. We've been talking about it.' She turned to Joyce. 'Peter thinks it's a good idea for us to have a joint wedding with you and Simon, if you don't mind sharing your day with us?'

Joyce's face lit up. 'There's nothing I would like more than to share my day with my best friends.'

Rose beamed before she burst out, 'You just don't want me to have two dresses, do you?'

They all roared with laughter.

Annie scooped up a forkful of cabbage and held it in mid-air. 'It's good to hear you laughing again, Rose.'

Rose nodded. 'It feels good, although I do feel a little guilty about it.'

Joyce shook her head. 'Well you shouldn't. The last thing Charlie would want is for you to be unhappy.'

Rose looked up. 'I know. That's what I keep telling myself.' She sighed.

Joyce licked her lips before placing her fork down across the centre of her plate. She glanced at her friends. 'Maybe we should see what's on at the pictures and have a night out.'

Rose shook her head. 'I'm sorry, I just have too much on at the moment.'

Joyce frowned. 'All the more reason to go. You need to have a break – you know, have some fun.'

Rose sighed. 'To be honest, I just can't afford to do anything at the moment.'

Annie studied Rose. 'I don't mean to be rude but you never go anywhere so you should be able to afford the pictures, not that it matters because I can always pay. I'm just surprised that's all.'

Joyce raised her eyebrows. 'Have you settled into working at Dickens and Jones? I mean they're paying you all right, aren't they?'

Rose gripped her knife and fork. 'The thing is I broke an expensive string of pearls. Mr Bowman was beside himself worrying about our jobs. Anyway he paid for them so our jobs are safe but I'm having to give him most of my wages every week to pay him back.'

'Oh how awful.' Joyce jumped up from the table. 'Why didn't you say something? We might be able to scrape the money together between us.'

Rose held up her hand. 'No, I shouldn't think we could ever afford to buy them in our lifetime.'

Joyce stared at Rose. 'But that means you'll be paying him back for years.'

Rose sighed. 'I hadn't thought of that.'

Annie placed her knife and fork down on her plate. 'Why don't you offer to sell your designs to him instead?'

Rose shook her head. 'They aren't worth anything. No, he saved my position so I shall have to stick to the agreement. To be honest I don't know how much they were. I shall have to find out.'

Their silence was broken by the scraping of the kitchen chairs across the tiled floor and the clatter of the dinner things being placed in the sink.

Rose picked up a damp cloth to wipe down the kitchen table. 'I'm not sure Mr Bowman is as clever, or maybe I should say as creative, as he makes out.'

Annie frowned. 'Why, what's happened?'

Rose looked thoughtful. 'When I was last at the Hardys I asked Mrs Hardy to show me a couple of dresses she really liked – you know, just to see what styles she favoured. Anyway, she brought a couple of dresses downstairs to show me, and said they were ones she loved.'

Silence hung in the air for a few seconds.

Annie pursed her lips. 'And?'

Rose twisted the damp cloth between her fingers. 'I think they were both from my drawings.'

'What?' Joyce frowned. 'But how is that possible?'

Annie's mouth dropped open. 'I don't understand. How can that be? Do you think Miss Hetherington was telling the truth then?'

Rose shrugged. 'It certainly seems that way. Oh, I don't know. If I'm honest one minute I think it's Miss Hetherington and then five minutes later I think it's Mr Bowman, but what I don't understand is how he could have got hold of them, unless of course she sold them to him.' She sighed. 'Maybe my designs aren't original and I've just got carried away thinking I'm cleverer than I really am.'

Joyce shook her head. 'I don't believe that, not for one minute. Did Mrs Hardy say where she got the dresses from?'

Rose gave a small laugh; there was no humour in the noise she made. 'That's just it; she bought them at Dickens and Jones. She said Mr Bowman had designed them, so they can't be my creations.'

Joyce stared at Rose. 'That doesn't make sense. How can that be?'

Rose shrugged. 'I don't know.' She paused. 'It means that Miss Hetherington was probably telling the truth.' She shook her head. 'I've allowed Charlie's fine words and all the praise I got for making Kitty's wedding dress to go to my head. That's shameful and means I got this job under false pretences.'

Annie shook her head. 'I don't know what to say.'

Rose fixed her gaze on the range. 'There's nothing to say. I have no proof of anything.' She sighed. 'I'm not even sure I can explain it, but either I'm not as good as I think or he has somehow got hold of my sketch pad and he could only have done that through someone at the theatre.' She shrugged. 'But that isn't based on anything at all.'

Annie looked thoughtful for a moment before shrugging. 'But who, if it isn't Miss Hetherington?'

Rose sat cross-legged on the soft plush pile of the dark green carpet in Mrs Hardy's sitting room. She was grateful Oliver wasn't in. Her mind was in turmoil trying to work out how he could be so kind in his work and with her, and yet, potentially, be violent to his daughter. Her scarring haunted her. Her fingers clenched around the scissors. He wouldn't be the first. She glanced at Catherine; she appeared to be a happy child, so how could she be suffering at the hands of her father or grandmother?

She desperately wanted to help in some way, but she wasn't sure what to do or say. Rose wanted to ask Catherine about them, but was struggling to find the right words. Sighing, she realised that all she could do was keep an eye on her. She tucked her skirt under her knees and concentrated on the pattern laid out in front of her, smoothing out the creases with her hand. 'Right, before I cut it, are you sure this is the colour you want for your teddy bear?'

Catherine ran a hand over it. 'Yes, it's wonderful.'

Rose giggled. 'The material is lovely, it's the colour I'm questioning.'

'My pa would say it's very girly. But I like it.' Catherine tucked her hand inside a pocket of her dark green skirt; she pulled out a thin piece of red ribbon. 'Look, it's to tie round its neck.'

Rose looked back down at the material. 'It'll go nicely, but pink's an unusual colour for a bear.'

'But isn't that the point of making things? They're all

brown in the shops.' Catherine ran her fingers down the ribbon. 'I love it.'

Rose nodded. 'Well, that's good. I just wanted to check.' Opening the scissors, she began cutting round the pattern.

Catherine sat silently watching Rose. 'What was the first thing you ever sewed?'

Rose stopped cutting and peered across at Catherine as she thought back to her childhood. 'I tore my skirt climbing trees. I got into a lot of trouble and my mother told me I had to repair it. She said if I didn't do a good job I wouldn't be allowed out again.' She smiled. 'I think she was more annoyed I'd been climbing trees. It wasn't very ladylike.'

Catherine giggled. 'My grandma wouldn't be happy if I did that. She's always telling me I need to act in a ladylike manner. I get told off if I don't sit properly, or if I speak out of turn. She's always telling Pa that his father used to say, "Spare the rod, spoil the child."'

Rose forced a smile. 'What does your pa say to that?'

Catherine shrugged. 'He doesn't say anything; at least I've never heard him.'

Rose frowned; she wanted to ask more questions but glanced down at the material instead. Was that why she had those scars? 'We have to remember our family try to have our best interests at heart. If my ma hadn't made me repair my skirt I probably wouldn't have learnt how to sew, and if I hadn't learnt to sew I wouldn't be here cutting out this teddy bear with you.'

Catherine nodded. 'So we have your ma to thank.' She continued to watch Rose cut round the pattern. 'I can't believe it's going to be a teddy bear.'

Rose smiled. 'It's not just going to be any teddy bear, it's going to be one you've made and you'll cherish it forever, no matter how it turns out.' She continued to work in silence before leaning back and sighing. 'Right, I'll pin it together and then show you how to do the back stitch.'

'When grandma comes downstairs she's going to be so proud of me.' Catherine frowned. 'I hope I don't mess it up. Remember, I've never done it before.'

Rose shook her head. 'Don't worry, it's all part of learning and the trick is not to give up.' She picked up the needle and threaded some pink cotton through the eye.

Catherine watched her closely. 'Can I be excited and scared all at the same time?'

Rose laughed. 'Of course. It's just nerves. Watch me, then you can try.' She pulled the thread down to a desired length before cutting it and tying a knot to hold the two ends together. 'Now, Catherine, you need to make tiny stitches otherwise your teddy will fall apart.'

Catherine leant in as Rose tilted the two layers of material; stabbing in the needle she pulled the thread through several times.

'I want to try it… if that's all right?' Catherine didn't take her eyes off the needle and thread.

Rose nodded. 'Of course. Please be careful; the needle's sharp and you don't want to prick your finger. Just follow what I did, and don't worry, it can all be undone so it doesn't matter if you make a mistake.'

Catherine bit down on her lip as she concentrated on where to put the needle.

Rose watched her. It took her a moment to realise she was holding her breath. 'Well done. That's a lovely small stitch, so carry on like that and sew all around the body.'

She used her fingers to show her where to sew. 'The neck is left open so we can stuff it. Let me know if you get stuck.'

Catherine's face lit up. 'I can do it, I can do it.'

Rose chuckled. 'Of course you can. It's not that difficult, it's just practice.'

An hour later Catherine shrieked, 'I've done the body and the head. What's next?'

Rose beamed and placed the trousers she was turning up beside her on the chair. Reaching out, she took the material from Catherine. Moving it slowly through her fingers, Rose examined the stitching. 'Well, you've done a wonderful job. Now, you get to do the fun bit and bring it to life.'

Catherine beamed and clapped her hands together.

Rose watched Catherine pick up small pieces of the fine silk stuffing and push it into one of the legs of her pink teddy bear.

Catherine glanced up. 'How much stuffing do I need to put in?'

Rose leant down and squeezed the teddy's legs. 'They need to be firm, so you can squash a bit more in and then you keep going until the body is so full you can't get any more in.'

Catherine sighed.

'Don't get impatient now – it's nearly finished and if it's not stuffed properly it will be too floppy.'

Catherine giggled. 'Maybe that's what I'll call him: Floppy.'

The sound of heels clattering on the tiled floor of the hallway caught Rose's attention. The sitting room door swung open and Mrs Hardy strolled in.

Catherine looked up and grinned. 'Grandma, you look lovely.'

Mrs Hardy beamed. 'Why thank you, Catherine. Rose, this dress is beautiful. What do you think?' Mrs Hardy turned round slowly.

Rose stood up, looking at it with a critical eye. 'Hmm, it doesn't seem to fit too bad. How does it feel?'

Mrs Hardy beamed. 'I love it.'

Rose smiled and stood aside. 'Do you want to sit down to make sure it's comfortable?'

Mrs Hardy stepped towards the armchair by the fireplace and lowered herself into place.

Rose frowned at Mrs Hardy's pensive expression. 'Is that how you normally sit down?'

Catherine giggled. 'Grandma, you look so scared. It's just a dress.'

Mrs Hardy chuckled. 'I'm worried it will split.'

Rose eyed the woman who was normally full of confidence, and yet here she was worrying about splitting the dress she was sitting in. 'Then it must be too tight, but that's why you're having a fitting. Do you mind standing up again?'

Mrs Hardy slowly lifted herself out of the chair.

Rose couldn't help smiling as she watched her easing herself out of the chair. From what she'd heard from Catherine, and seen for herself, Mrs Hardy was clearly a clever, formidable woman and yet she looked quite vulnerable at that moment. Rose stepped forward and ran her fingers over the shoulders of the dress before standing back and studying it. 'It fits fine around the neckline and the waist. Maybe the tulip-style skirt isn't for you; perhaps you'd feel more comfortable with a fuller one.'

Cold air rushed into the room as the front door slammed shut. 'It's not getting any warmer out there.' Oliver strolled in.

Rose's jaw dropped slightly at the sound of Oliver's voice.

Catherine dropped her teddy and jumped up. 'Pa, you're home.' She threw herself at him and hugged him tight. 'Sit down and I'll show you my teddy.'

Oliver smiled, scooping his daughter into his arms. 'My goodness, you're getting too big for me to pick you up.' He turned to Rose, watching her as she studied the dress his mother was wearing. 'Hello, Rose.'

Rose blushed as she looked up. 'Hello, Doctor Hardy, I'll be on my way once we've decided what needs doing to this dress.'

Mrs Hardy glanced at her son. 'What do you think?'

'It looks lovely.' Oliver gave Rose a sideways glance. 'Although, I don't know why you're asking me. I know nothing about ladies' clothing.'

Mrs Hardy sighed.

Rose frowned. 'You don't have to know to have an opinion.' She gasped. 'I'm so sorry, I crossed the line and forgot you were a customer.'

Oliver frowned. 'I'm not surprised; we've worked together under many guises and I like to think we're more friends than seamstress and customer. Besides, you are quite right.' He chuckled. 'It's not very often someone puts me in my place; apart, of course, from the women in this family.' He eyed his mother for a moment. 'Well, let's see. That shade of purple really suits you, and it looks a good fit. Although, I'm not sure how you'll manage to walk very far in it.'

Mrs Hardy grinned. 'Thank you, and that's exactly what we were discussing when you walked in.'

Rose nodded. 'Personally, I feel clothing should be comfortable. With Kitty's wedding dress the lace overlay was separate so she could wear the dress again. It's no good having beautiful clothing if you can't wear it because it's uncomfortable.'

Oliver chuckled. 'Don't let Mr Bowman hear you talk like that; he likes his ladies to keep spending their money regardless.'

Rose smiled. 'Well that's business, and I'm not sure I fit into that way of thinking.' She paused. 'Maybe it's just my upbringing – you know, the old make do and mend.'

Mrs Hardy rested her hand on Rose's arm. 'That's not a bad thing; after all, it's given you your needlework skills. I'm quite envious of anyone who can create such beautiful things.'

Rose blushed. 'Thank you. I'd be happy to help you to sew along with Catherine.'

Mrs Hardy laughed. 'I'm getting too old in the tooth to learn such things. Anyway, my eyesight isn't what it used to be. I'd never get a needle threaded but it's very thoughtful of you to offer.'

'We all have our strengths. From what Catherine has told me you've taught her, she can be anything she wants with hard work. She knows all about the suffragettes so you are giving her the gift of believing in herself.' Rose took a breath. 'So, what would you like me to do about this dress?'

Mrs Hardy looked down and kicked her leg out. 'I think you're right, Rose. Would you mind making it fuller for me?'

Rose smiled. 'Of course not. Is the length all right?'

Mrs Hardy peered down at her calves. 'Yes, it's quite a modern length. Shall I take it off?'

Rose nodded. 'Yes, I'll make the alterations and then, if you don't mind, perhaps you could try it on again.'

'Of course.' Mrs Hardy turned and shuffled out of the room.

Oliver watched his mother leave before turning to Rose, and nodding at the sewing on the chair. 'Are those trousers from the refuge?'

Rose picked them up. 'Yes, I thought I'd alter them while watching Catherine stuff her bear. They just need a couple of more stitches and then they're done.'

'Yes, come on, Pa, I want to show you my teddy.' Catherine tugged at his hand.

'Of course, Cat, I'm sorry. I got caught up with Grandma's dress.' Oliver laughed. 'Let me see what you've done.'

Catherine giggled. 'He doesn't have a head yet, but that's because I haven't finished stuffing him.'

Oliver reached out and took the bear from his daughter. He brushed his hand up and down the material. 'He's lovely and soft.'

Catherine beamed. 'He's going to be very cuddly when he's finished.'

Oliver peered inside at the stuffing. 'I think you are a very clever girl to have sewn this. When will the head go on?'

Rose smiled. 'We have to add the eyes and nose to the face and then the head will be the last thing to be sewn on.'

Catherine looked up expectantly. 'Can we do that tonight?'

Rose laughed. 'It might have to wait for another day.'

Oliver watched his daughter's look of disappointment fix firmly on her face. 'I think between us we take up quite a lot of Rose's time. She must think we're taking over her life one way or another.'

Rose's gaze shifted from one to the other. 'I don't mind. It keeps me occupied, and trust me that's a good thing.' She finished off the thread in the trousers before cutting them loose. 'Perhaps you could take these back to the refuge when you go.'

'I'm going on Sunday so maybe you could come with me.'

Rose neatly folded the trousers. 'Ordinarily I would love to come but I need to try and find someone that I haven't seen since Christmas. I know that's only just over a month ago but I used to see him around most days so I'm a little worried something might have happened to him.'

14

Bert held the front of his jacket together as he got caught in the February crosswind outside the Lyceum Theatre. The street sellers' voices travelled up Wellington Street as they shouted and joked with everyone who passed their barrows.

'Come on, ladies and gents, if I don't get this bread sold my family will have to have it for their dinner tonight, tomorrow and the day after!'

'Now come on, ladies, never mind his bread – what about my flowers? They'll die if they're not given a good home. You gents could get in the wife's good books if yer went 'ome wiv a bunch. Come on, everyone deserves a treat, even in these 'ard times.'

Bert smiled as he listened to the sellers competing with each other. He tightened his grip on the cup as he ambled down the steps, stopping only to look across at Michael wrapped up in his old coat. He marched towards the unkept man. 'Here, I've bought yer a mug of 'ot tea. Get it down yer while it's still 'ot. It's blooming freezing out 'ere.'

Michael looked up at the man who'd probably saved his life when he handed over the heavy coat that was wrapped around him. 'Thank you.' He reached up and clasped his hands around the cup, letting the warmth filter through his cold fingers.

Bert watched him holding the cup close. 'Is there no family yer can stay with instead of suffering out here?'

Michael glanced along the street before looking back at Bert. 'I'm just one of many. It's no different for me than it is for them.'

Bert shook his head. 'Why don't yer come inside, even if it's just for a little while; at least until yer get warm?'

Michael didn't look up. He lifted the cup to his lips and the steam warmed his face. 'I can't do that, but thank you for offering.'

Bert frowned. 'I don't understand. Anybody else would bite my 'and off for that offer.'

Michael sipped his tea, feeling the warmth cascade down his throat. 'I do appreciate it; I just don't want to get anyone into trouble. It's a very grand theatre and I'm sure they don't wanna see people like me inside it. To be honest, I'm surprised I get away with sitting in the corner out of the wind.'

Bert lowered himself to sit on the steps next to Michael. 'Yer don't have to worry about that. The worst that will happen is I get my knuckles rapped and I'm 'appy for that to 'appen if it gets yer out of the cold for a little while.' He wriggled on the cold damp step. 'Anyway, there's only one or two who would complain and they're regular moaners so yer don't need to worry about that.'

Michael turned to look at Bert. 'I take it Miss Hetherington's one of those? I only ask because I know she upset Rose.'

'Yeah, she's so angry all the time. I've never met anyone

like 'er before. She just 'ates everyone and consequently no one likes 'er either.'

Michael frowned. 'I suppose it's easy to judge people when you don't know what's going on in their lives; we're all guilty of that. I expect people make decisions about me, and others like me, every day.'

'Is that what got you 'ere?' Bert studied him for a moment. 'I expect people do judge yer, because of the way yer look and the fact that yer living on the streets.'

Michael nodded. 'You get used to it. It becomes a vicious circle: I can't get a job because I have nowhere to live and I have nowhere to live because I can't get a job.' He shrugged. 'It's just the way it is.'

Bert's eyes narrowed. 'I suspect that's true, which makes it all quite sad.' Frowning, he glanced at him. 'But having said that, and yer've never had to deal with 'er, but she's mean-spirited and doesn't 'ave a kind word to say to anybody. Someone has clearly wronged 'er in 'er life, and she's making us all pay.'

'That's a terrible thing to carry.' Michael stared ahead, and remained silent for a few minutes. 'Maybe she lost someone important to her and she's never got over it.'

Bert nodded. 'Maybe, but that's not our fault. Yer can't go around taking your problems out on everyone yer meet. That just ain't right.'

Michael's lips tightened. 'No, you're quite right; after all, we would all be at war with each other all the time and, in my opinion, there's already enough hate in this world.' Michael gulped a mouthful of tea down. 'You make a good cuppa, I'll give you that.'

Bert smiled before lowering his head, and staring hard at

the steps. 'I expect everything's made worse because of your injured arm.'

Michael sat in silence.

Bert looked up as three men left the public house arguing with each other. 'I'm sorry if I spoke out of turn but I noticed that yer wouldn't put the coat on until we'd left yer on your own. I watched yer struggle with the movement of your left arm. Is that why you're living on the streets?'

'The injury is thanks to the war.' Michael gave him a sideways glance. 'I... I once fell in love with a beautiful woman, and I believe she loved me too, but her parents didn't think I was good enough for her and if I wasn't then I certainly wouldn't be now.'

Bert's eyes narrowed. 'Did she not fight for yer love?' He shook his head and laughed at the sound of his words. 'I think I've been working in the theatre for too long.'

Sadness swept across Michael's face. 'Her father was a strong individual. He controlled everything around him and I believe she was too scared to stand up to him. That's why I feel quite strongly about judging people when we know nothing about them or their lives.'

Bert nodded before shrugging. 'I can see that, and to a point I think yer right but it's very 'ard not to when someone is so 'ateful to yer day in and day out. If yer like, I can take yer inside and yer can see for yerself.' He laughed. 'I'm sure she'd 'ave something to say about yer being inside the theatre.'

Michael handed Bert the empty mug. 'I don't think that would be a good idea, but I really appreciate the cup of tea, thank you.'

Bert looked down into the empty mug before sighing.

'Yer know it makes me very sad to 'ear that yer missed out on your love because I wouldn't be without my missus. She is a diamond in the rough.' He chuckled. 'But if yer ever meet her I'll deny I said that.'

Michael laughed. 'Don't worry, your secret's safe, and don't fret about my lost love because she's not totally lost to me. I know where she is every day, so even if she doesn't see me, I see her.'

Bert studied Michael. 'Yer do know that sounds a little scary and maybe yer should be locked up.' He stood up and brushed down the seat of his trousers. 'Having said that I saw yer with Rose so I know you're a good man. Yer may have lost your way but something tells me you'd never hurt anybody.' He glanced back at the theatre to see Miss Hetherington looking up and down the road. 'I've gotta go before she gets me the sack.'

Michael followed his gaze and didn't speak for a moment. 'Yes, I wouldn't want that to happen, and thanks again for the tea.'

Rose flicked the bottom of the dress and stood back, casting a critical eye over the gown that looked perfect on the mannequin. It was her first completed evening dress. She tilted her head one way then the other as she moved around it. She couldn't believe it was all her own work on a mannequin in Dickens and Jones. Rose wanted to pinch herself.

The sewing room door creaked open and quickly slammed shut again. 'Well, it doesn't make sense to me.' Mr Bowman's voice carried over the noise of the sewing machine treadles moving back and forth and the needles moving up and down. 'I make sure every length of material is accounted for. You can check my books.'

Mr Woodford frowned. 'I will. Something is wrong and I'll catch whoever is stealing from us.'

Mr Bowman nodded. 'Of course, maybe the dresses have gone missing from the shop.'

Mr Woodford suddenly stopped near Rose. 'This looks a good addition to the collection.' He turned to Mr Bowman before glancing back at Rose. 'Are you the new seamstress?'

Mr Bowman cleared his throat. 'This is Miss Spencer.'

Mr Woodford smiled. 'Ah yes, my wife and daughters haven't stopped talking about the wedding dress you made for the actress.' He smiled as he turned to Mr Bowman. 'You need to be careful – you have competition here.' He chuckled as he moved away.

Mr Bowman scowled at Rose before taking large strides to catch up with Mr Woodford. 'That is one of my designs she's working on. Miss Spencer has a lot to learn before I let her put anything into a collection for us.'

Rose shook her head. She couldn't believe what she was hearing. Why would he deny her the recognition for her first dress in a collection?

'Morning, Rose.'

Rose turned round. 'Hello, Marion, is it that time already?'

Marion smiled. 'No, I've come in early. I love sewing and the idea of creating something from a length of material brings me joy. My father's always telling me I have ideas above my station in life.' She shrugged. 'But one day I'd like to be able to sell the clothes I make.'

Rose smiled. 'Keep going, you'll get there, and if I can help in any way just say.' She walked with Marion to the many colourful dresses hanging from the rail. She lifted off the next coat hanger. Running her hand down the soft silky material, Rose was impressed with the way it flowed and folded so naturally. She glanced over Marion's shoulder. 'Mr Bowman is here.'

Marion grabbed the next coat hanger. 'I better get on; I don't want to risk losing this opportunity. Perhaps we can catch up later?' Without waiting for an answer, or looking at the dress, she marched to her designated sewing machine.

Rose nodded before returning to stare at the note, which had been hooked over the hanger, to see what needed altering on the dress. Wrinkling her nose, she squinted as she tried to read it but her thoughts jumped to Mr Bowman's lie about the dress on the mannequin.

'Is everything all right, Miss Spencer?'

Rose turned at the sound of Mrs Todd's voice. 'Yes, I'm trying to understand this note. I wonder if it would be better to have a piece of paper with boxes on it; assistants could add a tick or cross.' She paused. 'You know, maybe a box if it needs turning up, taking in, or anything else we can think of. And then we'd only need to know by how much.'

Mrs Todd glanced over her shoulder to see Mr Woodford striding out of the sewing room. 'That's not a bad idea.'

Mr Bowman suddenly appeared next to them. 'Ah, Miss Spencer, I need a word.' He turned to Mrs Todd. 'Maybe you could do that alteration while I speak to Miss Spencer.' He took the dress from Rose and handed it to Mrs Todd.

Rose's gaze shifted between Mr Bowman and Mrs Todd. 'I'm sure I can do it after you've spoken to me, unless of course you're going to give me the sack.' She gave a nervous laugh as she looked back at him.

Mrs Todd frowned. 'No, you may be employed as a seamstress and I may be senior but Mr Bowman is in charge of us all so if he wants me to alter the dress then that is what I must do.' She pursed her lips. 'I'm quite sure he has no intention of sacking you.'

'No I don't. I just want to talk in the office about some future designs I'm working on.' He threaded his arm through Rose's and turned her in the direction of his office.

Rose's whole body tensed at his overfamiliarity. She took a breath and his citrus and woody perfume hit the back of her throat. Her throat tightened as she tried to stop the cough from escaping, but it wasn't long before the raspy noise broke free.

Mrs Todd watched them go into the office.

'Are you all right?' Mr Bowman pushed the door shut as he followed Rose inside.

Startled by the thud, Rose glanced over her shoulder, wondering why the door was shut. 'Yes, thank you. Something just caught in the back of my throat.' She fought the urge to add that he wore too much scent. Instead she turned back and gazed at the many material samples and sketches, which were strewn all over the desk. In awe of what she was privileged to be part of, she turned and peered out of the window and into the busy sewing room. There was no sound of the sewing machines or the murmur of voices. She looked back into the office, and at the walls holding pictures of different styles of clothes. 'All this must give you great inspiration, Mr Bowman. I mean being surrounded by wonderful fabrics and drawings.'

Mr Bowman walked around the desk. 'I must admit I do find it more difficult these days to come up with something different. I get there in the end; it just takes me longer these days.'

Rose looked back out at the sewing room and caught Mrs Todd staring in their direction. 'Do you ever have help with your designs; that is, if you don't mind my asking?'

Mr Bowman frowned. 'Unfortunately, Miss Spencer, not everyone has your design eye so it tends to be rather a lonely task.'

Rose nodded. 'I know what you mean, but Mrs Todd seems to have quite an eye for clothing and Marion, I mean Miss Simpson, wants to learn too.'

Mr Bowman looked down at his desk, fidgeting from one foot to the other. 'Yes well, Miss Simpson is employed here as a sales assistant, and Mrs Todd doesn't have the imagination she thinks she has so she will always be a seamstress and nothing more. You, on the other hand, have a great eye for detail and I want to make use of it. After all, that's what brought you here in the first place.' He grinned as he indicated the chair next to his desk.

Rose sat down, again thinking of his earlier conversation she'd overheard with Mr Woodford. She frowned as she waited for Mr Bowman to say what was on his mind, watching him prowl restlessly before closing the curtains at the sewing room window. 'Is that necessary?'

'Most definitely – we don't want anyone stealing our designs, do we?'

Rose's eyes narrowed. Who could see the drawings through the window? None of it made sense. It begged the question: how did her designs get into the hands of Dickens and Jones? She shook her head; she hadn't met Mr Bowman before Kitty's wedding and didn't recall ever seeing him at the theatre. No, the only people she knew who could have connected the two were either Kitty or Miss Hetherington. She was confident Kitty was too supportive to have done it. That left Miss Hetherington. Everything seemed to point back to her.

Mr Bowman walked back around the desk and sat down on the large padded chair. 'Now, I have done some sketches so tell me what you think of these.' He passed over some loose pages that had drawings with little notes attached to them.

Rose stretched out her hand and took the papers from him, immediately recognising them. Although none of it was in her handwriting.

Mr Bowman stared at her. 'Is everything all right?'

Rose could feel the colour draining from her face. 'Yes, yes of course. I just thought for a moment I recognised them, but I must be mistaken.'

Mr Bowman jumped up. 'Indeed, that's not possible when they are brand-new designs.'

Rose quickly shook her head. 'Of course, I'm obviously getting confused.'

Mr Bowman slowly sat back down again. 'I should hope so. I can't have you working here if you are going to throw doubt on my work. My reputation is everything.' His nostrils flared. 'None of you people would have a job if it weren't for me. I'll not stand by and let you ruin that. Nor will I allow Mr Woodford to think you are the saviour of the ladies' department. I heard him admiring the gown you were working on, and trust me he'll think differently when he hears about the pearls.'

Panic trampled across Rose's face. 'Of course not. I'm sorry, that wasn't my intention. The sketches just look familiar.' She glanced down again at the paper. 'I brought in one of my pads to show you. I thought it was the least I could do after you helped me out paying for the pearls.'

Mr Bowman grinned. 'Excellent. I'm glad you are finally realising we are a team. I shall take a look when we have finished here.'

Rose noticed his smile didn't reach his eyes. 'What would you like me to do?'

Mr Bowman's face lit up in a way she hadn't seen since she had started working there. 'I just wanted your professional opinion.' He picked up a couple of fabric samples. 'I wondered whether you could add something to them or had a view on the sort of material that we should use.'

Rose pushed open the creaking front door to the refuge. After dropping the bags of clothing she was carrying, she turned to thrust the long length of string back through the letterbox. The key rattled against the wood as it fell. The walls of the hall were white with no pictures or mirrors on them. 'Hello?' Rose shouted as she removed her gloves and coat. She opened the large cupboard that dominated the narrow space and hung it up before closing the door again.

Ruby came striding towards Rose, wiping her hands down her apron at the same time. 'Rose, I thought I heard the door. I wasn't expecting to see you today, not that I'm complaining.'

'No, I hadn't planned to come, especially not straight from work but then I thought why not; after all, the men are probably waiting for their clothes.'

Ruby smiled. 'Ah, bless you; you're a good girl. You must be so tired. You never seem to stop.'

'Don't worry about me. I'm enjoying doing my bit to help.' Rose breathed into her hands and rubbed them together. 'It's freezing outside. It wouldn't surprise me if it snows later.'

'I'm sorry the fire's not lit yet. I'm trying to keep track of my spending more and save money where I can. Everything is getting so expensive, and that includes coal.'

'Yes, we've noticed prices going up. It makes you wonder how we're all going to survive this war.' Rose turned around and picked up the bags she had dropped when she first came in. 'Anyway, I've done these alterations. I hope they're all right but if not I can correct them.'

'Thank you, you're a godsend.' Ruby paused. 'A friend of yours has taken a room here. He tells me he's doing some washing up in a restaurant so he can pay me a little for his rent. Bless him; he can't afford to pay anything really. It's such a shame because he appears to be desperate to look after himself. Although, I can't help feeling there's more to it than that.'

Rose's eyes widened. 'Do you mean Michael?'

Ruby beamed. 'That's right.'

Rose shook her head. 'We did say he could stay with us for free but he's a proud man, too proud to take what he considers to be charity.'

Ruby nodded. 'There's a lot like that; in fact I'd say more than not. The trouble is they feel worthless with nothing to offer.'

Rose's lips tightened. 'He practically said as much to me, but don't they understand it should be us thanking and looking after them after everything they've sacrificed?'

'I agree but they don't seem to see it that way.'

Rose shook her head and picked up one of the bags. 'Peter also gave me a bag of fruit and vegetables for you. There's not loads but hopefully it will help.'

'Oh bless him. You're all so kind. I've never met Peter and yet he's donated food. It was certainly a lucky day for us when Oliver brought you here.'

Rose blushed. 'Peter has a stall on the market. I keep hoping he and Annie will get married soon.'

Ruby nodded. 'Bless them, here's hoping; after all, who doesn't love a wedding?'

Rose frowned. For the first time she allowed herself to dare to wonder what her own wedding to Charlie would have been like. She shook her head as sadness engulfed her. She didn't want to think about it. That wedding was no longer going to be and she chased her thoughts to the corner of her mind. She needed to concentrate on others and not on her own loss. There was nothing to be gained from thinking about such things. 'It's all quite sad. To think they thought it would all be over by Christmas. They couldn't have got that more wrong. Here we are over a year later and there doesn't seem to be any end in sight.'

Ruby reached out and threaded her arm through Rose's. 'It's best we don't think about it, lovey. All we can do is try to help those who need it the most.'

Rose patted Ruby's hand. 'You're right. It's depressing if we think about it for too long.' She took a breath. 'Right, what can I do to help?'

'Hello, I thought I recognised that voice.' Michael beamed from the end of the hall.

'Michael, how lovely to see you. We've been worried about you.' Rose grinned. 'But, I'm so pleased you have a room here. Make sure you look after Ruby.'

'Always.' Michael grinned at his landlady before frowning back at Rose. 'I didn't mean to make you worry. I assumed Joyce would tell you.' He walked towards them.

Rose nodded. 'Joyce told us you were working at the restaurant, but never mentioned where you were living, and Annie hadn't seen you at the theatre. I didn't think – I should have checked again with Joyce.'

'Let me take that. It looks heavy.' Michael reached out and took the bag of food from Rose. He glanced at Ruby. 'I'll put it in the kitchen.'

'Thank you, Michael. I'll come and make us all a cuppa.'

Michael stepped aside so Ruby could get past him. 'Joyce kindly gives me a loaf to bring home every day and sometimes we get pies as well.'

Rose beamed. 'She never said, but I'm not surprised – she has a good heart. I'm glad you've found somewhere to live.'

Michael nodded. 'I'm lucky Ruby doesn't turn anyone away.'

Ruby chuckled. 'We no longer have a sitting room; it's got four single beds in it. I need to find someone to do some building work so the men can have some privacy.'

'I don't think you should worry too much about that.

We're just glad to be off the street, especially in this weather.' Michael moved the shopping bag to his other hand.

Rose nodded. 'How are George and Jack?'

Ruby glanced over her shoulder. 'They are out looking for work at the moment but they are doing well. I particularly worry about Jack because any sudden noise and he's unable to cope, so I'm not sure he will ever find work.'

Rose's eyes widened. 'Yes, I remember that from the first time I came here with Oliver. I must admit it scared me a little but I didn't know what to do to help him.'

Ruby held the kettle under the tap and twisted it to turn it on. The water gushed out, rattling against the inside of the metal kettle, bouncing off its sides as it filled up. 'All you can do is try and reassure him. He usually calms down after a while. The trouble is those noises put Jack, and others like him, back on the front line. I can't help worrying what the future holds for him and Brian.'

Michael dropped the bag onto the table, and potatoes began to roll out. He quickly grabbed the handles and the potatoes. 'Sorry.' He picked the bag up again and propped it against the larder door.

Rose looked pensive for a moment. 'Perhaps we could find out what interested them before the war and then we might be able to find someone who's sympathetic and prepared to give them both a chance.' She sighed. 'Charlie would have helped. He would have taken Jack on to help repair the bicycles. He was all about the community.'

Ruby reached out and squeezed Rose's arm. 'You do know you can't help everyone? I'm not saying Jack can't be helped but he has limitations to what he can do. For example, he can't work outside because the cars and vans would be too much for him, or even inside if there's likely to be any sudden noises. I can't imagine Brian will ever be able to work again. The war has left him so volatile and to be honest I can't see how that will change anytime soon.'

Rose nodded as she remembered his distrust verging on anger when she first went there with Oliver. 'But there must be something. We've got to try or at least give it some thought.'

Ruby smiled. 'Anyway, I'm so glad you're here. I wanted to extend my thanks for saving the men from starving when I wasn't well over Christmas.'

Rose beamed at the small grey-haired lady. 'I can assure you it was our pleasure to help where we could.'

'Well, the men have been very good.' Ruby leant in and lowered her voice. 'They're helping around the house where they can, although some of them are quite limited in what they can do but it all helps.'

Rose stepped forward and hugged Ruby. 'That's wonderful news.'

Ruby smiled and stepped back. 'It made me think though. It's all right me providing them with a roof over their heads but they need to learn to look after themselves – you know, work, cook, and clean.'

Rose chuckled. 'Good luck with that. My ma's been trying to get my brothers to do that for years. Although, I expect now she would do anything to have them back home again.'

Sadness crept across Ruby's face.

'Sorry, I didn't mean to speak out of turn.'

Ruby shook her head. 'There's no need to be sorry. Thanks to this war we've all lost someone, and these men feel like they've lost everything. Some are too injured to get their old jobs back. To be honest I don't know what to do to help them.' She paused. 'If I do nothing they will always be dependent on places like this and that's not what I want.'

Rose pursed her lips. 'You're already doing a grand job but I'll put my thinking cap on and see what ideas I can come up with.'

Ruby forced a smile. 'Thank you, any help is gratefully received.'

Rose lowered her eyes, studying the grain of the kitchen table. 'Have you spoken to Oliver about it?'

Ruby nodded. There was a clatter of crockery as she grabbed the cups from the cupboard. 'Only in passing. He's a lovely, kind man and does so much good already. He's always so busy that I'm grateful he comes here at all. The men couldn't afford medical bills so his free advice is always welcome.'

Rose looked up as Ruby placed the teapot on the table, quickly followed by the cups. 'Have you known him long?'

Ruby sighed and closed her eyes. 'I was a friend of his late wife's mother.' Her eyes snapped open and she smiled. 'The family doctor wasn't available. I can't remember why, so I ended up delivering his little girl; of course Oliver wasn't a doctor then. When his wife became ill I think he felt quite useless – you know, unable to help, so when she died he trained to become a doctor.'

Rose stared down at her cup. 'I didn't know.'

Ruby took the lid off the teapot, and clattering the spoon against the china, she vigorously stirred the hot brown liquid inside. 'Why would you? He's a good man and he adores Catherine.'

15

The Dickens and Jones' steps to the sewing room were shadows in the darkness of the early morning. Holding her breath, Rose gripped the banister as she tiptoed down the stairs. A thud made her stop and stare over her shoulder. She waited to see if anyone was coming her way while trying to behave like it was normal for her to be in so early in the morning. After all, Mr Bowman was adding pressure to get the outfits finished for the coming season. Biting her lip, Rose slowly pushed open the door at the bottom of the stairs. The door creaked, screaming out in the silence. She wondered why she hadn't noticed the noise it made before.

Rose shivered as the cold March morning caught up with her. Peering left and right, she tentatively walked in and looked around. 'Thank goodness, no one seems to be down here.' Walking on tiptoes, fearing her heels would be heard clattering on the floor tiles, Rose pushed open Mr Bowman's office door. Again she looked over her shoulder before stepping into his office to stand by his desk. She glanced around at the many books on the shelves and the paperwork stacked high on, and around, his desk. Nothing obvious stood out to her, but she was aware she didn't want to get caught rummaging through his things.

She took the couple of steps nearer to the shelves and ran her fingers along the spines of the books; it would be easy to hide a sketch pad amongst them. Five minutes later, she sighed. There was no sign of it. 'I wonder if he would be arrogant enough to leave it in the office, or would he have taken it home?'

Rose walked back to the desk and began lifting pieces of material and paperwork to see what was underneath them but again there was no sketch pad. 'Maybe I've got it wrong, maybe it isn't him.' She shook her head. Her mind was in turmoil. How had all her designs ended up being for sale in this shop? It didn't make sense – none of it did. Walking around the desk, Rose sat in Mr Bowman's chair, looking out into the sewing room. She pulled open the desk drawers one by one. Her fingers rummaged through them but didn't find what she was looking for. She sighed at his many ties and handkerchiefs that were stowed away in his desk.

Maybe she was totally on the wrong track. Was it Mrs Todd? Rose didn't like the thought of that; it left a bitter taste in her mouth. 'No, I can't believe it's her. Something tells me it's Mr Bowman. I've just got to find proof.' Her eyes scanned around the office again but she was running out of places to look. Maybe he'd taken it home – that would be the sensible thing to do.

She moved her legs to push herself out of the chair when her foot hit something hard. Rose bent down to look under the desk to see a box. Was it in there? She peered back up and looked out onto the sewing room. She was still alone. Maybe she'd have time to just have a quick look in the box. Rose pulled the box forward and lifted the lid. Her heart sank at the sight of more paperwork and sashes of material. The paper rustled as she rifled through the many pages. Rose gasped as she came across one that had her name and address on it. Picking it up, she began to read it. It was quite clear she was employed as a seamstress and not a designer. Sighing, Rose ran her gaze over it again. It seemed he had lied to her from the beginning. Her eyes narrowed as she started to look at the other paperwork again. It was all unpaid bills from his tailor, his gentlemen's club, a wine merchant...

'Hello, is someone in the office? Is that you, Alexander?'

Rose held her breath, wondering what she was going to do. Time was getting on and she just needed to come clean to Mrs Todd that she was there. She quickly thrust the paperwork back in the box and replaced the lid before slowly sitting upright to see Mrs Todd standing in the office doorway.

'What are you doing, Miss Spencer?'

Rose took a deep breath. 'I'm sorry, Mrs Todd; it isn't what it looks like. I came in early to try and get some of the work done on the dresses but I couldn't find Mr Bowman's original drawing so I came in here to see if it was on his desk.'

Mrs Todd raised her eyebrows. 'But you weren't looking on his desk – you were under it.'

Rose could feel the colour rush into her cheeks. 'I... er... I was trying to sort my shoe out, I laced it too tight this morning.'

Mrs Todd folded her arms in front of her. 'Well, you shouldn't be in here at all – not without either myself or Mr Bowman.'

'I'm sorry, it won't happen again.' Rose stood up and walked around the desk.

Mrs Todd moved aside to allow Rose to step past her into the sewing room. 'What were you looking for? And don't tell me it was a drawing. I have been watching you and some of your reactions to the dresses tell me something isn't right.'

Rose frowned; her hands clenched by her sides. 'I don't know what you mean, Mrs Todd. I've liked everything I've seen. Mr Bowman is clearly a very clever man.'

Mrs Todd took a step nearer to Rose. 'You know, his last collection was quite spectacular compared to previous ones. I even think he could have been on the verge of losing his job if that collection hadn't been so successful.'

Rose spun round to face Mrs Todd. 'Why are you telling me this?'

Mrs Todd shrugged. 'I don't know. It just feels important that you know. Mr Bowman was beside himself with worry that he wouldn't get you here in time for the next collection. Don't you think that's strange in itself?'

'Maybe, but maybe he was just lacking confidence.'

Mrs Todd laughed. 'Does he strike you as that sort of man?'

Rose shook her head. 'I don't know what you want me to say.'

'I don't want you to say anything, except the truth. You were looking for something. I've been watching you.'

Rose took a deep breath. 'Well, if I'm going to get the sack you might as well know the truth. I was looking for my sketch pad; it had a number seven on the spine and on the front. I have many of them at home and I always number them so I can see if I'm improving. When I worked at the theatre the pad was always with me but then it went missing. I even accused Miss Hetherington of stealing it when she came into work wearing one of my designs, but she told me she had bought it from a shop. I didn't believe her, but since working here I've recognised quite a few of the dresses.' She shrugged. 'I understand if you want to get rid of me. I should have been honest, but the trouble is I don't know who I can trust, or if I was imagining it all.'

Colour began to rise in Mrs Todd's cheeks and her gaze darted around the room. 'You're not going to get the sack. If, and it is only if, Mr Bowman has stolen your work then he should be reported to the board.'

'The trouble is I don't know if he did steal it because I can't figure out how he would have got hold of it from the theatre, so I'm going round and round in circles, which is why I haven't said anything. I can't go around accusing people. I've just gotta get over it.'

Mrs Todd studied Rose for a moment, her eyes narrowing. She coughed to clear her throat. 'How did you feel being in the office when Mr Bowman closed the curtains?'

Colour rushed into Rose's cheeks. 'I don't know why he did that. I did question it, but he said something about the designs being a secret and having to be careful about who saw them.' She shook her head again. 'Not that anyone could see from the sewing room. They were just sketches on his desk.' She paused. 'I don't want you to think anything happened because it didn't.'

Mrs Todd looked pensive and bit down on her lip.

'Is everything all right?'

Mrs Todd took a breath. 'You know I used to think

Mr Bowman was teaching me about design, helping me to improve, but I clearly misunderstood his motives.'

Rose stared at the lady in front of her. 'That's awful, especially if he misled you on purpose. How can you continue to work with him?'

'It's not as simple as just walking away.' Mrs Todd frowned. 'I have to put my own feelings aside. After all, I need the money and my job here.'

Rose shook her head. 'You're a talented lady and you could get work anywhere.'

Mrs Todd's lips tightened. 'This conversation wasn't about me. I just wanted to warn you.'

Rose took a deep breath. 'That's very kind of you, especially as I thought you didn't really want me here in the beginning.'

Mrs Todd's eyes lit up as she chuckled. 'That's called plain old jealousy. Mr Bowman used to talk about you all the time.'

Rose reached out and touched Mrs Todd's arm. 'Please trust me, you have no reason to be jealous on my account. I'm only here because my boyfriend thought I could achieve more than repairing costumes.' She closed her eyes for a moment. 'When he died I felt I owed him to at least try; plus I was very unhappy with the lady who managed me at the theatre. She was quite mean.'

'I'm sorry about your boyfriend, and he was right, you are very talented.' Mrs Todd's eyes narrowed. 'Is that still Miss Hetherington, or has she got married?'

Rose frowned. 'Oh my goodness, don't tell me you know her and I've put my foot in it.'

Mrs Todd threw back her head with laughter. 'I do know

her, but she became withdrawn when she lost the love of her life.'

'I always knew there had to be a reason.' Rose paused. 'But never thought it was that. I can see how easily it could happen, especially when it's unexpected. If it hadn't been for my friends, and Oliver, who knows...'

Mrs Todd reached out and squeezed Rose's hand. 'Jane didn't lose the love of her life in the way you did, as far as I know he's still alive. I believe he had an accident at the boot factory, which caused him to lose half a finger. I don't know what happened to him after that. Her family never thought he was good enough, and she wasn't brave enough to fight for him. I don't know where he is now – it's all quite sad.'

'That's terrible. Why didn't they fight for each other?' Rose shook her head in disbelief. 'Mind you, I ran away from Charlie when he proposed...' She sighed. 'You know there's nothing I wouldn't have done for him, but we tend to think we've all the time in the world and that couldn't be more wrong. I take comfort that he knew I loved him and wanted to marry him before he died.'

Mrs Todd frowned. 'Unfortunately, it's not always possible to change what's been said or done, and that was probably the case with Jane.'

Tears pricked at Rose's eyes. 'That's so sad, and it explains a lot.' She paused. 'I wonder if we could find him? Not that I'd know where to start.'

Mrs Todd shook her head. 'I'm not sure it's wise to interfere with other people's lives. Jane wouldn't thank you after all this time.'

'I've seen a crumpled photo she keeps with her. I did wonder who that was. She got angry when I picked it up.'

Rose's eyes widened. 'I've just remembered Bert told us she dresses up about the same time every year. Do you think that means something to them? Maybe they were going to run away together and something went wrong?'

Mrs Todd smiled. 'I think you're getting carried away.'

Rose laughed. 'Maybe, but wouldn't it make a wonderful love story if they finally found each other again?'

Mrs Todd chuckled. 'Come on, we've got to get on, otherwise we'll be in trouble.'

Rose's excitement bubbled to the surface. 'Maybe you and I could talk to her?'

Mrs Todd's eyes widened. 'There's no chance Jane will talk to us about Michael.'

Mr Bowman's voice bellowed from the sewing room doorway. 'Every time I see you two you're standing around gossiping.'

Rose looked around the Breaking Bread restaurant, remembering how hard everyone had worked to make it happen. Simon's many paintings hung on every wall. The large portrait painting of Joyce with her family was proud and centre on the wall that faced her. She had been so happy back then; her life with Charlie had stretched in front of her. She glanced back at her friend. 'We have all come a long way in the last couple of years. So much has happened, and we're all so grown-up now.' She paused. 'Do you enjoy having your own restaurant? Does it live up to your dream?'

Joyce placed her knife and fork on her plate. 'You're right – a lot has happened.' She looked up and beamed at her friend. 'It's more than I ever thought I would achieve. None of it would have happened without you and my father. You started the ball rolling by telling Simon about my love of cooking, encouraging me to follow my dreams when I was too scared to think it was possible. You did the same for Annie. You actually told her not to marry your own brother. You have been instrumental in us all achieving the best we can in what we want to do, but what about you, Rose?'

Rose looked down at her half-eaten roast chicken dinner but said nothing.

Annie glanced at Joyce and frowned. 'I know you left the theatre because you couldn't face going back, and I do understand that, but I'm not convinced you're any happier at Dickens and Jones.'

Rose avoided looking at Annie as she took a breath. 'Are you making enough money out of the restaurant to live on, or do you think you'll have to continue baking for Peter's stall?'

Joyce's eyes narrowed; she bit her lip as she studied Rose. 'I don't mind making the pies and the bread for the stall; after all I love baking.' She gave Annie a sideways glance before taking a breath. 'What's going on, Rose? You worry about the men and Ruby but please understand we worry about you in the same way. I know you're not at war, you're not fighting with guns, but you are fighting inside your head and you don't talk about it. I'm not convinced you're happy at work and I know you wanted to do what Charlie thought was best for you but maybe he was wrong.'

Rose scowled as she peered from one young woman to the other.

'Don't look at us like that.' Annie tilted her head to one

side. 'Maybe, just maybe, you misunderstood what Charlie wanted for you?'

Rose shook her head.

Annie sighed. 'I'm not saying Charlie was wrong. I'm just saying he clearly thought you were more capable than repairing theatre costumes, which is definitely true. But maybe he wanted you to find what made you truly happy and I don't think working for Mr Bowman is that.'

Rose raised her eyebrows and took a deep breath. 'I can't help feeling Mr Bowman is not the person everyone thinks he is. He's like Jekyll and Hyde. One minute I'm convinced he has my sketch pad, but I don't know how he's got hold of it and I can't prove it, and the next he's trying to help me.'

Annie frowned. 'In what way? I mean, I know he helped you get the job at Dickens and Jones but that's it, isn't it?'

Rose stayed silent for a moment before whispering, 'And with the broken pearls.'

Annie studied her friend's pale features. 'Of course, he definitely has a real hold over you. There must be something we can do, it can't be as helpless as it seems.'

Joyce looked around the restaurant she was so proud of. 'There must be a way we can find out if he's got your pad or not. Let us help you like you've helped us.'

Annie tapped her finger on her lips. 'I wonder if Mrs Todd could help in some way?'

Rose's mouth dropped open. 'Definitely not. I have no desires to involve anybody else and whatever happens she has to continue working there with him so it wouldn't be fair.'

The girls nodded in agreement.

'Then I don't know how we can find out.' Annie shrugged.

'There must be a way, and let's face it if he's a thief then he should be stopped.'

Rose picked up a fork and pushed her potatoes around her plate. 'The trouble is I don't know where to start. I've even gone in early and searched his office, but I didn't find it. Although, I did find my details and I was hired as a seamstress and not a designer.'

Annie pursed her lips. 'So he's lied to you from the beginning. He's just using you.'

'Mrs Todd caught me, so I told her about my sketch pad.' Rose shrugged. 'She told me that Mr Bowman used her as well, but she didn't say how and I didn't like to ask.'

Joyce watched them both. 'We need a plan; perhaps we could set a trap for him. Maybe Kitty will help us; after all she's always encouraged you so she might be glad to help.'

Annie beamed. 'That's a wonderful idea, Joyce. She could ask Mr Bowman to bring a sketch pad of his ideas with the thought she might pick something from it.'

Rose laughed. 'He would definitely fall for that, but whether he would pop along with one of my books I'm not so sure. You'd like to think he wouldn't be that arrogant.'

Excitement rose in Annie's voice. 'But if he's as bad as Mr Butterworth he'll think he's untouchable so he probably would fall for it. If you don't mind, Rose, I will ask Kitty to help me set the trap?'

Rose studied her friend for a moment. 'I'm not sure it's a good idea to involve others. Let me think about it for a couple of days. After all, I know it's unlikely but Kitty might have given it to him.'

Annie gasped. 'She would never have done such a thing.'

Rose put down her fork. 'I think you are right but the trouble is I don't know who I can trust anymore.'

Joyce nodded. 'I can understand that.'

Rose forced herself to smile. 'On a lighter note, Mrs Todd knows Miss Hetherington very well.'

'Oh my goodness, you didn't put your foot in it did you?' Annie raised her eyebrows. 'You don't want to upset her as well.'

Rose smiled. 'No, although I thought I had.' She closed her eyes for a second, recalling the conversation they had. 'She was telling me how Miss Hetherington had lost the love of her life, and now I know what that feels like it makes me feel a little more sympathetic towards her.'

Annie nodded. 'I do understand that, but I don't think that gives her an excuse to be so horrible to everyone around her. A lot of people lose someone they love, and no one is ever ready for it, but that doesn't give anyone the right to be mean all the time.'

Rose nodded. 'I agree, but he didn't die, which is what I thought happened when she was telling me. Apparently, her parents didn't think he was good enough and she didn't fight for him. I can only guess that she's now full of regret.'

Joyce shook her head. 'That's so sad. I'm assuming she's never married or met anyone else, and that would make it worse.'

'That's what I thought.' Rose sat silently for a moment.

Joyce's eyes narrowed. 'I wondered whether it would be possible to find him, but I wouldn't know where to start.'

'Nor me.' Annie's gaze darted between her friends. 'Maybe she already knows where he is, and wouldn't thank you for bringing him back into her life. After all he may not want to be. He might be married with children by now. You could open up a whole can of worms if you're not careful.'

'I know.' Rose lowered her eyes. 'It just sounds so sad, that I've the urge to do something about it.' She paused. Her eyes narrowed. 'There's more. Mrs Todd said his name was Michael. Do you suppose it could be—'

'Surely not.' Annie gasped.

Rose shook her head. 'It might explain why he's always on the steps of the Lyceum. It would mean he'd be able to see her every day.'

Joyce's eyes widened. 'It can't be him. Surely he would have spoken to her, wouldn't he?'

Rose shrugged. 'He doesn't feel like he has anything to offer anyone, let alone a woman like Miss Hetherington.'

Annie sighed. 'I can't believe it.'

Rose's gaze shifted between her friends. 'When Michael came downstairs at Christmas and had shaved off his beard I thought he looked familiar.' She paused and looked at Annie. 'Do you remember when Miss Hetherington dropped her papers and I picked up a photograph of a young man?'

'Oh yes, she was so angry that you were looking at it.' Annie's mouth dropped open. 'Do you really think Michael is her lost love?'

Rose's lips tightened. 'I don't know, but it would make sense of some things.'

Joyce clapped her hands in front of her. 'Oh my goodness, we need to find out, and if it's true we should try and bring them together.'

Rose smiled at her friend's excitement. 'Mrs Todd said he lost half his finger in an accident in a boot factory, and I noticed that Michael has half a finger on one hand.'

Joyce beamed. 'We definitely need to try and bring them together, and sort out the mess they're making of things.'

Rose sat on the top step outside the Lyceum Theatre next to Michael. The roof of the elegant building gave them some protection from the wind and the rain. It was late afternoon but it was already dark. She lifted her hand to cover her mouth as a yawn escaped. It had been a tiring day at work. Rose couldn't wait for the warmer days and the lighter evenings to arrive. As she sat there it dawned on her there was a time when she couldn't have come to the theatre without weeping about Charlie being ripped away from her so suddenly. She had moved on more than she'd realised.

Michael stared at Rose. 'Are you happy in your new job?'

Rose watched the people walking by, not noticing them sitting on the theatre steps. She shrugged. 'If I'm honest I'm not sure it's for me but I'm doing it for Charlie.'

Michael took a breath. 'But what about what you want?'

Rose frowned as she turned to him. 'I could say the same to you.' She was silent for a moment. 'I have thought about going back home, I have nothing to keep me here. My friends are getting married so their lives will be moving on with children and all that.'

'Is that what you want?'

Rose sighed as she pulled up the collar of her coat. 'That's the trouble – I don't know what I want. It all feels a bit meaningless. Well, apart from altering the men's clothing. I must admit I get a sense of pride at doing my small bit to help someone.'

Michael nodded. 'You need to think about what makes you happy.'

Rose glanced across at Michael. 'And what makes you happy?'

Michael shrugged. 'I'm as happy as I can be sitting here every day watching the world go by. Joyce has given me hope that I might be able to earn enough money to rent my own room.'

Rose's eyes narrowed. 'I think you sit on these steps every day just to try and catch a glimpse of the love of your life but do nothing to talk to her.'

Michael lifted his chin as he stared straight ahead. His voice took on a harsh quality. 'Do I? It sounds like someone's been gossiping.'

Rose shook her head. 'No, no one's been gossiping, but something clearly brings you to the Lyceum every day.'

Michael gave a humourless laugh. 'I can't deny it, but I have nothing to offer her. Trust me when I say don't do what I have done. I wasn't brave enough to fight for the woman I loved and life has passed me by.'

Sadness washed over Rose. 'It's never too late. Look at Arthur and Dot. You don't know them but they lost a child and he took to the drink. In the end Dot left, but they have been given a second chance because they talked, listened and realised the love they felt for each other was more important than money and material things. The trouble is we all get caught up in things and forget what's important. You shouldn't take the choice away from her. You are depriving her when in reality if you really love each other none of it matters.'

Michael sat in silence for a moment before turning to look at Rose. 'I've heard it said that Dr Hardy has a soft spot for you. Apparently he appears to be happier than anyone has ever seen him, and he's never brought anyone to the house before. Are you going to give yourself a second chance at love?'

Rose laughed. 'You men are just romantic fools. You need to find something to occupy your minds.'

Michael eyed her. 'Do you like him?'

Rose listened to the sellers shouting at their barrows for a moment. 'We get on well. He's a kind man, but I don't really know him.'

Michael nodded. 'Is he kind like Charlie was?'

Rose smiled. 'Yes, I suppose he is, although in a very different way.'

'Then you should let him in. Charlie wouldn't expect you to be alone.'

Rose shook her head. 'Oh my goodness, you have a nerve. There's you and Miss Hetherington both miserable, and have been for years, all because you haven't found the courage to talk to each other, never mind anything else.'

Michael gave a wry smile. 'You're right, but that's just it: I don't want you to make the mistakes I have and then have to live with the regrets afterwards.' He paused. 'Life is too short. If I've learnt nothing else I know you have to grab it with both hands and let it take you where it may. Don't waste your time doing things that give no fulfilment. Within reason, you should do what makes you happy.'

Silence sat between them for a while.

Rose looked at Michael. 'Is that what you're doing?'

Michael's lips tightened. 'I deserve that.'

'You don't deserve any of it but you're telling me to do things you're not prepared to do yourself.'

Michael shook his head. 'I suppose what I'm trying to say in my clumsy way is that you're never going to get over losing Charlie. I say that assuming he was your first real love, but you will learn to live with that loss. You're young and shouldn't spend your life avoiding finding a new love. It will never be the same but it might be better. You may not be able to see that now, but if you don't try you will never know.'

Rose stared down the street taking in the everyday tasks that people had to do just to survive. She wondered what secrets they all held close to their hearts. She turned and studied Michael. 'The same could be said for you. Actually, you are more of a coward because Jane is still alive and you've wasted such a lot of time being apart when you could have been happy.' She looked heavenward. 'As you say, and as Charlie used to say, life is too short. It's time you practised what you preach.' She sat lost in her thoughts for a moment. 'I can also say don't make the mistakes I made. It can all be ripped away from you without any warning at all.'

16

The Seven Dials roundabout was just ahead. The clock was just visible in the darkness. A dustbin lid rattled as it hit the ground, almost drowning out the cats hissing and growling at each other as they fought for the rewards. Several dogs barked in the distance, while rain blew in the wind.

Rose tugged at the collar of her coat. 'I know it's April and winter is meant to be over but there's definitely a chill in the air. Oliver, it's lovely of you to walk me home but maybe you should have stayed in the warm with your mother and Catherine.'

Oliver looked across at her all tucked in with a scarf wrapped round her neck and a woollen hat sitting neatly on top of her head. 'You certainly came to my house prepared for the thick of winter. You do know it's spring now, don't you?'

'Of course but I feel the cold, and you must admit the weather isn't wonderful at the moment.'

Oliver chuckled as they walked along side by side. 'Thank you for doing all the alterations. Cat tells me you are doing some of them while you are watching her sew.'

Rose smiled. 'Yes, I might as well. Your daughter is quite independent so I'm only there in case she runs into problems. Now the teddy is finished she wants to learn how to embroider, but I haven't had the chance to sit with her yet.'

Oliver shook his head. 'Don't take any nonsense from her. She likes you a lot but don't let her take advantage of you, because she will.' He paused and gave her a sideways glance. 'I've arranged for a sewing machine to be delivered tomorrow so you don't have to do all the sewing by hand while you're watching Catherine. Hopefully it will make life easier for you.'

Rose gave him a wide-eyed look as she shook her head. 'Please, that expense is not necessary. I'm used to sewing by hand.'

Oliver smiled. 'I thought you would say that but if Catherine carries on enjoying sewing she will eventually start using it. And, anyway, I understand you are there almost as much as I am.'

Rose shook her head. 'My goodness, I don't want people to get the wrong idea.'

Oliver jutted out his chin. 'You know the more I get to know you the more you don't seem like the girl Charlie described to me.'

Rose frowned as she looked up at him. 'Well obviously I don't know what he said but if I am that different, maybe it's just as well we didn't get married.' Her throat tightened as she tried to commit to her words.

'I don't believe you think that for one second. He loved you so much and I know you loved him. There's nothing like the feeling of being with the one person who makes you feel so special. My wife did that for me so I know what you're missing.'

Rose stared down at the wet pavement; the puddles were glistening in the dark. A shiver ran through her as she tried to fight her tears and gather her thoughts. 'Charlie obviously saw me differently than you do.'

Oliver blew out an exasperated breath. It was grey as it hit the cold air and it swirled up into the night sky. 'I think you are the same person who Charlie fell in love with, but I think you have lost yourself with the grief that holds you in place. From what Charlie told me the Rose he knew would take on the world, and didn't care what people thought of her.'

Rose gave a humourless laugh. 'That Rose has gone. Charlie made me believe I could achieve anything I wanted but without the person you love it all seems meaningless.'

Oliver nodded. 'Has she gone to the point that you can't find her, or don't you want to? I have no desires to make life difficult for you; it just feels odd that my daughter is overfamiliar and calling you Rose, and you and I are quite formal at times, and I would like us to be friends.'

Rose gave a faint smile. 'I can see that; maybe your daughter should call me Miss Spencer.'

Oliver gave a hearty laugh. 'Good luck explaining that to her. Have you not noticed my daughter is how you used to be only younger?'

Rose shook her head. 'I don't think that can be the case. Your daughter is a lovely girl and you've obviously done a good job bringing her up, whereas I was always getting into trouble for speaking out of turn.'

Oliver gave her a sideways glance. 'So you are the person that Charlie described to me. So now I would like to ask you to call me Oliver all the time, and, if it's all right with you, I shall call you Rose.'

Rose opened her mouth to speak but said nothing.

'After all, Charlie and I were good friends and he wouldn't expect me to address you formally and neither would he expect you to address me in that way, so in honour of Charlie I think we should work at being less formal and more friendly with each other. I mean, we have spent quite a bit of time in each other's company and I know how relaxed you can be with Cat. I've heard you giggling with her, and that's how I'd like you to be with me. There's no ulterior motive. I know your heart will always be with Charlie just like mine will always be with my wife. I want you to know that I do understand but we can still be friends.'

Rose nodded. 'Thank you. When you put it like that it seems churlish to not agree to it.'

They were both deep in thought as they approached the Seven Dials. 'You know you didn't have to walk me home. I mean, I do appreciate it, but it is quite cold tonight and you have to walk back again.'

Oliver laughed. 'I was brought up to be a gentleman and no gentleman worth his salt would let a young lady walk home by herself at night; plus it gave us a chance to chat without my daughter, or my mother, listening to every word. I don't want you to fret because I'll probably get a taxi home.'

Rose laughed. 'And there was I feeling sorry for you.'

Oliver studied Rose for a moment. 'Trust me when I say

I will never be looking for sympathy from you or anyone else, and I suspect you are exactly the same.'

Rose looked up, not sure what she was seeing in his eyes, but decided not to question it. 'I know it's none of my business but I… I wondered what happened to Catherine. I saw the scars on her back. They look so sore, and I just…'

Oliver's eyes narrowed for a moment. 'I don't think I've ever been so scared, except when my wife died. I don't know how I would have coped if Catherine hadn't needed me.'

'Can I ask what happened? Obviously, if you don't wish me to know then just tell me to mind my own business or shut up. I do understand.'

Oliver stopped walking and took both her hands in his. 'We were at the Lyceum when the bomb went off.'

Rose gasped. 'I didn't realise.' She closed her eyes for a moment as she was transported back to the sight, sounds and smells of that terrible evening. She bit her lip while her mind relived the aftermath of the explosion. Her emotions caught her out and tears immediately ran down her cheeks.

Oliver pulled her in close; her body shuddered against his as the grief she had held together for months racked her body. He stroked her back as he held her tight. His tone was low when he spoke. 'It's going to be all right. Let it all out. I won't let you go.'

Rose could feel the whispers of his breath on her neck and knew she should pull away but found comfort in his soft coat and his safe arms as she held on to him. 'I'm sorry.' She sniffed. His musky scent wrapped itself around her. 'I don't know where that came from.'

Oliver held her tight, and Rose didn't struggle. 'It's called grief. It catches us unawares and sometimes it's the slightest thing that sets us off.'

Rose pulled back slightly; she looked up with red blotchy eyes and a tear-stained face. 'I'm sorry, it was so painful to think about I decided to try and block that night from my mind.' She sniffed. 'I didn't realise you were there. You never said.'

Oliver shook his head. 'I couldn't bring myself to talk to you about it. You were reliving it in every waking hour; you certainly didn't need me to remind you of it.' He lifted his hand and stroked her cheek, gently wiping away the dampness her tears had left behind. His gaze didn't leave her face.

Rose no longer had the urge to talk but the alternative was too dangerous, and she guessed he didn't either. She stepped away, breaking the spell that held them together.

Oliver cleared his throat. 'Catherine was knocked unconscious and ended up half buried under debris. Thankfully I was only slightly hurt so I managed to dig her out and carry her to my car to get to the hospital.'

Rose shook her head as she remembered the scars on Catherine's back. How quick she had been to judge him. Thank goodness she hadn't mentioned it. She ran her gloved fingers over her eyes, the wool scratching at her skin. 'Charlie was buried as well. He told me to run and I did thinking he was behind me but he wasn't. He had stayed to make sure everyone got away; he stayed to save others.'

Oliver nodded. 'I know. It must have been him I heard shouting but at the time I didn't make the connection. It was only afterwards, when the ringing in my ears stopped and I had time to think about it. It was thanks to Charlie that Catherine was saved.' He paused and closed his eyes as he relived that night. 'I will always be grateful to him, and I'm so sorry he didn't make it. I should have stayed, but all I could think about was getting Catherine to hospital.'

'I never realised. It would have been awful for you to have lost your wife *and* your daughter.' Rose frowned as she stepped away from Oliver. 'Wait, was it you I saw running with her in your arms? The child looked limp and was wearing a bright yellow dress. It was the brightness that caught my attention, but not for long because I was worrying about Charlie.'

Oliver lowered his arms; he folded them tight in front of him. 'Yes, that was me and Catherine was definitely limp in my arms. She had run on ahead to get a drink.' He shook his head and sucked in his breath. 'I might be a doctor but I was convinced I was gonna lose her that night.'

'I'm so sorry. I've been quite selfish making it all about me.' Rose thrust her hand through his arm, and squeezed it tight.

Oliver clasped his hand over hers. 'Not at all – you've been grieving, and that's very different.'

Rose looked up at Oliver. 'I'm glad she came through it, and her scars will fade with time.'

Oliver nodded. 'She's been through a lot, but she's here and that's all that matters.'

Rose glanced at him. 'Charlie really did die a hero when he managed to get people away from the theatre. My friends kept telling me that but I suppose I was too upset with him for not following me when he told me to run to see it. It's time I started feeling proud of him instead of feeling so alone and lost.'

Oliver nodded, and they carried on walking in silence. 'When I thought we might have a chat while I walked you home I didn't mean for it to get so serious. I'm so sorry I made you cry.'

Rose gave a faint smile. 'You didn't. It's this whole situation. Innocent people are dying, or coming back injured in many different countries and for what? I don't suppose there's many families that aren't touched by this war.'

'Well, we're here, Oliver. Thank you for walking me home.' Rose paused. She could feel the colour rising up her neck as she remembered sobbing in his arms. 'I'm sorry I cried all over you.'

Oliver shook his head. 'Don't be embarrassed or sorry. It's good to get it all out of your system and I'm here whenever you feel the need.' He stood at the end of the path and gazed up at the house. 'It's quite late – at least later than I realised.'

'Yes, the time certainly flew by.' Rose shivered as the wind whipped around her. 'Before I go in I just want to say thank you for all your help with everything. I'm sure Charlie would be pleased with what you've done, and as unexpected as it was I really appreciate it.'

Oliver frowned. 'It's been my honour and I'm sure Charlie would have done the same if the roles had been reversed.' He smiled. 'Anyway, it's the least I can do, especially now you've been manipulated into teaching Catherine to sew.'

Rose smiled. 'I don't mind. She's lovely and eager to learn.'

Oliver's chin dipped down as he studied the ground in front of him. 'Listening to her sometimes I think I've spoilt her, but she's my life so it's hard not to.' He cleared his throat and looked up. 'Now I know exactly where you live I can drop the alterations round or, of course you can pick them up from my house, if you don't mind being kidnapped by my daughter.' He chuckled.

Rose nodded.

'Would you like me to see you in, or will you be all right?'

Rose smiled. 'No, thank you, the girls will have a field day if I walk in with a man.' She laughed. 'Their imaginations would run away with themselves.'

Oliver chuckled. 'I have a mother who's exactly the same. She can't wait to marry me off again even though I say I'm not interested.'

Rose looked up at him. 'I'm sure she means well; after all, that's what mothers do.' She glanced over her shoulder at the house. 'I'd better get inside before they come out looking for me.' She laughed. 'Besides which, you still have the walk home.'

Oliver nodded but didn't move to walk away. 'I hope you now feel you can talk to me as a friend.'

Rose remembered the feel of his arms around her and colour flooded her cheeks. 'Thank you, although I'll try not to cry all over you next time.'

'If the need arises my shoulder is always available.' Oliver smiled. 'Maybe I'll see you at the house, or at the refuge.' He reached out and took her hand in his. 'Please remember you're not on your own so don't feel that you are.' He squeezed her hand before letting go. 'I suppose I should go.'

Rose nodded. 'And I should go inside.'

They both stood there for a moment, waiting for the other to make the first move.

Oliver gave a small chuckle. 'I'm definitely going now.' He turned to walk away, and then stopped and looked over his shoulder. 'Goodnight, I'll see you soon.'

Rose lifted a hand to wave. 'Goodnight, take care going home.'

Oliver waved before walking away.

Rose pushed open the letterbox and pulled out the string. The key clattered against the inside of the door as she pulled it through. She pulled off a glove and her fingers gripped the cold metal of the key and inserted it in the lock. It grated as she turned it. She pushed against the door to open it. She leaned against it and the hinges groaned as it flew open. The cold air rushed in, filling every nook and cranny. Rose quickly removed the key, and pushed it back through the letterbox and shut the door. Leaning against it, she closed her eyes and tried to figure out what had happened.

'Ah, Rose, I've been waiting for you to get home.'

Rose's eyes snapped open at the sound of Annie's voice.

Annie frowned. 'You haven't been working at Dickens and Jones until now have you? If you have that's worse than being at the theatre.'

Rose shook her head and began to undo the buttons of her coat. 'No, I've been round at Dr Hardy's house, teaching his daughter to sew and doing some alterations while I was there.'

Annie watched Rose closely. 'That's good. What is she sewing?'

'She was so excited when she made a pink teddy, which

was a good start and something she can be proud of, but now she wants to learn to embroider.'

Annie laughed. 'You're not teaching her to darn then?'

Rose chuckled. 'I have a feeling Catherine will never have to darn anything in her life.'

Annie nodded. 'You're probably right, but it's still a good skill to learn and you never know when fortunes might change.'

'That's true.' Rose slipped her coat off and hung it on the peg.

Annie reached out and picked up a wad of envelopes that had been sitting on the console table next to the church candle. 'I have some exciting news. All of these letters arrived for you today.' She waved them around in front of her.

Rose's eyes widened. 'Oh my goodness, they're not from my brothers are they?'

Annie passed the envelopes over to her. 'You'll have to open them to find that out.'

Rose flicked through the envelopes, fanning them out to examine them. 'I recognise the handwriting. Thank goodness, I was beginning to think they'd forgotten about me.'

Annie stepped forward and wrapped her arms around her friend. 'They could never forget about you, Rose, you're their little sister, and anyway once met never forgotten.'

Rose stepped back and tore open the top envelope. She quickly pulled out the single sheet of paper and unfolded it. 'Oh my goodness, it is from my brother.'

Dear Rose,

I hope you are keeping well, Ma tells me that you are enjoying London. Please try and keep safe. I don't want to get a letter to say I've lost a sister. Thank you for the parcels that we receive with great regularity. We all share the chocolate so everybody gets a lift from it. The socks that you knit are always welcome, even though they look a little strange. I'm afraid I can't tell you where we are, but I can tell you we are all safe, well as safe as we can be in the trenches. We are often knee-deep in water, and very cold, so the change of socks is a real welcome. I also wear the scarf that you sent me because it's really cold. The book you sent is doing the rounds. We often swap and share the things we receive.

I'm afraid I don't have much to tell. We have to be careful in case our letters are read and also in case they get into the hands of the enemy. I miss you and the family like crazy. What I wouldn't do to be on the farm right now. Hopefully, it won't be long before we are all home and digging up those fields that we used to moan about so much. Stay safe, little one, and I will write again soon, I promise. Please keep sending the parcels, as we all love them.

Lots of love, your darling brother, John xx

Rose swiped her fingers across her face. She hadn't realised she had been crying as she read the letter. 'Oh, Annie, at least they're safe and that's all that matters right now.'

Every movement since Rose had got up that morning had been a great effort. Her bloodshot eyes and the dark lines under them hadn't escaped her attention as she had stared at her reflection in the bedroom mirror. She had sat up most of the night reading and rereading the letters from her brothers. She was pleased they were getting the parcels she sent every week. Although her mother had written to her and told her they were very happy with them she had never understood why they hadn't written to her themselves. A smile spread across her face as she realised they had and she'd just not received them until now.

Rose unbuttoned her coat as she walked into the sewing room of Dickens and Jones. She hung her coat on the peg and unwrapped the scarf from around her neck before thrusting her hand inside the coat pocket to pull out her clean white handkerchief. A couple of small pearls fell out. Gasping, she remembered when the necklace fell apart and finding them on the floor when she was going home. She had frantically picked them up and hidden them in her pocket. She looked around hoping no one had noticed before quickly bending down to pick them up. Sighing, she ran her fingers round the small beads and felt a small chip in one of them. Raising her hand, she scrutinised it and realised the coating was coming away. It wasn't a pearl at all! How could that be? Why did Mr Bowman tell her they were?

'Miss Spencer.'

Rose jerked round at the sound of her name and saw Mr Bowman staring at her. Her heart sank; she didn't feel able to be bubbly today. 'Good morning, Mr Bowman, did you want to see me?' She thrust the fake pearls into her coat pocket.

'You look tired. I hope that's not going to affect your work. Come into the office.'

Rose shook her head. 'It won't, sir.' Her eyes widened as

she thought about saying more but she bit her tongue and decided against it.

Mr Bowman studied her for a moment. 'That's good. I don't feel I've made the most of you since you've been here so I think it's time to correct that.' He turned to walk away from her. 'Follow me.'

Rose groaned. 'Yes, sir.'

Mr Bowman entered the office, and immediately walked over to the window that allowed him to look into the sewing room. He pulled the curtains shut.

Rose watched him go through his now familiar routine. 'Is it necessary to close the curtains? After all, we're all working for the same company.'

Mr Bowman arched his eyebrows as a disdainful look trampled across his face. 'You have no idea how easy it is for people to steal your ideas.'

Rose's eyes narrowed as she studied him. 'You'd be surprised at what I know.'

Mr Bowman cleared his throat and marched around to his side of the desk. 'Well, we're not here to discuss what you know; we're here to discuss the new designs that are due out in a few months.'

Rose nodded and her gaze fell on the rolls of material that were astride his desk, and the sketches that she had seen the last time she was in this office. 'What is it you'd like me to do?'

Mr Bowman picked up pieces of paper and put them back down again. He moved material this way and that, concentrating on his desk. 'I want you to work with Mrs Todd to get the garments finished on time.'

Rose looked at him, unsure how to react. 'Have you spoken to Mrs Todd about this?'

Mr Bowman shook his head. 'No, not yet, but she's very good at what she does and I'm sure she'll support you.'

Rose gasped. 'Support me? Surely it should be me supporting her?'

Mr Bowman's eyes narrowed as he stared at her. 'I don't think you understand your position here. I want you to design clothes, so Mrs Todd will support you.'

Rose glanced over her shoulder at the closed curtains before looking back at him. 'I'm sorry, sir, I have no desires to tread on her toes and she thinks I'm employed as a seamstress, not a designer, so I would rather support her.'

Mr Bowman glared at her. 'This isn't about what you would prefer; this is business and Mrs Todd will do as she is instructed, as indeed will you.'

Remembering the paperwork she'd found in the box under the desk, Rose took a deep breath. She opened her mouth to argue against his decision but decided against it, recognising she had the ability to antagonise him without really trying.

'Now, Miss Spencer, if you would like to call Mrs Todd in, it's time to get started.' Mr Bowman watched her reluctantly walk towards the door.

Rose peered over her shoulder before twisting the handle to open it. She stepped into the sewing room and walked over to Mrs Todd. 'I'm sorry to bother you, but Mr Bowman would like to see us both.' Rose noticed Mrs Todd's expression gave nothing away as she walked towards the office.

Mrs Todd stepped through the open doorway, quickly followed by Rose. 'You wanted to see me, Mr Bowman?'

Mr Bowman looked up. 'Yes, come in.' He waved his hand, beckoning them in. 'Come on, shut the door.' He stared at Mrs Todd. 'I would like you to support Miss Spencer in getting this new line ready to show in a couple of months. I don't have to tell you how important this is and we need to get it right, so I want you to work together and run me up the first versions of the garments. I don't want either of you working on alterations or anything else. This has to take priority.' He picked up a couple of the sketches that were sitting on his desk. 'Obviously, patterns will need to be cut as well, and it goes without saying none of these designs should be discussed or shown in a public area, not even to our own seamstresses.'

Mrs Todd nodded. 'I do know what needs to be done. I've worked on new lines for several years and in the past we have been quite successful, particularly the last season's dresses you designed.'

Rose frowned. 'Mrs Hardy showed me some dresses as samples of styles that she liked. I wonder if they were from your last season's design?'

Mrs Todd peered at her. 'Mr Bowman's designs are still available upstairs in the shop.'

'Yes, yes, we're not here to discuss last season's designs; we're here to get to work on the new ones so can we have less talking and more doing. I have work to do so I'm going to leave you two to work together.' Mr Bowman walked around his desk towards the office door. 'And when I get back I hope to see some progress.' He turned the handle of the door and pulled it open, grabbing his hat as he marched into the sewing room.

Rose bit her lip as she glanced over at Mrs Todd. 'I'm happy for you to lead the way and I will follow your instructions.'

Mrs Todd's lips tightened. 'Oh no, you heard what he said.'

Rose jutted out her chin and pulled back her shoulders. 'To be honest, I don't care what he said. I have never produced new designs for a shop. I have no idea what's involved and you do, so I think it's important you take the lead and if I have any questions I'll ask them but we need to work together.'

Mrs Todd gave a faint smile. 'That's very kind of you to say so, but I have no desire to get on the wrong side of Mr Bowman.'

Rose chuckled. 'Nor I. That just means we need to be careful about what we say and how we say it. He doesn't need to know the detail of how we make our decisions. I would like us to work together to get the job done.'

Mrs Todd raised her eyebrows. 'You've got some backbone – I'll say that for you.'

Rose shrugged. 'So I've been told, but I do believe I lost it for a while; however, it's time I found it again.' She picked up the sketches that Mr Bowman had piled together on the desk. She stared at them, struggling to keep her dismay hidden at the familiar drawings. 'I suppose we have to decide on the parts needed to make up these garments and cut out the pattern.' She passed them over to Mrs Todd. 'How do you want to do this? Should we work on one garment together, or should we do a garment each?'

Mrs Todd looked at all the sketches in turn. 'Mr Bowman's excelled himself this year. They look really good and not like anything he's ever produced before.' She dropped the pieces of paper onto the desk. 'I am happy to do either but maybe, for speed purposes, we should try and take a garment each and come together to discuss any problems we have.'

Rose nodded. 'That sounds like a good idea. I also think if we feel they can be improved in any way we should also discuss that as well. After all, Mr Bowman made it plain to me this morning that he bought me here to design, so that is what I shall do.'

17

Rose pushed open the front door of the refuge, screwing up her face as the hinges creaked. 'Ruby, it's Rose. I can't stop as I'm going to be late for work.'

'Stop, listen to yourself.' Ruby's nervous voice rang out from the kitchen.

Rose stood frozen for a moment.

Rose wondered if she should leave. She didn't want to intrude on their personal lives. But what if it was more than that? Ruby could be in trouble.

'Ruby, stay out of it,' a man's deep voice shouted out. 'He comes in here and starts painting walls. I see him giving you money when none of us can. He has no idea what it's like for the rest of us.'

'Look, Brian, I was only trying to help Ruby. I'm very grateful for her not turning me away, for giving me a chance to improve my life. And if the pittance I give helps then that's a good thing isn't it? Doesn't it help all of us?'

Rose gasped and held her breath as she tiptoed nearer to the kitchen door. It sounded like Michael. She looked around wondering what she could do. Should she do anything? Ruby's words bounced to the forefront of her mind. *Brian was volatile.*

'Brian, why don't we sit down and have a cup of tea and I might be able to rustle up a biscuit somewhere?' Ruby spoke in a low whisper. 'You know I can't have you here if it's going to be trouble; life is hard enough as it is. We all have to get on for this to work.'

Brian growled. 'I don't think you understand, Ruby; this man has come in and taken over. We were happy until he arrived, and I know I'm not the only one who feels like that. The difference is no one else is saying anything.'

The floorboard creaked as Rose took another step forward. She held her breath, fearful that Brian would come running into the hall.

'I'm sorry, Brian, that was never my intention.' Michael paused. 'I don't think you understand how grateful I am, so I was just trying to repay that kindness. I certainly didn't mean to tread on anyone's toes.'

Ruby cleared her throat. 'Brian, I'm going to put the kettle on. I beg you to put the knife down because no good can come of this.'

'No, Ruby, he's got to go.'

Rose jerked as a hand rested on her shoulder. She froze, wondering who it was.

'Rose, what's going on? Why are you standing here looking so worried?' Jack's voice whispered in her ear, his breath tickling as he spoke.

Rose spun around on her heels. 'Thank goodness, Jack; I don't know what to do. I think Brian's got a knife, but I'm not sure. He wants Michael to leave. He's saying none of you are happy with him because he's come and taken over.'

Jack shook his head. 'Brian shouldn't be living here. I

know I have issues but Brian is different altogether.' He paused, tilting his head to listen. 'I'll go in there and see what I can do.'

Rose grabbed his arm. 'Please, don't put yourself at risk. It's bad enough Ruby and Michael are stuck in there.'

Jack's lips tightened. 'Don't worry, we can't stand here in the hall and wait until Brian's committed murder. Wait here and I'll try and sort it out.' He took a step forward and pushed open the kitchen door. 'Hello, what's going on here then?'

Rose stepped forward so she had sight of the room now the door was wide open.

Brian waved the large kitchen knife around. 'Get out, Jack. This has nothing to do with you.'

Jack shook his head. 'I have to say, Brian, I disagree, and you're waving a knife around in front of Ruby.'

Brian stared at Jack. 'I would never hurt Ruby. She's a saint. But I have to protect her from the likes of him.'

Jack frowned. He quietly took another step forward. 'What does that mean, from the likes of him? Michael's all right – he's only ever tried to help Ruby. You need to put the knife down before any real harm is done.'

'Don't come any nearer, Jack. I don't want to hurt you but I can't let him stay here any longer. Look at him – he's got a job and he's wearing nice clothes. He's a real ladies' man, ain't that right, Ruby?'

Ruby took a deep breath. 'Brian, I don't know what you're talking about. Michael is wearing the same clothes that you wear. Rose has altered them to fit him properly just like she did yours, remember?'

Brian's eyes narrowed as he waved the knife around. He

moved his head from side to side. 'You're making it up, Ruby. You're already taking his side.'

Jack took another step forward. 'Ruby's not making it up, Brian. Please don't let everything that's happening confuse you. Rose altered all our clothes, including yours.'

Michael pulled back his shoulders and stared at Brian. 'I'm not a ladies' man. I have only ever loved one woman and I only ever will, but it doesn't mean I can't be kind to people. Brian, I'm really sorry you feel I'm wrong to help, and I'll find somewhere else to live if it solves this situation.'

Brian made a humourless noise. 'Of course you will. Why would you do that when you're onto a good thing?' He suddenly lunged forward and plunged the knife into Michael's stomach and pulled it out again.

Ruby and Rose screamed in unison as the crimson blood dripped from the knife to the floor.

Michael dropped like a stone.

Rose ran into the room and knelt down by Michael's crumpled body. 'Jack, we've got to get Michael to the hospital. See if you can find someone who will take us. Be quick.'

Jack stood frozen.

Rose screamed. 'Jack, I know it's difficult but please, you could save this man's life.'

Jack jerked and ran out the kitchen.

The knife clattered to the floor.

Ruby grabbed a towel and pressed it onto the wound. 'We need to press down hard to try to stop him from bleeding to death.'

Rose nodded. 'Stay with me, Michael. We'll soon have you at the hospital.'

Brian dropped to his knees and began to sob.

It was an unusually warm day for May. Rose was breathless when she pushed open the heavy stage door of the Lyceum Theatre.

'Well I never – are you a sight for sore eyes. You look flushed. Are you all right?' Bert jumped up from his chair and opened his arms as he sped towards Rose.

The pain in Rose's chest gripped her as she tried to gulp down the air her lungs were screaming for. 'Hello, Bert.' She gulped. 'It's been a while.'

'Been a while? It feels like it's been forever. I miss seeing your smile around the theatre and finding out what mischief you've been up to.' Bert wrapped his arms around her and squeezed her tight.

Rose nestled against his soft white shirt and breathed in his woody scent. 'Bert, I can't breathe. I need to catch my breath.'

Bert chuckled as he pulled back from her. 'I'm sorry; I'm just so pleased to see you. I take it you didn't rush in just to see me?'

Rose stepped back from Bert and peered up at him. The pain in her chest was slowly easing. 'I've missed you, Bert, and your teddy-bear hugs, and I don't mean to be rude, but can we catch up later?'

Bert raised his eyebrows. 'Of course. What's wrong? And don't say nothing.'

Rose forced herself to smile. 'I've come to see Miss Hetherington.'

Bert frowned. 'They're words I never thought I'd hear you say.'

Rose tightened her lips. 'No, me neither, but I need to speak to her urgently. I promise we will catch up later.'

Bert nodded. 'Well, you get along to the sewing room, not that I can say she's in there.' He smiled. 'And if you can't find her you'll have to chat with me for a while. Kitty and Annie are on stage rehearsing at the moment, at least they were. I shouldn't think they will be long though.'

Rose sighed. 'Do you mind? Only it's important I speak to her.'

'My dear girl, you don't have to ask. You belong here, and this will always be your home.'

Rose stepped forward and gave the man who had become her firm friend and father figure a hug. 'Thank you, Bert, it means a lot to me.'

The clatter of heels coming along the corridor made Rose pull back from Bert. They both looked in the direction of the noise.

Bert's lips tightened. 'I'd know that walk anywhere. Your favourite person is about to be upon us.'

Rose took a deep breath as Miss Hetherington came into view.

Miss Hetherington's eyes narrowed as she gave Rose a cold stare. 'Good day, Miss Spencer, and to what do we owe this pleasure? Have you come looking for your job back again?'

Rose forced herself to smile, reminding herself she was here for Michael. 'No, Miss Hetherington, but I do want to talk to you.'

Miss Hetherington eyed her suspiciously. 'Would you indeed? I can't imagine we have anything to say to each other.'

Rose flexed her hands by her sides. 'No, I would expect that from you but I do have something to say, which you might find interesting.' She turned to look at Bert before glancing back at Miss Hetherington. 'Of course I am quite happy to say what I've got to say here but you might prefer it without an audience.'

Miss Hetherington's expression didn't change. 'I suppose you'd better follow me then. The sewing room is empty at the moment so we can sit in there.' She turned on her heels and began walking back down the corridor.

Rose trotted behind her expecting Miss Hetherington to look back over her shoulder to see if she was following her but she didn't.

Miss Hetherington pushed open the sewing room door and stepped inside. 'Right, what do you wish to see me about if it isn't to get your job back?'

Rose stepped through into the small room; memories of making Kitty's wedding dress and chatting to Dot as they sewed flooded her mind.

'Well?'

Rose smiled. Nothing had changed. 'First, I wanted to say I was sorry for accusing you of stealing my sketch pad.'

Miss Hetherington frowned. 'I should think so too. It's disgraceful how you accused me like that, and especially as you had no evidence apart from the frock I was wearing.'

Rose nodded. 'You're right; I should never have done it. The trouble is, while it's no excuse, I couldn't see how you had one of my designs without the pad. And what's more I didn't believe you when you said you'd bought it. I'm very sorry, and I can't apologise enough.'

Miss Hetherington looked a little stunned at Rose's admission. 'I'm a lot of things but I'm not a thief.' She pulled out the nearest chair and sat down.

Rose also sat down and faced Miss Hetherington. 'I've come to realise that my pad was more than about one single dress, but I can't get to the bottom of it without making more accusations with no proof. Having done that once and been wrong I have no desire to do it again.' She paused as she watched Miss Hetherington. 'The manageress where I work is someone who knows you.'

Miss Hetherington looked straight-faced. 'Really.'

Rose kept her gaze fixed on her old adversary. 'It's Mrs Eileen Todd.'

Colour started to fill Miss Hetherington's face. 'I haven't heard that name for many years. We used to be friends.'

Rose nodded. 'Yes, she told me.'

Miss Hetherington's eyes widened.

Rose held up a hand. 'And before you say anything we weren't talking about you. Well, I told her you didn't like me very much and she told me about Michael.'

Tension was suddenly between them again. Each waited for the other to speak, but remained silent for a few moments.

Rose gripped her hands in her lap. 'I can promise you we weren't talking about you but I wondered why you were so angry with everyone. She told me how you shut yourself away. You didn't want to mix with anyone, but she was sure you were still in love with Michael.'

Miss Hetherington's lips tightened. 'Well, it sounds like

you know my life story. Michael's gone, and gone for good. There's nothing we can do about that. We both should have been braver at the time, but particularly me.'

Rose was suddenly overcome with sadness at Miss Hetherington's plight. 'If Michael was still alive, would you have him back if you could?'

Miss Hetherington stared down at the floor.

Rose had the urge to shake her but remained seated. 'Losing Charlie has made me realise that you have to grab life with both hands. Life is too short to throw it away and be miserable.'

Miss Hetherington looked up with watery eyes. 'What makes you think Michael would want me back? It was entirely my fault it went wrong. Anyway, he's probably married with children by now.'

Rose wanted to wrap her arms around Miss Hetherington but knew she wouldn't want that. Her features had softened and she looked vulnerable for the first time since Rose had met her. Was that why Michael fell in love with her? 'I don't think that's the case, and it's hard to go against a father's wishes. Then pride gets in the way. Michael probably thinks he's not good enough because you didn't fight for him, and he won't fight for you for the same reasons. One of you has to make the first move.'

Miss Hetherington shook her head. 'What makes you think that you know Michael?'

Rose shrugged. 'When I picked your photograph up off the floor, remember you got so angry with me for touching it, but it had clearly been looked at a lot. That tells me that you still love him, and if he hasn't moved on either, he must still love you.'

Miss Hetherington's eyes narrowed. 'Have you seen him then? Where is he and why hasn't he come to see me if he still loves me?'

Rose took a deep breath. 'He has sat on this theatre's steps every day to catch a glimpse of you coming and going.' She watched the colour drain from Miss Hetherington's face. The older woman gasped for air.

Rose reached across and rested her hand over hers, feeling Miss Hetherington's hands shaking under hers. 'I'm taking a chance coming here but I couldn't not come. I pray to God I'm doing the right thing.' She took a deep breath. 'Michael is unconscious in hospital. I think it's quite serious. He's been stabbed. Let me take you to him.'

Miss Hetherington folded her arms around her and rocked backwards and forwards in her chair. 'Oh God no!'

Rose stood up, hoping and praying she was doing the right thing. 'Come on, let me take you to him.'

'Why didn't he speak to me?'

Rose shrugged before leaning forward to take Jane Hetherington's hands in hers. 'I suppose it's pride. He thinks he has nothing to offer you. He's homeless, he has no job, and he watches you from a distance. That is what he has settled for but I can't let that just be. Life is too short. I miss Charlie every day but I know he would want me to be happy and you have a chance of that because the man you love is still alive and close by.' She took a breath. 'I pray to God I'm right; otherwise I'm raising hope where there isn't any and if that's the case I'm truly sorry. I want you to know that whatever has gone on in the past I have no desire to hurt you.'

Miss Hetherington sat in silence for a moment and closed her eyes.

Rose watched her closely.

'I don't want to live my life like this anymore.' Miss Hetherington's eyes snapped open. 'I can't take the risk of losing him a second time just because I'm too scared. I won't let any chance of finding him go by.' She paused. 'I need to take control. It doesn't matter to me whether Michael has a job or not; I just want him in my life.' She took a deep breath. 'I want to see Michael.'

Rose smiled and squeezed Miss Hetherington's hands. 'Come, I'll take you to him.' She paused as the magnitude of what she was doing suddenly hit her.

Men's groans drifted around the hospital ward, mingling with the whispers of conversation.

The strong smell of disinfectant hung in the air, catching at the back of Rose's throat as she stood next to Miss Hetherington staring down at the man lying unconscious in the hospital bed. She was desperate to know if she had done the right thing or not. Would he survive? Would they forgive each other for all the wasted years, or was she putting this woman through unnecessary pain?

When Miss Hetherington spoke her voice was barely audible. 'I want to stay with him.' She slowly slumped down onto a hard wooden chair next to the bed.

Rose gasped, not realising she had been holding her breath waiting for her to speak. She coughed into her arm before resting her hand on Miss Hetherington's shoulder. 'I'm sure it will be all right.'

Miss Hetherington slowly lifted her hand and rested it on the bed. She tentatively moved it nearer to his but quickly pulled it back again.

Rose could feel the tears pricking at the backs of her eyes. 'Don't be frightened. He loves you and your touch might help to bring him round.'

'Does he?'

Rose smiled. 'I believe so.'

The rustle of a nurse's uniform and the squeak of soft shoes made Rose look behind her. 'Good, you found him.' She stood on the other side of his bed and peered at his notes.

Rose glanced across at the nurse they had spoken to when they first rushed into the hospital. 'Is it all right if Miss Hetherington stays with him?'

The nurse looked up. 'Are you a relative?'

Miss Hetherington opened her mouth to speak but Rose immediately squeezed her arm.

Rose jumped in. 'She's his fiancée. They have been engaged for some time but the army and now the war have kept them apart.'

The nurse's gaze travelled between Miss Hetherington and her patient. 'It would be churlish of me to say no. However, you might have to step away when the doctor comes to see him and his bandages are being changed. You will also have to go home before the lights are turned off.'

Miss Hetherington looked up for the first time. 'Thank you. Can I do that every day?'

The nurse's headdress rustled as she nodded. 'I will let everyone know. Try talking or reading to him. He has lost a lot of blood and hasn't come round since he was stabbed.'

Rose's bottom lip trembled. 'Will he make it?'

The nurse looked from one to the other. 'The honest answer is I don't know. He could be unconscious because his mind is trying to protect itself against the pain and what has happened, but to be honest we don't know enough about these things.'

Miss Hetherington's tears began to roll down her cheeks.

The nurse's tone softened. 'We are doing the best we can. Thankfully the knife didn't hit any major organs, and the wound has been stitched. It will be cleaned and the dressing will be changed every day. We are monitoring him closely because of the amount of blood he has lost, and we're keeping him comfortable.'

Rose nodded. 'Thank you.'

The nurse reached out and touched Miss Hetherington's hand. 'Talk to him. Let him know you are here. Tell him how much he means to you. Give him a reminder of why he needs to wake up.'

Miss Hetherington gazed down at Michael. 'Will he be able to hear me?'

The nurse gave a faint smile. 'There have been reports that patients can hear and it's something I want to believe is so.' She paused and placed the notes back on the bedside locker. 'If there's any change, or anything you are worried about, let someone know.'

Miss Hetherington peered up at the nurse. 'I will, thank you.'

Rose watched the nurse move on to the patient in the next bed. 'Are you all right?'

Miss Hetherington slowly nodded. 'Thank you for

bringing me. I can't believe I'm actually looking at him. I never thought the day...'

Rose squeezed her eyes tight in a bid to stop the tears from falling. 'If he can hear you let him know how you feel. Thanks to your father you've both wasted so many years.'

Miss Hetherington didn't take her eyes off Michael.

Rose studied Michael for a moment. 'I truly hope he comes round, Miss Hetherington.'

Miss Hetherington glanced up. 'Please, call me Jane.'

Rose bit down on her lip, wondering if she could ever call her Jane.

Miss Hetherington let her hand creep across the rough, itchy grey blanket before gently wrapping her fingers around his.

Rose had the sudden urge to leave. She had no desire to play gooseberry even if Michael was unconscious. 'I had better go. Will you be all right if I leave?'

Miss Hetherington didn't look up.

Rose fidgeted from one foot to the other. 'I need to tell Ruby, his landlady, how he is, and I should try and get to work as well.'

Miss Hetherington's head jerked up. 'Work? Oh my goodness, they will wonder where I am and if I'm here who's going to make sure all the sewing gets done?'

Rose took a deep breath. 'Don't worry about a thing. I'll help out at the theatre and I'll let them know that you are here because a friend has been injured.'

Miss Hetherington let out her breath. 'I can't thank you enough. I'm not sure I deserve all the kindness you have shown me, but please know I appreciate it more than you will ever know.' She took a breath. 'Regardless of what happens here, if there's anything, anything at all I can do for you, please just say.'

Rose nodded. 'I'll pop back later to see if there's been any change. Tell Michael I said hello.'

Miss Hetherington pushed herself up off the chair and threw her arms around Rose, clinging on to her like her life depended on it.

At a loss for words, Rose slowly put her arms around Jane and held her tight. 'Hopefully, he'll be able to say hello to you soon.'

Jane stepped back and ran her fingers across her glistening cheeks.

Rose nodded and turned away before her tears began to fall. She heard Jane's tearful voice and glanced over her shoulder.

'Michael, how I've wished for the moment I could see you again.' Jane sniffed. 'You know I've gone to the same tea room every week just in case you came and I wasn't there. If only I had known you were at the theatre the whole time.'

Rose shook her head and wiped her eyes before she carried on walking out of the ward.

18

Rose stood on the Lyceum Theatre steps and took a breath, sending up a silent prayer that Michael would pull through. Her body started shaking, her legs were like jelly and she wasn't sure if they would hold her up anymore. She stretched out her arm to one of the pillars, taking a deep breath as she stumbled towards it. Rose sighed, closing her eyes as she felt the reassurance of the hard pillar against her back.

'Rose, are you all right?'

Rose slowly opened her eyes to see Lizzie running up the steps.

'Take my arm; you look like you're going to pass out. Let's get you inside. Are you all right to walk if you lean on me or shall I get Bert?'

Rose took a breath. 'I should be all right... to walk.' She closed her eyes again. 'Everything's just a bit hazy... and my legs feel like jelly... I'm hot.'

Lizzie put her arm around Rose. 'Lean on me. We don't have far to go.'

Rose peered out of hooded eyes.

'Don't worry, I've got you.' Lizzie took a step forward,

half dragging Rose with her. 'Try and lift your legs a little. I'm not as strong as I think I am.'

A man appeared by Lizzie's side. 'Allow me. Where are you taking her?' He scooped Rose's limp body up with ease.

Lizzie eyed the man in uniform and breathed a sigh of relief. 'Thank you. I was just taking her inside the theatre, through the stage door.' She guided him round to the side of the building. 'Bert.' She yelled out. 'Rose has collapsed.'

Bert came running through the open door, just stopping short of the soldier holding Rose in his arms. 'Bring 'er inside.'

Rose groaned.

Lizzie gasped. 'Thank goodness, she's coming round.'

The soldier gently lowered Rose onto a chair. 'Do you want me to find a doctor or something?'

Bert knelt next to the chair. He put the palm of his hand on Rose's forehead. 'Lizzie, keep an eye on 'er while I fetch some water.'

Lizzie nodded, kneeling down where Bert had been. She gave the soldier a small smile. 'I don't think that will be necessary, thank you. She's probably just fainted, and you've done so much already.'

The soldier nodded. 'If you're sure.'

'Thank you for your kindness. I don't know why I thought I could get her indoors by myself.' Lizzie sighed.

'I'll be off then. I hope your friend will be all right.' The soldier turned on his heels and marched out of the theatre.

Bert came running towards Lizzie, carrying a china cup. 'Here, get 'er to sip this.'

Lizzie took the cup and peered inside at the clear liquid. 'It is just water, right?'

Bert gave her an indignant look. 'Of course it is. What do yer take me for?'

Lizzie laughed. 'Just checking.'

The sound of heels clipping the floor made Bert turn around. 'Ahh, Mrs Tyler, it looks like Rose 'as passed out.'

Rose's eyes flickered.

Lizzie pulled the cup back from Rose's lips. 'I think she's coming round.'

Kitty studied Rose's pale features. 'Bert, can you carry Rose to my dressing room and lie her on my chaise longue?'

Bert nodded. 'Of course.'

'I think she'll be more comfortable there.' Kitty turned to Lizzie. 'Can you go and get Rose something to eat? Maybe some soup, or whatever you can find – it doesn't matter what.'

Lizzie jumped up and passed the cup to Kitty. 'Yes, I'll go now. She's going to be all right, isn't she?'

Kitty briefly looked away from Rose. 'Don't worry, we'll look after her. She's family.'

Lizzie nodded and almost ran out the theatre.

'Don't run,' Kitty yelled. 'I don't want you hurting yourself. I've only got one chaise longue.'

Lizzie immediately slowed down but didn't look back.

Bert scooped Rose into his arms and walked along the corridor to Kitty's dressing room. He pushed the open door with his elbow and stepped inside.

Annie jumped up. 'What's happened?'

Bert lowered Rose onto the chaise longue. 'I think she fainted but she appears to be coming round. Lizzie must have found 'er outside and a soldier carried 'er into the theatre. It was lucky young Lizzie was there.'

Kitty stood aside, listening to Bert.

Annie rushed over to the sink and turned on the tap. As always the water sprayed everywhere. She turned it down and put a tea towel under the cold water to give it a good soaking before wringing most of the water out. After quickly turning the tap off she rushed back to Rose's side and placed the cold cloth on her friend's forehead for a moment before moving it to dab at her cheeks. 'Rose, can you hear me? It's Annie. Everything's all right.'

Rose's eyes flickered open.

Bert breathed a sigh of relief. 'Thank goodness.'

Rose moved to get up but Annie pressed her hand on her shoulder. 'No, you lie still for a while. I'll make you a drink in a minute but I don't want you moving just yet.'

Kitty stepped forward. 'I'll keep an eye on her while you make a drink. You're better at that sort of thing than me.'

Annie laughed.

'I'm all right.' Rose moved to sit up but was once again pushed back down by Annie. Her voice faltered. 'I was coming to see Stan.'

Kitty frowned. 'Why? What's happened?'

Rose took a deep breath, trying to steady her voice. 'Miss Hetherington probably won't be in for a few days; well actually I don't know for how long.'

Annie frowned. 'I don't understand. I noticed she seemed to have disappeared. Have you spoken to her?'

Rose nodded. 'I'm sorry, I need to sit up. I feel quite sick.'

Annie helped her friend up before going to the cupboard and collecting the biscuit tin. 'Here, have a biscuit. It might help.' She pulled off the lid and stared inside. 'There's not a great deal of choice but there's a couple of Lincolns in there – they should help with the nausea.' She thrust the tin towards Rose, who dutifully took one. 'I'll make you a cuppa.'

'Wait, I've just left Miss Hetherington at the hospital.' Rose paused, biting her bottom lip.

Annie's mouth dropped open. 'What's happened? Is that why you fainted?'

There was a light rap on the door. Lizzie poked her head round. 'Thank goodness you've come round, Rose. I managed to get you some soup. I'll be honest I'm not sure whether it's pea or vegetable.'

Kitty took the cup from her and lowered her head to smell its contents. 'It doesn't smell too bad, although it's probably not the best thing I've ever smelled.' She held out the cup for Rose to take.

Rose gave a faint smile as she took it. 'I think I fainted because I haven't eaten or drunk anything since early this morning, and I've been rushing around a lot. I suppose it just all got too much for me.'

Annie shook her head. 'So what were you doing at the hospital?'

Rose took a deep breath. 'I was at the refuge when Michael was stabbed.' She paused. 'Anyway, we got him to the hospital but he's lost a lot of blood.' Her words tripped over each other. 'I came and got Miss Hetherington. She's at the hospital with him now.'

Annie's eyes widened. 'Is he going to be all right? Is he conscious?'

'He's not at the moment, and only time will tell whether he'll come round or not.' Rose sighed. 'But I thought if he doesn't make it at least she can sit with him so he doesn't die alone.' She looked up at everyone staring at her. 'I've been back to the refuge to let Ruby know, but no one knows whether he will live or not. She's heartbroken but Oliver had popped in so I know they are all in good hands.'

Annie turned away and picked up the kettle. 'They may well be, but you look dreadful.'

Rose put the cup down and nibbled the dry biscuit. 'That may be so, but I came back here to let you all know that Miss Hetherington wants to stay with him so she doesn't know when she will be back.'

Lizzie moved closer. 'I don't know what's going on but I can work longer hours to try to get the work done.'

Rose closed her eyes for a moment.

Kitty smiled at the young girl. 'That's very kind of you, Lizzie, and we may well have to take you up on that.'

Rose glanced round at everyone in the room; she had forgotten they were always there for each other, even for Miss Hetherington. 'I can do some repairs after, or before, my day at Dickens and Jones.'

Annie shook her head. 'You can't do everything, Rose. You're already busy every evening altering the clothing for the soldiers.'

Rose held up her hand. 'Hopefully, it won't be long before it's good news and he wakes up. I want to do this for Miss Hetherington. I will find the time.'

Rose wrinkled her nose as the familiar antiseptic smell flooded the ward. She had been kept busy the last couple of days and now she held her breath as she stood behind Jane Hetherington. Should she talk to her? She didn't want to intrude but she wanted to be there for her should the worst happen.

Jane suddenly peered over her shoulder. 'Did he know you were going to talk to me about him?' She fumbled for a hanky in her skirt pocket and dabbed at the corners of her eyes.

Rose shook her head. 'No, I hadn't planned to talk to you about Michael. I was always going to apologise about the dress, but when he was stabbed I felt compelled to try to bring you together.'

'No matter how painful this may turn out to be I'm glad you did decide to tell me.' Miss Hetherington gave a faint smile before patting the back of her hair. 'Do I look all right?'

Rose tilted her head and smiled. 'You look fine, and he has seen you every single day, morning and night, so he won't care what you look like. You need to prepare yourself because he has been homeless but he's now living in a refuge and washes up in Joyce's restaurant. I think he was trying to get his life back on track so he could talk to you.'

Jane sighed. 'I can't believe I never noticed him. That says something about me, doesn't it?' She arched her back. 'I'm so grateful the hospital staff are letting me stay all day, even if the chair is incredibly uncomfortable.'

Rose quelled the urge to hug Jane, knowing she wasn't one for displays of emotion. 'Are you all right?'

Miss Hetherington nodded. 'I can't believe I'm doing this. I've waited for so many years and now I'm terrified what he'll say if... when... he wakes up.'

Rose nodded. 'That's understandable, but I will stay by your side for as long as you want me to.'

Miss Hetherington pushed back her shoulders and lifted up her chin. 'That won't be necessary. I have to be braver now, otherwise how will I ever get him back in my life? But thank you.'

Rose could almost touch the tension in the air. Her head began to throb. 'Hopefully it won't be long before he comes round.'

Fear trampled across Jane's face. 'I'm so frightened he won't want me but this also feels like something I must do. If he opened his eyes now I don't know what I'd say to him.'

Rose nodded before peering at Miss Hetherington as she stepped nearer the bed. 'Don't think about it too much because I expect whatever is in your head will just come spilling out.'

Miss Hetherington took a deep breath and nodded.

Rose frowned as she glanced down at Michael lying so still. 'Come on, Michael, it's time to be brave.'

Miss Hetherington gasped. What little colour she had drained from her face. 'Is he… is he waking up?'

Michael's eyelashes fluttered.

Rose stared at him for a moment before shaking her head. 'I don't think so but I'm hoping the sound of our voices will stir something inside him, even if it's only fear. But I know Michael will love seeing you.' She leant in further. 'Come on, Michael, the love of your life is here. She's waiting for you to open your eyes and see the love shining out of hers.'

Michael was still.

Jane glanced at Rose. 'Does that mean he doesn't want to see me?' A tear ran down her cheek. 'Does it? Does it mean I should go?'

'No.'

The two women stopped and stared at Michael. His eyes were still closed, he wasn't moving, and yet surely that was his voice they had just heard. Wasn't it?

Rose immediately stepped away to find a nurse. 'Can someone help please; I think he's coming round. He spoke.' She paused. 'I'm sure he did…'

Jane stared at Michael, reaching out and resting the palm of her hand on his face. 'Michael, it's Jane. I'm here. We have a lot of catching up to do; that is, if you still want me in your life.'

Michael's eyes slowly fluttered open.

Jane gripped the cup of water on his bedside table. 'You must be dry; have a sip.' She held the cup to his lips and gently thumbed away the water dribbling down from the side of his mouth.

A nurse stopped at the foot of the bed. 'Hello, Michael, it's good to see you awake.' She moved to the side of the bed and took his pulse, checking with the watch attached to her uniform. 'No sudden movements, please, and I will let the doctor know you have come round.' She nodded to Jane and Rose. 'This is good news but don't let him get too excited.'

Rose nodded. 'Thank you, nurse.'

The nurse moved to the bed opposite.

Rose watched the fear in his eyes fighting with the love that he was obviously feeling at seeing Jane up close. It had been the right thing to do and she was thrilled. 'Jane Hetherington, may I introduce you to Michael Dean, and let me just say please don't waste another moment.'

'Michael, I can't believe I'm here talking to you after all these years.'

Michael nodded. His voice was hoarse when he spoke. 'Yes, I've been sitting on the theatre steps every day. Happy to just get a glimpse of you as you go in and out of the theatre.'

Jane sniffed, quickly wiping away a tear that was rolling down her face. 'I wanted to come and meet you all those years ago but my father locked me in a room so I couldn't get out and when I finally did I couldn't find you.'

Michael licked his lips. He blinked quickly as his eyes welled up. 'I guessed it was your father who kept us apart but I joined the army to lick my wounds.' He shook his head. 'So many wasted years.'

A tear dropped onto Jane's cheek. 'Is it too late? I love you as much now as I've ever done but can you forgive me for not being braver?'

Michael shook his head. 'There's nothing to forgive. I have never stopped loving you but I have nothing to offer. I have no home or real employment. I only have my love and the question is would you take a chance on someone like me?'

Miss Hetherington moved to throw herself on him but suddenly stopped. She gripped his hand and sobbed. 'Trust me when I say there's no greater gift than your love.'

Rose slowly walked back to the ward door. She looked over her shoulder and smiled, knowing they would work it out.

Mrs Todd scowled. 'I gave you everything. Yes, I've done things I regret but I realise now I was being selfish. I shouldn't have done it and I'm now riddled with guilt.' She spat out her words. 'I allowed you to get inside my head but you care about no one but yourself.'

Rose watched and listened in horror. She knew she should leave, after all no one was expecting her to come into work early, but instead she stood rooted in the doorway of the sewing room.

Mr Bowman gave a humourless laugh. 'You enjoyed the attention so don't act the innocent with me because it doesn't wash.'

Mrs Todd clenched her hands by her sides. 'You promised me the world, remember? But I realised, when it was too late, you were never going to deliver. Is that what you've done to young Rose? I won't stand by and do nothing, no matter what it costs me.'

'Don't threaten me. You have too much to lose, like your job.' Mr Bowman sneered at her. 'I haven't promised anyone anything. If you were better at your job I wouldn't have to bring in Miss Spencer.' He took a step nearer.

Mrs Todd stepped backwards, feeling the hard wall against her back. She ran her clammy hands down the sides of her skirt.

'You have nowhere to go.' Mr Bowman scowled. 'So be careful what you say; after all, we wouldn't want your little secret to come out.'

Mrs Todd's voice broke. 'I'm not going to carry on like this… It's wrong… and you're not going to keep holding it over me.'

Mr Bowman laughed. 'Do you seriously think I can't get rid of you? The power lies with me, not with you. I thought you understood that but clearly you need reminding.' He stepped nearer.

Rose couldn't believe what she was hearing. How could he threaten her like that? She stepped forward; her anger surged through her. 'Mr Bowman, it sounds and looks to me like you're threatening Mrs Todd, and no one deserves to be spoken to in the way you've spoken to her.'

Mr Bowman smiled at Rose. 'With all due respect, Miss Spencer, this has nothing to do with you. This is between me and Mrs Todd.'

Rose noticed his smile didn't reach his cold eyes; she pulled back her shoulders and jutted out her chin. 'And with all due respect to you, Mr Bowman, if you pick on someone in a public place you deserve to be questioned over it. Mrs Todd works hard for you and she achieves the best she can with the time you allow her. She certainly doesn't deserve to be bullied by you.'

Mr Bowman scowled. 'You have no idea what you're taking on, Miss Spencer. You haven't been here long enough to be throwing your weight around, and I will not put up with it. You are a seamstress and an unreliable one at that.'

'I've already explained what happened and apologised for not coming in a couple of days ago. I came in early this morning to make up for my absence, and I'm glad I did, especially if this is how you treat people when you think no one is around.' Rose's lips tightened slightly. 'And you're right – I am a seamstress, despite you lying to me when you employed me. If I recall correctly you said I was being employed as a designer, but none of that matters now. I will not stand by and watch you berate somebody in front of me.'

Mr Bowman's eyes narrowed. His indecision on how to react was there for all to see.

Rose watched the conflict running across his face with interest. She smiled. 'You don't know what to do, do you? You would like to give me the sack but you need me; you need my designs. They're all over the shop and in the sewing room. I must say you have some gumption to think you could get away with it.' She hesitated. 'However, I can't prove you stole them—'

'Are you accusing me of theft?' Mr Bowman's face flushed with colour as he sucked in his breath. 'I can assure you I don't need to steal yours, or anyone else's designs, thank you very much.'

Rose scowled. 'I've met your sort before. You're a bully and no better than the likes of Mr Butterworth – the shopkeeper back home. You're just posher, with your fancy suit, fancy pink tie and matching band around your fancy hat. I'm not afraid of you, Mr Bowman, and I will not stand by and watch you bully Mrs Todd just because you feel she should be able to produce the collection quicker, and if need be I will report you to anyone who will listen.'

Mr Bowman's gaze flitted between the two women standing in front of him. 'Miss Spencer, you are skating on very thin ice. I do not bully my staff. I'm under immense pressure with this new collection.'

Mrs Todd coughed. 'It's my own fault. I produced some designs for the last couple of collections but I don't seem able to do it anymore.'

Rose stood silent for a moment before studying Mrs Todd. 'You'll never produce ideas if you're under pressure all the time.'

Mrs Todd gave a small smile. 'You are too kind but it's—'

'Look.' Mr Bowman sighed. 'Mrs Todd and I have

history. I have to make sure she is delivering what I ask of her. That's my job.'

'Pressure or no pressure it seems to me, Mr Bowman, that you have gone too far. You need to treat your staff kinder than you do because I'm sure the owners of the shop wouldn't want anything to reflect badly on them. Nobody likes a bully, and if it is because of the collection then you are clearly in the wrong job. Taking it out on others is not the answer.'

Mr Bowman frowned. 'I do not have the time to stand here discussing the whys and wherefores of getting a collection out with someone who has no idea what's involved, so I suggest you both get on with your work before you are both out of work. Miss Spencer, you need to understand that your job depends on this collection being a success. Let alone a change in your attitude. We will discuss this after the collection has been completed, in private.' He turned and marched out of the sewing room, slamming the door on his way out.

Mrs Todd turned to Rose. 'Thank you, thank you so much. I should stand up to him more but when his temper is up he scares me a little and then I'm frightened of losing my job.'

Rose stared straight ahead. 'It doesn't matter. I don't want to get you into trouble, or worse – the sack.' She sighed. 'It's thrilling and heartbreaking to see my designs here but it's just a sketch pad and I've allowed it to get out of hand. I'm never going to find it so therefore I can't prove it. It probably isn't here at all. He may have taken it home and if that's the case I'll definitely never find it. I'm definitely going to confront him about the pearls though.'

Mrs Todd's eyes widened. 'Pearls?'

Rose scowled. 'Yes, it's a long story but I do believe he's making me pay for something I broke that isn't real.'

'Oh my, perhaps we should take it further?'

Rose shook her head. 'I don't want you getting involved. I shall sort it out, don't worry. He isn't going to get away with it.'

Mrs Todd lowered her eyes and took a breath. 'I don't know what to say, except I'm sorry.'

Rose shrugged. 'Thank you.' She tilted her head. 'Anyway, back to the dresses; maybe we should start including Marion, especially as we are under so much pressure to get everything finished. She has a love for material, a great eye, is eager to learn, and is a very good seamstress.'

Mrs Todd nodded. 'That's a good idea, although Mr Bowman won't like involving anybody else.'

Rose shook her head. 'No he won't, but he can't have it all ways. He can't moan that we're behind and not give us help. To be honest he doesn't even need to know. He's only concerned with the outcome.'

Mrs Todd's eyes widened. 'You're a brave young lady. I don't think I've ever met anyone like you, especially when you consider how timid you were when you arrived.'

Rose chuckled. 'I am not as brave as you think I am, but I've never liked someone picking on someone else. Some of the owners of the village shops where I come from were so rude and mean to my friend and I struggled to keep my mouth shut.' She smiled. 'Consequently, I was always getting into trouble.'

'Would that be Mr Butterworth?' Mrs Todd smiled.

Rose nodded.

Mrs Todd lifted her chin slightly. 'You're right though – the more we let people get away with it the more it happens.'

Rose frowned. 'Don't be hard on yourself. When you need to keep your job it's a very different feeling. I need a job but I'm lucky enough to live in my friend's house; so while I need to earn money, if I can't for a week or two it's not the end of the world. I could probably go back to the theatre if I really wanted to.' She smiled at Mrs Todd. 'Come on, don't look so worried. Let's get this collection finished so he doesn't have to talk to me ever again.'

Mrs Todd chuckled. 'You're like a breath of fresh air.'

19

Rose placed a cushion under her head and closed her eyes, nestling into the armchair. Sighing, knowing she should go up to bed, she snuggled down further. Climbing the stairs seemed too much of an effort. The front door slammed shut. Startled, Rose jumped out of her chair and marched into the hallway.

Annie was leaning against the door and her eyes were squeezed shut.

'What's wrong, Annie?'

Joyce came running along the hallway. 'Hello, Annie, I heard the door and thought something must have happened when it banged shut. Did the wind take it?'

Annie opened her bloodshot eyes. 'Peter's been called up. He has a couple weeks and then he has to go for his medical.'

The girls gasped, and rushed forward as one.

'Oh no, when did he find out?' Rose shook her head. 'Take no notice of me – it doesn't matter. It was a stupid question.'

Annie lowered her head. 'I don't know when he heard. I only found out today.'

Joyce threaded her hand through Annie's arm. 'Come and sit down. I'll make us all a cup of tea.'

Annie allowed herself to be guided into the sitting room. 'I can't believe it. I was hoping he would get away with not having to go. But, I suppose that was never going to happen with conscription.' She slowly lowered herself onto the chair, clearly dazed by the turn of events.

Rose knelt down by Annie's feet. 'How's Peter? I know he's never had the urge to enlist. I mean he was more concerned about looking after his family. What will happen to his stall?'

Annie just shook her head.

Rose clasped Annie's hands in hers. 'I'm so sorry for asking so many questions.' She paused. 'You look quite pale and I want to help where I can.'

Annie stared straight ahead. 'I'm so silly. It was obvious really, but I thought we had no rush to worry about our future together.' She turned to look at Rose. 'You were right – you kept saying don't wait.' She sucked in her breath. 'Peter wants us to get married before he has to go. He hasn't said as much but I think he's quite frightened.'

'That's understandable.' Rose frowned. 'Who wouldn't be? Let's face it, the men who went early didn't realise what they were getting into but it's different now that we have injured soldiers coming back and lots of men have been lost because of this rotten war.' She squeezed her friend's hand. 'You can still get married before he goes, if you want to. I can make your dress. It won't take long but you'll need to tell me what you want. We can write to your family and mine so they can feed the chickens for a few days.'

Annie smiled. 'Rose, I don't want you to do that. It's not fair.'

'I'm not listening, Annie. If you don't tell me what you want I'll just make something I think you'll like.'

Joyce pushed open the sitting room door and walked in carrying a tray of tea things. She glanced at her friends, who were huddled together. 'Get this tea down you. Remember we decided our mothers were right – saying a cuppa solves everything.' She handed them each a cup. 'So, we have a wedding to plan, and quickly.'

Annie shook her head. 'What about you, Joyce? We were going to get married together.'

Joyce smiled. 'Don't you go worrying about me; we need to get you organised.' She sat on the nearest chair. 'First thing we need to do is to sort out your dress so Rose can get on and make it.'

Rose looked between her two friends. 'You can both still get married at the same time. I will just have to get started as soon as possible. Annie, if you go to the church in the morning, sort out a date and then you can write to your father. I'm sure they can stay here for a couple of days. I know it'll be a tight squeeze but at least it'll keep the cost down for them and you get to see them.'

Annie smiled at the sparkle that had appeared in her friend's eyes. 'You're enjoying this aren't you?'

Rose frowned. 'I'm not enjoying the idea of Peter going off to war but I'm definitely enjoying finally talking about your wedding.' She glanced up at the clock on the mantelpiece as it struck half past ten. 'Did you see Peter on the way home from the theatre?'

Annie looked down at her hands gripping her cup of tea. The warmth was filtering through her fingers. 'He brought the letter to the theatre.' She paused. 'I tried to be strong but I cried like a baby.' Colour flooded her cheeks. 'Kitty heard Peter say he wanted to get married before he left.' Her gaze flitted between her friends. 'She offered me her wedding dress.'

Rose nodded. 'That's kind of her. If you're happy to do that it will probably fit you because I don't think there's much between you in size, but you'll have to try it on.'

Annie smiled. 'It's a beautiful dress.' She turned to look at Joyce. 'Will you and Simon still get married with us? We would like you to but I know it will be quicker than you would probably want.'

Joyce smiled. 'It will be an honour, Annie, and we will make it a good day.'

Rose nodded. 'So we just have the dresses to sort out. I can start making Joyce's and I'll come to the theatre to see you in Kitty's.'

Annie sucked in her breath. 'Will you be all right doing that? I mean, things were different when you last saw the dress.'

A shadow passed over Rose's face before she forced herself to smile. 'This isn't about me, Annie. You two are much more important. It's time I stepped forward, even if it's only for now. As Charlie used to say life's too short to keep putting everything on hold.' She paused. 'Joyce, if you let me know later about your style of dress then it won't take me long to make it. I can ask Oliver if I can use the sewing machine he bought. That will speed things up a bit.'

Joyce tilted her head. 'It's very kind of you, Rose, but I

don't really know how you are going to fit it in, what with going to work and doing all the alterations you've taken on for the men.'

Annie nodded. 'Let alone the work you're doing because Miss Hetherington hasn't returned yet.'

Rose chuckled. 'Don't you worry about that. It will all get done.'

Rose took a deep breath and forced a smile as she walked through the open door into the theatre, which looked dark after the brightness of the sun.

'Ah, Rose, a sight for sore eyes.' Bert smiled. 'We never 'ad a chance to chat last time – 'ow are you doing?'

Rose smiled. 'I'm much better, thank you.'

Bert raised his eyebrows. 'Last time I saw yer 'ere yer didn't look so good. Yer frightened us all.'

Rose blushed. 'I'm sorry; it must have been the lack of food, water, and rushing around. It wasn't one of my better days.'

Bert nodded. 'Yer got to look after yerself. How's Miss Hetherington doing? It's quite strange. I miss her scowling at me.'

Rose laughed. 'She's doing well, and more importantly Michael will be out of hospital soon.'

Bert beamed. 'That's wonderful news. He's a kind man, although I'll never understand 'ow he fell in love with old Hetherington, but it's each to their own.'

Rose smiled as she shook her head. 'It doesn't do for us all to be the same, and everyone deserves to feel loved by someone.'

'Yer right there. I shouldn't be so mean.' Bert looked contrite for a moment. 'If they're both 'appy and can actually sort themselves out then that's all that matters. He must love 'er to sit on those blooming steps in all weathers; 'e's a better man than me.'

Rose nodded. 'Trust me, they are truly in love and I think they will start their lives together as soon as Michael can leave the hospital. I don't know for sure but it probably explains why she used to dress up on certain dates. She kept hoping he would return without realising he was here all the time. It's all quite sad.'

Bert sighed. 'It is. Yer better be careful because I'm on the verge of feeling sorry for 'er.'

Rose tilted her head. 'So you should.'

'Maybe.'

Rose giggled. 'Do you know if Annie and Kitty are in their dressing room?'

Bert nodded. 'Annie said earlier you might pop in but she wasn't sure.'

'Thanks, Bert. I'll go along to Kitty's dressing room and see them and then we can have a good old chat.'

Bert grinned. 'Go on then, don't be long.'

Rose rushed along the corridor trying to hold her memories at bay. Standing outside Kitty's dressing room she took a deep breath before knocking on the door.

Annie's voice called out. 'Come in.'

Rose opened the door and gasped.

Kitty glanced over her shoulder at Rose, spinning round she threw her arms around her.

Rose was engulfed with Kitty's orange blossom perfume as she returned the hug.

'Hello, Rose, I'm so pleased you are here. I want to talk to you about Jane and Michael but first...' She beamed, looking back at Annie. 'What do you think? Doesn't it look lovely?'

Annie stared at her reflection in the mirror. 'I feel like a princess.' She frowned. 'I don't think I should wear this. What happens if I have an accident and it gets torn or something gets spilt down it?'

Kitty shook her head, waving away Annie's fears. 'It's just a dress, a very beautiful dress but just a dress.'

Rose stepped further into the room. 'You look wonderful, and it looks like it fits you perfectly.'

Annie turned to face her friend. 'You did such a good job making this dress and it feels wonderful on.'

Rose looked at it with a critical eye. Her hands pulled the material here and there. 'It is a lovely fit.'

Kitty smiled. 'That's it then, you shall wear it. Everyone should feel like a princess for at least one day in their lives.'

Rose nodded. 'If you are worried about wearing Kitty's dress I can make you a different one.'

Annie frowned. 'No, you're making Joyce's, and this is without doubt a beautiful dress.' She studied her reflection. 'Thank you, Kitty, I promise to look after it.'

Rose smiled. 'You look beautiful. It doesn't look like it needs altering, so shall I help you out of it?'

Annie nodded. 'I would love to wear it all day, but yes, I should take it off.'

Kitty walked over to Rose and put her arms around her. 'I'm sorry, I haven't asked how you are? That's very rude of me.'

'I'm well, thank you – keeping myself busy.'

Kitty stepped away and picked up her packet of cigarettes. 'From what Annie tells me I don't know how you fit it all in. I understand you're doing some clothing alterations for wounded soldiers. Now that's very worthwhile.'

Rose beamed as she walked over to help Annie out of the wedding dress. 'Yes, Ruby is quite remarkable and wants to put her money into helping the men. Although, Oliver is trying to raise money to help fund the refuge and he wants to find work for the men.' Her smile faded. 'Some of the injuries, and by all accounts the nightmares, are horrific.'

Annie shook her head. 'It doesn't bear thinking about; at least I don't like to think about what our brothers have seen and heard. I'm sure they won't come back the same men and now Peter's going as well.'

Rose could feel the tears pricking at her eyes. 'You're right of course, but it's best to not think about it otherwise you'll go out of your mind with worry.'

Kitty's gaze travelled from one to the other. 'Maybe we can help raise some money, perhaps a charity performance.' Her fingers tapped the unopened cigarette box. 'And I'll speak to Stan because he's always looking for people who can help backstage – you know, painters and cleaners, there may be other jobs as well.' Her eyes sparkled. 'I'll definitely talk to him later.'

Rose stepped forward and wrapped her arms around Kitty. 'Thank you so much. Oliver will be pleased.' She stepped back. 'When he's not at the hospital he's at the refuge looking after them.'

Kitty studied Rose before turning to Annie. 'You never told me Rose had found someone special.'

Annie's mouth dropped open.

Rose blushed. 'I haven't. Oliver is a good man and Charlie's friend who has helped me a lot.'

Kitty nodded. 'I'm sorry. I didn't mean to speak out of turn.'

Rose shrugged. 'No, you haven't. He's just given me a reason to carry on. I just feel like I'm doing something worthwhile.'

Kitty eyed her. 'Well, I'm very happy you have found your niche. Is everything going well at Dickens and Jones?'

Rose lowered her eyelashes as she fought with her conscience. She had no desire to lie but she didn't want to talk about it either. 'I'm sure you know everywhere has its ups and downs.'

Rose smiled; she loved wandering around the ladies' department of Dickens and Jones. It was almost as good as the haberdashery department. The ladies' fragrances all mingled together as they walked past her. She could hear murmured voices of delight as customers searched through the many different styles and colours of the beautiful gowns on the hanging rails. Rose pulled out a coat hanger. Her eyes widened as she stared at the dress.

Mrs Todd frowned. 'What's the matter? Don't you like it?'

Rose's gaze moved to study Mrs Todd's puzzled expression. 'Yes, it's quite beautiful.'

Mrs Todd's face immediately flushed with colour. 'It was my pride and joy. Although, I now realise that my pride is misplaced, but I did do all the work myself and Mr Bowman loved it so he put it in his collection.'

Rose reached out to touch the familiar gown. Her fingers caressed the soft material that flowed gently through them. 'It's beautiful.' She glanced at the tag inside the dress that showed it was part of Mr Bowman's previous collection.

Mrs Todd fidgeted from one foot to the other. She gripped her hands together in front of her. 'It means a lot that you like it.'

Rose shook her head as everything became jumbled up again. Her heart was pounding. How could Mrs Todd have got hold of one of her designs? She licked her dry lips. 'Why hasn't Mr Bowman given you credit for it?'

'I'm not a name. They all come here for his designs, which I do understand.' Mrs Todd gazed at the dress for a moment before putting it back on the rail. 'That must be how you felt when you made Miss Smythe's wedding dress.'

Rose nodded. 'Yes, the only difference was it was all my own work and no one claimed it as theirs.' She paused. 'Have you ever been to see Miss Smythe with Mr Bowman?'

'Ah, Miss Spencer, how lovely to see you again.'

Rose spun on her heels to see Miss Allen heading her way. 'Good morning, Miss Allen. I trust you are well and are still happy with the gowns I made for you.'

Mr Bowman scowled, his voice barely audible when he spoke. 'What's going on here?'

Rose sucked in her breath, but kept her smile fixed, as Mr Bowman's stern voice startled her.

Miss Allen beamed. 'Oh yes, darling, they were a hit with all my friends and it wouldn't surprise me if you get some more work coming your way.'

Mr Bowman lifted his chin and cleared his throat. 'Ladies,

I can assist this customer as your attention is required elsewhere.'

Rose forced herself to smile. 'Please forgive me, Miss Allen—'

'It's not a problem, I must get on. I don't need assistance.' Miss Allen turned on her heels and glided out of the ladies' department.

Rose watched her go, wondering if she could ever be that elegant.

Frowning, Mr Bowman took a couple of steps away from them. 'There's no time for you two to be amusing yourselves around here. There's work to be done.'

Mrs Todd glared. 'We weren't amusing ourselves; we were checking what was on the hanging rail. If you remember that's part of my job.'

Mr Bowman stopped in his tracks. He turned round to face them before hissing, 'It might be part of your job but it's not part of Miss Spencer's.' He frowned at Rose. 'When did you get permission to make clothes for Mrs Bowman, or Miss Allen as she now likes to call herself?'

Rose pulled back her shoulders, hoping she would look more confident than she felt. 'I didn't know I needed permission. It was all in my own time and I didn't know she was your wife.'

Mr Bowman's gaze darted around the shop before he whispered through gritted teeth, 'Ex-wife! Is that where you were when you didn't come to work, when you claimed your friend had been stabbed?' His eyes blazed at her.

Rose clenched her hands by her sides. 'You make it sound like I was lying, and I wasn't.'

Mr Bowman eyed Rose. 'Well, you're clearly secretive because you never mentioned going to my home and working for my wife.'

Rose lifted her chin. 'It wasn't a secret and I didn't know she was your wife. As for me telling you, well I'm not sure I need to when it's in my own time – at least I was never told I had to.'

Mr Bowman arched his eyebrows and turned his anger on Mrs Todd. 'Did you know about this?'

Mrs Todd shook her head. 'Why would I?'

Mr Bowman nodded. 'So it was a secret then.'

Rose could feel the hairs on the back of her neck rising as the injustice of this conversation took hold. 'Mr Bowman, I do a lot of sewing away from here. I alter injured soldiers' clothing and I'm currently making my friend's wedding dress. Are you saying you need to know every time I pick up a needle and thread or a pencil, every time I sketch out an idea?'

Mr Bowman flared his nostrils. 'This isn't the time or the place to discuss it but it isn't over.' He turned to walk away.

Anger flowed through Rose's veins. 'No, it isn't, Mr Bowman.' She followed him down to the sewing room and into his office and slammed the door behind her. 'I'm not interested in what your game is but you have involved me so, unfortunately, that makes it my business.'

Mr Bowman stared at Rose. His eyes held a steel-like quality. 'You need to watch your step, young lady, or you are going to be out of work. I took a chance employing you and this is how you show your appreciation.'

Rose's eyes widened. 'Show my appreciation? You have stolen my ideas, you are making me pay for a very expensive necklace, which wasn't even real, and you are selling dresses from here to a market trader.'

Mr Bowman pulled himself upright and puffed out his chest. 'How dare you come in here with all your accusations. I think you need to collect your things and leave. I don't want you working here; you are nothing but trouble with all your accusations. I've a good mind to call the police.'

The door suddenly burst open and Mr Woodford strode into the office. 'Miss Spencer, I'd appreciate it if you could leave Mr Bowman and I to talk for a moment.'

Mr Bowman sneered. 'Miss Spencer is just leaving.'

20

It was early but the warmth of the sun was already filtering through the kitchen window. Rose stared outside, while sitting at the table deep in thought. She had no idea what to do next, but she did know she had behaved recklessly without a thought to the consequences. She was not in the village now, and there were no parents to tell her what to do.

Annie picked up her china cup and wrinkled her nose as she sipped the strong, tepid tea. 'Everything all right, Rose? You look deep in thought.'

Joyce scraped the butter across her slice of toast, glancing up at the clock on the mantelpiece. Holding her knife in mid-air, she peered across the table at Rose. 'Aren't you going to be late for work this morning?'

Rose lowered her eyes. 'No.' She took a breath. 'I didn't tell you last night but Mr Bowman sacked me yesterday.'

Annie's cup clattered down onto the matching saucer. 'Why didn't you say?'

Rose's mouth tightened.

Joyce gasped. 'What? I don't understand. What happened?'

Rose was silent for a moment. She could feel her friends'

eyes boring into her. Sighing, she raised her eyebrows. 'I don't really know what happened.' Rose paused. 'That's a lie; to be honest I was probably a little too impetuous. I've been thinking about it for most of the night and in the cold light of day I'm not surprised I was sacked for the way I spoke to Mr Bowman.'

Annie's eyes widened. 'What did you say?'

'You know me, Annie, I can't stand a bully and he was talking to Mrs Todd like she was the dirt on the bottom of his shoes.'

Annie shook her head. 'Well, it's not surprising. We've experienced all that before.'

Rose nodded. 'That's the thing, isn't it? I just can't stand by and listen to it.' She paused. 'Of course, there's more to it than that. Miss Allen came in to Dickens and Jones and told Mr Bowman I had made some gowns for her. I don't think she was trying to get me in trouble, but she did cause a stir. He wasn't happy.'

Joyce raised her eyebrows. 'Why? Are you not allowed to make clothes for other people?'

Rose shrugged. 'I'm not sure but it turns out Miss Allen is Mr Bowman's ex-wife and he accused me of all kinds of things.'

Annie's mouth dropped open. 'Oh my goodness, did you know that?'

Rose gave a wry smile. 'No, but even if I did I could hardly say I'm not going to finish the dresses.' Her voice rose slightly. 'And she wasn't calling herself Mrs Bowman.'

'It sounds like you were in a difficult position.' Joyce crunched into her almost-dry toast.

Rose sighed. 'I'm sorry, Joyce. I'll put every penny I earn

from the alterations into the household pot. Hopefully, I'll be able to find another job soon.'

Joyce studied her for a moment. 'I'm not too concerned about that, Rose, I'm just sorry it didn't work out for you.' She hesitated for a moment. 'Do you think Charlie was wrong to encourage you to leave the theatre?'

'No, if I hadn't gone, I wouldn't know whether it was for me or not. I think Charlie had my best interests at heart. I just think it wasn't the right time for me to make decisions like that, and I clearly made the wrong one.'

Joyce nodded. 'I'm sure you're right about that, but you've tried it and if it's not right for you it's not right for you.'

Annie watched her friend closely. 'Charlie told you to find yourself and to do that you have to try different things. You encouraged me to take the job as Kitty's dresser, which I didn't want to take, but now look at me. They have become like family to me.'

Joyce smiled. 'You also told Simon I was an excellent cook and had dreams of being one, and now thanks to you, my family and friends, I am. It's time for you to do what's right for you and it's our turn to help you achieve that.'

'The trouble is I was never like you two. I never knew what I wanted to do.' Rose frowned.

Annie smiled. 'I think you did but you were always too scared to admit it. That's why you kept your grandma's presents a secret. Charlie was the driving force for you to change and admit what you really wanted.'

Rose sighed. 'It's hard still seeing Charlie's shop boarded up, especially as it's where he proposed to me. It will always hold a special place in my heart.'

Joyce tilted her head slightly. 'I can see how it's a daily

reminder for you. Maybe you should open it up yourself, or, of course you could go back to work at the theatre.'

Rose stayed silent for a moment. 'You may have something, Joyce.'

Joyce smiled. 'They would probably be glad to have you back, especially with Miss Hetherington not leaving Michael's side at the moment.'

Rose shook her head. 'No, I won't be going back to the theatre. I don't mind helping out until she returns but I have no desire to be there every day.'

Joyce frowned. 'But I thought you just said—'

'I don't know what I'm going to do. The only thing that's certain is I need to earn money, and I want to be happy in what I do. One thing I do enjoy is altering clothing for the soldiers.'

'I can see why you would get some satisfaction from that.' Joyce dabbed her mouth with a napkin. 'After all, you're doing what you do best. You're helping people and using your sewing skills at the same time.'

Rose looked thoughtful. 'Actually, maybe Charlie was right about me spreading my wings. If I hadn't worked at Dickens and Jones then I wouldn't have met the Hardys and it was Oliver who encouraged me to help out at the refuge and by altering clothing for the patients at the hospital, so maybe I'm where I'm meant to be.'

Annie watched Rose's eyes sparkling. 'So, how does Oliver fit in?'

Rose frowned. 'He doesn't, he's become a really good friend but that's it. I'm not looking for love.'

Joyce put down her knife. 'But he might be, how do you know he isn't?'

'Who says he is?' Rose shook her head and laughed. 'You're terrible, and such a romantic. Apparently, Oliver's mother has been trying to find him a new wife for years and he is having none of it, and I'm sure I wouldn't fit the bill even if I wanted to.'

Joyce shrugged. 'You could be right. I just want you to be as happy as Simon and I are. It took us a long time to get where we are, and when I look back I do think what a lot of years we wasted because we were too scared to take the next step. I know I've said it before but I will say it again, I owe you a lot because you were the first person to notice the love that we had for each other and while it was embarrassing when you pushed us together I will always be grateful. Please don't make the same mistakes that I did.'

'Don't worry, Joyce, I'll be all right.' Rose laughed. 'And it gives me more time to make your wedding dress.'

Joyce's lips tightened. 'You're always putting others first but we are here to make sure you are all right.'

Rose nodded. 'I'm truly blessed to have such good friends, but I want you to understand I'm not looking for love.'

Joyce smiled. 'And that's usually when it comes knocking.'

Annie laughed. 'Love life aside we need to figure out where you go from here.' She paused before tilting her head. 'Maybe Joyce has something; perhaps you could make use of Charlie's shop. I don't know how yet but it's an important place for you, him, and even Oliver, so it's a shame to leave it empty.'

Ruby took a handkerchief out of her apron pocket and began to mop her brow. 'It's hot in here, what with the range on and the sunshine. If this carries on it's going to be a hot summer.'

Familiar cooking smells filled the kitchen; in some ways the refuge reminded Rose of home. The men in and out and her mother always seemed to be cooking or cleaning and every day was a washday. Rose smiled at the woman who had become like a mother to her. 'And it's only June.' She looked around her. 'It's quiet today. Is there anything I can do while I'm here?'

'I think most of the men have gone out, and since I had that fall they've all tried to do so much more around the house.' Ruby reached out and rested her hand on Rose's arm. 'You are a good girl, Rose; you've helped more than you could ever know. You've helped give the men back some of their dignity, and that's so important.'

'That's kind of you to say so. I wish I could do more.' Rose glanced at Ruby. 'Is Brian going to be all right?'

Ruby sighed. 'I think so. Unfortunately the police are looking into what happened so that probably won't help him very much. I had a word with Oliver to see if he could find him somewhere that was more appropriate for his needs. I didn't want to but after what he did to Michael I couldn't put the other men at risk, let alone people like yourself.'

Rose picked up her teaspoon. 'I popped into the hospital and Michael will be discharged soon and Miss Hetherington has barely left his side. It's lovely that the hospital made a special allowance for her to stay all day.'

A teaspoon clattered on the china as Ruby put her teacup down. 'I expect they allowed it because they thought it might help him recover.'

Rose nodded. 'At least she has found him. It's so sad to think about all the years they have lost. It makes you wonder how many people are in that situation.'

Ruby cut a thin slice of sponge and carefully placed it on a tea plate, sliding it across the table to Rose before handing her a cake fork.

Rose held the fork between her thumb and fingers, ready to dig into the sponge.

Ruby smiled. 'Sorry, it's a Victoria sponge but without enough eggs or sugar and no jam.'

Rose chuckled. 'It still looks delicious.'

Ruby tilted her head and smiled. 'I was very lucky to spend many happy years with my husband. I miss him every day but I know he would approve of what I'm doing. We weren't lucky enough to have any children. It obviously wasn't meant to be, so we always said we would give back to the community when the time came.'

'You've a very kind heart. Charlie was all about wanting to do more for the neighbourhood, and he did what he could with what he had but who knows what he might have gone on to achieve.'

Ruby nodded. 'It's so sad that we've all lost some good people. And who knows what they might have achieved if they'd lived out their lives.'

Rose's lips tightened. 'It saddens me that his shop is boarded up. It's a constant reminder that he's not here.'

Ruby gave Rose a sideways glance. 'Perhaps you should make use of it.'

Rose looked down at her slice of cake. 'I've been wondering about that but I'm not sure whether I could cope with the constant reminder of him not being there.'

Ruby nodded. 'I can understand that but we are all stronger than we realise, and it's only when we're tested that we move ahead and achieve great things.'

'Is that cake I can smell?' George sniffed the air as he strolled into the kitchen.

Rose forced a smile to her lips. 'It certainly is, George, and I'm sure it will be very nice too.'

Ruby chuckled. 'I don't know how you manage it, George. You must be able to smell cake from miles away.'

The three of them laughed as Ruby cut George a small slice.

'Hmm, lovely Victoria sponge, my favourite.' George licked his lips.

Ruby placed the slice on a plate. 'It would be better with some jam filling.'

George shook his head. 'Don't you go worrying yourself. It's lovely.' He sat down at the table, scratching the chair legs across the tiled floor. 'The doc is in the front room with Jack; I've left them to talk in private. I think Michael getting stabbed has affected him the most.'

Ruby frowned. 'Do you think I should take him a cup of tea?'

George shook his head as he balanced a piece of cake on his fork. 'No, he said he would come and find you when he's done.' He glanced up at the large wall clock. 'I don't suppose he'll be long. They've been on their own for nearly an hour.'

Rose raised her eyebrows. 'I didn't realise we had been talking for so long.'

George smiled at Rose. 'The doc has checked in on Michael and he's probably going to be discharged in the next couple of days.'

Rose breathed a sigh of relief. 'That is good news. I knew he had come round but I didn't know how the healing was going.'

George nodded. 'Apparently he was lucky that the knife didn't do more damage. Poor old Brian. I know Michael is in hospital but Brian needs help and prison won't give him that. Believe it or not he's a good man.'

The three of them sat in silence for a few minutes.

George took a breath. 'Anyway, young lady, how are you bearing up? I don't suppose you'd ever witnessed anything like that before.'

Rose pursed her lips. 'No, I've watched my father kill our chickens.' She smiled. 'As a child that was quite awful to see but we were always brought up not to see them as pets so it was expected I suppose. I remember crying all day the first time it happened.'

Ruby studied the young woman in front of her. 'I suppose us city dwellers don't think about the food we eat in the same way as people in the country.'

Rose looked up. 'I don't know about that but the picture in my head has never left me, although that's nothing after Charlie dying in the bomb blast.'

George nodded. 'I know it doesn't really help but at least you know he saved lives that day, including yours.'

'It doesn't help because I know he could have achieved so much. He was such a caring man.'

'Evening, everyone.' Oliver smiled, as he looked at them all sitting at the table. 'Hello, Rose. I was just talking to Jack and wondered how you were doing.'

Rose smiled. 'I'm not doing too bad, thank you. More importantly, how's Jack?'

Oliver sighed. 'I'm not sure Jack will ever get any better than he already is but, all things considered, he's not coping too badly.'

Ruby stood up. 'Thank you for popping in, Oliver. I'll make us a fresh pot of tea.'

Oliver beamed. 'It will be most welcome, thank you.'

Rose sighed and scraped back her chair. 'I should get home. I need to talk to Joyce.'

Oliver frowned. 'Is everything all right?'

'Not really, I have some serious thinking to do.'

Oliver raised his eyebrows. 'Is it anything I can help you with?'

Rose shook her head. 'Unfortunately not.' She turned and watched Ruby. The noise of the water hitting the sides of the kettle seemed to fill the room. 'Actually, Ruby, is it possible you and I could have a conversation? I have something I would like to run by you. It's a very cheeky one so don't feel you have to say yes.'

Ruby turned round and smiled. 'That's caught my interest, and it all sounds intriguing. I'll make the tea and we'll leave the men and go and talk in private.'

Rose gave a nervous smile. 'Thank you, I know you'll be honest with me.'

Rose sat on the edge of her bed listening to the intermittent dripping coming from the ceiling echoing as it landed inside the metal bucket. She needed to speak to Joyce about getting the leak looked at before the ceiling came down on her. Sighing, she realised she should have reminded Arthur before he left, and now she needed to get another job so she could pay her share of the housekeeping. 'Oh, Charlie, I've made a right old mess of things.'

Rose leant forward and opened her bedside cabinet drawer and stared at the folded piece of paper. She remembered finding it amongst Charlie's paperwork. When she'd brought it home she couldn't bring herself to read it without crying so she hadn't got past the opening line. Instead she had hidden it away in her bedside drawer. Sighing, she turned it over in her hands. Now it was time. The faint thud of the doorknocker reached her but she ignored it. Whoever it was would be gone by the time she ran downstairs. Rose didn't take her eyes off the letter. Taking a deep breath, she unfolded the white paper. She stared down at Charlie's handwriting; the distinctive loops and hooks on his letters made her smile.

My dearest Rose,

I'm writing this letter because I get tongue-tied when I'm with you, and I'm now scared of frightening you with my feelings. I shouldn't have proposed when I did, I realise that now. I shan't make any excuses for it, except I love you more than life itself and my feelings got the better of me. I now know you have no desire to be married, at least not to me, but it doesn't lessen my feelings for you.

The day I proposed wasn't a good day for me. I also got a telegram to say my brother had died and it brought home to me how quickly things can change. I realised then I couldn't just let you go, at least not without fighting for you.

It's important to me that you are happy and if you

can't find love with me please find love with someone else, and be brave enough to marry and have a family. Life is too short so grab it with both hands. Be happy with the path that you find yourself on, ideally with me. God will guide you and you'll eventually end up where you're meant to be.

I will always love you.

Charlie xxx

Rose blinked rapidly to stop the tears from falling, knowing she had to take comfort that he died knowing she loved him and did want to get married. The floorboards creaking carried up the stairs. She quickly folded the letter and placed it back in her drawer. She fixed a smile on her face and turned to look towards her bedroom door, which stood ajar. The door swung open. Rose gasped. She jumped up as she took in his sinister smile. 'What are you doing here? How did you get in?'

Mr Bowman raised his eyebrows. 'I've come for something you kept promising to give me.' He stepped nearer to her. 'It's time you paid me for giving you a chance.'

Rose stepped back while eyeing the door, wondering how she could escape, knowing she was in the house by herself. She lifted her chin. 'You need to leave, now.'

Mr Bowman scoffed. 'Or what?'

Rose's gaze darted around the room. 'I'll let the police know you broke into my home.'

Mr Bowman stepped nearer. 'They will never believe you; after all, I am a man of standing.' He glanced at the shelf that held her books. 'It's time to hand them over.'

Rose pushed back her shoulders and clenched her hands

by her sides. Fear ran through her. 'No, you are a liar and a cheat. You never gave me a chance. It was always about you. That's why you took me on as a seamstress. You just wanted my designs. I don't know how you got hold of them but that doesn't matter now. You are certainly not stealing any more.'

Mr Bowman smiled. 'It's no good you pointing the finger at me. You need to ask Mrs Todd how they came to be in my possession.'

Rose moved to stand in front of the shelves as Mr Bowman stepped nearer.

Narrowing her eyes, Rose yelled at him, 'I'm not going to stand by and let you take them.'

Mr Bowman glared at her, steely-eyed. 'I've lost my job, thanks to you, so don't think your idle threats are of concern to me.' He glanced over his shoulder. 'I must admit I used the doorknocker and when no one answered I thought it was safe for me to pull the key through and let myself in.' He looked back at her. 'It's too bad you're in, but that's not going to stop me taking what I came here for.'

Rose held her arms out to stop him from getting any closer.

Mr Bowman gripped one of her wrists and squeezed it tight. 'I will not allow you to get in my way.'

Rose screwed up her face. 'You're hurting me.' The iron taste of blood seeped into her mouth.

Mr Bowman gave a humourless laugh. 'Not as much as all you women have hurt me.' He pulled her towards him and twisted her arm behind her back before pushing her flat against the wall. He reached up and grabbed several of the books with his other hand and threw them on her bed before reaching up for some more. 'Miss Spencer, it's time you learnt you are no match for me.'

Rose was suddenly being pulled backwards. Squeezing her eyes tight, she stumbled and fell to the floor. Shaking, she wondered what was going to happen to her, how this was going to end. She opened her eyes to scan close by to see what she could grab to hit him with.

Mr Bowman was suddenly being pulled away from her. 'I don't know what you are playing at but the police are on the way.'

Rose breathed a sigh of relief as Oliver's firm voice washed over her.

'Are you all right?' Oliver took in her pale features and trembling lips. 'Has he hurt you?'

Rose looked up, wrapping her arms around herself as she began to shake uncontrollably. She shook her head. 'Thank God you're here.' Her tears began to fall as she watched him grab a scarf off her chair and tie Mr Bowman's hands to the end of her bed. 'I... I thought I was going to die.' She brushed her clammy hand across her face and smeared the blood from her nose across her cheeks.

Oliver rushed towards Rose, and crouching down, he wrapped his arms around her. 'Are you all right, apart from your nose bleeding that is?'

Rose pulled back. 'You're going to end up with blood on you if you're not careful.'

'I don't care about that – you're all that matters.' Oliver reached inside his trouser pocket and pulled out a white handkerchief and passed it to her before pulling her close again. 'Do you hurt anywhere?'

Rose smiled. 'Only my pride, and my nose.'

Oliver squeezed her tight before pulling back to study her. He took her hands and pulled her to her feet as footsteps could be heard running up the stairs.

A policeman came rushing in. 'Are you all right, miss?'

Rose nodded.

The policeman glanced at Mr Bowman tied to the metal bed frame before turning to Oliver. 'I see you apprehended him, thank you.' He paused. 'I'm Constable Albright and this is my colleague Constable Appleton' He indicated to the woman in the dark blue uniform standing next to him, who was patrolling with him for the first time.

Oliver nodded to them both. 'He broke in and assaulted Miss Spencer. I got here just in time; otherwise who knows how this was going to end.'

The policeman looked at Oliver as he took his notepad and pen out of his pocket. 'Can I take your name and ask you how you got in, sir?'

Oliver nodded. 'I'm Doctor Hardy and Miss Spencer alters clothing for the wounded soldiers at the hospital. I'm here on the off-chance I could pick up the work she had done.'

The policeman was nodding as he made notes in his notepad.

'When I got here the door was open. I stepped inside and I heard Miss Spencer shout out.' Oliver paused as he looked across at her. 'I went next door and asked them to get the police and then I came back in here.' He sighed. 'By that time Mr Bowman here had her pinned up against the wall. As you can see that has resulted in a nosebleed.'

Constable Appleton stepped nearer to Rose. 'Do you need to go to the hospital?'

Rose shook her head. 'No thank you, I'm more shaken up than anything else.'

Oliver nodded. 'I'll stay and look after her.'

The two police constables nodded.

Constable Albright turned to Mr Bowman. 'Well, sir, you are under arrest for breaking and entry and assaulting this young lady.'

Mr Bowman's face screwed up. 'Are you going to believe these two nobodies? I am a man of standing and I'll get you fired for this.'

Constable Albright untied Mr Bowman. 'Come on, you're going to the station where you'll be charged.'

Constable Appleton looked at Rose. 'Perhaps you could come to the police station later and make a formal statement.'

'Of course.'

The policewoman turned to Oliver. 'We'll also need a written statement from you, sir.'

'I'll bring Rose with me and we'll do it together.'

The policewoman nodded. 'Tomorrow will be fine.' They turned on their heels and walked out of the room with Mr Bowman between them.

21

Joyce stood still on the three-legged stool, rigid like a soldier standing to attention. The clock on the mantelpiece chimed nine times. 'It's about time I emptied the cabinets and dusted the figures. It's a job I used to love but I always seem so busy these days.'

Annie peered up from her knitting. 'I don't know where the time goes.'

Rose glanced over her shoulder at the cabinets. 'It's not just your place to do the housework; any of us can do it.'

Annie smiled. 'I have time tomorrow so I'll do it before I go to the theatre.'

'You can breathe, Joyce.' Rose laughed. 'After all, you will be breathing when you go down the aisle.'

Joyce giggled. 'I didn't realise I was holding my breath.'

Rose tugged at the white material and inserted a pin. 'Have you lost weight? I'm sure I cut this out in your right size and yet it feels too big.'

Joyce shook her head. 'No, I don't think so and all my other clothes seem to fit all right.'

Rose sighed. 'I must've cut it out wrong then. It doesn't matter – I can easily take it in. It's better it's too big than too small.'

Annie sat in the armchair watching them both. 'You're going to look lovely, Joyce. I'm so happy for you and Simon.'

Rose chuckled. 'I am too, but I was beginning to think neither of you were ever going to walk down the aisle.'

Annie took a breath. 'We were only thinking of you, Rose.'

Rose raised her eyebrows and peered at Annie. 'Well, whatever the reason I'm pleased it's finally happening.'

A smile played on Annie's lips as her eyes locked with Rose's. 'So, I was quite taken aback by Kitty's remarks.'

Joyce peered over her shoulder at Annie. 'What remarks? Have I missed something?'

Rose groaned. 'No, you haven't. It's only Kitty getting carried away with herself.'

Annie chuckled. 'Hmm, the more I think about it the more I think she could be onto something.'

'Think about what?' Joyce waved her arm in the air. 'Please tell me what's going on.'

'Rose, do you want to tell Joyce, or shall I?'

Rose kept her eyes fixed firmly on the dress and the job at hand. 'Well, you might as well because it's only going to go on all night otherwise.'

Annie clapped her hands together and kept her eyes fixed firmly on Joyce. 'Kitty thinks Rose has found someone special in Oliver.'

'Oliver.' Joyce's eyes widened.

No one said a word, waiting for Joyce's reaction.

'Why does she think that? She's never seen the two of you together, has she? I don't understand.' Joyce's gaze dashed from one to the other.

Annie leant forward in her seat. 'Rose was talking about

him and his work at the refuge.' She smiled mischievously before carrying on. 'According to Kitty, Rose's eyes were sparkling when she was talking about him. I can't say I saw it, I was too busy admiring the wedding dress and feeling every inch a princess at the time.'

Rose shook her head. 'It's all nonsense; it was embarrassing.'

Joyce peered down at Rose, who was kneeling at her feet pinning up the hem of her dress. 'Why were you embarrassed? It's quite feasible; after all, you have been in his company and you always say what a kind man he is. It sounds like you could do a lot worse.'

Rose sighed. 'There's lots of reasons, Joyce. The main one is I'm not looking for a man. I don't want to be in love. He's a doctor for goodness' sake. Do you not think he has a choice of women who would fall over themselves to have him as a husband?' She shifted her position to move further around Joyce.

Joyce chuckled. 'Rose Spencer, you are no different to me. To think all this time I thought you were braver than me. Wasn't it you who told me it was obvious that Simon and I were in love? It makes me feel a lot better because it shows none of us can see what's right under our noses. We all think we're not good enough or have nothing to offer someone. Look at Michael and all those wasted years and all because of his pride.' She pursed her lips. 'I know you've lost the love of your life but it doesn't mean you can't love again. There's nothing better than feeling that someone will always be there for you no matter what's going on. I know as friends we are always there for each other but my love for Simon is different. I can't explain it but if you loved

Charlie the way I love Simon you'll know what I mean.' She paused before lowering her voice. 'I'm just saying don't deprive yourself of that again.'

Rose stayed silent and concentrated on pinning up the dress.

Joyce glanced over at Annie, who shrugged.

The sound of the front doorknocker thudding down made them all look at the clock on the mantelpiece.

'It's quarter past nine.' Joyce frowned. 'Who's that at this time of night?'

Annie pushed herself out of the chair. 'There's only one way to find out.' She strolled towards the hallway.

The creaking of the front door opening could be heard in the sitting room. It was followed by muffled voices.

Joyce frowned. 'Can you hear what they're saying?'

Rose looked up and shrugged. 'No, but I'm sure Annie will tell us when she comes in.'

Joyce shook her head. 'I hope nothing's wrong? Please God don't let it be bad news.'

The bang of the front door closing told the girls they were about to find out. Annie stood in the doorway of the sitting room. She hesitated for a moment. 'Rose, you have a visitor.' She stood aside and Mrs Todd walked in.

Frowning, Rose jumped to her feet. 'Mrs Todd, what are you doing here? I didn't even realise you knew where I lived.'

'Please call me Eileen.' Mrs Todd looked awkward as she fidgeted from one foot to the other. 'I'm sorry to intrude on your evening but I needed to talk to you. I knew I wouldn't sleep until I had.'

Rose frowned. 'That doesn't sound good.' She indicated to a chair. 'Come in and take a seat. I'll get you a cup of tea.'

Mrs Todd perched down on the edge of the nearest chair. 'Please don't worry about the tea. I don't wish to take up your evening and I can see you're busy.'

Rose smiled as she glanced at Joyce. 'I'm making Joyce's wedding dress.' She turned back to Mrs Todd, who was gripping the handles of her handbag with both hands as it sat on her lap. 'Anyway, what can I do for you?'

Mrs Todd didn't say a word. She quietly opened her handbag and pulled out a sketch pad with a number seven emblazoned on it. Shaking her head, she handed it to Rose. 'You were half right about Mr Bowman, and I feel dreadful and am really sorry. This is your property and I'd like to return it to you.'

Rose took the pad; she gazed at it in disbelief. 'I'm sorry too, Mrs Todd… Eileen. I truly didn't want to believe it but I knew in my heart he had taken it. I just hadn't figured out how.'

Mrs Todd sucked in her breath. 'No, he didn't take it from you; he took it from me.'

Stunned silence filled the room.

Rose's gaze switched from Eileen to her friends, and back again. 'I… I don't understand.'

Eileen avoided looking at Rose as colour crept up her neck. 'Mr Bowman and I visited Kitty Smythe at the theatre on a couple of occasions… but it was me who picked it up, while we were in her dressing room.'

Rose frowned. 'But, why?'

Eileen looked up, her eyes blurry with unshed tears. 'I've always wanted to design clothes and Mr Bowman did include a couple of my gowns in his collection. After that I was under pressure to produce more; at least I felt I was.

That's not an excuse because what I did was inexcusable and I can't apologise enough. I wanted to tell you on so many occasions but I was frightened, even though you were so nice to me all the time.'

Rose knelt down by Mrs Todd. 'Don't look so worried. I'm grateful to have it back and I won't say anything. In that regard you, the shop and Mr Bowman are quite safe.' She flicked through the pages before hugging it. 'Thank you for returning it to me, although it doesn't seem so important now but it's good to know what did happen to it.' Rose paused. 'Wait, is that what you and Mr Bowman were arguing about? Was this the secret he was holding over you?'

Eileen nodded. 'There's more.' She bit down on her lip. 'I felt terrible after you left so I searched Mr Bowman's office and found it hidden behind some books. I took it to Mr Woodford and told him what had happened. He now knows all the clothing in Mr Bowman's last couple of collections were your designs.' She took a deep breath. 'I'm so sorry, Rose; you didn't deserve to be treated in such a bad way. I let my own want take over. The dream became more important than anything else. I hope you can forgive me.'

Rose stared wide-eyed at her. 'Please tell me you haven't lost your job as well?'

Eileen shook her head.

'Oh thank goodness. I know you regret your actions; it's written all over your face.'

Eileen blushed. 'They've asked me to take over and I said I would as long as you came back.'

Rose studied Mrs Todd's face; there was tension in every

line. 'I'm genuinely so happy for you. You deserve the recognition, but I don't want to come back. I love to design clothes but I have no desire to pander to people. I don't have the right temperament for it.'

Annie slowly lowered herself onto a chair. 'Are you sure, Rose? You need to work.'

Rose looked around at the three anxious faces. 'I've never been more sure of anything in my life. You should give Marion a try. She has a good eye.' She paused. 'Charlie was right when he said I was wasted repairing costumes. What he didn't realise was I'm at my happiest helping people. I love making a difference to the injured men – you should see their faces when they get a shirt that takes into account they only have half an arm.'

Annie smiled. 'If I remember rightly, he told you to find yourself and it sounds like that is what you've done.'

Mrs Todd gazed around at the girls and opened her handbag again. 'I had a feeling you might say something like that so when I went to the board about Mr Bowman I opened your pad to show Mr Woodford—'

'Oh, you didn't, did you? How embarrassing.'

Mrs Todd smiled. 'Well, if you can cope with a little embarrassment I have something for you.' She thrust her hand inside her bag and pulled out a bundle of five-pound notes. 'They liked everything they saw and are prepared to pay for your designs, now and in the future.'

Joyce flopped down onto a chair. 'Oh my goodness.'

Annie beamed. 'Rose, this will enable you to do whatever you want.'

Rose looked at the money. 'I don't want it, Mrs Todd... Eileen... give it back. It wasn't Dickens and Jones' fault. Or give it to charity where it can do some good. To be honest it feels tainted and while they were my designs I would never have got them into a shop like that – at least not for years – so in some strange way it doesn't feel like I've worked for it so I don't deserve it.'

Annie shook her head. 'You could ask Oliver where it would be most useful. That way you are putting it to good use somewhere that interests you.'

Mrs Todd nodded. 'That makes sense, and you don't have to give it all. You will still have things to pay out.'

Joyce stared at Rose. 'What about your other books?'

Rose jerked round.

Mrs Todd smiled. 'Do you have other designs? They told me to find out. They will pay you for any designs they use. I've also asked for your name to be on every ticket that's sewn in each garment.'

Rose's mouth dropped open. 'I can't believe it. So I can draw out designs and they will look through them and pay me accordingly?'

Mrs Todd laughed. 'Yes, I suppose that is what I'm saying. Mr Bowman has been asked to leave, because of his… your designs and Mr Woodford overheard some of his comments and wasn't happy. The police also came to see Mr Woodford about him coming here and assaulting you—'

'What?' Annie and Joyce chorused as one.

Rose shook her head at them. 'I'll tell you later.'

Mrs Todd frowned as she stared at the girls. 'I feel like I started this chain of events, and I'm so sorry. I would like you to come back.' She gave a small smile. 'Also, I'm not sure I can do this job on my own.'

Rose clasped Mrs Todd's hands in hers. 'You've done

more than enough, and such honesty takes a lot of courage, thank you. However, you can do the job. You're so clever; Mr Bowman relied on you. Take Marion under your wing, let her be your apprentice. She's a quick learner and she'll do you proud.' Rose stood up. 'I'll go and get the other books but please try not to laugh at my early scribblings because that's all that they were. I don't want anything for them; they are my gift to you and Marion. I will continue to sketch out designs and pass them on to you, if that's all right?'

'Of course it is, and thank you for the lovely offer, but please understand you will definitely be paid so start thinking about what you can do with the money.' Mrs Todd put the bundle of notes down on the side table next to the chair she was sitting on.

Annie grinned as she took in Joyce's wide-eyed expression. 'Rose, this means you can now do whatever you want to do.'

Rose beamed. 'I won't be long.' She rushed out the door and headed for the stairs.

Rose stood outside Charlie's boarded-up shop. She shivered as the early morning breeze caught her. Butterflies flitted around her stomach. The palms of her hands were damp. A smile slowly formed on her lips. 'This is it, Charlie, it turns out your dream and mine are exactly the same. I just never realised it.' She thrust her hand inside her skirt pocket and wrapped her fingers round the cold metal key. Pulling it from her pocket, she stepped forward.

'Oh good, we're not late.' George's loud voice carried

above the cars passing by and the sellers shouting out about their wares.

Rose spun round. Her mouth dropped open for a moment. 'What are you two doing here?'

George chuckled. 'Yer didn't fink we were going to let you do it all by yerself did ya? Even Jack has braved the outside world to come along.'

Jack waved as he cowered behind George, his smile belying the fear that was in his eyes.

George turned to pull Jack forward. 'Come on, Jack, you've done well. Let's get yer indoors.'

Rose stared at them both. 'I don't know what to say.'

George chuckled. 'Ruby told us about yer plan so here we are. I think the doc will be along later with Ruby.'

Rose's eyes widened. 'I can't believe it.'

Close by there was a loud thud as boxes hit the pavement. Jack dropped shaking to the ground, gripping George's leg.

'It's all right, lad, it's just some boxes – yer safe.' George pulled Jack up. 'I've got yer.' He turned to Rose. 'So, are yer going to open the door then?'

'Yes, yes, of course.' Rose turned on her heels before glancing over her shoulder at the two men. 'Thank you; thank you both so much. Jack, I know this is difficult for you and it means a lot that you came to help.' She put the key in the door, which took some force to turn, before it grated against the lock.

George watched Rose struggle. 'It looks like the first thing is to oil that door.'

Rose pushed it open. She wrinkled her nose at the musty smell. The dust swirled up as the breeze forced its way in, making her sneeze.

'Bless you,' the men said in unison.

'Thank you.' Rose stepped over the various papers that were lying on the doormat, and propped open the door. The breeze rushed in, chasing out the staleness that hung in the air.

George and Jack followed her.

George wrinkled his nose. 'Shall I open the back door and get some fresh air blowing? And then we can decide what we're going to do first.' Without waiting for an answer, he marched out to the rear of the shop.

Rose nodded. 'If I'm honest I don't know where to start.'

George walked back into the shop and signalled to Jack to help him remove the boards from the shop window and door. Light flooded in, showing layers of dust everywhere.

Rose walked over to Charlie's counter and ran her fingers through the dust settled there. 'It looks like it's cleaning first and then maybe finding a couple of tables from somewhere, one for a sewing machine to sit on. We also need to think about a sign for outside.'

Jack nodded. 'I used to make signs and paint things before the war started so I could do something like that easily enough.'

Rose smiled. 'I don't have much money so it's all about cost.'

'If George will come with me, I can try and scavenge some bits from where I used to work; after all, it's for a good cause.'

Rose frowned. 'Wouldn't they give you back your old job?'

Jack shrugged. 'Probably, but I'd struggle to get across London.'

Rose shook her head. 'Maybe, when this is sorted out,

you could do some work here. We could set you up out the back so you are furthest away from the street noise. Do you think they would pay you to do some work for them, maybe by the job?'

Jack's eyes narrowed. 'I don't know.'

George grinned. 'That's a wonderful idea and we won't know until we ask, will we? Let's face it, the worst they can do is say no.'

Rose beamed at the two men standing in front of her before frowning. 'It's a lot to expect you to go and ask for help. Do you think you can do it?'

Jack stared at Rose. 'I want to try.' He turned to George. 'Will you come with me?'

George nodded. 'I wouldn't have it any other way.' He glanced at Rose. 'Shall we go now, or do you want us to stay and help first?'

Stepping away from the counter Rose unbuttoned her jacket. 'I'll be fine; I'd like to get most of the heavy work done before it gets too hot. I'll start with the cleaning while you go off, but please take care. I'll worry about you until you get back.'

George patted Jack on the back. 'Don't worry; I'll look after him. Come on then, Jack; the sooner we go the sooner we get back.'

As Jack and George turned to go, Joyce and Annie peered round the doorway.

Annie gasped. 'Rose, what are you doing here? I thought you had given back the key. What's going on?'

'Hello, I remember you from when Ruby had her fall.' George looked from one to the other. 'Do you want us to stay?'

Rose shook her head. 'No, George, everything's all right. I just need to confess my secret now.'

George nodded. 'We'll be as quick as we can.'

Rose watched George and Jack leave the shop before looking guiltily at Joyce and Annie. 'Don't be cross with me. I had this mad thought to open Charlie's shop as a place for the community. I spoke to Ruby and she loved the idea and helped to make it happen. That was before I knew I could earn money in the future from my designs so that's all extra money, but it does mean this place could be used to give to those in need of a helping hand.' Rose's eyes widened. 'We could maybe have food available, not that I've spoken to anyone about how I'll achieve that, but I could buy a few loaves and cut them up to make them go further or ask Peter if he has any fruit or vegetables that he feels he can no longer sell. I don't know, to be honest I haven't worked out the details. I have all these ideas running around my head. I can do free repairs. I could ask Oliver to see patients without charging them. We could even do bicycle repairs, if I can find someone who knows about such things. The possibilities are endless.'

Joyce and Annie were grinning from ear to ear.

Rose stared at them. 'What? Do you think I'm mad?'

Joyce giggled. 'Now you've found yourself, of that there is no doubt. You look so alive.'

Annie laughed. 'Oh yes.'

Rose beamed. 'So you don't think I'm crazy then?'

Joyce nodded. 'Yes, most definitely, but you are Rose. Welcome back.' She glanced around the shop. 'Right, I have to go and bake some pies for Peter. He's already got the bread and then I'll be back to help.'

Annie nodded. 'If you see Peter, make sure you tell him about Rose's idea so he can think about how he can help too.'

Rose rushed forward and hugged her friends. 'Thank you. I'm so happy, if a little scared.' She stepped back. 'Wait, Annie, I assume you must have been going somewhere to be out this early?'

Annie smiled. 'The only place I ever go is the theatre. It's like a second home to me, but it wasn't for anything that can't wait so I can definitely spare a few hours to help.'

Joyce giggled. 'Right, I shall leave you two because as George said the sooner I go the sooner I can get back.' She turned to walk towards the door. 'Oh, and you won't have to buy any bread.' She paused. 'You know, I've just had a thought. What if I cooked something like a stew every day? It'll be more vegetables than meat at the moment, but we could offer a free meal to the children.'

Rose nodded. 'You're thinking of that brother and sister you met, aren't you?'

Joyce frowned. 'I can't help wondering what's happened to them. To be homeless at their age must be terrifying. If only I could have persuaded them to come and live with us.'

'Remember, they were frightened of being separated.' Annie rested her hand on Joyce's arm. 'Your idea is wonderful though and they might turn up once word gets around. What do you think, Rose?'

Flushed with colour, Rose was bursting with excitement. 'It's all coming together; it's going to be amazing. Thank you, Joyce. Right, I've got to get started otherwise nothing is going to happen.'

Joyce nodded. 'I'll see you as soon as I can.' She turned and waved as she left the shop.

Annie removed her jacket. 'What do you want me to do?' She looked around her. 'I'll sweep the floor first and then we can start washing everything down, including the windows.'

Rose's eyes followed Annie's gaze. 'All right, while you sweep I'll clean the kitchen so we can take a break later.' She moved to walk away but immediately stopped. 'Do you think I'm mad for trying to do this?'

Annie giggled. 'No, I think it's wonderful.'

Rose scanned the shop, and smiled with the amount of work that had already been done that morning. Oliver and Annie had helped her clean everything in sight, and they were all still smiling.

There was a rattle of crockery as Ruby walked through from the kitchen carrying a tray. 'It's a good job I brought some cutlery and crockery with me, otherwise you wouldn't be able to have a cuppa.'

Rose shook her head. 'I didn't think about that. I'll buy some.'

Ruby rested the tray on the counter. 'There's no need. You can keep it all. In fact I'll have a sort-out to see what else I can bring. There's no point in buying anything new if I have spares.' She lifted the teapot lid and began to noisily stir the tea.

'So this is where you're all hiding? They said at the refuge I might find you here.'

Everyone looked in the direction of the door.

Ruby grinned as she stepped forward to throw her arms

around Michael. 'I can't begin to tell you how pleased I am to see you. Thank goodness you're well. I can't forgive myself for putting you, and the other men, in that position.'

Michael shook his head as he gave her a bear-like hug. 'Ruby, it wasn't your fault so please don't torture yourself anymore.'

The girls grinned and clapped their hands together with excitement.

Rose stepped forward, taking in his shaved appearance. 'Michael, it's wonderful to see you up and about. You look well, and I do believe you've had a haircut.'

'Yes, it was a must if I'm going to be a married man; after all, I want my wife to be proud of me.' Michael nodded. 'I've brought someone to see you.' He moved aside so Jane could step inside.

Rose gasped. 'Does that mean...'

Jane nodded.

Rose ran forward and threw her arms around Jane and then Michael. 'This is wonderful news. I'm so happy for you both.'

Annie stepped forward. 'I'm so happy for you, Michael, and you, Miss Hetherington.'

Jane's face lit up. 'Please call me Jane.'

Michael grinned. 'Jane won't be a Hetherington for much longer. She has agreed to become Mrs Michael Dean.'

Rose giggled. 'This day is just getting better and better.'

Jane turned to Annie, and frowned. 'I owe you and others an apology. I shouldn't have taken my misery out on everyone. Please forgive me.'

Annie smiled. 'Only if I can give you a hug to congratulate you.'

Jane opened her arms. 'There's nothing I would like more. I had forgotten how good it felt to have a cuddle.'

Annie's eyes became watery as she stepped forward and wrapped her arms around Jane. 'Congratulations, I hope you'll both be very happy.'

'Annie, is Annie 'ere?'

Annie stepped back from Jane and saw Peter in the shop doorway. Fear ran across her face. 'What… what is it?'

Peter grinned. 'I failed me medical.'

Everyone cheered.

Annie ran into his open arms with tears streaming down her face. 'Thank goodness.' She suddenly pulled back, her brows pulled together. 'Wait, wait, does that mean you're dying or something?'

Peter laughed. 'No, but it turns out me eyesight is pretty poor so I can't go.'

The tears rolled down Rose's cheeks.

Oliver rested his hand on her arm before whispering, 'Are you all right?'

Rose nodded. 'These are happy tears.' She brushed her fingers across her cheeks.

Oliver glanced around the shop. 'Charlie would be so proud of you.'

Rose smiled. 'I actually think he would be.' She stepped nearer to Oliver and rested her hand on his arm, squeezing the soft white material of his shirt. 'But not just me, I think he would be proud of all of us.'

Oliver studied her for a moment. 'You know you mean a great deal to me—'

'Sshh, I know.' Rose stood on tiptoes and brushed her lips against Oliver's cheek. 'You have managed to make me see what's important, albeit not intentionally. I think Charlie would be happy because I am.'

Oliver didn't take his eyes off her as he reached out to take her hand in his.

George strode through the open shop doorway, grinning as he looked across at Oliver and Rose. 'It's about time. I was beginning to think it was never going to happen.'

Joyce glanced at Annie and noticed her smile matched her own.

Rose blushed as she glanced at all the happy faces watching them.

George slapped Michael on the back. 'Hello, it's good to see you. I don't mind admitting I thought you were a goner.'

Michael nodded. 'I understand I owe everyone here a great deal of thanks for their quick actions as it probably saved my life.'

George nudged Michael. 'Right now, if you're well enough, we need your help to unload the van.'

Rose's eyes widened. 'Van?'

'Yeah, Jack's old company gave us a few bits that you might need and they brought us back with it all.'

Oliver's face lit up. 'That sounds like good news.' He followed George out the door.

Half an hour later the van was unloaded and the shop had a couple of tables, several chairs, boxes for storage and an old shop sign.

'This is wonderful. If you give me their address I will write a letter of thanks to them.' Rose looked around wondering how best to arrange the furniture. She suddenly turned to Jack. 'Did you ask them about working from here?'

Jack beamed. 'George did most of the talking.'

George laughed. 'Jack asked them first but then I pushed them on a decision.'

Rose clapped her hands together. 'And?'

Jack laughed at Rose's excitement. 'They said yes, but we've got to go back next week to sort out the details.'

Rose rushed forward and wrapped her arms around Jack and George. 'That's wonderful news.' Pulling back, she looked around. 'I wonder where we can fit you in?'

Ruby was quietly watching everyone and listening to the excitement. 'I am so happy for you, Jack; it's wonderful news.' She turned to Rose. 'I don't know if I told you but I bought this property for a very good price, mainly because the owner hadn't managed to rent it out again.'

Rose's mouth dropped open.

'Anyway, what I was thinking was maybe George and Jack could live upstairs and one of the rooms could be used for Jack's work as well. What do you think?'

Rose shook her head. 'Won't you miss them?'

Ruby laughed. 'Of course, I'm not kicking them out. They can live with me for as long as they want but it would mean Jack wouldn't need to go out any more than is necessary and George likes to keep an eye on him so they will have each other.'

Rose smiled. 'I think it's a wonderful idea but it's not my decision.'

Jack frowned for a moment before glancing up at George. 'What do you think?'

George put his arm around Jack's shoulder. 'I'm happy to give it a go if you are?'

Jack's face lit up as he nodded. 'Ruby, if I struggle with it will I be able to come back?'

Ruby beamed. 'Jack, you and George will always have a home with me but I think you are ready to take this next step. Don't you, Oliver?'

Oliver peered at Jack. 'You've come a long way since moving in with Ruby, and it would be a good thing to give someone else that chance too.'

George nudged Jack. 'Shall we go upstairs and pick which room is going to be used for what?'

Jack chuckled and raced on ahead. 'Come on then.'

Oliver turned to Ruby. 'That's a lovely idea, and it frees up two of your rooms. That's if you're willing to take on a couple more?'

Ruby smiled. 'Of course – just send them my way when you're releasing them from hospital.'

'Right, I had better get back to putting this shelf up.'

A smile played on Rose's lips as she watched Oliver working on the far wall. 'Shall we call it Helping Hands or Helping Hearts?'

Oliver tilted his head slightly before peering over his shoulder at her. 'I think Helping Hands sums it up. What do you think, Ruby?'

'I agree, Helping Hands tells everyone exactly what this shop stands for.'

Rose stood near the doorway of Charlie's bicycle shop and remembered how she had wondered if she would ever think of it as anything else. Without her realising it, life had moved on. Her eyes were drawn to the photograph on the wall of Charlie standing outside surrounded by his bicycles. 'Thank you, Charlie. You were my first love, and you'll never be forgotten. Oliver has done you proud. This isn't just for me; it's for you too. We're working together to give something to the community so your dream will also come true.'

Taking a deep breath, Rose picked up the framed photo of Charlie and stared at it. Looking up, she let her gaze wander around the room. Sighing, she looked back at the picture. 'This bedroom was my prison for what seemed an eternity. I was heartbroken when I lost you; it's a day I'll never forget. But it's time; I've learnt to laugh again.' A tear gently rolled down her cheek. 'It doesn't seem right to say it out loud, to be happy again. It's important you know you'll never be forgotten.' She brushed her hand across her damp face. 'You showed me a love I've never known before, and what's more you believed in me. You might not have been in my life for long but there will always be a place for you in my heart.' She pulled the photo in to her chest and hugged it tight for a few minutes, before stretching her arms out and smiling down at it again. 'I hope you are proud of what I'm – or perhaps I should say we – are trying to achieve. I couldn't have done it on my own.' She ran her finger over the picture before placing it back on the bedside table.

Sighing, Rose pushed herself up off the bed. The springs twanged as she stood upright. She caught sight of her reflection. It was time to put on her best frock. Opening her wardrobe door she glided her fingers across the clothes that were hanging there before pulling out a red dress. She had made it when she worked at the theatre, but once Charlie had gone, there had never been the right time to wear red. She took off her dressing gown, letting it drop to the floor. She stepped into the calf-length dress before she slipped her feet into the curved-heeled black shoes.

Rose studied her reflection in the long narrow mirror. Reaching up, she touched the delicate silver cross and chain around her neck, remembering when Charlie gave it to her. 'I will never forget your words. "Take a leap of faith," you said. It's been an honour to be loved by you, and now I'm taking another leap of faith. This one I'm certain is the right decision.'

'Rose,' Annie's voice shouted from the other side of the bedroom door, quickly followed by a knock.

'Come in.'

The door handle squeaked as it turned. Annie beamed as she caught sight of her friend. 'You look stunning. I'm so pleased you changed into that dress.'

Rose blushed. 'I should have done something with my hair.' She picked up the hairbrush.

Joyce strode through the open doorway. 'Rose, how wonderful you look. That red is so striking; it really suits you.'

Annie reached out and hugged Rose. 'You are beautiful, inside and out, so stop worrying about your hair.' She took the brush from her friend and put it on the chest of drawers before picking up the perfume bottle. 'Lift up your chin and hold out your arms.' She watched Rose do as instructed and then dabbed the floral scent on her.

Joyce sniffed the air. 'That smells lovely.' She smiled. 'It's been a very busy and exciting week for you and this evening will be just what the doctor ordered.'

Rose giggled. 'I'm sure it is. Do you think I'm mad for opening the shop?'

Annie smiled. 'No, you've just taken helping others beyond your friends to the whole of the West End, which is wonderful.'

Joyce clasped her hands around Rose's. 'There's no doubt you are doing the right thing. I've never seen you look so happy as you have this week. Helping others has always been who you are.'

'Thank you; it feels right.' Rose smiled.

There was a loud thud at the front door. Joyce leant in and hugged Rose. 'I'll get the door.' She clapped her hands as she ran out the room.

Rose shouted after her. 'Go carefully. I don't want you falling down the stairs.'

Annie studied Rose for a moment. 'Are you ready?'

Rose took a deep breath. 'I think so.'

Annie followed Rose out of the bedroom.

Rose slowly took each tread of the stairs, stopping only when Oliver came into view.

He looked up and walked nearer to her.

Everyone was silent as Rose took the next couple of steps.

Oliver reached out to take her hand. 'You look beautiful.'

Colour flooded Rose's cheeks as she placed her hand in his.

Joyce's gaze moved from one to the other, looking every inch like a proud parent as she caught Annie's gaze.

Oliver held his breath for a moment. 'Are you ready?'

Rose nodded. 'I'm ready.'

About the Author

ELAINE ROBERTS had a dream to write for a living. She completed her first novel in her twenties and received her first very nice rejection. Life then got in the way until she picked up her dream again in 2010. She joined a creative writing class, The Write Place, in 2012 and shortly afterwards had her first short story published.

Her first novel was published in 2018, followed by five more:

The Foyles Bookshop Girls
The Foyles Bookshop Girls at War
Christmas at the Foyles Bookshop
The West End Girls
Big Dreams for the West End Girls
Secret Hopes for the West End Girls

Elaine and her extended family live in and around Dartford, Kent, and her home is always busy with visiting children, grandchildren, grand-dogs and cats.

Acknowledgements

The encouragement and support I've had since my debut novel, *The Foyles Bookshop Girls*, was published has been unbelievable. For very personal reasons I have found my sixth book, *Secret Hopes for the West End Girls*, difficult to write. It touched my heart in a number of places. I wonder if my readers will be able to tell where. It's been a strange couple of years, with people working from home and having to find new ways to entertain ourselves. As an author, and already working from home, you'd think my life would have just carried on but I found, at times, my focus and concentration just wasn't there. I would like to thank my wonderful family for being so encouraging and supportive, their guidance is always appreciated.

My research into World War One and the home front has brought home how the women stepped up against all odds to support their men on the frontline. It was through their endless hard work that they gained respect, and eventually the vote. I have the utmost respect for them.

A big thank you, and a lot of love, must go to the people I have never met, the virtual friends on social media and readers who have sent me messages, saying how much they have enjoyed my writing and are looking forward to the next book. I have had huge support from them, both in my writing and personal life, and that means the world to me. It's the ultimate act of kindness.

Also, my gratitude must go to fellow writers, editors and agents. They are a special breed of people and are happy to share experiences, good or bad, offering guidance and advice, which I'm most appreciative of. I have been fortunate to meet quite a few on my journey.

A huge thank you must go to the team at Aria, who have published The Foyles Bookshop Girls series and The West End Girls series. They have believed in me and encouraged me to fine-tune my novels. They have been a pleasure to work with and gave me space when I needed it. I truly hope everyone who reads *Secret Hopes of the West End Girls* enjoys it.

If you wish to talk to me, here are my details:

Facebook: www.facebook.com/ElaineRobertsAuthor/
Twitter: www.twitter.com/RobertsElaine11
Website: www.elaineroberts.co.uk